The Pharaohs of Atlantis

Larry N. Stewart

First Edition

Copyright 2010

Larry N. Stewart
Silver Spring, Maryland

ISBN 13: 9780615423494

ISBN 10: 0615423493

Dedication

This book is dedicated to Corinne,
the Collective Intelligence needs you desperately.

The Pharaohs of Atlantis

Synopsis

Indiana Jones meets *The Da Vinci Code* in this Tom Clancy-Dan Brown style thriller.

Can a long-dead Pharaoh travel through time to warn a 21st century civilization of impending disaster?

Is time travel possible via reincarnation?

Is it possible to remember past lives?

Have we all lived before?

Are there warnings and messages contained in our genetic code?

These mysteries and more are explored when Sean and Corinne meet in a prestigious Washington, DC, watering hole. Corinne is a human genome analyst on the verge of discovering the key to the future. Is it immortality or the gene-splice that leads to a super-race of human beings?

Sean is a DHS national-threat analyst on the trail of a merciless killer who is targeting scientists and prominent members of the government. From the moment they meet, these two know their destinies are linked.

Sean and Corinne attend a secret meeting held in the basement of the Smithsonian Institution. The meeting is sponsored by a quasi-secret society of leading scientists called The League of Red-Headed Men. The League is determined to save the planet from a consortium of inept government leaders and corrupt billionaire industrialists.

The meeting is focused on the amazing Necropolis found beneath the Great Pyramid.

The Ancients have left a secret message in the hieroglyphics on the wall of the tomb. The Necropolis of Atlantis is 10,000 years old and contains the mummies of the pharaohs. But before the pharaoh's hidden message can be deciphered and revealed, the US Government stages a security crack down and arrests the attendees.

Sean and Corinne barely escape the crack down but now they are on the run. Who will catch them first—the government's secret agents or a cold-hearted, greedy billionaire industrialist?

They must get to the Great Pyramid to uncover the pharaoh's truth, but the chase will take them across Europe and the Mid East—from Washington, to London, to Spain, to a science ship in the Mediterranean, and ultimately, to Cairo. An act of explosive sabotage traps them beneath the Great Pyramid with no way out. Now they know the pharaoh's secret, but will the secret die with them buried beneath the Saharan Desert or will they live to alert the world to the coming Life Extinguishing Event that is hovering like the Sword of Damocles above humanity's head? Will the Pharaoh's warning be heeded?

Is our civilization lost? Will our heroes fail? Will the pharaoh's secret remain buried? Has time run out? Follow Corinne and Sean to the end and learn the shocking truth.

Table of Contents

The Pharaohs of Atlantis

The Past as Prologue

As Pharaoh's royal yacht drew near its destination, Lord Kontar jumped off the ship and onto the dock. He immediately stepped aboard the waiting chariot. The whip whistled and the horses sprang forward. It was a short trip to Pharaoh's court from the center of Atlantis. Lord Kontar was Pharaoh's royal architect and the site manager at the Giza Plateau. He was late for a royal meeting with Pharaoh's Science Council.

Lord Kontar was responding to a royal missive to provide a construction report on the Great Pyramid project. But what Lord Kontar didn't know was that Pharaoh's science minister didn't want a construction report. He intended to levy yet another construction change on the royal architect.

Lord Kontar assumed that one of Science Minister Al jer's spies had reported the construction delay, and thus he had been called to Atlantis to answer the charge.

There was no doubt that the pyramid construction project was off schedule. The delay was due to material and labor shortages beyond Lord Kontar's control, and to get back on schedule would require additional resources. But Lord Kontar didn't know the science minister was ignorant of the construction delay. Lord Kontar was cagey enough to play the game in small increments until he could gauge just how much the science minister knew. Lord Kontar knew better than to give the royal council any direct construction or schedule delay information. Any disappointing information would be used by Pharaoh's science minister to gain position in Pharaoh's court.

When the chariot arrived at the administration building, Lord Kontar hit the ground running, waived to the guards, and went straight to the Council Chamber. Lord Kontar was a popular overseer at Pharaoh's court. He entered the chamber and addressed the council immediately, "A thousand pardons Minister Al jer, and I know the hour is late, but the Nile was a most unforgiving mistress today."

Minster Al jer said, "Lord Kontar, please. Enough of the Nile! Present your report!"

Lord Kontar began, "My lords, the royal Necropolis and Science Center is nearly complete and the royal funerary artisans have reinterred all Pharaohs and family members from Atlantis to the Necropolis at Giza.

The royal monuments overseer is now concentrating on relocating the noble families to the Giza Plateau Necropolis."

Minister Al jer cautioned, "May I remind you that the equinox is just a month away and the Priests of Ra plan to conduct sacraments and bless the site during the equinox. The ceremony must be delivered from the top of the Great Pyramid so that the assembled multitude can all be blessed at the same time to initiate the Festival of Ra."

Lord Kontar said, "Minister Al jer, with all respect, if I suspend work on the pyramid's interior to complete the exterior, I will have to build ladder work to provide the Priests of Ra access to the top of the pyramid because the interior staircase is not yet completed. This means work currently being done must be postponed until after the Festival of Ra dedication. The science and prayer rooms and the interior access to the top of the pyramid, where the Crystal of Ra will be installed, will have to be delayed until after the completion of the work on the outside of the pyramid. All of these activities will invite construction delays and costs will go up."

Minister Al jer ignored Lord Kontar's observations and asked, "Please present the status of the crystal installation. When can the signalmen of Atlantis establish daily communication with the signalmen of the Necropolis and Science Center?"

Lord Kontar replied, "The cutting and polishing of the Great Crystal is on schedule. The polishing and shaping of the mirrors that focus the light of Ra to the crystal is just a week off schedule, but all mirrors are expected to be complete and in place in two weeks."

"Once the crystal installation at Atlantis is complete, the two sites will be able to communicate instantly by shuttering the sunlight to the crystals. Pharaoh's royal signalmen will use coded signals to create a communication link between Atlantis and Giza."

Minister Al jer said, "I trust your progress reports will be more current when the crystals are in place?"

Lord Kontar replied, "With the crystals in place, my progress reports will be timely. But, may I remind the minister that redirecting the workmen to the exterior will delay crystal installation and consequently, crystal communication."

Minister Al jer bellowed, "Enough! The Pharaoh of Ra has spoken! It will be done!"

Lord Kontar knew the meeting was over. He bowed low and as he retreated from the room he repeated, "The Pharaoh of Ra has spoken."

When Lord Kontar entered the hallway he began muttering to himself about the inefficiencies of the government bureaucracy. He couldn't help but think that, while the Pharaoh of Ra can work miracles with slaves and soldiers, the miracles come a little slower when cutting granite and limestone is involved.

Overall Lord Kontar was very pleased with the outcome of the meeting. With Minister Al jer's redirection of efforts, all existing delays and cost overruns would be conveniently buried. Now he could attribute all construction delays on changes dictated by the royal science minister. His royal decree would allow the pyramid project to get back on track and no one would be the wiser. Yes, life was good for Pharaoh's royal architect.

Lord Kontar stopped in the Public Works Administration Building to enjoy the chef's renowned recipe for Nile tilapia. As he was drinking a cup of wine, a child approached the table and handed him a wooden puzzle box. When he solved the puzzle and opened the drawer, he immediately recognized Pharaoh's scarab cartouche seal impressed in the wax on the papyrus. When he broke the seal and unfurled the scroll he read, "I must see you before your return to Giza. Come to my chambers immediately."

Lord Kontar smiled and signaled the waiter, "I must cancel lunch due to pressing business. Please serve the tilapia to your staff, courtesy of Pharaoh's royal architect."

The palace was a short walk and when he arrived, the guards raised their swords in salute and admitted Lord Kontar to the interior. Pharaoh's vizier was just closing the doors to the royal chambers. He threw up his hand and motioned for Lord Kontar to join him.

The vizier said, "Greetings, Kontar! Pharaoh is impatient today, go right in."

Lord Kontar headed for the royal chambers and, looking over his shoulder, asked, "When is Pharaoh not impatient?"

The vizier smiled in response.

Lord Kontar opened the massive doors and entered the royal chambers, but Pharaoh was not seated on the throne. Lord Kontar walked over to a table where a basket of fruit was setting and selected a handful of dates. At that moment Pharaoh emerged from behind the hanging drapes. Lord Kontar looked up and smiled.

Pharaoh thundered, "Kneel in the presence of the Pharaoh of Ra and look at the Earth for you are not worthy to look upon the face of Ra!"

Lord Kontar immediately dropped to his knees as ordered. Pharaoh proceeded to circle the kneeling lord and then drew the royal sword and placed it on the back of Lord Kontar's neck. Pharaoh then carefully slid the blade under Lord Kontar's tunic strap and with a quick flick, cut through the strap.

Pharaoh then said, "Rise."

When Lord Kontar stood up, his robe and tunic fell to the floor and he stood nude with his back to Pharaoh.

Pharaoh commanded, "Turn around!"

As Lord Kontar turned around, he could see that Pharaoh wore nothing but a golden scarab amulet with a highly polished black stone in the center.

Pharaoh squealed, "Oh Kontar, I missed you like the Earth misses the morning sun."

Kontar said, "Zahra! My heart is yours as always, come to me!

Three hours later as Kontar and Zahra were bathing, Zahra asked, "How did the progress report to Minister Al jer go?"

Lord Kontar replied, "Minister Al jer added yet another delay to my construction schedule by adding new requirements. The latest delay is to satisfy the Priests of Ra and you must know that it will drive up the project cost, too."

Zahra said, "You know very well if we are to control the people we must remain in partnership with the Priests of Ra, for they control the will of the people and we all serve Ra."

Kontar scoffed, "They are a bunch of self-serving, holier than thou hypocrites and we need to get them out of the line of authority!"

Zahra said, "Yes, of course, but you weren't complaining about the Priests of Ra when they were recruiting the artisans, stone cutters, and masons to donate time to your project at the Science Center."

"Wait! I didn't say they don't have a place, but the Royal Necropolis of Ra should be the Royal Science and Astronomy Center of Ra that just happens to be near a cemetery. Perhaps your Royal Ka, in your next incarnation, will separate the priests from the government, and we can lead the people of Atlantis with science and philosophy rather than ancient superstitions."

Kontar continued, "If we apply the principles of science to advancing Pharaoh's plans, rather than superstitious unproven methods that rely on smoke and mirrors and suspending common sense, we will accomplish more."

Kontar looked up to see if Zahra was in agreement only to see that Pharaoh was reclining on the pillows still wearing nothing. She seemed to be lost in thought as she was stroking and admiring the scarab amulet. In the center of the solid gold amulet was a jade scarab. In the middle of the scarab's shellback was a highly polished black stone. The black stone was creased down the middle to simulate the scarab's shellback. Under the scarab was a cartouche containing the hook symbol to signify ruler, the ankh symbol to represent eternal life and at the bottom was the hieroglyphic symbol for Z. This cartouche was Zahra's personal hieroglyphic seal that she had designed as a child, before she ascended to the throne of Atlantis. Her royal name was also contained in the cartouche, but it was twenty symbols long. The royal cartouche was prominently displayed on all monuments, including her royal sarcophagus at Giza.

Pharaoh said, "I wish you would reveal the name of the artisan that created my scarab amulet. It is my favorite piece of jewelry. I never take it off. It is my good luck charm and it always protects me."

Kontar smiled and said, "Dearest Zahra, if you want more jewelry from this artisan, we must honor his wish for secrecy or there will be no more golden trinkets."

Pharaoh frowned and Kontar thought, *If I tell her it was me, I'll never have another free minute as long as I live. I'd have to spend each waking moment making trinkets for her.*

Zahra looked up and said, "After speaking with Minister Al jer, I realize I must make a royal tour of inspection of the Necropolis and Science Center. I have ordered the royal yacht made ready for an early evening departure today."

"We will have tonight aboard the royal yacht and every night leading up to the Festival of Ra. Are you not surprised and delighted?"

Kontar said, "Every moment spent with you, my love, is a moment spent in heaven. But remember, during the day, I will be on site at the Great Pyramid and we will only have the nights together."

Zahra said, "I live for our nights together!"

Pharaoh summoned the vizier and asked him to move the Pharaoh's entourage to the royal yacht and to prepare for the trip to Giza.

Pharaoh's entourage would occupy three ships. The lead ship would contain archers and foot soldiers, as would the ship bringing up the rear. There was no real danger because the civilization of Atlantis was orderly and peace ruled the land. Still, security was something never left to chance by Pharaoh's vizier.

The royal yacht was nearly a hundred cubits in length with an accompaniment of thirty oarsmen and thirty archers along with the ship's crew and Pharaoh's personal slaves. There was a royal cabin and several sleeping compartments for the royal entourage.

The voyage from Atlantis to Giza was easy. Each ship was rigged with a square sail. Although the Nile flowed north and emptied into the Mediterranean, the prevailing winds were from the north so the oarsmen had little work when going in either direction.

Sunrise on the Nile was beautiful. Pharaoh's royal yacht was making good time on the calm waters in the spring of 2807 BCE. The rhythmic slap of the water on the hull was a soothing sound to the sleeping royalty.

It happened to be the 10th of May and the annual Nile flood wouldn't occur until sometime between July and September, but the Priests of Ra were predicting the flood to be on the 15th of August this year. By 21 June the Festival of Ra would be history and Pharaoh would be back in the royal place in Atlantis and Lord Kontar would be working feverishly to complete the Great Pyramid project at Giza.

Distant thunder awakened Lord Kontar. He looked to his left to see the beautiful Zahra, sleeping like the princess he had known since they were children playing together at her mother's royal court. He and Zahra had always known they would marry one day. But neither had anticipated that Zahra's twin sister would die young in a chariot accident and that Zahra would become Pharaoh. Zahra's ascension to the throne had delayed their wedding plans. Once the Great Pyramid project was complete Kontar would be free to return to Atlantis and marry the love of his life.

There was another clap of thunder and Zahra stirred restlessly. Kontar noticed that she was holding the scarab amulet, even in her sleep. Kontar slipped out of the sleeping silks and made his way to the ship's bridge. The captain waved and motioned Kontar to the tiller.

Lord Kontar observed, "Captain, look how dark the southern sky is! What's going on? Are we in for a storm?"

The captain replied, "I've been making this run for 35 years and I've never seen a storm or a dark sky like that!"

Lord Kontar said, "Pharaoh's safety comes first; head for shore and get everyone safely on dry land."

At that moment they heard fifty bare hands and twenty-five heads slapping the deck at the sight of Pharaoh. Pharaoh looked at the southern sky and asked, "Are the Gods angry?"

Lord Kontar replied, "The Gods indeed may be angry and we may be in for a heavy storm. I have ordered the captain to make for dry land. Pharaoh's life must not be placed at risk on a stormy sea."

At that moment a bright light appeared in the dark southern sky. It was a fireball and it was streaking across the sky from west to east. From the deck of the royal yacht it looked like a piece of the moon was falling. A smoky tail was trailing the fireball, and it was miles in length. The fireball was a thousand miles south of the royal yacht, but the unusual sight alarmed everyone. The slaves had abandoned their oars and were screaming and praying. The current swept the ship back toward Atlantis. The captain shouted orders and the oar master whipped the men back to their positions and ordered them to pull for the shore.

Pharaoh commanded, "Wait! The fireball is an omen from Ra that our journey and the Festival of Ra are blessed! Captain, continue the journey to Giza. Let us show these ignorant slaves that Pharaoh is blessed by Ra!"

The captain countermanded his order and the royal yacht returned to its course for Giza. Lord Kontar had an eerie feeling that Pharaoh was making a mistake, and he wanted to discuss the decision with her, but he knew he had to wait until they were alone. Before he could suggest returning to Pharaoh's quarters, the sky began to clear and the sun broke through. A loud shout of joyous relief went up from the crew, and the ship's master cadence drummer began to beat out a steady rhythm once again.

Kontar turned to Pharaoh and whispered in her ear, "Hey, are you ready for breakfast?"

Pharaoh smiled.

As they were having breakfast in the royal cabin, Kontar could feel the wind's growing intensity. Through gaps in the drapes, he could see white caps on the river as the wind blew the tops off the wave crests.

A loud crack of thunder startled everyone. Kontar noticed that the sky was growing dark again and that it was beginning to rain. Pharaoh's personal slave immediately lit the lamp in the cabin. As she was lighting the lamp, Kontar caught her eye and he could see stark fear in the girl's face. Kontar glanced at Zahra and she appeared unconcerned and completely at ease.

By noon the rain was a torrent and the sky was pitch black. Kontar excused himself and returned to the bridge of the ship. The high wind and pounding rain made it difficult to cross the deck to the bridge. Lord Kontar shouted, "Change course immediately and pull for the shore! That is a direct order from Pharaoh!"

The captain ordered the helmsman to come about. As the flagship turned, the other two ships reversed course too. With the new course back toward Atlantis and the wind at his back, the captain ordered the mainsail set.

All three ships immediately began a very fast course toward the nearest shore. For the first time since the weather turned bad, Kontar felt a glimmer of hope. He thought, with luck, they would make shore before the main storm hit. Lord Kontar decided to remain on the bridge for the time being.

Still, the weather seemed to be getting worse. The sky was as dark as a moonless night, and the slaves couldn't keep the navigation torches lit because of the wind and blowing rain. Lord Kontar's glimmer of hope was once again replaced with a feeling of impending doom.

Lord Kontar was certain they were just on the fringes of a massive storm and he knew it would only get worse. The thunder seemed to be drawing closer and the sky was ablaze with lightning strikes.

Lord Kontar didn't want to leave the bridge, but he was afraid for Zahra's safety. Pharaoh's quarters were at the bow and he was helping the helmsman maintain course by leaning on the tiller. Just when his fears were peaking, the storm began to lessen in intensity and he felt that he could steal a moment to check on Zahra. As he was making his way forward, lightning struck the ship's main mast. The mast was split down the middle and the mainsail was blown away. With a sickening lurch the ship tore partially in half at the base of the mast. He was on the back half and Zahra's quarters were on the front half of the ship. As the storm reintensified, the two halves began to wrench apart.

Kontar screamed, "Zahra! Zahra!"

Through the tossing waters and blinding rain and in a bright flash of lightning he saw Zahra clinging to the rail of the ship.

"Zahra! Zahra!"

Kontar began to scramble along the remaining pieces of the ship that were still attached to the front half. Just as he reached Zahra, the two pieces of the ship separated.

In a flash of lightning, as their eyes met, they both knew they were facing eternity.

They struggled toward each other and Kontar grabbed a rope and wrapped it around their waists. He then lashed the end of the rope to the remains of the bow of the tattered ship.

The storm howled and blew and then, in an instant, the Nile became deathly still with no wind. The blackness of the night was complete, even during what should have been broad daylight. As the lightning flashed, their faces became visible for a few moments. During one lightning flash, Kontar could see Zahra's hands tightly wrapped around the scarab. Kontar, trying to be positive, said, "You better let go of that scarab and hold onto me!"

Zahra replied, "Kontar, you know I treasure this scarab as a symbol of our love. I will never let it go, and I want you to hold the scarab with me."

Kontar immediately cupped his hands around hers.

Zahra said, "I know this is the end of the world and I know we don't have much time left together in this life. I don't know how we offended Ra, but he is displeased and he is ending the world."

"My wish and hope is that we spend eternity together and that someday, somehow, we are reincarnated and will find each other again."

Kontar said, "Zahra, don't say those words. We are not dead yet and we will survive this storm, I promise."

Zahra said, "I only want one promise. I want you to promise that you won't lose me or the scarab."

"I promise."

She looked up at him and said, "Kontar, I know you are the artisan that made the scarab."

Kontar smiled.

First, the thunder returned. Then, the frequency of the lightning strikes increased.

Once again the driving rain pounded the ship's remains. Then, the hurricane force winds were back.

As the tiny remnants of the royal barge were tossed about, Kontar and Zahra began to hear a sound that grew in volume and intensity with every second. It was a sound no living creature on Earth had ever heard before. It was the sound and fury of a mega-tsunami roaring down the Nile Valley.

A 400 foot high wall of water, pushing a valley-wide pile of debris and rubble, was laying waste to all in its path. It took the tsunami thirty minutes to pass the Giza Plateau but the blackness lasted for three weeks.

The rain continued, on and off, for three months. The rain produced flood levels unknown on Earth in millions of years. The floodwater submerged two thirds of the 480 foot tall Great Pyramid for six months.

Then one day, the falling rain began to lessen. Then the waters began to recede and sunlight once again began to peek through the darkness. A new dawn was breaking.

People lucky enough to be above the flood waters began to emerge from safety and to put their lives back together. They were the nomadic tribesmen, herdsmen, and peasants. No one living near the Nile or the Mediterranean survived.

Lord Kontar, Zahra, the scarab, their lives, and their Atlantean civilization were all lost to the flood. The memories of the dominant Atlantean civilization became a legend, and then Atlantis itself became a myth. The people of Atlantis, their stories, and the contributions of their civilization would now be lost forever in time's abyss.

Chapter 1

The Friendly Skies

A news reporter was interviewing the eyewitnesses that called in to report the plane crash that hit the 14th Street Bridge that morning. Most people heard the plane before they saw it. The aircraft was making a high pitched screaming sound which drew their attention to the western sky.

"I looked up and saw this plane going like a thousand miles an hour. I thought it was going to hit the Washington Monument. Then suddenly, it veered toward the river and struck several cars on the bridge. I lost sight of it then, but I heard an awful explosion and I could see smoke and flames in the distance."

The news anchor voice-over droned on, "Just after dawn this morning a charter flight from Denver, Colorado, struck several inbound cars on the 14th Street Bridge before coming to rest in a burning pile of scorched metal and tangled hurricane fencing on the apron of Ronald Reagan Washington National Airport. The pilot and co-pilot were pronounced dead at the scene; four survivors were transported to a local hospital with non-life-threatening injuries. The names of the victims and the survivors have not been released."

Sean Thornton was a Department of Homeland Security (DHS) federal employee and he was watching the morning news report before leaving for work. Only in this case, the latest news was from three months ago. As he glanced over the top of his newspaper at the large-screen monitor and viewed the wreckage, he was munching on dry breakfast cereal and drinking a glass of orange juice. Sean was watching a previously recorded news report of the plane crash and reading a print-out of the Safety Board's final report of the plane crash.

As the news anchor continued, the crash scene images were playing on a continuous loop. The firefighting and emergency medical vehicles kept arriving at the crash scene over and over. The first responders found the fuselage in three pieces, with the cockpit located a hundred feet down the runway from the main crash site. The tail section was located at the point of initial ground impact, where it had separated due to damage caused by the impact with the cars. The main cabin and the wings made up the third and final chunk of the plane.

Even now, Sean thought it was a miracle there were any survivors at all. All four passengers had been transported to the Washington Hospital Center. While they sustained injuries, their lives were never in danger.

The plane crash had been particularly disturbing to Sean because the DHS Director and his family were aboard the plane. Of course, nearly everyone at DHS knew the director personally, or indirectly, and it was with great concern that they followed the news events of that morning three months ago.

The director had recovered quickly and returned to work after a few weeks with no ill effects. Still, Sean was anxious to hear the NTSB report to try to understand what had happened. Pilot error is often cited in small plane crashes, but equipment failure or weather can be contributing factors.

Sean knew only the cockpit crew could really answer the "what happened" question and they were both dead, so Sean was reading the safety report with great interest.

The safety investigators managed to retrieve fragments of the cockpit conversation between the pilots at the time of the crash. The Gulfstream's black box had been damaged, but it retained the vital information associated with the plane's speed, direction, and altitude.

Sean turned his attention from the screen back to the newspaper's report.

The plane had been flying at 45,000 feet in the clear blue skies of an early morning sunrise. What was unusual was that the plane was still in autopilot so close to the airport. The plane was on course and an hour ahead of schedule. The DHS Director, Tom Delaney, his wife, Mary Lou, and their two children were asleep in the passenger cabin. They were returning to Washington from a week-long ski vacation in Aspen.

The black box verified that Daniel McCann, the pilot, had engaged the autopilot from the pilot's seat. The investigators speculated that James Stephens, the co-pilot, might have been dozing because the co-pilot controls were disengaged and the cockpit conversation record supported that conclusion.

The National Weather Service confirmed that the jet stream had presented a strong tail wind the morning of the flight, and the strong wind contributed to the plane being an hour early.

Safety investigators could only speculate about what might have happened on the flight deck by comparing the data from the black box, the conversation transcripts, and the autopsy reports.

Investigators usually establish a disaster timeline and then integrate critical disaster events into the timeline to verify proposed scenarios. The speculations are used in the same way that a crime scene investigator will recreate a crime scene to test various theories in order to determine criminal intent and possible perpetrators. The principal NTSB investigator proposed the following scenario:

The pilot checked the chronometer on the cockpit's dash, compared it to his wristwatch, and recognized that he would need to contact the Reagan tower and update the flight plan because they would be landing an hour early.

The pilot may have been feeling a little sleepy as he reached for his thermos and poured hot coffee into his cup. The pilot's thermos had been found in the wreckage without a lid and the co-pilot's thermos was untouched. The pilot then engaged the autopilot about 200 miles outside of Washington.

The medical examiner's autopsy report determined that Daniel McCann and James Stephens had died in the plane crash. The report also noted a congenital aneurysm in the pilot's brain. The autopsy report did not speculate on the role the aneurysm may have played in the pilot's health during the last few moments of the flight, but the NTSB report did.

The NTSB released the transcripts from the flight data recorder: "Jim! Jim, wake up! My head is killing me."

"What the hell? Oh, Christ!"

The investigator's scenario suggested that the pilot might have tried to regain control of the aircraft by disengaging the autopilot at that point because the plane immediately began to descend at an acute angle. The speed was 500 miles per hour and should have been at 100 miles per hour for approach and landing at Reagan. The noise level in the cockpit was significantly elevated due to the speed and the plane's close proximity to the ground. Further cockpit conversation couldn't be isolated.

The Reagan Tower's voice records verified that the air traffic controller had attempted to contact the plane numerous times prior to the crash, with no response. The air traffic controller alerted Reagan's Emergency Crash and Rescue Team and was given special recognition for contributing to saving the passengers lives.

The NTSB report indicated that the co-pilot seized the controls thirty seconds before the crash. He immediately throttled back and banked right to avoid downtown Washington. The plane then stalled. In response to the stall, the co-pilot immediately shoved the throttles forward to gain air speed and pushed the stick down, but it was all just seconds too late. The co-pilot's attempts to control the plane changed the crash site from somewhere in Washington to the bridge and airport apron. The co-pilot's emergency efforts managed to scrub off enough air speed to allow the passengers to survive.

The NTSB determined that the crash most likely occurred after the pilot suffered complications from a grade six aneurysm that resulted in unconsciousness. The autopsy verified that Mr. McCann's aneurysm was a congenital defect that had gone undetected for years during his annual flight physicals. The NTSB closed the case on the crash.

At the Center for Disease Control in Atlanta, a data analyst had reviewed and entered the data from the death certificates for Mr. McCann and Mr. Stephens in the appropriate database. The official listed the cause of death for both men as being from a plane crash. Mr. McCann's aneurysm was not mentioned.

The CDC's "Causes of Deaths Contributing to Changes in Life Expectancy Category" is a vital information database that is routinely monitored by many government agencies, life insurance companies, health care providers, and drug manufacturers to support their business areas. True causes of death are important to the database users.

Database users access the data to specifically correlate the "Cause of Death" category to age and to occupation in order to establish trends and develop actuary tables. For example, the mortality factor for airline pilots versus mine workers was quite good. Whereas airline pilots versus government workers was not as good. The major variable in the data in the CDC database lies with the medical examiner and the death certificate. There is no real standard for citing cause of death. Cause of death determination is up to the individual coroner.

Sean checked the time on the media LCD and noted that it was time to leave for work. He clicked off the TV, pushed the auto button on his key remote, grabbed his brief case, and headed out the door. The convertible was sitting at the curb with the top going down and the motor running. Sean vaulted into the driver's seat. He pushed the home security button, and the house door locked and the alarm activated. As he drove along he couldn't help but think how close the department had come to losing one of its own.

Sean arrived at his office building and parked in the secure underground parking facility. When he exited his car, the top immediately closed and the alarm activated automatically. As Sean approached the elevator the infrared security camera verified his identity and opened the doors to convey him to his top floor office. The elevator doors opened directly into the lobby of the DHS Threat Analysis Office. As he approached the door to the office suite, the infrared security camera automatically verified his identity, his security level, and his access approval authority, and automatically released the door to the office suite. No one was in the office at this hour but Sean. As Sean entered the office the coffee machine activated to produce Sean's favorite blend and he waited for the cup to fill. He grabbed the coffee and sat down at his desk as his computer activated and verified his identity and checked his password.

Sean preferred to arrive early in the morning and to get his work hours in early so he could avoid rush hour traffic in both directions. DHS was flexible about work hours as long as employees were available during the core hours between 10:00 A.M. and 2:30 P.M.

Sean's specialty was categorizing, analyzing, and assessing threats to the homeland. Threats could include nuclear war; conventional war; terrorism; chemical/biological warfare; and a wide range of potential contingencies such as emerging military trends, regional threats, narcotics, and others yet to be categorized. One of the uncategorized threats that Sean thought was worth pursuing was what he believed to be an alarming trend in lowered life expectancy.

While he could easily accept that a rogue nation or a seriously disturbed individual might wish to influence the life spans of Americans in a negative way, he just didn't know how a reduction in life span could be covertly implemented.

Sean had been regularly tracking the CDC's databases to assess trends associated with raw data, and he had developed some theories on what to him was an apparent negative trend in life expectancies.

It was well established that human life expectancy had increased decade after decade during the 20th century, but Sean believed that today's raw statistical data was trending toward 19th century levels.

Sean had discussed his pet theories with his fellow analysts. His co-workers thought the negative data was an insignificant spike and that up and down spikes were consistent with the normal cycle and could be expected over the short term. They believed Sean was attaching too much meaning to the early 21st century results. His colleagues noted that the causes of death were all over the place too, with genetic defects playing a role and people simply not taking advantage of the medical treatments and life extending longevity treatments that were available to nearly everyone.

Sean recognized that using raw data to draw conclusions was problematic, and he knew that he would need at least ten years worth of data to make a concrete case. He knew very well that a large study would need to be conducted and the data carefully selected to reach any conclusion that could be identified as a certified threat. Nevertheless, while Sean knew he was courting a long shot he had a gut feel that something was wrong. Sean clicked the CDC bookmark to access his favorite database.

As he reviewed the fresh data added since his last visit, he thought, *people are dying young—way too young.* The average life span for human beings seemed to be trending still lower and lower. Again, the actuary tables and the raw statistics were showing a downward trend.

Sean thought his analyst colleagues were missing an early critical data point. While their cyclical answer was reasonable, he just couldn't buy it.

Sean's systems analyst job with DHS didn't charge him with saving humanity. All he had to do was show up, analyze the data and review the trends, and leave the cause and effect relationships to the PhDs and the government think tanks. But, Sean was concerned that someone, or some enemy of the USA, might be behind the trend. Of course, he wouldn't dare elevate his pet theory on diminishing life trends to the next level based only on a gut feeling. He needed something concrete that just wasn't on the horizon. But still, he would keep an eye on the data points.

While his life and his job relied heavily on computers and information technology, he believed there was no substitute for the human brain when it came to leaps of sudden enlightenment or the "eureka" moment. Search functions associated with interactive browsers inevitably have to search all available data and still they only present data. It is left to the human mind to make sense of the data returned.

The human brain has the ability to instantly draw a conclusion, skip untold steps, and arrive at the eureka moment. Sean believed that the eureka moment, with regard to a negative trend in life expectancy, was just outside his grasp, but he was certain it was hovering near.

Even though Sean was a full time analyst his true passion was philosophy, world history, archeology, and, oh yeah, drinking a few beers with his friends while solving the world's problems at the same time.

Sean lived a bachelor's life in an old Victorian home in Maryland's Garrett Park neighborhood, but his office was located in Georgetown. In his off hours he surrounded himself with an eclectic collection of antiques, fossils, yard sale furniture, old clocks, old books, and old cars. He also had a passion for the opposite sex.

Sean often spent the weekends looking for antiques and fossils, and if his girl friend liked antiques that was a plus, but by no means a deal breaker. He usually combined his activities because some of the best junk shops and mom and pop antique stores were on Maryland's Eastern and Western Shores. Both shores were excellent for fossil hunting, too, especially the Calvert Cliff area near St. Mary's City on Maryland's Western Shore and Tilghman Island near St. Michaels on Maryland's Eastern Shore. If his girl friend d'jour preferred sailing and sun bathing to antiques and fossils, then he could work those activities into the mix very easily because he moored his sailboat at his friend's dock in Chestertown, Maryland.

Chestertown was just across the Chesapeake Bay Bridge on Maryland's Eastern Shore. Sean didn't care if the girls liked antique hunting or if they preferred fun in the sun. At sunset everyone likes a nice dinner, a little wine, perhaps some dancing, and frolicking in the hot tub.

Sean's favorite author was Sir Arthur Conan Doyle, and he considered himself, like Sherlock Holmes, a keen observer of people, places, and events. It was his downtown place of work and eclectic collection of interests that led Sean to bring his thoughts on the upcoming weekend, and his keen observation of people, to the happy hour crowd at Clyde's of Georgetown. Clyde's was a daily stop for Sean since his college days at the University of Maryland. When his afternoon physics lab was done, he and his lab partner, Bill O'Hara, would adjourn to Clyde's to enjoy the "Afternoon Delight" menu.

Some college bad habits are hard to break and Clyde's Afternoon Delight menu was no exception. Today, Sean and Bill the bartender, his old lab partner, were shooting the breeze and nursing a couple of beers. Sean activated his keen observational skills as he appraised a particularly striking brunette sitting at the end of the bar.

He thought to himself, hmm, the long hair, professional business attire, and high heel pumps means she is not a tourist and she probably works nearby.

The long hair suggested that she took her time getting ready for work rather than the "quick shower, short hair, blow dry, and out the door look" that many lawyers or corporate executives display.

Sean thought that she definitely considers herself a woman in the professional environment rather than a competing colleague in a man's world. The fact that she is wearing pumps rather than running shoes means a professional appearance is more important than comfort, not to mention style. Then he thought, there I go again over analyzing the situation.

Sean continued with his internal review and began to check off the pluses. No ring on her left hand—check! Bright blue eyes, check; and, oh how blue they are, check! Wow! She's beautiful!

Sean knew by the color of her security badge, still pinned to her lapel, that she was a government employee.

Sean had never seen her in Clyde's before. Bill followed Sean's gaze and raised his eyebrows appreciatively.

Sean left the bar area monetarily to answer his personal digital assistant (PDA) and when he returned to the bar he took a seat two stools away from the girl. Sean motioned for Bill and ordered a draft beer. Sean and Bill began to shoot the breeze about sports in general and the Georgetown Hoyas in particular. The Hoyas were a national contender again, and they were a perennial threat in the NCAA tournament during March Madness.

Sean said, "Bill, there is no doubt in my mind that Georgetown is a better sports school than it is an academic school."

Bill replied, "I can't argue with you there, that's for sure. They're definitely a sports-first school."

That unfounded declaration forced the brunette beauty to interject, "Just a minute there. I know Georgetown is a stellar academic institution, and sure they are under the gun to produce winning sports teams just like UVA or any other school, but at Georgetown scholastics are number one."

Sean said, "Well, wait a minute, consider the evidence. Georgetown, like most schools, is more focused on publicity, expanding enrollment, and sports crowns than seeing that the members of the sports teams graduated on time."

Her blue eyes flashed as she replied, "Your facts are uncoordinated. Georgetown's sports teams routinely graduate 80% of their players compared to the national average of less than 50%."

Someone called Bill's name, he gave Sean a wink, and moved off to the other end of the bar to serve other happy hour customers. Bill's absence gave Sean room to operate. This was a game Bill and Sean had played before. The important part of the game was to establish a rapport with the lady that dodged standard pick-up lines.

Sean introduced himself and held out his hand. She did the same and smiled. "I'm Corinne Cannon," she said. They proceeded to discuss the local sports teams and the various teams' prospects for the fall basketball season. Sean said, "I find it interesting that you know so much about Georgetown, yet you're a University of Virginia alum. Do you prefer the Atlantic Coast Conference to the Big East Conference?"

Corinne raised an eyebrow and said, "I do prefer the ACC, but I have many interests."

Sean's keen Sherlock Holmes technique had not seen that one coming. He was beginning to think Corinne had other mysteries that were not easily deduced as well.

There was a flurry of activity behind them as a party of four vacated a booth when they were called for dinner.

Sean said, "Let's move to that empty booth over there. I'd like to hear your ideas on what you think colleges can do to improve their graduation rates. Hey Bill! Can you bring us two martinis? Sean turned to Corinne and asked, "Is a Gibson okay with you?

Corinne asked, "A martini? Why a martini and what's a Gibson?"

Sean said, "I know you are interested in college traditions and I wonder if you like historical quotes too?

"Sure, what do you have?"

"H. L. Mencken, the Sage of Baltimore, observed: 'The martini is the only American invention as perfect as a sonnet.'"

Corinne replied, "Who am I to doubt? Maybe Mencken is right. Okay, I'll try one."

Sean called to Bill, "Make that two Gibson's, and very dry, please."

As they settled into the booth Corinne asked, "What's the difference between a martini and a Gibson? I know a martini is made with gin or vodka, a shot of white vermouth, and three olives."

Sean replied, "A Gibson is a horse of another color and there is a subtle but real difference between a gin martini and a gin Gibson. The Gibson is served with cocktail onions and it has a magic that the martini lacks."

Sean could tell by the look on Corinne's face that he wasn't getting anywhere.

"So the difference is cocktail onions rather than olives?"

"Well, onions are an important distinction, but according to General George S. Patton the main difference is that the gin bottle should be pointed in the general direction of Italy to honor the vermouth. Oh, and the three pickled cocktail onions are a must, too."

Bill brought the Gibsons and Sean proposed a toast, "To the Hoyas, Mencken, and General Patton!"

Corinne took a sip and said, "Oh my God! This is awful! I can't drink this thing."

"Trust me! Give it the old college try and have two Gibsons with me. If you still can't appreciate the Gibson's magic after two, we won't order a third. Remember, it takes two Gibsons for the magic to work."

"Okay, I'll try!"

By the time they finished the second Gibson, Corinne's eyes were very shiny and the conversation had turned from sports teams to the plane crash and the NTSB report and the subject of God vs. evolution.

Corinne said, "I remember the plane crash like it was yesterday. I had just climbed out of the shower and turned on the hair dryer when I heard that awful screeching sound when the plane passed over our townhouse. At first I thought it was my hair dryer and then I heard the explosion. The morning news broadcast was interrupted with scenes from the crash, while I was still putting on my make-up. I just know it was the hand of God that saved those people that morning."

Sean said, "I think it was luck and the last second tug on the controls by the co-pilot, along with the airport's rescue team, that made the difference."

Corinne said, "You may be right, but all of those people are God's handiwork too."

While Corinne's Catholic faith gave her the confidence to believe in God without a doubt, her science education gave her the will to doubt the Bible's infallibility.

Sean asked, "Couldn't the science that created the jet airplane and the medical technology that saved those people's lives be a property of the natural evolutionary progression of life on this planet? In other words, evolution the way Darwin and the fossil record indicate? By the way, how do you like that Gibson now?"

Corinne's face crinkled into a grin and she said, "Okay! I get it! I get it! This is the best damned cocktail I've ever had, let's have one more! My God! Mencken was a genius! I feel like I need to get a book of Shakespeare's sonnets and see what I missed the first time around."

"I knew you'd like it! I love it when the magic works!"

Corinne said, "I believe the Bible and Darwin's theory of evolution are not mutually exclusive. If you considered the Bible as a metaphor, then Darwin's theory and the Bible's metaphor could occupy a seat together on a cross-country bus trip without feeling the need to change seats before St. Louis."

Sean laughed and said, "I see what you mean, but I agree with Carl Sagan. As far as Carl and I are concerned, we are simply the product of star stuff striking the primordial soup. What I mean is when the meteors and space debris hit the Earth all those million years ago, the result was a chain of self-replicating proteins. You see, I think life's history on this planet is simply a product of the enormous amount of elapsed time since the dawn of the self-replicating proteins and the dawn of modern man."

It was Corinne's turn to laugh, "Well, you and Carl may have a point but it fits with either Darwin's theory or the Bible's explanation. And on top of that, it doesn't fit with the evidence that, in my mind, shows the hand of God has given rise to man's intelligence."

"Who's to say how a supreme being would implement his will. Would he simply "think a reality" and it would instantly occur or would he be constrained by the physical laws of the universe the same as we are? In other words, might he not, by the strength of his intellect, nudge the meteors and space debris from an outer obit toward the Earth for the creation of life in the primordial soup?"

"Corinne, that's an interesting concept for a Catholic. Are God and God's work supernatural, or are God and his work an integral feature of science? Must God operate within the same laws of the universe as we do?"

Rather than answer, Corinne excused herself to go powder her nose. Sean couldn't take his eyes off her as she walked the length of the bar toward the ladies room. Sean decided not to order another round of Gibson's. He remembered what his old Air Force buddy, Harry, always said about Gibsons, "Gibson's are like women's breasts; two are not enough and three are too many." Sean thought, *I need to be on top of my game with this girl.*

While Corinne was in the ladies room, Sean was thinking that Corinne was charming, intelligent, and perceptive; plus, she had great legs. He also thought that everything else about her was turning out to be pretty super too. As he waited, he wondered if he should share his pet theory about God, DNA, and the double-helix conspiracy. Plus, was he sober enough to make a case. Then again, maybe they should now adjourn to the Crazy Horse Saloon for some dancing before the night was lost or she determined that he might be too far out or just plain crazy.

At that moment Corinne returned from the ladies room and picked up her jacket and said, "Hey! Let's go dancing!"

Corinne's suggestion gave Sean the focus he needed and off they went. Sean slapped a twenty down on the bar as they were going out the door; he didn't have time to wait for change. The Crazy Horse was a short walk down M Street, and when Corinne's high heel snagged in a crack between the cobblestones Sean caught her to keep her from falling. As they came face to face and inches apart there was an awkward moment before Corinne gave Sean a quick "thank you" kiss on the cheek, and they launched back into their debate on the meaning of life.

Corinne asked, "Isn't the real argument whether God has a hand in men's lives or whether he simply created life and remains hands off?"

Sean said, "No, to me the real argument isn't whether God did or didn't create the universe or even if there is a God. What is the nature of God? Or what is the "nature of the force" that humans mistakenly interpret as God. For example, every civilization has assumed there was a power greater than itself and has created a religion to honor or worship their God. In every case they believed God to be in the sky above them and they built monoliths, buildings, or temples up toward the sky or the heavens."

"The Bible depicts man's attempt to reach heaven by constructing the Tower of Babel."

Corinne replied, "Now you are making my case for God by admitting that the hand of God has been evident since the beginning of known time in all of man's recorded civilizations."

Sean said, "Whoa! You are leaping to a conclusion and putting words in my mouth. What I mean is that I don't doubt that the natural laws of the universe represent intelligence, I'm saying that early civilizations have mistakenly attributed the order of the universe to a supernatural being that directs the daily affairs of men."

"My point is that mankind's existence may not be the result of a supernatural being invoking his will on nature and creating Adam and Eve in his image. Mankind's existence may simply be a secondary derivative of the application of the natural laws of nature."

Corinne said, "So, you are not buying the 'God created Adam in his image to be ruler of the universe' part of the Bible?"

Sean said, "That's a good way to put it. I believe that Genesis represents not the 'word of God' but highlights the arrogance of the human scholar that composed Genesis. The arrogance of the scholar or the officials of the Vatican is again demonstrated when the Vatican felt compelled to persecute Galileo during the 16th century."

"Galileo insisted on proving, in a public forum, that the Earth-centered Ptolemaic view of the universe was wrong and the sun-centered, Copernican universe was correct. I understand the Vatican's reluctance to admit Galileo was correct because to do so would fly in the face of the Bible's infallibility."

"As science has proved, the Earth is not the stationary center of the universe. Eventually, the church had to accept the truth."

Corinne asked, "Don't you have faith in God?"

"I don't want to wear out Mencken, but he said 'faith may be defined briefly as an illogical belief in the occurrence of the improbable.'"

At that moment two men stepped out of the shadows with knives drawn and demanded, "Quickly, your money or you die!"

Before Sean could act Corinne threw her jacket in the face of the first man and kicked the other man in the groin.

Sean grabbed Corinne by the hand and pulled her into the M Street traffic. Horns blared and tires screeched. When they reached the other side of the street, they looked back and both robbers had disappeared into the darkness of the side streets.

Sean asked, "Are you crazy, you could have been hurt or killed?"

"The hell with those punks, I may be somebody's target, but I'll be damned if I'll be somebody's victim, at least not without a fight!"

They high fived each other and began to laugh. They crossed back across M Street, picked up Corinne's jacket, and walked on toward the Crazy Horse.

As Sean listened and watched Corinne as they walked, he began to think, *I want to know this woman a lot better. Thank God she wasn't hurt.* Then he caught himself and he had to laugh.

Sean began to think, maybe going to dinner would be better than dancing in a loud club. Soft music, dinner, and intimate conversation would be perfect.

Sean asked, "Hey, Corinne are you still in the mood for dancing or would you rather catch dinner? I know this perfect restaurant just a few blocks north of M Street. What do you think?"

Corinne turned around and gave him the look.

Chapter 2

Midnight in Old Europe

"Hey, that's a great idea! A quiet dinner after all this would be perfect."

"Super! Wait right here in front of the Crazy Horse and I'll pick you up. My car is just around the corner in the parking garage. I'll be back in a second."

Corinne heard Sean before she saw him. There was a low rumble of the high performance exhaust pipes of a powerful V8 engine reverberating off the bricks and the buildings on M Street and Sean pulled up, jumped out, and opened the door for her. Corinne said, "Thank you, kind sir. Can I be sure you are in compliance with the environmental and fuel standards with this car?"

"Not to worry, this is a classic car that is exempt from those standards."

Sean blipped the throttle and made an illegal left turn onto Wisconsin Avenue and headed north. Sean pulled up in front of the restaurant. The Old Europe was a favorite haunt of Sean's because the food was great and priced right, and the booths provided a little seclusion and anonymity.

The valet, Jimmy, opened the door for Corinne, while Sean applied the parking brake and left the engine running. When Jimmy came around to the driver's side Sean said, "No joy riding this time, parking only."

Jimmy said, "Mr. Thornton I was only filling it up with gas to surprise you."

Sean laughed, "Yeah sure, but don't surprise me this time."

The maitre'd, Günter, met them at the door, greeted Sean with a handshake and asked, "Your usual table, Sir?"

"Good evening Günter. Is the booth in the back available? We've had a little too much of Georgetown's night life already."

Günter showed them to their table and took their drink orders, Beck's on draft in frosty mugs this time.

When the drinks arrived, Sean hoisted his glass high and said, "To Corinne! Your courage, fast thinking and quick action saved our lives tonight!"

Corinne held up her glass and added, "And to Sean for making sure we weren't killed in traffic and, most importantly, for retrieving my jacket." They laughed, clinked glasses, and took a sip.

Sean observed, "You know we made a pretty good team tonight?"

"I was thinking the same thing. Somehow I feel like I know you better than I should. After all we just met for the first time a few hours ago."

Sean said, "I feel the same way about you. Isn't it funny how sometimes you meet someone for the first time and yet it feels like you are old friends? It is almost a deja vu moment but with people rather than places."

Corinne said, "Some people call the sensation remembering the future."

Sean said, in a sing song voice, "So where did you grow up, where did you go to school, and what sorority did you pledge?"

Corinne said, "Okay! You asked for it! My parents worked for the State Department's diplomatic core and we spent time in England, Germany, France, Italy, Spain, and the District of Columbia. Of course, while technically Washington, D.C., is not a foreign country it does have a separate language and culture of its own. I grew up in Alexandria and spent my teenage years in and around Washington. I attended almost as many embassy parties as my parents did."

Corinne's parent's friends included a diverse group of people from many cultures and Corinne felt comfortable in most any social setting.

Corinne said, "When it came time to select a college, the University of Virginia was a given because my mom and dad are both UVA alumni. I graduated with a Master's in genetic research. During the summers I interned at the National Institutes of Health in Bethesda with Dr. Addison Paige. When I graduated, Dr. Paige asked me to continue my work on the genome project."

"It's the perfect job for me. As an intern I worked on data correlation, and now I have a chance to really get into the research side in depth."

Sean said, "I attended a seminar on the life and times of Francis Crick and James D. Watson at the Smithsonian a few years ago and I was struck by the sheer size of the molecule and the enormous amount of data contained within the code."

"I have a feeling that we, as human beings, are far more programmed by our genetic code than we realize. There is no doubt in my mind that we have free will to alter our behavior, but I often wonder if some brilliant idea or insight that comes into our consciousness as a eureka moment might have been preprogrammed in the genetic code."

Corinne replied, "I've read virtually everything that has been written on Crick and Watson. They're my professional heroes. Sean, you don't know how unusual it is to meet someone that has an interest in DNA. Most people are only familiar with DNA when the police have used it to connect a suspect to a crime scene or perhaps to free someone from prison that has been wrongfully convicted of a crime that they did not commit."

Sean said, "Corinne your behavior tonight, in the crisis with the muggers, may well have been in your genetic make up; you may not have had a choice once the situation exceeded the threshold of the 'fight or flight' decision."

"You may be right, but then we both may be simply A-type personalities. Whether we are A's or B's may have more to do with our environment than with our genetic code."

Sean said, "Of course! That's the elementary argument of nature or nurture."

Corinne said, "I suspect that if we examine our childhood environment and our home life we will find that we have far more in common than genetics. Now that you've had the thumbnail sketch of my background, let's hear your story!"

Sean began, "I was born to career military parents and we moved around a lot."

Corinne remarked, "See, the same as my parents."

Sean said, "Corinne, you're getting ahead of the story. My parents were killed in a terrorist attack in the Mid East when I was three years old and I was raised by my grandparents on a farm in Indiana."

Corinne replied, "I'm so sorry. I...I...I...."

Sean laughed, "Take it easy Corinne it happened a long time ago, and I don't remember anything about it. My grandparents were Mom and Dad. They've passed on, but I still think of them often."

"When high school was finished, I just couldn't face four years in college. I needed to see the world my mother and father knew and, I wanted to know the world's people on a first name basis. I didn't have a career in mind, but I knew I could be successful in whatever career I tackled."

"However, saying you want to travel and see the world is one thing, but financing it is something else; so I joined the Navy."

"As a kid I was really interested in computers, software, electronics, and all things involving artificial intelligence and robotics. The results of my Navy aptitude tests pushed me toward the digital data fields. I attended two years of the Navy's electronic and IT technical schools. The schools were eight hours a day and five days a week."

"Once school was complete, I served aboard intelligence gathering ships. I met intelligence officers from the US Navy but also from our NATO Allies."

Corinne said, "So you were a secret agent! Wow! That sounds like fun!"

Sean replied, "Fun is not the right word. But secret agent is more correct than you know. I was at sea for nine months at a time, mostly in the Mediterranean. I met a lot of strange people, but I also met a lot of nice people."

"Typically, my division stood four hour watches with eight hours off. During the off-watch time through out the cruise, we performed maintenance on the exterior communication and electronic counter measures equipment. So, men shared berthing areas, meals, recreation activities, daily work, and liberty too. I met some folks that I still call my friends. I have some military friends that, even now, if I needed them, would come running."

"When it came time for me to make the decision to reenlist or leave the service, my friends advised me to take advantage of the GI Bill to earn a college degree and then to consider returning to the Navy as an officer."

"I was stationed at the Pentagon when I made the decision to leave active duty, but I decided to remain in the Naval Reserve to keep my options open."

"The Pentagon employees include active military, civil service workers, and defense contractors, also known as beltway bandits."

"The beltway bandits provide defense electronic equipment experts as technical representatives to the ships to install and groom the equipment prior to the ship's deployment, so I was familiar with the companies providing the service to the fleet and I already spoke their technical language."

"My Navy resume and my intelligence background made the transition from active military to civilian contractor easy. As recommended, I enrolled at the University of Maryland and earned an undergraduate degree and a Masters in Computer Science. I then accepted a position with the Department of Homeland Security as a systems analyst."

Sean said, "So there you have the thumb nail sketch. Your parents were diplomatic corps professionals, highly educated and traveled in high society, while my grandparents lived on a farm in Indiana. My childhood couldn't have been more opposite than yours. Yet here we are crossing paths professionally, academically, and, hopefully, romantically."

Corinne said, "So you think that because we had dissimilar childhoods your case for genetics and the double helix is made?"

"Well, I don't think it makes my case, but I think it is a data point that supports my theory. Yes, we would need to do the research and gather the data and we would need to observe some control groups over a long period of time that would probably exceed our lifetimes by perhaps a factor of a hundred. Oh! By the way, you didn't mention romantically."

Corinne smiled and said, "Perhaps we need to gather more data to support that hypothesis."

With dinner over, a shot of Drambuie with coffee and the night drawing late Sean said, "Tomorrow is Saturday and, unless you have to work, you might want to think about the "Attic in the Street" flea market off Knowles Avenue in Kensington. I never miss it! I always find some treasure I can't live without."

Corinne said, "Kathy, my room mate, and I always hit the Georgetown Flea market on Sundays but I've never heard of the Attic in the Street. Is the flea market held every Saturday?"

"Oh no, just once a year and that's what makes it so special. Garret Park is chock full of retired diplomatic corps people so there's always an unusual collection of stuff to choose from. I once bought an Arabian long rifle that had a goat's skull nailed to the rifle butt so that the gun would be easier to hold to the shoulder and fire from horse back."

Corinne said, "Yew! I hope they are sold out of those! Thanks for the tip. Maybe Kathy and I will check it out."

Sean offered, "I can drive you home or to your car. What works for you?"

Corinne replied, "My car is under the NIH satellite office building in the parking garage. If you could drop me off at home in Georgetown I'll ask Kathy to take me to get my car tomorrow morning."

Sean pantomimed starting a car to Jimmy. Jimmy nodded and went to bring the Corvette around to the door.

Minutes later as they were motoring down Wisconsin Avenue, Sean said, "Corinne even with all the excitement tonight it has been a delight meeting you and I would like to see you again, is that possible?"

Corinne said, "Well, you did save my life and buy me dinner. Maybe I can trust you with my number. If you call and no one picks up please be careful how you word your message; remember I have a room mate and she may be screening calls."

"No problem."

Corinne shared a Georgetown brownstone with a girl friend from college.

They arrived at Corinne's brownstone and Sean leaped out to open the car door and walk her to the front door. They were standing on the doorstep just staring at each other and smiling. Sean leaned in toward Corinne and kissed her slowly and sweetly on the lips and Corinne returned the kiss. Sean said, "See you soon. I'll call you."

And Corinne thought, *I wonder if he will call?*

Chapter 3

Time is on My Side

The next morning at breakfast Corinne told Kathy about the big adventure. Corinne was seated on the couch with folded legs and she was very animated. Kathy heard every detail about ten times. And that was okay with Corinne because she loved talking about every moment over and over. Kathy asked, "Do you think he'll call?"

Corinne said, "I'm sure he will, because he seemed as interested in me as I was in him. What is the rule on calling a girl? Does he have to wait a week or what?"

Kathy said, "I don't think those rules apply any more. Why don't you call him?"

"Some rules may not apply but I would never call a man I met at happy hour. It just isn't done, at least not by me."

"If he doesn't call, you can always go back to Clyde's and bump into him."

"Not me! If he sees me again, he'll either have to call me or it will have to be by accident because I won't return to Clyde's and have him think I am interested in him."

Kathy roared with laughter!

Kathy dropped Corinne at her car at the garage. Corinne waved thanks and drove off in a tiny little hybrid car. As she drove along she remembered the flea market in Garret Park and decided to check it out. By this time it was afternoon and she knew you had to arrive early to find the good stuff, but it was worth a look anyway. *After all,* she thought, *I don't care if they are all out of goat skulls and rifles.* Thirty minutes later she had parked the car behind the Garret Park Town Center, in the church parking lot.

The town center faced the "Attic in the Street" event so Corinne stepped from the town center and into the crowd.

She thought, *Wow! Sean was right, just look at this stuff!*

As she approached one set of tables she saw several antique clocks for sale. Sean had mentioned his clock collection, so she was thinking Sean might have missed the event after all. She thought, *I'll just check the price on this little Seth Thomas clock; it would look great in the hallway.* She didn't see anyone but she heard water running and she looked up toward the garage. A man, with his back to the street, was washing a shiny red classic corvette.

Corinne said, "Excuse me. Is this table yours?"

The man put down the hose and turned around and said, "It sure is. Which one do you like?"

They instantly recognized one another and both laughed.

Sean thought sometimes a subtle suggestion is all you need to make the improbable seem coincidental.

"I see you decided to take my advice on the flea market."

"I just happened to be in the neighborhood. Wow! What a beautiful Victorian home you have."

Sean said, "This old thing? You'd be surprised what an Indiana farm, a little bit of sweat equity, and a half million dollars worth of fix-up can do for an old run down house. Would you like a tour?"

Corinne replied, "I would like a tour, if it's not too much trouble."

"No trouble at all. I love showing off my collection of stuff."

Sean said, "I bought this old house several years ago with the inheritance from my grandfather's estate. It was run down and in horrible shape or I wouldn't have been able to afford it. I took my time restoring the house, doing it bit by bit as my budget allowed.

"On the inside and out it looks pure 1880s, but the insulation, roof, windows, and HVAC are the latest in energy efficient stuff."

"Come on, I'll show you the inside, but remember it doesn't have the benefit of a woman's touch."

The predominant decorating theme was time and timekeeping. Sean's collection of clocks covered most of the available wall space on all levels including the bathrooms. The collection included everything from precision regulator clocks to novelty clocks where Lady and the Tramp's eyes followed you with every tick tock.

Sean said, "Here is an 'Attic' find, check this out."

Sean raised the top on the beautiful mahogany Victrola to reveal a bright green velvet turntable with gold plated needle holder. Sean wound the Victrola with the crank on the side, placed a record on the turntable, and set the record spinning. He gently lowered the needle on to the record and the sounds of "God Bless America" filled the room. Corinne listened, mesmerized by the sound.

When the record finished Sean said, "This old Victrola is an example of why I love antiques. There is nothing like the textured sound that is reproduced without electronics and amplified by the aged mahogany of this antique cabinet."

Sean then placed the love song Irving Berlin wrote for his wife on the turntable. The words began: "I'll be loving you always, with a love that's true always...." Sean held out his hand to Corinne and they danced around the parlor.

Corinne said, "This is the dance we missed last night, but I think the wait was worth it."

The next stop on the tour was the family room. As they entered the room the fireplace immediately blazed up. Located on one side of the fireplace was the biggest wall clock Corinne had ever seen. It had glass advertising panels offering meals at the White Swan Tavern in Chestertown, Maryland; official rail road time for the Washington, Baltimore and Philadelphia Rail Road Company; and advertisements for the Chestertown Transcript. To Corinne the most amazing parts were the three rotating advertising cylinders that changed advertisements every five minutes.

Sean said, "You might think of this clock as the 19th century mechanical version of the 20th century neon sign."

Corinne said, "I know Chestertown, it's on Maryland's Eastern Shore. But just where?"

Sean said, "It's easy to find. You cross the Bay Bridge and stay on Route 301. Look for the sign to Chestertown then make a left. I keep my sail boat at my friend's dock in Chestertown."

Corinne noticed a little shadow box with a golden beetle in the middle, surrounded by what looked like dinosaur teeth.

Corinne asked, "I know you like antiques and fossils; are these actual dinosaur teeth?"

"No, they're not dinosaur teeth. Those are fossilized shark teeth from an ancient great white shark that was forty feet long and probably lived at the same time as the dinosaurs."

"What is the golden beetle in the middle?"

Sean said, "That is an Egyptian scarab necklace that I bought in a Cairo bazaar when I was in the Navy. Here, try it on!"

Sean picked up the necklace and stood behind Corinne as he lowered the necklace over her head and fastened the clasp. As Corinne looked in the mirror at the shiny scarab, their eyes met and Sean's clocks began chiming 2:00 P.M.

Corinne said, "Holy cow! What does it sound like at midnight? How do you sleep?"

Sean said, "I love to hear the chimes and if one clock doesn't chime, the silence will wake me. The ticking and chiming is very soothing like the natural rhythm of the universe or your heartbeat. Time is the heartbeat of the universe. If you think about it, the initial big bang was like the first strike heard at the beginning of time and the universe has been counting time ever since with each orbit of the planet around the sun. The Earth and sun are gears in the great clock of the universe."

After the house tour, Sean invited Corinne to go for a road trip in the Maryland countryside. The flea market was winding down so Sean and Corinne quickly carried the stuff to the garage and they were on the road in the Corvette in no time. Sean decided to follow the Potomac River north towards Harper's Ferry to enjoy the beautiful unspoiled countryside.

They stopped at the Chesapeake and Ohio Canal's aqueduct where the canal and towpath cross the Monocacy River via an elevated bridge, just before the Monocacy flows into the Potomac River.

The canal towpath provided a flat walkway for a romantic stroll under the canopy of trees along the sun-dappled canal. It was a beautiful stroll with the occasional hiker or biker passing by. The rolling cumulus clouds framed the distant Sugarloaf Mountain cliffs.

Corinne said, "I've always been fascinated by the contrast nature provides to the concrete and steel of the city. When we are tied up in the frantic pace of our jobs in Washington, we lose sight of nature and perhaps the true meaning of life. Thanks for bringing me here."

Sean said, "It's too late today, but sometime in the future I would like to take you to the top of Sugarloaf Mountain. We'll sit on those cliffs among the clouds and have a glass of Merlot. You'll feel like you are on top of the world as you look down on the Potomac valley and see the hawks circling below, looking for lunch."

Corinne said, "Pencil me into your day planner; I'd love to." They continued to enjoy the afternoon stroll as they headed north on the towpath. They covered about a mile when Sean suggested that they should head back to the car.

As they were climbing back into the car, Sean recommended dinner at the "Old Angler's Inn," located south of Great Falls overlooking the C&O Canal. As they were driving south, Sean called ahead and made reservations for an upstairs table with a perfect view. Over dessert Corinne marveled at how truly unique and quaint the Old Angler's Inn was.

"Sean this restaurant seems like the perfect mixture of antique architecture, old world style, elegance, and fresh seafood."

Sean asked, "What do you like best, the ambience or the chef's specialty?"

Corinne responded. "I think it is the perfect combination and the good company that creates the perfect ambience."

Sean said, "A toast to nature and the beautiful C&O Canal!"

As they leaned forward to clink glasses Corinne saw her candle lit reflection in the window and noticed she was still wearing Sean's scarab necklace and said, "Oh gosh!" and reached up to remove the necklace.

Sean said, "Don't take it off now. As a matter of fact you can wear it whenever you like because it is a gift from me."

Corinne said, "Oh no! I couldn't."

Sean said, "When I found that necklace in that Egyptian bazaar years ago, I thought it couldn't be more beautiful. Seeing that scarab on you tonight just proves how wrong I was. That scarab has never been more beautiful than it is right now, gracing your neck. Please accept it!"

She smiled and said, "Thank you Sean. That is very touching and I will always treasure it. What kind of stone is this?"

Sean said, "The shop owner insisted that the stone was very precious, of great age, and very valuable. Of course I didn't believe him for a minute. When I got back to the ship I realized the stone was attracted to a magnet and magnetic attraction means high iron content. My geologist buddy said the stone was indeed iron and was very old, in fact, millions of years old. It turns out that the stone is an iron meteorite that some Egyptian must have picked up in the desert and polished to make the scarab jewelry. The stone is really not worth much and is certainly not precious, but it is from another planet."

Corinne smiled, "Well, it's precious to me! How cool! Imagine the improbable journey for this little piece of meteorite from millions of miles out in space to around my neck millions of years after beginning its voyage."

The waiter approached the table and asked if they'd like coffee and Sean said, "Yes please, but we'll have our coffee in the lounge downstairs."

Sean turned to Corinne and said, "There is usually a fire going in the field stone fireplace and there are some comfortable sofas and easy chairs to relax in.

Corinne thought relaxing in front of the fireplace sounded like a good idea. She followed Sean to the iron spiral staircase and they wound their way down to the lounge. There was no one in the lounge so they had their choice of seats, and Sean chose the love seat directly in front of the crackling fire. The concierge came over and added a log to the fire and their waiter brought the coffee. Sean ordered two shots of Kahlua to add to the coffee and they sat back to enjoy the fire.

Sean said, "I know you probably already have plans and this is a little late to ask but would you like to go on a hike tomorrow to Maryland Heights?"

Corinne smiled and said, "Let me think," As she placed a finger to her lips and pretended to be lost in thought, "Okay! But what is a Maryland Heights, and where is it?"

"Corinne, have you ever been to Harpers Ferry?"

"No! But I do know where Harpers Ferry is."

"Harpers Ferry is located at the confluence of the Potomac and the Shenandoah Rivers. Maryland Heights is the high point of the gorge on the Maryland side of the Potomac River. The hike to the top is fairly easy because there is an old military road dating from the Civil War that gets you almost to the summit. The view of the little city, the two rivers, and the railroad bridges from the summit is just spectacular and is well worth the hike. You can either meet me at my house or I can pick you up. Either way is fine."

Corinne said, "You can pick me up. What time will I see you?"

Sean said, "Let's plan on nine in the morning. Hey! I've got an idea! You know, it is getting late and the Old Anglers Inn is closer to Georgetown than it is to my house. Unless you need something from your car I can drop you at home tonight, and you can leave your car at my house. When we complete our hike and picnic tomorrow and return to Garret Park, you can retrieve your car then."

Corinne said, "Sounds like a plan!" and they slapped hands.

They made their way to the mighty Corvette and Sean zoomed down McArthur Boulevard towards Georgetown. This time they spent a little more time on the doorstep than the night before. Neither one of them wanted the evening to end. During the tenth good night embrace Kathy flashed the porch light a few times.

They laughed and Corinne said, "I think that means Kathy would like to meet you and say hello."

Sean said, "I'd love to but I have to run." Sean gave her a last kiss. "See you at nine."

Sean was up early packing sandwiches, chips, cheese, dip, wine and wine glasses, and a linen tablecloth. When he pulled up in front of the townhouse, Corinne was standing at the door waiting. As she ran to the car Sean could see that she was stylishly dressed in hiking shorts, boots, broad brimmed hat, neckerchief, and her shirt was tied in a knot with her bare mid drift showing. Sean thought, wow! Does she ever know how to put a look together! Corinne opened the door and jumped in the car, before Sean could get out and open the passenger door.

"Good morning, Sweetie. You look fantastic!"

"What? I just threw together this outfit of old clothes. Thanks, you look great too."

And they were off. Maryland Heights was an hour away because Sean preferred country roads to interstates. They made their way up Route 28 through Darnestown, Bealsville, Point of Rocks, Brunswick, and finally to the base of Maryland Heights. Sean parked the car under the bridge where Route 340 from Frederick crosses into Virginia. They hiked from the car to the base of the 1,000 foot mountain and began the climb to the top. The mountainside was covered with pines, maples, walnuts, and oaks, so there was plenty of shade and the going was pretty easy because of the old military road. There were some sections that were fairly steep, so they stopped to rest a few times.

Sean said, "Imagine trying to drag horses, wagons, and large cannons up this road." Sean pulled the bottled water from his backpack and they shared a drink.

"Harpers Ferry played a significant roll in the Civil War and the city changed hands eight times during the war."

Corinne said, "I enjoy world history, but I must confess I don't really know all that much about the Civil War."

Sean said, "When it comes to wars, the one I've studied the most is WWII. I didn't pay too much attention to the Civil War until I moved to Washington. I just started to stumble across the history, on a piece-meal basis, as I explored Washington and the surrounding areas. The fascinating part of the Civil War is that all participants were Americans. The officers, on both sides, attended the same schools and often married sisters. More than that, however, they weren't particularly pissed off at each other. Still, the United States was nearly destroyed by well meaning and honorable men."

"Harpers Ferry is so beautiful and quaint. It is like one of those untouched Swiss towns where time has stood still. At least from a distance it is. Thomas Jefferson described the view of Harpers Ferry as 'worth a voyage across the Atlantic.' Up close it is a National Park and is a little too over done for my taste. Are you ready for some more climbing?"

Corinne frowned.

Sean said, "Come on just a little more. We are almost there, just a little further."

Corinne said, "Man! I'm getting tired."

"Hold onto my belt and I'll pull you along. Don't worry, the top is flat as a pancake and the return trip is all down hill. All the rest is flat. Close your eyes. Are you ready? Okay! Now you can look."

Corinne opened her eyes and saw a fairy tale city in the distance. The Shenandoah River on the left, the Potomac River on the right, and the little town of Harpers Ferry nestled on little hills between. It was like a tiny San Francisco with the cable cars replaced by railroad cars. Corinne could see two railroad bridges that entered the town from Maryland. The C&O Canal was visible along the Potomac River and there was traffic on the two rivers.

Corinne said, "No wonder this little town played such an important part in the Civil War. Didn't John Brown, the abolitionist, begin his rebellion here at Harpers Ferry?"

Sean said, "Some believe his 1859 rebellion helped make the case for abolition of slavery that finally led to the Civil War. He was hanged in Charles Town for treason and conspiring with slaves to over throw the government. In his final words he said something to the effect that 'you might easily dispose of me but you will yet have to resolve the slavery question and there will be more blood shed.'"

"Of course, the Civil War began a couple of years after his execution. As a world history buff you know that many empires, especially the Roman Empire, crumbled from within. Let's hope the world's civilizations have learned the lessons of the past better than the Romans."

Sean unpacked their picnic lunch and spread the linen tablecloth over the remains of a Civil War gun platform that made a perfect table. Sean uncorked the Merlot and Corinne nodded approvingly.

When he produced the wine glasses she said, "Hey this is better than the Old Anglers Inn. I just wish there was a spiral staircase to get me back to the Corvette."

Sean proposed a toast, "To John Brown and all the soldiers that fought for what they believed in, and to those that dedicated their lives to preserving the Union and ending slavery!" They hoisted their glasses high.

Corinne said, "Sean you make everything interesting and fun."

At that moment Corinne brushed away a butterfly that had landed on her nose. The butterfly then promptly landed on Sean's nose.

Corinne said, "Wow! Did you see that? The same butterfly landed on both our noses! What a funny coincidence!"

Sean said, "I don't believe in coincidences and neither did my grandmother. Grandma Corinne swore that if a butterfly landed on your nose and your girl friend's nose, it meant that you would have a happy and prosperous life together."

Corinne said, "Wow! Is that true?"

Sean said, "No, I just made that up but its fun to think so, isn't it?"

Then Corinne asked, "Your grandma's name wasn't Corinne either was it?"

Sean looked a little sheepish and said, "Well, not legally!" They both laughed and Corinne giggled as Sean tickled her.

Then Sean asked, "Corinne, I'd like to see more of you. Do you think that is possible?"

Corinne replied, "Sean, I don't know. What would your grandma think about that?"

Chapter 4

Time, Speed, and Distance

With Sean's grandma looking on, they began to see more and more of each other. They toured the wineries in the Virginia and Maryland countryside and they frequented the Blue Ridge Mountain "get-a-ways."

One of the ways Sean liked to enjoy nature's beauty was to combine his passion for the country road with his passion for driving the Corvette by participating in the Sports Car Club of America's sponsored Time, Speed, and Distance Road Rallies. The rallies were usually conducted once a month. While Sean enjoyed an occasional road rally, he didn't have time for more than two or three rallies a year.

Sean's success in the rally depended on how experienced his navigator was and how committed she was to the rally. The road rallies were sixty miles in length and took three hours to complete. Sean really didn't care if they won, just as long as they had fun.

Sean and Corinne were early to the starting checkpoint, so they had time to grab a quick lunch and to go over the instructions.

Corinne read through the instructions twice and observed, "Wow! These rules are pretty intense. I hope I can keep up."

"Don't worry about it. The only person that really gets pissed off if he doesn't win is John Applegate."

Corinne asked, "Is he a professional rallyist?"

"Nope! He just has more money than he knows what to do with, and he thinks money always wins the day."

Corinne said, "Well, doesn't it?"

"It usually does but attention to detail, instinctive decision-making and common sense can be worth more than money in the right situation. You know the saying that money is just a way of keeping score? Well, when you are a multi-billionaire you need a different way of keeping score. That's why the outrageously rich engage in philanthropic activities, build America's Cup sailboats, or sponsor near-Earth spaceship development. John does all those things, but he is also extremely competitive with classic cars and road rallies too."

"Remember, a road rally is not a road race and there is no speeding, it is a test of your ability to follow instructions along a road course, and to do it at the correct speed. You don't want to hit the checkpoints too early or too late. It is more like a game of golf. It is you against the course and your competitors against the course. If you finish first, you only win bragging rights."

"It sounds like fun to me! Let's go!"

The rally started at Luray Caverns and ran along Virginia's stunning Skyline Drive with the last leg through Virginia's county roads. The final checkpoint ended, as usual, at a tavern with a large parking lot.

At the beginning of a rally, everyone synchronizes their watch to the rally master's watch. Then, the first ten miles of the course is set-up so you can synchronize your car's odometer to the rally master's odometer. That way everybody is using the same reference points. Like a crossword puzzle, the more familiar you are with the course creator and his bag of tricks, the easier it is to decipher the instructions.

They were three quarters of the way through the course and Corinne knew they were doing pretty well. Her calculations showed they were only a few seconds off the pace when they came to the final "T."

Corinne said, "Okay! Make a right here."

Sean started to make a right and then quickly made a left instead.

Corinne said, "Oh, oh! I think we goofed."

Sean said, "I think we almost fell for a built-in trap. If you read ahead a couple of instructions you will see if we had made a right, we would be off course. We were supposed to keep turning left until we arrived at the 'Big T' and then make a right. Look! Here it is now. The quotes around the 'Big T,' in this case, mean it is a fast food restaurant and not a 'T' in the road."

"How was I supposed to know that?"

"You weren't supposed to know. This is a standard trap that the rally master uses to confuse the novice. Only the experienced rallyist would know."

When the final scores were tallied, Sean and Corinne came in first and John and his navigator-friend, Larry May, came in five seconds off the winning pace. The thing that particularly annoyed John was that he was driving a million dollar Ferrari prepared by the best technicians in the country and his navigator was a national rally champion. It galled him that Sean was driving a production Corvette that he had restored and prepared in his own garage. To make it worse, Sean's navigator was a first-timer. John didn't like to lose at anything. During pizza and drinking beer, John proposed a toast to Sean and the winning Corvette.

Sean said, "Hold on! Let me modify that toast first. I propose a toast to my capable navigator, without whom I would have come in last, and to the Corvette."

John said, "Here! Here! I'll drink to that!"

Sean pointed out that the difference in winning and coming in second wasn't the car, it was the navigator.

John said, "Corinne's skills as a first rate navigator are only exceeded by her beauty," as he hoisted a drink and acknowledged her with a slight salute."

Applegate just knew in his black heart that Sean and Corinne must have cheated somehow.

"Oh, by the way, I'm having a little BBQ at the ranch next Sunday, and I would love for you two to attend. I want you to meet Jennifer and I'd like to show-off my car collection, too. I have a rare Sunoco-blue Grand Sport Corvette in the collection that should be right up your alley. Check your calendars, and if you can make it let me know."

Corinne and Sean looked at each other and Sean said, "Yeah, John we don't have anything scheduled. What time, and can we bring anything? Also what's the dress code?"

"Oh, that is terrific! No, just bring yourselves, and there is no dress code beyond golf casual. The festivities will begin around 3:00 in the afternoon. You'll meet some new people, but you'll recognize some familiar faces from the League of Red-Headed Men too."

"The BBQ is being held at our Talbot County cottage on the Eastern Shore. It's an easy drive across the Bay Bridge and we're located a little south of Easton, just off US 50. Sean, I'll email you the directions."

Sean knew that John lived in Leesburg, Virginia, and he knew John had a weekend place on the shore, but until he received John's email with the address, he didn't know where it was located. With address in hand, he did a Google search. The search turned up a satellite view of the cottage along with a description and a history of the property.

"Hey, Honey! Listen at this description: The original plantation dates to pre-revolutionary times when it was a very busy shipyard that produced many of the ships that the privateers used to harass British shipping during the Revolutionary War. The privateers would lay-in-wait in the Chesapeake tributaries until a British merchantman was sighted, then they would surround the ship and demand the cargo or a ransom. If the captain refused, they would confiscate the cargo, burn the ship, and release the crew on the shore."

"Oh, my gosh! Sounds like quite a little cottage."

On Sunday, Sean and Corinne loaded the Corvette and headed for the shore. As they crossed the Chesapeake Bay it looked like every sailboat in Annapolis was taking advantage of the beautiful weather. The bay looked like a rush hour with sails.

Forty-five minutes later they were south of Easton, Sean checked the GPS navigator display and said, "Okay, it says that we make the next right."

Corinne replied, "It can't be this right, it's an old gravel road."

The simple entrance to the estate from the highway belied the presence of an upscale plantation. But then, that was the point of the rundown fence, the old broken down mailbox, and the gravel road in the first place.

Sean said, "This has to be the place," and turned into the lane.

Corinne asked, "Are you sure we have the right address?"

Sean replied, "We sure do. I checked it on Google, remember?"

About a mile from the highway they came to electronically controlled gates monitored by John's security team via CCTV. As Sean stopped at the gate, Larry May said, "Sean and Corinne, welcome to the BBQ. Hey! It's Larry May from the Luray Cavern rally. Good to see you guys. Drive straight ahead. See you soon."

The gates swung open and as Sean drove through he said, "Well, we were certainly expected. What a set-up! This is the first time I've been invited to the inner sanctum. I have crewed for John a couple of times on the bay when he was sorting out one of his cup contenders, and we've butted heads on the various road rallies, but this is my first visit behind the curtain of secrecy. I wonder if you are the key to the invitation today."

Corinne said, "Oh, Sean! You're a nut. Get real!"

Sean laughed but he knew John Applegate always had an angle on everything. He believed John was probably aware that Corinne was working on the human genome project.

Sean said, "Keep an eye on John today, especially around the BBQ. I bet you never see him take a bite of food. John is a fanatical health nut, and he eats one regular meal a week. He'll drink beer or alcohol on occasion, but he usually drinks imported mineral water from Northern Italy. Most of the time he only consumes vitamins, powdered protein mixed with mineral water, and the purified foodstuff NASA has been developing for voyages to the outer edges of the solar system. John is convinced that human beings can live beyond the century mark, if they restrict their diets to the essentials and vigorously exercise. John is always coming up with new and bizarre diets."

"One of his goofy adventures involved fielding a team of researchers to investigate a little village in Northern Italy where the people routinely live beyond a hundred years old. His team investigated diets, lifestyles, work, stress, family, minerals, vitamin intake, genetic profile, and a thousand other variables. He now imports their mineral water to mix with the powdered protein."

"How did he get the people to cooperate? He probably had to pay dearly to collect that data. Plus there must have been people that simply wouldn't play along."

Sean said, "He was far from subtle about it. He constructed a hospital, staffed it, and offered free medical coverage. It was an offer the people couldn't turn down. His research team was up front about what they wanted to accomplish, and everyone cheerfully participated. The whole operation was detailed in the Smithsonian Magazine."

"Wow! What was the conclusion of the research?

"There were no grand conclusions beyond the need to have the same genetic profile as the people of the village. Long life just happened to be part of their genetic make up."

Corinne said, "The 800 kilogram gorilla in this question is: What part of their genetic profile is different from ours, and if we knew, can we change or augment our genetic profile?"

Sean said, "If you open this subject with John he might end up adopting you. He might even offer you a job."

"Thanks anyway, but I'm very happy working with Dr. Paige. And I'm beginning to think that John is a real nut case."

"Wait a minute, Corinne. The rich are eccentric. Only the poor are nut cases."

"Oh, I'm sorry. I mean John may very well be delightfully eccentric."

"Now that is a better way to describe your host."

Eccentric or not, Sean and Corinne had a wonderful time with John and Jennifer at the BBQ. Jennifer gave Corinne a tour of the house and gardens. Jennifer was particularly proud of her rose garden. Her green house and rose garden were larger than most professional garden centers.

When they rejoined the men at poolside, the discussion was about the up-coming League meeting. Corinne only caught portions of the discussion, but it had to do with recent archeological finds in Egypt. Corinne made a mental note to ask Sean later about the discovery.

As they were headed home after the BBQ, Corinne remarked, "You know, except for John and Jennifer's multi-million dollar car collection and their grand lifestyle, you'd think they were regular people."

Sean said, "They were regular people before they became outrageously rich via the computer and software field. Did you notice the building in the distance when you look due west?"

"Oh yeah, I did. Is that the tower of the local airport?"

Sean said, "Well, sort of. It's the tower of John's airport where he keeps his Gulfstream 750."

"When will it stop? A private jet; now that is rich."

"The Gulfstream 750 is capable of supersonic flight and has a range of 8500 nautical miles. You can't beat it, when you're in Washington and you have a golf date in the Bahamas."

Corinne laughed, "Hey, our new best friends are really well heeled!"

Sean said, "The Applegates may live large, but they also give back a lot to the community. Even if John's motives in Northern Italy weren't entirely altruistic, it was still an incredibly generous thing to do. All in all, they are nice people. Please don't hate them because they're filthy rich."

"On the contrary! What do we have to do to get a ride to the Caribbean?"

Sean mused, "Let them win the next road rally?"

They both laughed.

Chapter 5

Ferry Cross the Potomac

It was Saturday night, a few weeks later, and Sean and Corinne had just finished dinner with the Applegates in a restaurant near their home in Leesburg. Over dessert and coffee the talk turned to careers and Corinne mentioned that she worked with Dr. Paige at NIH. John remarked that genetic research was a pet project of his. He then gave a brief description of his Northern Italy project, but he didn't bore in on Corinne as Sean thought he might.

Everyone said their good-byes in the restaurant's parking lot. In parting, John asked, "Sean, do you plan to attend next month's meeting at the Smithsonian?"

Sean said, "I plan to, unless I get a better offer," and he winked at Corinne.

"Maybe I'll see you there. My schedule is not firm yet." John replied.

Sean added, "I'm interested in the details concerning the Egyptian find, that is, if there are any."

John said, "We'll have to wait and see what the professor decides to tell us. He is usually very open. Good night guys and have a safe trip home. It was good to be with you."

As Sean drove out of the parking lot he had his eyes on the traffic monitors, but as soon as he reached Route 15 he pushed the pedal down. Sean was hoping to make White's Ferry before the ferry boat to Maryland closed for the night. The ferry closed at 1:00 A.M. on Friday and Saturday nights. He wasn't too concerned, but if he missed it he would have to drive an extra 37 miles out of the way, so he preferred the ferry. As Sean made the last turn before the ferry landing, he began blowing the horn to let the ferryman know he was almost there. The ferry gave a short whistle toot in response and Sean relaxed.

Corinne asked, "Are we going to make it?"

"Sure! No problem."

As they pulled aboard the ferry, the gate closed and the ferry began chugging toward the Maryland ferry landing. Sean and Corinne got out of the car to enjoy the night sky and the smells of the river. Sean pointed out the North Star and Orion's belt in the night sky.

He said, "The stars always look so brilliant when you get just a little bit into the country."

Corinne said, "When I'm in the city, I don't even think to look up."

The ferryman let the motor idle and the ferry crunched softly into the concrete ramp. The operator lowered the safety chain and waved good night. Sean drove off onto the country road towards Poolesville.

Corinne said, "I think I ate too much at dinner; I can't keep my eyes open. Talking about appetite, did you see John putting the food away tonight? He must be on a new diet kick because he ate everything on his plate, including dessert."

"Yeah, I did notice. He's got something new up his sleeve. Why don't you close your eyes and take a power nap; we'll be home in about thirty or forty minutes."

The road veered to the right and then there was a straight stretch where Sean gunned the Corvette to enjoy the feel of the horses. He could see lights in the trees ahead so he knew a car was headed his way. Before he saw the car, Sean took his foot off the accelerator and let the Corvette return to the posted speed limit.

The on-coming car emerged out of the foliage and entered the straight stretch about three quarters of a mile in front of Sean. Sean heard a horn and saw headlights flash as a second car began to pass the first. Sean gauged the distance between the Corvette and the approaching cars, and while he knew he wouldn't have attempted to pass with so little a margin of safety, he wasn't worried. He knew, if he had to, he could slow to add an additional safety factor.

What Sean didn't know, and couldn't see, was that there were two cars executing the pass simultaneously. There was no room for the second car to complete the pass. The second car and the Corvette would collide head-on.

The flashing headlights woke Corinne, and she looked up to see the blinding high beams of the on-coming car and she screamed. At the same time, Sean glimpsed the second car and realized the danger. The road was barely a two-lane country road. It was black top, but there were ditches and fences on both sides, with no place to get off the road. Nevertheless, the ditch and fence were preferable to a head-on collision. Sean quickly jerked the steering wheel right and luckily got out of the way of the second car. The Corvette's incredible disc brakes brought the car to a safe stop astraddle the ditch, teetering between the fence and the berm of the road.

Corinne was nearly hyperventilating as Sean backed the Corvette back onto the road, put it in gear, and with squealing tires launched the car toward Poolesville.

As Corinne's breathing returned to near normal Sean turned to her and said, "Now that was too close!"

A jumble of thoughts tumbled out of Corinne as she exclaimed, "Oh my God! I thought we were dead! I didn't even have time to pray! Something or someone stepped in and saved us and I don't know who or what! Thank God we're alive!"

Sean said, "I know."

"Know what?"

"I know who saved us."

"Okay, who saved us?"

"I did!"

"I've found that when you leave things in God's hands and don't pitch-in to help, you often end up on the wrong side of the equation. I love the Ben Franklin quote: 'God helps those that help themselves.'"

The rest of the drive home was made in silence as Sean focused on the road ahead and Corinne stared out her window at the darkness. Corinne's head began to clear and she became more focused. She couldn't help but think that Sean's quick reactions were movements that had been assisted by God. She could understand how Sean could believe that they were saved directly by his actions and, of course, that was true. Still, she thought Sean was a little wrong-headed in not recognizing that all good things are derived from God.

They spent the following weekend in Middleburg, Virginia, at the Red Fox Inn. After a wonderful dinner they retired to their room for lovemaking and after dinner drinks, in that order. Corinne stepped into the hot tub with the drinks. While waiting for Sean to join her, she was reflecting on how much fun she was having with Sean, and how much life meant to her. She heard a scramble of feet and out of nowhere Sean did a cannonball into the hot tub, spilling the drinks and nearly drowning her. Corinne was fuming and having a hissy fit. Sean was laughing and mocking her when she burst into raucous laughter too.

They hugged and kissed and began to get passionate all over again when Corinne pulled away. She began to fiddle with the scarab around her neck with one hand and to twist her hair unconsciously with the other hand as she stared at Sean.

Sean said, "Hey Baby, where are you going, come back here, I want to whisper some secrets into your ear and kiss your neck."

Corinne said, "Just a minute, round two can wait."

Corinne was serious, and serious is the part that all bachelors dread because it takes away from playtime.

"Sean, I'm a Catholic and you know I believe in God but you once said that you didn't believe in God. I find that knowledge uncomfortable and disturbing, and I want to know how you really feel. Please tell me how you really feel!"

Sean said, "Baby, now is not the time for that kind of discussion. Let's wait until the cold light of day, when we are both sober, and we can discuss it in depth on my sun room couch."

She said, "Oh, no you don't. Start talking."

"Corinne we've done a lot of 'What if' philosophizing over the last few months, but because you've asked a serious question, I'll give you an answer that describes how I feel based on my observations rather than wild theories. Let me start by saying these are my feelings and my feelings are based on a little bit of science, a little bit of common sense, a little bit of my faith in the scientific method, and a little bit of my own gut feelings. I don't claim to have the final answers, but I'm always asking questions and revising my conclusions."

"Okay, here goes. I think all the world's religions are based on the golden rule and none of the additional dogma is necessary. The dogma is simply someone's concept of reality based on his or her place in time and the civilization they were trying to conceive at the time."

"The religions of the world should be viewed within the context of the place and time in which they were conceived. Each religion is essentially that particular group's Declaration of Independence and Constitution for their respective civilization. If you strip out the fairy tales and the supernatural part of the dogma of the various religions, you are left with the golden rule and the basic common laws applicable to all for promoting education, commerce, and civilization."

"I think America's Founding Fathers did the best job for modern people in stripping out the supernatural. The Declaration of Independence and the Constitution essentially say these are the rules and regulations for commerce and civil law. You are free to be as nutty as you like with your selection of your individual religion. A friend of mind once said, 'Religion is the only socially acceptable form of mental illness there is!' and I believe he is right."

Corinne asked, "Don't you believe in God as described in the Bible?"

Sean asked, "Which God, the Old Testament God, or the New Testament God? They are both materially and philosophically different."

She said, "Either or both!"

Sean said, "I don't think the question is that simple. Let me answer this way: I believe in, and adhere to, all the rules and commandments as presented in both Testaments, but I don't believe in a reward system for good behavior or a punishment system for bad behavior. I think that if you start with the golden rule and you add the ten commandments you have a viable road map for civilization."

Corinne said, "Then what is the point in keeping the rules and commandments, if there is no pay off and no punishment?"

"Ah! That is the difference between philosophy and religion," said Sean, "because you can use the power of persuasion, inductive reasoning, and deductive reasoning to make the case for civilized behavior versus a shaky reward system of eternal life or eternal damnation."

Corinne said, "Okay, but that still doesn't answer the question of whether or not you believe in God?"

Sean replied, "Einstein said that God reveals himself in the order of the universe. I believe that is a keen observation because without order there is chaos. Clearly the universe has order and life on this planet has order and a life cycle."

"My corollary to Einstein's observation is that I believe God's natural order is revealed in the life on this planet. To me, life on this planet is the DNA structure and the complex double-helix molecule. It is clear to me that the double-helix molecules are bound together and communicate within an individual creature. Further, I suspect that all the double-helix molecules on this planet, whether plant or animal, are connected on some level and that together they form a Collective Intelligence that is inclusive of all life. I think that when most people think of God they are actually referring to the Collective Intelligence, rather than the supreme intelligence, that may be behind the creation of all matter and the universe. I think the Collective Intelligence on this planet exercises free will by shaping changes to the DNA and thus the genetic code for life."

Corinne listened intently as Sean answered her most difficult question. After he finished, they were quiet for a few minutes with only the soft gurgle of the hot tub breaking the silence. Slowly, Corinne's eyes softened and a warm smile formed on her face. Sean thought to himself that she had never looked more beautiful.

Then Corinne stood up with the water glistening on her breasts and said, "Sean, my darling, that's close enough to believing in God for me. Come here, lover, it's time for round two."

Chapter 6

The League of Red-Headed Men

Sean and Corinne had packed the Corvette, checked out of the Red Fox Inn, and were on the road by noon. Sean was thinking about the League of Red-Headed Men's quarterly meeting, scheduled for later in the day. He was contemplating inviting Corinne but he really hadn't clued her in on the League activities. Yet he was sure the members would be delighted to have Corinne attend, especially with her NIH Genome research background. Sean's main concern was Corinne's steadfast Catholic faith versus their kind of issues that are routinely discussed by the members. He didn't want the less-than-politically-correct language to come across as crude.

Sean knew Corinne's faith wouldn't be shaken by what she heard; he just didn't want her to feel uncomfortable. But then, on the other hand, he also knew she had a very open mind. So he decided to invite her.

Sean asked, "Corinne, remember when we were at the BBQ at John's place and we were discussing the archeology find in Egypt?"

"Oh, yeah, I remember. Wasn't there a formal presentation scheduled sometime in the future?"

"You're exactly right and that presentation will take place tonight at the League's meeting at the Smithsonian. Would you be interested in checking it out with me? The meeting starts around seven."

Corinne asked, "By the way, why do you call your club the League of Red-Headed Men? I remember reading the Sherlock Holmes mystery "The League of Red-Headed Men," but you don't have red hair so may I assume red hair is not a prerequisite for membership?"

Sean said, "Oh it's just a pet name that goes back a number of years to when Sherlock Holmes was popular in literature and the movies. And no, you don't have to have red hair to join, nor do you have to be a man. It's an informal group and there are no by-laws or rules other than that to belong, you have to be invited by one of the members."

"Sean, I don't want to intrude or be in the way, so what's on the agenda and what do you guys really discuss?"

"Dr. Death chairs the meeting and he maintains contact with League members world wide, so he has information that's not available elsewhere."

"Dr. Death? Why do you call him that?"

"Dr. Death is Dr. Grant K. Ackkingbach. We affectionately refer to him as Dr. Death because he believes man's time on Earth has run out, and that mankind is destined for the DNA scrap heap, just like Neanderthal man."

Corinne roared, "I don't know what's worse, Dr. Death or Dr. Achingback!"

"That's Ackkingbach not aching back."

"Oh, excuse me! That makes a big difference," said Corinne laughing. "What makes Dr. Death think that we, as a species, are on the DNA off ramp?"

"Well, he predicted a decline in the actuary tables back in the 1980s in his PhD thesis. While his thesis is available at his alma mater his research has never been published in a scientific journal and is not common knowledge in scientific circles."

"What's his premise?"

Sean replied, "Many geneticists believe that genetic research has proven that Homo sapiens are descended from one village, tribe, or civilization—likely out of Africa. All people alive today bear the same genome, such that for at least the last couple of million years, we have, for all practical purposes, been inbreeding. The theory is that Homo sapiens wiped out or killed off competing species like the Neanderthal or Homo erectus. There is no DNA evidence to suggest that Homo sapiens interbred with Neanderthal man or any other species that may have coexisted at the same time. Dr. Death's colleague, Dr. Munkey, believes the inbreeding has produced a stagnant gene pool, and, like a poor photocopy, each iteration or generation is slightly worse than the last copy. Therefore, as a species, we are in decline and destined for the DNA scrap heap."

Corinne said, "That's an interesting concept, but what evidence do they have?"

Sean replied, "Okay, but before we get to the evidence, let me expand on Dr. Munkey's position. Also let me tell you up front that the man's name is not monkey but is Munkey. And yes, he is that 'Dr. Eugene Munkey.' Dr. Munkey directs the President's National Scientific Research Project Foundation."

"Dr. Munkey believes the scientific and medical research community should manipulate the human genome by restructuring the DNA strands to enhance the genome, and to map the future of the species to a positive trend. He's convinced the body, and more importantly the brain, can be improved. For example, the skull or brain box could be genetically enlarged, thus allowing the gray matter to expand."

"On the other hand, Dr. Death sees no purpose in increasing the size of the brain because artificial intelligence can accommodate any requirement for greater memory or increased processing speed in a better and more manageable way than a biological solution."

"Dr. Munkey believes once we have the human genome mapped, it will be time to start considering improvements. Conversely, Dr. Death believes that human beings are not ready to design their own replacement. Dr. Death quotes Dr. Stephen Hawking's 20th century caution as: 'Laws will be passed against genetic engineering with humans. But some people won't be able to resist the temptation to improve human characteristics such as size of memory, resistance to disease, and length of life. Once super humans appear, there are going to be major political problems with the unimproved humans, who won't be able to compete. Presumably, they will die out, or become unimportant. Instead, there will be a race of self-designing beings, who are improving themselves at an ever-increasing rate.'"

Sean said, "Naturally, the world's religious leaders would be outraged by the concept of manipulating the genome or 'playing God.' Because America remains a predominately Christian nation, Dr. Munkey has been very low key with his theories and publishes his official position as being against any interference with the human genome. His true feelings are that we must do something, but Dr. Death and Dr. Munkey have yet to come up with a concept of what to do because they are still arguing about who is right. Dr. Death believes we should do no more than correct apparent gene deficiencies and perhaps tinker with the various controlling gene sequences to insure positive gene mutations. Dr. Munkey, on the other hand, believes aggressive manipulation of the genome, up to and including the introduction of DNA strands from other species, should be pursued immediately. They both believe that the human life span can be extended indefinitely if we can define the gene sequence that has pre-programmed humans to an early grave."

Corinne said, "Sean, take a breath! I have mixed feelings about both points of view. I don't think we have the wisdom to play God either, but immortality would definitely be a good thing. Can't these guys reach a compromise?"

"To make matters even more interesting, the two doctors are long time rivals, old college roommates, and extremely competitive. I think their competitiveness goes beyond friendly, and while they may respect each other's intellect, they actually despise one another. Dr. Munkey believes Dr. Death's stature and influence in the world's scientific community is a danger to America's Human Genome Project. He also believes that Dr. Death's willingness to share his thoughts openly with the scientific community and the media will lead to a congressional restriction on genome project funding or possibly even lead to the project being shut down."

Corinne said, "Shutting down the Human Genome Project would be a tragedy that America might live to regret. I'm sure other countries would not shut down their genome projects. There is also the danger that whoever develops a technique to modify the genome first might put humanity itself at risk. If a rogue nation develops the immortality gene therapy first, the methodology will surely be marketed to the highest bidder."

Corinne thought, *Now I'm playing God! Because I'm thinking it would be a mistake to extend the life span of one hell of a lot of people.*

Corinne's mind raced as she thought of the various scenarios that an indefinite life span for the current generation might have on future generations. The current generation would manipulate and expand the human genome to develop what could only be called a new species of human beings, but with what attributes? Who would set the criteria for the new species, and who would determine success or failure of the species? What if the new species looked at us or the current species the same way Homo sapiens looked at Neanderthal man? Would the "New Man" think that the inferior copy should be eliminated? Would improving Homo sapiens end up being a self-fulfilling prophecy as implemented by Dr. Monkey?

Corinne could access all government funded and approved NIH human genome projects and studies, and she assumed everyone could access her projects, too. That is, all of her official projects. However, Corinne had a special pet project. Although the project was approved by Dr. Paige, it was not an "official" NIH project. Therefore, progress wasn't reported or tracked at NIH.

Corinne's project was based on trying to identify a common genetic marker among serial killers and mass murderers. The data Corinne included in her study group excluded those murders that were committed out of passion, greed, or revenge. She only studied those murders that were committed by the so-called compulsive or serial killer. She knew that preliminary data showed that there was a particular sequence common to all the murderers, but this same gene sequence was also present in all A-type over-achiever personality types. She was sure there had to be another controlling gene sequence that was absent in the murderers but was present in the A-type personality, and that controlling sequence remained to be identified.

Most people not associated with mapping the human genome didn't appreciate the scale of the project. With more than 3.1 billion letters in the human genome, understanding the cause and effect relationships among the various gene sequences was a daunting task.

If human beings had the life span of a fruit fly, it would be much easier to see the subtle changes to the genome. Gene splicing experiments, designed to identify the genes that control the on and off cycle of other genes, require the observation and verification of multiple generations.

Corinne suspected that all the movers and shakers in science, government, and politics were A-type personalities. Plus, she was sure she would have found the serial murderer gene sequence in Hitler, Stalin, and other heads of rogue nations that have ordered mass murder. She was confident that a faulty gene sequence had led to sanctioned and rationalized state sponsored homicide as perpetrated by the Axis powers during World War II.

Generally, democracies and republics have a better chance of weeding out the serial killer in political life, due to the possibility of election losses once the evil is revealed by their deeds. Dictatorships, on the other hand, are doomed once the serial killer gains the seat of power.

Corinne knew shutting down the Human Genome Project would also derail her special project and thus the possibility of developing a simple genetic test to detect the serial killer. Without the test, the world-at-large and future victims would remain in jeopardy, and history would continue to repeat the same scenario like a bad "do loop" from "The Twilight Zone."

Corinne was sure that, if a mass murderer genetic test had been available in the 1930s, today's gene pool would be very different. How many Mozarts, Einsteins, and Picassos were lost to humanity in the death camps of World War II?

Unknown to Corinne, Dr. Death and Dr. Munkey were aware of her special project. Plus both doctors had access to Corinne's NIH project files, so progress on her project was also known. They were anxious and hopeful that Corinne's project would soon bear fruit. The two doctors had vastly different plans for administering the serial killer test, should Corinne come up with a viable test.

Dr. Munkey would use the test privately to identify and rid society and the government of overly aggressive A-type personalities, judged to be in the way and/or harmful to the National Scientific Research Project's objectives and to promote and control those A types that agreed with the agenda. Of course, he rationalized his approach as "best for mankind" and he considered himself to be one of Plato's Philosopher-Kings.

Corinne, too, was keeping a secret. She already had a genetic test that could make the case for the genetic marker, that is, if she had a large enough sample of past and present DNA to test and cross correlate. Corinne assumed that anything in the NIH database was not secure. She knew database access from outside the government was possible, but she suspected that anyone inside the project could, most likely, access her private password-protected files.

She wasn't paranoid about her research; it was just that she didn't want people second-guessing her preliminary results before she had time to finalize her conclusions. So, Corinne never entered any speculative data in the database that she didn't want splashed all over *The Washington Post*. She kept her theories and speculations in the thumb drive memory of her PDA. As soon as she was certain of the data, she would post it to the NIH database for official file sharing.

Sean said, "Dr. Death and many members of the League of Red-Headed Men, including me, believe the DNA on this planet may be data sharing at some level. I suspect that the DNA data sharing facilitates communication of the environmental issues that life entities on this planet are facing as a group. We theorize that DNA and the double-helix genome are intelligent and are, as a collective, a self-aware entity. We refer to this entity as the Collective Intelligence, or CI. We believe the CI has an imperative, and that imperative is survival of the double-helix genome, but not necessarily the human genome."

Corinne said, "Now you are getting too far out for me! I know you said the Collective Intelligence concept is a theory, but do you have any empirical data to support the theory?"

Sean said, "The short answer is no, but when you superimpose the history of life on this planet over the Earth's timeline, you begin to see a pattern. The pattern suggests that the double helix meets the criteria for a separate identity, and that the CI has a will of its own!"

As they drove along Sean gave Corinne a quick outline of the League's concept. "You see, Dr. Death agrees with Darwin that humans and all life on Earth have evolved, but he doesn't think evolution was a result of natural selection, by Darwin's definition. Darwin defined natural selection as survival of the fittest. In other words the organism best adapted to the environment is the organism most likely to survive and transmit their respective genetic characteristics to the succeeding generation."

"There are too many instances in nature to assume a happy coincidence: for example, virgin births in fish or sharks, or starfish changing sexes to accommodate nature's environment. On the contrary, Dr. Death believes that the Collective Intelligence actually manipulates the genome to ensure survival of the double-helix molecule at the expense of the individual species. He also believes that the CI often reshuffles the double helix to wipe out either the current ruling civilization or species, as required, to take advantage of changes in the Earth's environment. Dr. Death believes world history lays this truth out in bold relief, if one takes the time to look."

Corinne said, "Hold on! You're going too fast again! These ideas are great for a science fiction novel, but this stuff isn't cast in stone, nor is there scientific evidence to support these conclusions."

Sean responded, "You're partially correct. The scientific evidence needs to be gathered to support the theories, but much of the evidence is indeed cast in stone. It is cast in the stone of the Earth and in fossil records."

"Let me continue. Dr. Death believes genome manipulation is a necessary consequence of an environment that can't be controlled by the Collective Intelligence. For example, Dr. Death believes that 65 million years ago, when all life on Earth faced a Life Extinguishing Event or 'LEE' and large land animals like the dinosaurs where destroyed along with their environment, the Collective Intelligence modified the double-helix molecule. The modified DNA molecule gave rise to humans with large brains and opposable thumbs and the Homo sapiens species has been reaching for the stars ever since."

"The human race has been trying to either find a way off the planet or a way to manage the asteroids and protect Earth from another LEE. The genetic imperative to reach for the stars has been the driving force for every civilization since then. Whether building pyramids, obelisks, tall buildings, the tower of Babel, or space exploration, each civilization has been compelled to focus on the heavens."

"Dr. Death believes that, as each civilization fails to achieve the goal of gaining control of the environment and/or near-Earth space, the Collective Intelligence modifies the controlling sequence of the aggressive gene and the civilization fails in favor of the next civilization or next species showing promise. Some historians believe the fall of many historical empires is a result of the people losing the will to power. Dr. Death thinks a better way to look at the decline of great empires is to recognize that the Collective Intelligence chose to try another civilization experiment."

Corinne gasped, "Holy crap! I'm sorry, but that whole concept sounds like you guys have had two too many Gibsons. No wonder you call your club the League of Red-Headed Men. Your goals and objectives have nothing to do with the Smithsonian Institution."

"That's right! Our goals and objectives are the survival of the species!"

"How can Dr. Death have Dr. Munkey as a member of the League, when they clearly are at odds with one another?"

"How could he not? It is better to have the two doctors under the same tent and sharing information, than to have the two off on different tangents that could only end in eventual gridlock."

Corinne said, "Having the two of them together amounts to conducting collaborative scientific research while handcuffed."

Sean said, "Not really. Their goals are the same until they have the data to chart the future. Then each believes he will be able to convince the other to make the right choice."

Corinne said, "If I get your explanation, what you are saying is that our species is being stalked by the very Collective Intelligence that created us! Our species may decline and fail because the double helix views our species as a threat to all life! I really need some time to turn all this information over in my brain a few hundred times. Okay! I need to attend the meeting to find out if there are members crazier than you are."

Sean said, "The League believes that if we can collect enough data to prove that our concept has merit, then as a species, we believe we can make the correction that gets our species and the Collective Intelligence working together to plan a better future for the planet and for the double-helix DNA molecule."

The meetings were held in the Natural History Museum in the Egyptian exhibit. Parking would be impossible now because they were running late. Sean decided to solve the parking problem by taking advantage of the late hour, so he eased the Corvette into the museum director's reserved parking space at the Air and Space Museum and cut the engine. Sean and Corinne had turned off their PDAs while they were parking the car. PDA interruption during the meeting was a no-no, plus the League of Red-Headed Men considered PDAs a security risk. Sean used his pass card to get into the Air and Space Museum building. They then took an underground electric shuttle to the Natural History Museum.

There were about thirty people at the meeting and Dr. Death was at the podium introducing a holographic presentation on recent* discoveries in the Old Kingdom in Egypt. The lights were dimmed for the holographic projection, and Professor Fitzgerald, on site in Egypt, was greeting everyone and explaining what he was about to present. Professor Fitzgerald's presentation had just started as Sean and Corinne entered the meeting room. They remained in the darkness and no one noticed they had entered the room.

Professor Fitzgerald said, "It is public knowledge that the recent discovery of an untouched tomb in the Great Pyramid has led to a better understanding of the first dynasty, but what I am revealing to you tonight is information held only by the research team here on site. This tomb has changed the history of everything we thought we knew about Egypt and its 5,000 year history. All the untouched tombs found down through history, including King Tutankhamen's, were, of course, Egyptian, but the Egyptian civilization may have been founded on the shoulders of a much, much older and more advanced civilization. The Egyptians did not construct the Giza Plateau, the Great Pyramid, or the Sphinx! And we have incontrovertible proof, in stone!"

Chapter 7

Trapped in History, Naturally

Professor Fitzgerald's holographic representation was so realistic that it looked like he was standing next to Dr. Death on the podium. The professor revealed that the new discovery was not another tomb in the Valley of the Kings. In fact, the find was located hundreds of miles from the Valley of the Kings.

The professor said, "We were researching and documenting the graffiti on the walls of the Great Pyramid when, by providence, a team member discovered a hidden door that led to a previously unknown chamber."

"The new chamber was littered with debris so the first step was to carefully catalog the litter and make sure we didn't accidentally discard something critical to the find. When we cleared the litter, we found a very narrow passageway that, at first, we thought might be an air duct. During monument construction the work crew often cut a ventilation shaft large enough to also serve as an escape passage. Once construction was completed the ventilation ducts were usually sealed with stone."

"After clearing the debris from the air duct, the youngest and most agile team member was able to navigate down the passage for a quick look. Our volunteer crawled down the 150-foot length and, as expected, found a dead end. The explorer shouted that it was a blind shaft, just as we had suspected."

"We later learned that the end of the air duct was slightly larger than the shaft, and it was just large enough for the explorer to turn around for the return trip. After all, it is much easier to crawl forward than it is to inch backward."

"As he headed back toward us his foot pushed on a block of stone that felt loose. He backed up and pressed on the loose stone, and he felt it give way. By pushing up on the stone, he was able to stand up. He waved his flashlight around the walls and realized the loose stone was actually a hidden door to a chamber. He pulled himself up and entered a chamber where he was able to stand. He called back to us, "There are hieroglyphs everywhere!"

"The chamber is a prayer station with granite benches and the walls are covered with hieroglyphs that represent ancient prayers."

Professor Fitzgerald continued, "The hieroglyphs are a particularly exciting revelation because these are the first hieroglyphs, or writings of any kind, ever found in the Great Pyramid, beyond graffiti."

"The hieroglyphs are stunning in detail and they are much older than those of the classic Egyptian dynasties. They are in magnificent condition. There are a number of symbols that are unknown and these symbols will need to be decoded before we can decipher all the information, but, at the macro level, many of the symbols are consistent with known Egyptian hieroglyphics. At the macro level the glyphs tell an astonishing story, and that is the story I want to share with you tonight."

"The hieroglyphs refer to a city in a lake that no one can correlate to either an existing or historical city. The city and the lake represent a city-state previously unknown to Egyptologists. The new city-state is located on an island or perhaps on a low-lying peninsula surrounded by a body of water."

"While the Gods depicted in the hieroglyphs are the familiar Egyptian Gods of Ra and other lesser Egyptian Gods, the city-state may be the mother city-state to the Egyptian cities located on the Nile. The hieroglyphs show all the Egyptian cities on the Nile paying tribute to the City in the Lake."

Professor Fitzgerald said, "Naturally, we refocused all team resources on the new chamber. As we scanned the chamber and established a physical inventory, we discovered another hidden door that led deeper into the bowels of the Great Pyramid."

"The hidden door revealed a staircase leading down below the base of the pyramid and into the bedrock foundation. We calculated that, at the bottom of the descending stairs, we were about 300 feet below the base of the pyramid. At the bottom of the stairs was a chamber that appeared to be a dead end. By this time we knew where to look for other concealed doors. It turned out that all the secret doors use the same release mechanism, so we were able to quickly gain access. When we opened the chamber door at the base of the stairs, we were unprepared for the sight beyond."

"The first chamber is the size of a football field, and it is cut from the living rock with a precision that would be hard to duplicate today. This tomb is actually a three-chambered Necropolis filled with 5,000 years of pharaohs in undisturbed sarcophagi."

"Unlike the tombs in the Valley of the Kings that have been sacked and robbed hundreds of times during antiquity, these chambers are pristine and untouched. The perimeter walls are covered with beautiful hieroglyphs that tell the story of the City in the Lake. The Pharaoh's Chamber is connected to a similar sized chamber that contains royal family members. A third chamber contains the important noblemen and members of the government. The entire Necropolis is an extensive underground complex that is more on the scale of an underground city than a tomb."

There was a commotion at the door and Dr. Death killed the holograph presentation. Twenty-five Secret Service officers entered the meeting room and ordered everyone to remain quiet.

At that moment Dr. Munkey stood up and said, "This meeting is being terminated on grounds of national security. No one is under arrest and no one is being detained or charged with any crime. However, everyone must board a bus for transport to CIA Headquarters in Langley, Virginia, for a security debriefing. After you have been debriefed you will be asked to sign a nondisclosure agreement."

Dr. Death began protesting but Dr. Munkey interrupted him saying, "My dear Dr. Death, please join me in the office so that I may share the security debrief with you personally and make you aware of the threat to national security."

Dr. Death tried to object, but he was ushered into an adjacent office by two Secret Service officers. The agent-in-charge reported to Dr. Munkey that the bus was loaded and ready for transport to Langley. Dr. Munkey asked if everyone on the list had boarded the bus.

The officer looked at his list and said, "Everyone but Sean Thornton and Corinne Cannon."

Dr. Munkey fairly screeched, "What? Find them! Cannon is first priority but we must capture them both alive. We must have the test!"

Sean took Corinne by the hand and they cautiously and quietly eased into the darkness of the Egypt display. Suddenly, all the lights in the Egypt exhibit came on. Sean quickly pulled Corinne toward a large pyramid display. He opened a maintenance hatch on the north side of the pyramid against the wall and pulled her inside, quietly closing the hatch behind them. Corinne started to speak but Sean pressed a finger to her lips. He pulled out a small notebook and a pen and wrote: "No sounds, no PDAs, no movement."

Corinne gave Sean the "a-okay" sign and they both looked for comfortable spots to settle down in while they waited to see what else Dr. Monkey might have up his sleeve.

Corinne took the notebook and scribbled: "Where did they get my name? I'm not a member of the League of Red-Headed Men."

Sean smiled and wrote: "You are now!"

They slept in fits and starts as the Secret Service officers moved in and out of the exhibit all night long. The museum opened for business at 8:30 in the morning and the noise level within the exhibit began to elevate. With the increased noise they felt comfortable enough to speak quietly. Sean said, "Corinne, you are a prominent genetics researcher at NIH. It's clear now that our activities have obviously been monitored."

"I agree but Dr. Munkey said, 'We must have the test!' How could he possibly know about the test? The only time I ever mentioned it was in the car on the way here? Even Dr. Paige doesn't know about the test."

Sean said, "Okay, conversation in the Corvette is off limits starting now. They must have accessed the Corvette's global positioning system to bug our conversation while we were driving here."

Corinne asked, "Isn't wiretapping private citizens without a warrant illegal? This is beginning to scare me. Munkey said he wanted us alive, which means death is not out of the question. Sean, what do we do next, and how do we get the hell out of here?"

"First, we'll get lunch in the museum cafeteria and make some friends with the tourists. Then we'll blend in with the crowd and just walk out with the noon-day surge. We should have no problem blending in because we are dressed like tourists already. Then, we'll catch the Metro Rail to the last day of the Air Show at Andrews Air Force Base in Suitland, Maryland."

Corinne asked, "Are you crazy? No one on the run eats lunch in the museum cafeteria and then leisurely goes sightseeing at the Air Show. Oh, I get it, hiding in plain sight! That's a brilliant plan."

The pyramid had one way mirrored view ports on all four sides that allowed light into the interior but, more importantly, made it possible for Sean to detect general museum traffic and whether members of the Smithsonian staff were in the area. Sean timed the CCTV security cameras and noted that the pyramid area was monitored regularly as the camera's red active light turned on and off at fifteen second intervals. At thirty minute intervals the lights in the Great Pyramid area dimmed, and the spot lights came on to depict the gleaming white, simulated limestone of the pyramid at night. The maintenance hatch was on the side of the pyramid that backed to the wall, so it was a matter of timing for them to successfully exit the pyramid with a high probability of not being spotted.

Sean said, "Now!" And Corinne pushed open the hatch and stepped out with Sean right behind her. They immediately began admiring the pyramid, commenting to one another while walking around it.

Sean said, "I'm getting hungry, are you ready for some brunch?"

"That sounds like a good idea, but first, let's find a restroom."

Sean knew where the closest restrooms were located. They both felt relieved to be out of the pyramid.

They went through the cafeteria line and each got a tray and loaded up. They selected a table right next to a noisy family of six. Sean struck up a conversation with the tourists. It turned out that the folks were from an Indiana town that Sean knew a little bit about and the family had gone to the last Indianapolis 500 mile race when Bobby Unsers' great-grandson won his first 500 mile race. The Stewart family was flying home that day and their car was packed and ready to go, except for the museum souvenirs they had just purchased. Sean offered to help get the gifts out to the parking lot, so Corinne and Sean picked up the packages and followed their new friends out of the museum. As Sean was giving Mr. Stewart detailed directions to Dulles International Airport and Mrs. Stewart was strapping the kids into the car seats, Corinne set her unclassified PDA to call home every two hours for the next eight hours and popped it in one of the Stewart's large suitcases in the trunk of their rental car. They all shook hands and agreed to meet at the next Indianapolis 500 and then the Stewarts were off.

Sean and Corinne parted company and both made their way to the Metro station to catch the next train to Andrews Air Force Base. They knew that security would be on the look out for a man and a woman that matched their description. The crowds were overwhelming, but once in the underground Metro station, they each took different routes, winding their way through the masses, to reach the same Metro car. The ride to Andrews was smooth and quick. Sean paid cash for a handful of disposable PDAs at the base 7-11. He thanked his lucky stars that he still had a large sum of cash left over from the weekend "get away." The money had gone unspent because they had spent so much time at the pool and in their room. Sean and Corinne knew that they couldn't use their PDAs, cell phones, ATM cards, or any electronic media because their location would be instantly pinpointed.

Sean said, "I bet Munkey has the train stations, bus stations, and commercial airports under close watch. He probably thinks we are headed to Reagan National Airport because it is just across the Potomac from the Smithsonian."

Corinne said, "Nope! I'll bet he's assuming Dulles."

"No! I'm sure he'll be working Reagan."

Corinne laughed, "No, I think he'll be surprised when he tracks down the Stewart's rental car and finds an empty trunk. Hopefully, the Stewart's plane is on time and, with my unclassified PDA calling home every two hours for the next eight hours, security won't have a clue until the plane's luggage is on the carousel at Indianapolis."

Now it was Sean's turn to laugh and he said, "You're a devious little minx, aren't you?" Corinne smiled and gave Sean a hug. She was beginning to feel much better about the whole nightmare.

Today was the last day of the Air Show and some participants would be leaving tomorrow, while others would be leaving at the end of the day. Sean and Corinne made their way to the hanger area and Sean looked up his old buddy, Air Force Captain Harry Kittle. Last week during a round of golf at Andrews, Harry had asked Sean if he wanted a ride in the new Super Sonic British Bomber. Harry was joking at the time, but he said his bother-in-law was the pilot. Sean was going to find out just how serious Harry really was about a ride.

Sean greeted Harry and motioned him aside and asked for a favor. Sean said he wanted to do something really special to impress his lady. He wanted to fly her to London and propose.

Harry started laughing and said, "You old dog, you'll never get married. But, this one must be really something. Give me a couple of minutes with Wing Commander Charles W. Rutherford, my bloody brother-in-law. Oh, by the way, we got smashed last night. You know the English are famous for being stuffy and pompous but the English pilots are famous for being nuts, so it just might work. Charlie is doing a pre-flight check right now. Let's walk out on the line and I'll check with him. Show your girl friend the plane. I don't think this will be problem since you are Navy reserve. Do you have your Navy reserve identification card with you?"

"Sure, I never leave home without it."

As the bomber stood on the tarmac for pre-flight inspection the crew hatch at the cockpit was open and so was the rear logistics hatch. Sean could see Charlie and Harry talking. The pilot gave Sean a crisp salute and headed toward the crew hatch. As Harry was walking back towards him, Sean knew it was a go and he said, "What'd he say?"

"Cheerio, mate! Climb aboard and strap in!"

Sean boosted Corinne through the logistics hatch and then pulled himself up and in. Sean could hear Harry dogging the hatch from the outside. Charlie climbed into the pilot's seat and looked over his shoulder and said, "Strap in mates! We're cleared for take off. We'll be wheels down in England in three hours. As soon as we reach cruise altitude at 60,000 feet, I'll give you guys a tour of the flight deck. Welcome aboard! I'm your pilot Wing Commander Charles Rutherford. Say hello to my co-pilot, Squadron Leader Clarence Warren!" Sean and Corinne introduced themselves and everyone shook hands. Squadron Leader Warren pointed out their seats and made sure the safety harnesses were secured correctly.

Charlie pushed the throttles forward and shouted, "Here we go!" The take off was fast and noisy and a little scary but once they began to climb out of Washington air space, it became reasonably quiet in the cabin.

Corinne said, "Sean! What have you gotten me into now, and where are we headed? Are we going to end up shot down? What's next? I haven't even joined the League of Red-Headed Men and I'm already on the most wanted list?"

"Corinne we're on our way to the Great Pyramid to look up Professor Fitzgerald, but we're stopping off in England on the way. With your handy, dandy genetic field test, and Professor Fitzgerald's 5,000 years worth of mummies, I think you will have enough of a sample to validate your genetic marker theory. Plus, we can test the League's theory on the genetic decline. We may yet be able to confirm or deny the existence of the Collective Intelligence. And if we're really on a roll, we may be able to determine if the Collective Intelligence has malevolent intentions."

"We'd better have access to the fastest computer in Egypt, if we hope to do all of that while in the field."

"Don't worry, our absence from Washington will give everything a chance to cool off around here, and it will give Dr. Death time to figure out what's really going on. I know we haven't done anything against the law, and I don't want to be told what not to do. So, if we're not available

The Pharaohs of Atlantis   69

for discussion, how can we end up with orders that conflict with our plans?"

"You know the old saying. It is better to beg forgiveness for something you've done, than to ask permission to do something and be told not to do it. That is always the approach I took with my grandparents when I was a kid, and it worked out well. If the double-helix genome decline can be proved, then it should be fairly easy to figure out what corrections need to be made in the genome."

Corinne said, "Hold on there! Who's the geneticist, me or you?"

Sean said, "You are, of course but you don't hold the power to change the genome. That power resides with the Death-Monkey."

Corinne laughed, "You do have a way with words!"

Sean took out one of the disposable PDAs and began typing. He said, "One of my intelligence officer friends from my Navy years, Sir Paul Gibbs, was a NATO exchange officer. You remember the guy that gave me the Act of Parliament clock? He has now rotated back to England, and he lives near London. If his spam blocker lets this text message through, we'll have a welcoming committee waiting for us. You'll be stunned by the beauty of their family home."

Suddenly a loud alarm began sounding in the cockpit and lights began flashing all around the aircraft. Charlie shouted, "Incoming missile!"

Chapter 8

A Night at the Museum

Sean and Corinne hadn't been the only League members arriving at the Smithsonian late that night. John Applegate's name was missing from Dr. Munkey's attendance list because he hadn't preregistered or signed-in before the start of the presentation. John was just about to exit the men's room when the commotion started and the lights came on. John immediately stepped back into the restroom, flipped the lights off, and opened the door a crack. He saw Sean and Corinne move behind the pyramid display and he heard the soft sound of a door being opened so he guessed they had slipped into the pyramid to avoid something or someone. John quietly closed the restroom door and made his way to the stall closest to the door and, leaving the stall door slightly ajar, climbed onto the toilet seat so, if someone gave the restroom a cursory look, his feet wouldn't be visible.

From the commotion and noise in the hallway he knew something was going down but he didn't know what. Then he heard the officer-in-charge say, "Check this bathroom and then tape the door so we know we checked it."

An officer entered the restroom, flashed his light around the room, and then flipped on the lights bending slightly to look under the stalls for feet. Seeing no feet, he reported, "All secure!"

"Good! Tape the door and let's move on."

John stepped off the toilet seat and sat down. He smiled to himself as he thought; *at least I'm in a better position to fill an hour in this restroom than Sean and Corinne are in that pyramid.* He wondered what the hell all the excitement was about. He quietly exited the stall and, in the dark, moved to the sink to splash a little water on his face, when he detected the faint sound of a conversation coming from the air duct. He put his ear close to the vent and recognized the voices of Dr. Death and Dr. Munkey. They were talking about DNA code and some test that Corinne had developed at NIH that they considered to be of national importance.

From what he could make of the conversation, that genetic test was behind tonight's security sweep. Apparently, Sean and Corinne weren't fugitives any more than he was, but something was up. Still, he couldn't imagine why Dr. Munkey had staged such a dramatic security crackdown. The voices in the air vent faded and John returned to his seat in the stall.

He was thinking, *Why not just request the information from NIH or ask Corinne? After all, it's not as if NIH could deny Dr. Munkey the information.*

As he sat there with nothing much to do, wild scenarios began to run through his head. There must be something about the genetic test that was far more important than Dr. Munkey was letting on to Dr. Death. But then, who knows? These government types were so egocentric that they were frequently caught up in their own self-importance, and were often overly dramatic in job performance.

As a prominent industry mogul, and also a member of the League, Applegate was privy to many classified government research programs. He knew that one or more of those programs were based on discovering the key factors contributing to the possible extension of human life and, hopefully, virtual immortality. John couldn't help but wonder if Corinne had stumbled onto the genetic secret to immortality. He thought, *I'd gladly trade my fortune for that information.* After all, what good is outrageous success if even very important people end up dead, just like the common people?

John knew that aging and death were controlled by genes that turned on and off, and eventually killed the living host organism. He knew that, if science could identify the point in the organism's timeline at which cells were no longer rejuvenated, then science could change the timeline or reverse the gene sequence. He hoped that finding that key point, and those key genes, would lead to immortality and eternal youth. The illusive fountain of youth might be discovered in his lifetime after all.

John decided to call Larry May and bring him up to speed on tonight's events. He wasn't worried about electronic spillage or his call being detected and traced because he didn't use a commercial frequency for his PDA. As a retired CIA agent, Larry had contacts all over the world, as well as in the local spook community. Larry wasn't with John at the Smithsonian because John considered it to be low risk. John didn't usually travel locally with a security entourage or use high profile automobiles, except for fun, because he didn't want to catch the attention of a casual, opportunistic thief. John was more concerned about international thieves or crime syndicates that had ransom and kidnapping on their minds.

John's friends didn't realize that Larry was employed as the head of John's security group. They assumed Larry was a family friend that happened to share John's interest in exotic cars and, occasionally, acted as John's co-pilot on the Gulfstream 750. Larry and John both believed that security was best managed as low profile, unless they were in a high profile public venue where a show of force was important.

John texted Larry, "Hey L, I'm unavail but I need you to send someone to the S and put a tail on my Corvette friends, S & C. Have someone here when the place opens and be on the lookout for folks exiting the Egypt exhibit. PS Use your best man and report progress. Do not detain."

Just before dawn John opened the door and pulled the tape off and flipped on the restroom lights. He then went back to the stall and waited until about 9:00, when he heard the noise of the building. Then he washed his face, combed his hair, and tried to look like a museum visitor. Just then he heard a knock at the door and a voice said, "Housekeeping?"

John replied, "Just a minute." He exited the restroom, left the building, and returned to his car. Leesburg and home was 45 minutes away.

Later in the day, John had the engine cover raised on the Ferrari when his PDA buzzed. He glanced at the message: "Too hot for text. I called Larry on the secure line and he has the scoop." Just then Larry walked into the garage and John turned to him and asked, "What's the story?"

"You're not going to believe it. They took the Metro to Andrews and they're currently aboard the British supersonic bomber, the star of the Air Show, and they're on the way to the bomber's home base at RAF Lincolnshire Air Station."

"What the hell is going on? Larry, this is probably a ridiculous question, but do you have any people on the ground in England?"

Larry said, "I do have a good man in London."

"Good! Have your man meet the bomber at Lincolnshire. Put a tail on the couple. It's the girl we are most interested in. If they get a chance to pick her up, do so, but don't make an international incident out of it. This mission is Operation Fox Hunt."

"Okay John, will do, but what's the plan?"

"Larry, I've had all night to think about this, and here's the concept. The ideal situation would be to set-up a jeopardy scenario using two action teams. The hostage team takes the Fox into custody and leads her to believe she is being detained until Dr. Munkey's interrogation team arrives from the US. This will make sense to her because she knows she is being pursued by the US government."

"The rescue team frees the Fox from the hostage team, sort of accidentally. The rescue team is composed of you and me and a couple of our guys from the America's Cup team. We just happen to stumble onto the kidnapper's safe house, when *Applegate's Dream* runs aground nearby. The safe house is that rental property just down the beach from our Cup headquarters. You may remember we rented that property to keep prying eyes away from the *Dream*. We come ashore in the dingy and beat on the front door of the safe house. The hostage team, on queue, assumes they have been found out, and they make a break for it, leaving the Fox behind. Maybe the hostage team fires a few shots in the air, for effect, while making their getaway. We suggest that the whole kidnapping scheme must have been some kind of actual ransom-based plan. We point out that if it were US government sponsored, the kidnappers wouldn't have abandoned their detainee. With sympathetic questioning, a grateful Corinne brings us up to speed on the whole Dr. Munkey security blitz, and why she believes they are trying to detain her."

Larry said, "Sounds like a hell of a lot of wishful thinking that will depend on all the dominoes falling in place at exactly the right time. It's not like we have a real plan at this time because there are too many variables. We'll need a lot of luck to get any of this done, even using retired CIA and retired MI5 operatives. After all, we aren't the Mission Impossible Force."

"You're right, Larry this is a fishing expedition, and I know it is a long shot, but I've always believed the sports analogy that 'luck happens when preparation meets opportunity.' We have absolutely nothing to lose at this point and perhaps a chance to gain immortality. If Corinne's secret turns out to be of little value, then we are simply rescuing her and helping to reunite her with Sean and friends."

"If the secret turns out to be related to the immortality question, then we gain their gratitude when we help them escape from the evil Dr. Munkey's clutches. Then we become de facto members of their merry band of co-conspirators and eventually share in the research results. If her research leads to an immortality potion, drug, or genetic modification, then we have won God's lottery!"

Larry said, "Okay John, I understand the concept, and we'll assemble a team that can think on its feet. I'll lay out the scope of the plan to my man in England, and I'll have him get two copters ready. One copter will be for the hostage team and the other bird for us, just in case we need it. I'll call the *Applegate's Dream* team manager and ask him to inform Captain Jason Smith that the boss wants to take a shake down cruise in the next day or so." Larry wasn't too surprised at John's wild scheme, because this surely wasn't the first time, but it was the first scheme that had kidnapping as a feature. Larry was beginning to wonder if John Applegate was transitioning from eccentric to certified nut.

John said, "Larry, take the Cessna and get to the Eastern Shore as soon as possible so you can prepare the Gulfstream for a transatlantic flight. I'll let Jennifer know that we're going to England to check on the progress of *Applegate's Dream*. As soon as I've tied up loose ends here, I'll drive to Dulles and take a charter flight to the plantation. Stay in touch via secure PDA, and let's get going."

Larry said, "We can't beat them to England but we'll be less than 48 hours behind them. Plus our guy will be on them the moment that bomber opens the hatch. Hey, John! I'm excited! This feels like a caper with my old company."

John said, "Larry, let's hope we execute the plan better than the typical CIA covert mission. I hope this doesn't turn out to be another Bay of Pigs disaster, with headlines splashed all over the front page of the *London Times*." They both laughed.

Larry got on the secure phone to his man in England, Tom Preston, and laid out the basics of the mission. Tom was requested to assemble a handful of operatives that could be trusted. Larry asked that the selection of operatives be based on former MI5 people, rather than rangers or commandoes. This mission was to be all finesse, with no brute force. In reality, and with all due respect to Ian Fleming, most spooks are technocrats rather than James Bond types.

The objective of the mission was to capture the Fox without a frontal attack. The mission must be stealth-based and all actions would be low profile, without gunfire or incendiaries. The Fox's safety was of paramount importance because the information she held could not be lost.

Tom Preston, as a life long spook, knew what he had to do. He and Larry had worked many clandestine missions together in their earlier days. As Larry was highlighting the mission elements, Tom was mentally down-selecting the potential operatives. All the old spooks and warhorses were anxious to get back into the game, so he had a crack group of specialists to select from. He knew he needed a man in place at Lincolnshire to identify the target as soon as she stepped out of the aircraft. Larry made things a lot easier when he indicated that Mr. "Deep Pockets" was funding the operation. Larry had impressed on Tom that Deep Pockets was willing to pay a substantial premium for a successful mission. Larry had already used his PDA to transfer mission funds from one Swiss Bank account to another, so all the pieces were in place to commence the launch of Operation Fox Hunt.

Larry was aboard the Gulfstream performing preflight checks when he heard chopper blades approaching. He looked up to see a commercial charter copter from Dulles making its approach to the Plantation. The copter had scarcely touched down when the door opened and John Applegate jumped out, waved to the pilot, and ran in a crouch toward the Gulfstream's hangar. Larry pushed the door button, causing the pilot's door to fold down and extend as a mini ramp, providing access to the plane. John climbed aboard and pushed the button to close the door behind him. Larry said, "All systems are go for take off."

John said, "Super! Let's start the engines and prepare for immediate take off. Did you file a flight plan with the Easton Airport yet?"

"No, I haven't yet. What do you want to tell them?"

John said, "England, of course we're to check on the *Applegate's Dream*."

"Aye, aye, Captain!"

As he taxied the Gulfstream to the runway, Larry sent the flight plan, via PDA, to the Easton Airport. He looked over at John in the captain's seat and asked, "Ready for takeoff, Captain?"

"Let her rip!"

Larry held the brakes and the turbines began to spool up on part throttle. The brakes began to slip in fits and starts, as the power built up. Larry simultaneously released the brakes and pushed the throttles all the way forward. The Gulfstream shot down the runway and with a whisper they were airborne for England. Larry retracted the landing gear as soon as they lifted off and the plane began to pick up speed rapidly. He then pulled back on the stick and they began a steep climb to the 60,000 feet cruising altitude.

On the ground in England, Tom Preston began assembling his team. Dave Davies was a crack copter pilot and worked out of Lincolnshire, so he was the first man Tom called. Plus, Dave had his own copter, although Tom and Dave agreed that it would be better to rent two copters for security reasons. Tom and Dave were in agreement on the two remaining team members as well. They both believed that it was always better to be over prepared and have greater firepower than you think you will need in order to ensure a margin of safety. They also knew they would need muscle for backup. Tom recommended using Steve Hicks, Tom's son-in-law, and Shamus Green, Steve's chum, for the muscle. They were former Army rangers and had just returned from Afghanistan, where they had been working for a security company. They were keen to pick up some extra cash and a little action too.

All four team members were on site in the hanger maintenance office at Lincolnshire when the bomber rolled to a stop. Tom said, "Well take a look at that, will you. It's Sir Paul Gibbs himself." They watched as Sean and the Fox climbed into the Rolls.

Dave Davies said, "They turned left when they exited the base, which suggests that they're headed for Stonehenge Manor. Let's take your chopper for a joy ride, Tom, to confirm their destination."

Tom and Dave jumped into the chopper and Tom immediately lifted off, flying in the opposite direction of the Rolls. As soon as they were out of sight of the Rolls, Tom turned left for a mile and then turned left again. Dave picked-up the binoculars and followed the Rolls and said, "No doubt about it, they're headed to the manor house. I've got some ideas. Let's head back to base and see what the rest of the team think."

Once they were on the ground, they began to discuss options. Dave said, "I'm familiar with Stonehenge Manor, and they have a pretty good security network in place. Sir Paul's security coordinator is Clancy Mason, and he is very good. Clancy upgrades the security network once a year to ensure that they have the latest technology. Plus, he doesn't use off-the-shelf stuff either. He customizes the network and adds little nice-to-have things too. Security at Stonehenge doesn't rely on low-tech devices. Breaching Stonehenge Manor's security, without being detected, would be next to impossible. If the security network is activated, we would never be able to slip past the net without running into old Clancy, face to face."

Steve Hicks said, "If we run into that bugger, we'll take him out."

Tom said, "Hold on Steve, remember, no violence. This is to be a covert sting."

Steve said, "No problem, Uncle Tom I guess I'm just a little too enthusiastic."

Dave asked, "How about this scenario? We get some of our mates to stage a car wreck in the front yard of Stonehenge Manor. Then we paste decals on our rental copter to make it look like a medical transporter. As the Stonehenge people respond to the emergency in their front yard, we land the bloody medical copter on their bleeding lawn. We then transfer the injured and bloody victims to the copter and head off to the hospital. With the distraction of the wreck and the medical copter, two of our boys slip across the perimeter on the west side and collect the Fox, while Clancy and his security force are on the lawn."

Everyone looked at each other and Tom asked, "Anyone have any comments or a better idea? At this point we know where the target is, and at least we know what we are facing. If we wait to see what pans out, we may lose track of the target and the opportunity to covertly collect the Fox. Dave, what time frame did you have in mind? How quickly can you assemble your car wreck mates, and do you have a ready source for the medical transport decals?"

Dave responded, "Tom, you know me well enough by now to know I wouldn't propose a plan that I didn't have the pieces to. I've got a friend that operates a traveling automobile stunt-show team that can move out with a phone call. He can also provide the medical transporter decals. It's all part of his show, you see? I think we should plan on staging our ruse just past sunset tonight."

Tom said, "I agree. Dave, take Shamus with you and execute your end of the plan. Steve and I will remain in constant communication via secure PDAs. As soon as you are ready, give the go, and we'll lift off immediately. Steve and I will man the extra chopper, and we'll plan on setting down on the west perimeter at the same time you set down on the front lawn. We'll slip across the perimeter and make our way to the house. It is likely that everyone in the house will spill out onto the lawn to view the commotion. We ought to be able to identify and grab the Fox quickly. We'll return to the chopper, lift off, and go directly to the safe house on the beach at Cowes. You mates lift off and ditch the copter fifteen miles in the other direction. As soon as you are in the car, head directly back to Lincolnshire and call in the missing copter as stolen. Okay! Off you go!"

Tom and Steve were getting their gear ready for the night's event. Tom carried a 9mm handgun strapped to his ankle, but it seemed like Steve had at least two of everything, from knives, to handguns, to automatic rifles and hand grenades. Steve said, "Uncle Tom do you have any black commando camouflage uniforms?"

Tom said, "No. But I have something better and more suitable. I have two black nylon running suits."

Steve looked at Tom with a frown and asked, "Are you having any second thoughts about this whole mission?"

Tom replied as he was sorting gear and getting everything ready, "Steve, I've never run an operation where I didn't have second thoughts. The only real apprehension I have about this mission is trying to pick Stonehenge Manor's pocket, and what Sir Paul Gibbs will do if the event is somehow traced back to us. I called this mission Operation Fox Hunt, but I hope it doesn't turn out to be Operation Dumb Ass. If we could have made the grab before the target entered the grounds of Stonehenge Manor, we would've had a better chance of success. The target was in Sir Paul's Rolls, so the retribution factor would have been the same, but the job would have been easier to pull off. We know now that a successful mission depends on the reaction of the people at Stonehenge Manor, which puts us at their mercy. If they respond the way we predict, everything will fall into place. If they respond in a way we haven't considered, then we will have to make real-time, on-the-field changes that put mission success in jeopardy. We have to get in, get out, and not leave a trail. I don't know what Sir Paul's connection to all of this is. If I had known Sir Paul and Stonehenge would be players in this little game, I would have turned the job down."

Tom looked up as he finished sorting the gear and saw Steve fully dressed and said, "Look at you! You look like a ninja in that running suit, with all your weapons. Hey! Wait a minute. No grenades."

Steve said, "No worries! These aren't grenades, they're smoke bombs."

A Night at the Museum

Chapter 9

England Swings Like a Pendulum Do

Wing Commander Sir Charles W. Rutherford killed the alarm and the lights and said, "Now! Do I have your attention? We have reached cruise altitude and we are about to achieve supersonic flight. You can watch the mach meter to check our speed. We are at .5 mach now on our way to mach 2. The water closet is in the rear of the ship, should you have a need. We'll be landing in Lincolnshire in about three hours. As soon as we reach cruising speed Clarence will break out the pop for a little refreshment, and you guys can join me on the flight deck."

"A-okay, Commander!"

Corinne said, "Whew! For a minute there, I thought I was going to need the facilities really quickly. Great sense of humor these English have."

"Just wait till you meet Sir Paul."

When Corinne returned from the water closet, Charlie called them to the flight deck. It was a little cramped, but no worse than a Concord. Charlie's Weapon's Officer, Clarence Warren, handed everyone a shot of Beefeaters.

Corinne asked Charlie, "Will there be a jolt or turbulence when we break the sound barrier?"

Charlie replied, "Did you feel anything? We're at mach 1.5 now and we'll be at mach 2 in two minutes."

"Oh, my! I didn't feel a thing. I guess I didn't think a supersonic bomber's ride would be so smooth and quiet. Did you have good weather for the trip over last week, too?"

Charlie said, "When we left RAF Coningsby last week, the sun had just set and the night sky was crystal clear. About two hours into the flight we caught up with the sun and experienced the phenomenon of sunrise in the west. Of course sunrises and sunsets can all look the same depending on the weather; but nevertheless to see a sunset and a sunrise within a couple of hours of each other is really something special."

Sean said, "Corinne, look! You can see the curvature of the Earth."

Corinne said, "How absolutely beautiful! It feels like we're almost in space."

Charlie said, "Okay guys, better finish your tea and strap in. We'll be landing soon."

Corinne said, "This is so much fun, and the scenery is unbelievable. Thanks a million, Commander."

Sean and Corinne returned to their seats to get ready for landing, and Sean checked his PDA for messages.

"Yahoo! Corinne, Sir Paul got my message! He'll meet us at the RAF Lincolnshire Air Station."

The rest of the flight was calm with no scary alarms. Twice the speed of sound was no different than a Boeing Dreamliner, except there was no piano bar. When the bomber rolled to a stop on the tarmac at Coningsby, Sir Paul V. Gibbs was standing next to the family's Rolls Royce Silver Cloud, waiting for them.

Charlie, Clarence, and Paul were Ministry of Defense colleagues, and Sir Paul greeted each man with a handshake.

Charlie said, "Keep your eye on 'em mate. Every time I looked in the back they were whispering in each other's ear. I think they can't wait to start the honeymoon."

Corinne said, "Hey wait! Honeymoon? What honeymoon? What are you talking about?"

Sean said, "Not now, Corinne! Our secret is out! There is no use trying to hide it. Let's get off the runway and let Charlie put the big bird to bed."

Sean and Corinne thanked Charlie and Clarence for the fast trip to England and the pleasant hospitality. Both men grabbed Corinne for hugs and wished her well on her up coming nuptials.

Sean and Paul shook hands and Sean introduced Corinne to Sir Paul and Randolph, the Gibbs' chauffeur. Randolph opened the limo's door and assisted Corinne into the automobile. Sir Paul and Sean climbed in from the other side. Sir Paul touched the intercom and told Randolph they were ready to return to Stonehenge.

Corinne asked, "Are we going to Stonehenge?"

Sir Paul laughed, "We are indeed going to Stonehenge. Stonehenge Manor is the name of the family's country cottage."

Sean said, "Country cottage? Just wait till you see the country cottage. It looks like the Queen's residence in an old British movie, except more opulent, if that's possible."

Sir Paul looked at Corinne and said, "Sean tends to exaggerate a bit, as I'm sure you must be familiar with by now. It's just the family's summer house to escape from the heat of London."

Sean said, "Corinne, you tell me if I've exaggerated when you see the 800 acre estate with its own security force."

Sir Paul said, "Well chums, I'm sure you can use a drink after what you've been through. Sean, why don't you pour a round of Gibsons for everyone?"

Corinne asked, "Is the Gibson the official drink of the League of Red-Headed Men?"

Sean said, "Well, not exactly, but it is for Sir Paul and me."

Sean asked, "Paul, has our little adventure made the *Times*?"

Sir Paul replied, "*The Washington Post* and the *London Times* each carried a minor story, on their back pages, about a security check at the Smithsonian. It was the standard release. An unnamed source at DHS indicated that, based on a tip, a security check had been carried out at the Smithsonian Institution. No terrorist activities or suspects were identified."

"There were no names mentioned, except for a request that Sean Thornton and Corinne Cannon contact their respective offices as soon as practical."

Corinne said, "I'll just bet they'd like us to contact our offices. If they hadn't tried to arrest us, we'd be at our desks and that damn monkey knows it."

Sir Paul said, "Slow down! Don't you mean Dr. Munkey?"

She said, "No! Monkey is what I said, and monkey is what I mean."

Sir Paul said, "Easy Corinne, I was just joking. There was no mention of names."

Both men laughed and Sean asked, "Was there anything about the League?"

Sir Paul said, "No, as a member, I'm sure Dr. Munkey didn't want to muddy the waters and have to field any questions from the inquiring press."

"Sir Paul, are you a member of the League, too?" asked Corinne.

Sean answered Corinne's question by explaining, "Sir Paul's great grandfather was one of the founders of the League of Red-Headed Men. You see, Sir Paul V. Gibbs is the third. Sir Paul the first and Sir Arthur Conan Doyle were best friends, and they founded the League of Red-Headed Men around 1900. Sir Paul and Sir Arthur described the League as a mystery writers club, but intelligence gathering and counter-intelligence activities were always the main focus. The League was especially effective during World Wars I and II, gathering intelligence and carrying out actions behind enemy lines. Sir Paul's father was lost on a classified mission behind enemy lines. Many Englishmen recognized the threat posed by the rise of Nazi Germany, and the League was dedicated to qualifying and quantifying the true threat."

"Sir Paul and I met when he was a North Atlantic Treaty Organization Intelligence Officer and we both were serving aboard ship during a Mediterranean deployment. It was common practice in those days, as it is now, for NATO to conduct joint tactical operations and to exchange officers and men across military units for the purpose of cross training."

"Once Paul and I discovered that we were both Sherlock Holmes fans we became close friends, both on duty and on the beach. It was during an Egyptian tour of the Old Kingdom that Sir Paul invited me to join the League of Red-Headed Men. Oh Paul, by the way, do you recognize Corinne's necklace?"

Sir Paul replied, "Indeed I do. That's the piece you bought from the shady antiquities dealer in Cairo. Corinne, I hope he didn't tell you he paid a small fortune for that scarab?"

Corinne said, "I don't care what he paid for it. The scarab is my good luck piece and my very favorite piece of jewelry. I never go out without it."

Sir Paul said, "Well it looks like the scarab has been working overtime for the two of you lately."

The Silver Cloud stopped briefly at the gate to Stonehenge Manor, allowing the CCTV to complete the security check before the electric gates opened. The gates were four meters tall and the stone pillars on which they were hung were six meters tall. Just outside the gates, adjacent to the driveway, stood a pair of English guardian lions that looked as if they belonged on the English Royal Coat of Arms. It took fifteen minutes to get from the gate to the manor house. Clancy Mason, the manager of Stonehenge, was waiting at the front door. Clancy helped Corinne from the car, and greeted them as if they were royalty.

Sir Paul said, "Clancy will show you to the Queen's suite so you can rest after the excitement of the last 24 hours. Lady Gibbs is engaged in a polo match today, and will return in time for high tea at four. Clancy will lay out fresh attire for you both. So you've got a couple of hours to relax and wind down, or is it wind up? See you on the veranda for tea. Now get some rest. Please, don't worry about the time; Clancy will call for you."

Sean and Corinne thanked Sir Paul for his gracious hospitality and they followed Clancy to the Queen's suite. Clancy invited them to choose the attire that pleased them, from the closets and dressers, and to ring if they needed anything. Clancy assured them that there was a range of sizes, and he was confident they would find suitable clothing.

Sean made a dash to the loo. He was anxious to scrub off the night in the pyramid and the grunge of the chase. When he returned to the living room, he could hear the other shower running and through the open water closet door he could see Corinne putting cream rinse on her hair. He kicked off his house slippers and dropped his towel and robe in a trail as he made his way to the shower. He slipped into the shower and reached around Corinne and cupped her breasts.

Corinne said, "Sir Paul! My God, we've just met! I don't think we know each other well enough for this kind of familiarity!"

Sean, in his best English accent, said, "Aye, the Squire of Stonehenge Manor has rights to all the comely young lasses!"

Sean swept Corinne into his arms and carried her to the bed and tossed her on it. He then jumped on the bed beside her and began to tickle her.

Corinne asked, "Now what's this stuff about nuptials and a honeymoon?"

Sean said, "We'll talk later. I just told Captain Kittle that the reason we needed to get to England was that I planned to propose to you, but I was, you know, just kidding him because, of course, we were on the run. He must have told Wing Commander Rutherford the same silly story."

"Oh? Silly story, you say! So you wouldn't want to be married to me, and you don't intend to propose, and you were just making that stuff up so you could have your way with me. Is that it?"

"Well wait, what I mean is, I ....I...."

There came a knock at the door and Clancy announced, "Sir, high tea will be served on the veranda in one hour. Ring when you are ready."

Sean said, "Come here, Baby!"

Corinne said, "Hold your horses; we'll be late for tea!"

Clancy returned to the security center and he and Sir Paul sat down to consider the anticipated security challenge the manor might have to face over the next couple of days. Sir Paul and Clancy had outfitted Stonehenge Manor with a sophisticated security network that included an underground perimeter motion and infrared detection system. The console operator could detect any perimeter breach and, using infrared imaging, the operator could classify the intruder as human or animal.

Clancy had also insisted on installation and monitoring of the air space around the manor with the latest radar technology. Most local airstrips had basic two-dimensional radars that tracked contacts in range and bearing only. Stonehenge Manor's radar system was three-dimensional and added contact height to the tracking model. The manor's radar system could track contacts out to twenty miles. The system was also equipped with an Identification Friend or Foe capability that could classify contacts as commercial or military aircraft, as long as their on-board IFF beacons were turned on.

Sir Paul briefed Clancy on the recent events surrounding Sean and Corinne. "Clancy, raise the Stonehenge Manor security level to number one for the next 48 hours. I don't know whether the threat will be physical or cyber. We could have operatives knocking on our door seeking information or experience an electronic attack."

"If you detect a security assault, don't hesitate to use deadly force to maintain the integrity of Stonehenge Manor. Depending on the scale of the assault, we may need to transfer our guests to a safe house. Make sure the chopper is flight ready. Hopefully, my concerns will amount to nothing."

Clancy said, "The chopper is ready for flight ops. I personally ran pre-flight checks this morning while you were at Lincolnshire. I've called in some extra help and all security consoles will be double manned for the duration."

Sir Paul said, "Clancy, you anticipate security threats better than anyone. That's why we've never had a breach at Stonehenge. Remind me to give all the security people bonuses. Sir Paul looked at his watch and said, "Almost tea time. Has Lady Gibbs returned?"

Clancy replied, "Lady Gibbs returned about 45 minutes ago, and she knows Sean and Corinne have arrived. I'll give the guests thirty minutes, and then I'll remind them of the hour."

Sean took a quick shower, dressed, checked the clock, and then rang for Clancy. Clancy escorted them down the back stairs to the veranda. The view was bucolic—a storybook picture with green pastures, horses, and a shimmering blue lake in the distance. Lady Gibbs and Sir Paul were standing at the fence rail, while Lady Gibbs combed the mane of her favorite horse. Introductions were made and they adjourned to the veranda for tea.

Lady Gibbs said, "This is all just so incredible! Paul told me about your adventure. You two have had just a frightful experience! I hope you feel safe now."

Corinne said, "Lady Gibbs, we will be forever grateful for your gracious hospitality."

"Oh please, call me Muffy. That stuffy Lady Gibbs hoopla just wears me out."

Sean noticed the dome of the observatory in the distance and he was reminded of Sir Paul's pet project, Mini-Argus.

Sean asked, "Paul, can you bring us up to date on Mini-Argus?"

Corinne said, "I know a little bit about Argus, in mythology, but I don't know anything about Mini-Argus. What's it all about?"

Sir Paul proceeded to explain, mostly for Corinne's benefit.

"Argus, of course, is the 100-eyed giant of Greek mythology. The astronomers chose Argus as the name for their night sky asteroid observance program. Argus is loosely funded by various government grants and donations from the public to purchase telescope time, actually camera time, on the various observatories around the world."

"The Argus agenda is to scan the night sky looking for objects large enough and on a trajectory that could put them on a collision course with Earth. No one wants a Life Extinguishing Event similar in magnitude to the one that surprised the dinosaurs 65 million years ago."

"It is impossible, due to limited computer memory capacity and processor technology, to track all moving objects in the night sky. Volunteers photograph the same night sky quadrants on successive nights, and then compare the negatives to pick up apparent movement of the lights. Once movement is identified, they assign a number and classify size and probability of the object's orbit intersecting with Earth."

Corinne asked, "If Argus is already performing this function, what is Mini-Argus doing?"

Sir Paul looked at Sean and said, "I wish my students at Cambridge were as attentive as Corinne. Good question!"

"The League of Red-Headed Men established Mini-Argus because we believe Argus is looking in the wrong part of the night sky. Plus, we didn't like sharing time with colleagues who have a different agenda than ours. We believe the Great Pyramid is more than a tomb for a dead pharaoh. We believe Egypt's ancient astronomers and engineers built the Great Pyramid in precise detail to align their observatory base with the night sky. We think the astronomers knew to look for the location of the next asteroid threat. For example, the Sphinx and the pyramid complex are in perfect alignment with where the constellation Leo in the night sky of 10,000 years ago. If you wind the clock backward 10,000 years, the positions of the stars change significantly. I believe there's no coincidence in the alignment of the Sphinx and the Great Pyramid complex with Leo. I believe the schism between science and theology was just as real then as it is today, if not more so. I believe the superstitious Egyptian priests feared instant death from the sky. The priests may have actually believed the Gods were administering a warning when they saw meteors in the night sky or punishment when they witnessed the meteors striking the Earth. The Egyptian astronomers, on the other hand, clearly knew where to look for comets in the night sky. I don't think the ancient Egyptian scientists believed the comets were designed by disgruntled Gods to punish Egypt, or that shooting stars were omens of good or evil. I suspect the astronomers recognized the comets as an act of nature."

Sir Paul noted, "In modern times, Halley's was the first comet to be recognized as periodic. Sir Edmond Halley, in 1682, compared historic sightings of comets by Petrus Apianus, in 1531, and Johannes Kepler, in 1607, and concluded that all three comets were, in fact, the same comet returning every 76 years. But the same comet was also seen in 240 BCE, 87 BCE, 12 BCE, 66 CE, 837 CE, 1066 CE, 1301 CE, 1456

CE, and so on. The most recent appearances have been in 1835; 1910 and 1986. Halley's comet will next return in 2061."

Corinne said, "I know some historians have suggested the 12 BCE appearance of Halley's Comet might explain the Biblical story of the Star of Bethlehem."

Sir Paul said, "You are correct. Twelve years one way or the other, when compared to ancient calendars, might as well be spot on."

"I suppose that, just like today, there was a division between science and theology. We think that the Great Pyramid was built to serve the ministers of Ra, but it was also designed by the engineers to take advantage of science, by providing an observatory where the scientists could work without being accused of being heretics."

"In primitive cultures, any shaman or medicine man that could explain or predict natural phenomenon became the sage that the people turned to for answers, blessings, or warnings. As some priests came to rely on science rather than superstition, a schism developed within the ranks of the clergy, between the smoke-and-mirror-based guys and the science-based guys. That schism between science and superstition continues unabated today."

"So we have been using computers to track the night sky backward and forward, and using the Great Pyramid's eye as the focus point for Mini-Argus. There are many asteroid or meteor impact sites around the world that are well documented. Science is still conflicted about which impact site might have been the one that wiped out the dinosaurs."

Corinne asked, "Isn't there some controversy regarding whether the dinosaurs and the other species were actually terminated by the asteroid?"

Sir Paul said, "Indeed, there are doubts that are fueled by the fossil record. The fossil record shows that many species were already becoming, or had become, extinct before the asteroid struck. There are several events documented in the Earth's fossil record that show unexplained deaths of many species. The "Great Dying" and similar events remain unexplained."

"Dr. Death and other League members have addressed the fossil record before the impact, but regardless of that red herring, we need to stay focused on the Life Extinguishing Event because that is where instant death and total civilization destruction comes from."

Sean observed, "It is the lack of explanation for the 'Great Dying,' and similar species die-offs, that support my contention that some force is periodically re-racking the life on this planet."

"As you well know there is no proof, but I still have concerns, as we've discussed before, regarding the Collective Intelligence and what role that entity may have played in the mass extinctions. Again, Darwin may say that there was a dramatic shift in the environment that resulted in the extinctions, but the fossil record doesn't show a big environmental change."

Paul said, "Sean, I believe in the concept of the Collective Intelligence, but we still need quantifiable proof. We know that Earth remains in the asteroid's line of fire and sooner or later we're going to get hammered again. I consider the asteroid threat to be a much more urgent threat than the Collective Intelligence."

Sean said, "I agree, but I can't help but believe the solution will be connected."

Corinne replied, "I know so little history about either threat that I can only stand here somewhat amazed at the information you have already collected and the multiple missions the League is engaged in. I am confident that only the League is giving either threat any scientific investigation. If I can help in anyway, I want to be a part of the investigation."

Sir Paul said, "Corinne, like Sean said, you are a member of the League, and your genetic research credentials will be invaluable in the days ahead. If I haven't said it before, welcome to the League of Red-Headed Men!

Corinne said, "Sir Paul, thank you for the vote of confidence. I am honored to be a member, I think."

Both men laughed!

Sir Paul said, "I know the European-Asian tectonic plate and the African tectonic plate may be largely responsible for the Mediterranean Basin. However, another possibility might be a large asteroid impact. I wouldn't be surprised if the biblical flood was caused by an asteroid impact in the Mediterranean Basin, or maybe an asteroid impact created the basin or isolated the basin from the Atlantic Ocean."

Corinne remarked, "The Old Testament says that it rained for forty days and forty nights and the flood lasted 150 days. Once the rains ceased and the Ark came to rest on Mount Ararat, it took an additional two months for the waters to recede. Does that time frame support an asteroid impact?"

Sir Paul said, "The damage and how it was felt would be directly proportional to the distance from the impact center. Remember, all recorded histories of the same timeframe contain a legend of a great flood. The impact could have been a glancing blow with damage limited to six months. The impact obviously wasn't a dinosaur surprise event, but it was a significant event. Unfortunately, we lack information to connect the data points on a realistic timeline. The Old Testament timeline, as extracted from the "begats," is a notoriously unreliable source. The events that have occurred in the night sky, that are corroborated by independent historians in the various civilizations, are limited to just a couple of thousand years. Even the fantastic Egyptian timeline is unknown when you consider the Sphinx may be 2,500 years older than the accepted build date for the Great Pyramid or perhaps vice versa."

Sir Paul explained, "The Observation Island is searching the Mediterranean Sea bottom to find crater evidence in and around the North Africa shores. If they find crater or impact zone evidence, they will take seabed core samples to determine the event's apparent age."

After dinner, Sir Paul invited his guests to join him and Lady Gibbs at the manor's observatory to test the clarity of the new telescope and to review some of the objects that Mini-Argus was currently tracking.

Sir Paul said, "Follow me to the lower level and we'll take the electric tram to the observatory. Muffy insisted that we not spoil the pasture land for the horses, so we had a tunnel put in."

When they arrived at the observatory, Sir Paul conducted them to the media room for show and tell. The facility's lights came on when they entered the media room. Sir Paul activated the presentation that gave an overview of the capabilities of the observatory and reviewed the goals of Mini-Argus.

Sir Paul said, "I'm going to have a Bailey's on ice, what can I get for everyone else?" Sean and Corinne both said fine, and Muffy requested a glass of Merlot.

Sean said, "Ladies, take a seat and I'll help Paul."

Sean handed the after-dinner drinks to everyone.

Sir Paul took a seat at the media console and said, "Okay, here's a status of where we are now. First are some images of the moon and nearby planets as we calibrate the telescope. They all have captions to describe what you are seeing."

"Wow! Are those really the canals on Mars?"

Sean started to laugh, "See! I told you Paul had a sense of humor. That's a fake slide from a science fiction movie he subjects everyone to."

Lady Gibbs shrieked, "Oh Paul! How could you?"

Paul looked at Corinne with a big grin on his face and Sean said, "You dog! You've let Muffy believe she was looking at the canals on Mars for the last three years?"

Paul said, "I can't help myself with Muffy; she takes everything I say literally. I start out saying something I know she'll never buy, but then she does. I always plan to let her in on the joke later, but sometimes I forget. Here are some images taken by NASA spacecraft that show the nature of comets up close and personal."

Corinne asked, "Paul where do the comets and asteroids come from, and is there ever a chance that the Earth will be out of danger from asteroid impact?"

Paul said, "The short answer is they come from the outer reaches of the solar system, specifically from the Kieper Belt and some from the Oort Cloud. As a matter of fact, the largest object in the Kieper Belt is the object formerly known as the planet Pluto. Pluto is not like the planets, and is on a highly elliptical orbit like the period comets such as to Halley. Many people believe our own moon is a refugee from the Oort Cloud or Kieper Belt that wandered too close to the Earth and was captured by the Earth's gravity."

"Short-duration comets, or those with orbits lasting 200 years or less, are generally believed to originate from the Kieper Belt. While long-period comets, such as Hale-Bopp, whose orbits last for thousands of years are believed to originate in the Oort Cloud."

"The period comets have a risk factor associated with them because they could be pulled apart by the forces of gravity and become smaller missiles. Yet they aren't the ones I worry about. Mini-Argus is about identifying and tracking the asteroids and comets that have a periodicity of thousands of years and new objects that may enter our solar system for the first time."

Sir Paul's PDA vibrated and he took a quick look at it and he said, "Come on over to the helo pad, I want to show you the new bird."

They jumped in the four-place golf cart and were at the helo pad in thirty seconds. Paul began releasing the tie downs and then climbed into the pilot's seat.

He said, "Come on gang! I want to take you for a quick spin around the estate."

Muffy said, "Oh Paul, it is too late. Let's not do it tonight, it's too dark."

Paul's voice took on an edge as he said, "No time to talk, get in!"

The rotors began to spin, the turbine began to wind up, and Muffy thought she heard fireworks in the distance. The helo lifted off, and Muffy said, "Look everyone! Clancy is setting off fireworks!"

The helo's lights went dark, and the turbine became a soft whistle. Paul punched a destination into the on-board navigator, put the helo on autopilot, and began to text a message.

The night was dark without a moon, and while those conditions are perfect for observing the night sky, those conditions are less than ideal for a helicopter voyage. Paul's helo was the most modern helo available, and its navigation system was second to none. Paul had been flying helicopters all his life, and Sean had no concerns whatsoever.

Corinne turned to Sean and said, "That wasn't fireworks was it?" Sean looked at her and just said, "No!"

England Swings Like a Pendulum Do

Chapter 10

The Ocean is Beautiful at Night

The sun was sinking below the horizon. Tom looked at his watch and thought, *Dave will lift off in about thirty minutes and send the signal for us to follow.*

He turned to Steve and said, "Let's head on over to the parking lot and pick up the rental car."

They drove from Lincolnshire to a parking lot near Tom's residence, where they switched to the rental car that Steve had rented earlier in the day. Then they drove to the commercial airfield to pick up the second chartered chopper. Steve gave the chopper the pre-fight inspection and climbed into the cockpit. Tom released the tie-down cables and Steve started the engine and brought the turbine up to operating temperature. Steve engaged the rotor and the chopper lifted into the air. The last streaks of red were dissipating as the sun sank beyond the horizon. Steve put the chopper through several maneuvers to get a feel for the ship and how it responded to the stick.

Steve said, "She's only got a few hours on the meter and she handles nicely. I think we have a nice ship here."

Tom had given Steve flying lessons when he was a youngster, but he had sharpened his skills flying combat missions for the Army. Just then, Tom's PDA began to vibrate. It was Dave's signal that they were in the air.

Tom picked up his secure phone and called, "Dave, we're airborne right behind you. I see three automobiles, in the distance, approaching Stonehenge. Are those your people?

Dave said, "Yeah, that's our guys. As soon as you see the crash, proceed immediately to the west side of the estate and set the ship down. There is only a tumbled down wall separating the moor from the manor property. You shouldn't have any problem climbing over the wall to access the Fox. Once the crash occurs, I'll set down on their front lawn within ninety seconds. When you see me land, run for the manor. You know what you're looking for. Good luck!"

Tom said, "Got it!"

They were in a slow orbiting pattern about a half a kilometer away and less than a hundred meters in the air. They spotted the three cars on the road, traveling at speeds that would put them at the gate of Stonehenge Manor in about thirty seconds. Two cars were approaching from the west and one from the east. All three vehicles collided and turned over. Two of the cars were on fire, and the third car was smoking.

Steve said, "This is going to be good. Oh, man! Look at that! If I didn't know better I'd think there must be a half a dozen people dead or bleeding in those three cars. Wow!

The smoke and fire effects are terrific! Okay, I'm going to take her down on the deck and move into the landing zone."

Tom said, "Set her down gently."

Steve came in twenty meters off the ground from the west and sat the chopper down easily. They were both watching the front of the estate through the trees and shrubs, and they could see the smoke and some of the flames licking into the air. They were on the ground behind the stonewall with the rotors turning slowly, when they saw Dave's chopper approaching the crash site with landing lights on and flashing red emergency lights. As the emergency chopper settled behind the trees Tom shouted, "That's our signal. Let's move out."

They left the engine idling and both men ran for the wall and scrambled over. Their side of the wall was only about one meter high, but the drop on the other side turned out to be more like two meters.

Steve whispered, "Damn! I think I sprained my ankle."

They began moving tree-to-tree and shrub-to-shrub to get closer to the house. They saw no one, and there still was no activity from the house. They heard sirens approaching in the distance and they could see activity around the crash scene, but no one came out of the house.

Tom said, "Let's get closer, maybe we'll see movement in the house through the windows. Steve picked up the night vision binoculars and began to scan the property.

Steve said, "Someone is moving to the back door. They're opening the door. I can't tell if it's a man or a woman. Let's get closer. Holy Crap! They just let the dogs out."

Steve immediately turned and ran as fast as he could toward the wall, limping as he went, and shouted, "Come on, before those dogs get here!"

Tom cried in a high pitched whisper, "Come back! Wait for me, maybe they're just pets."

Then Tom saw two Doberman's on a run, heading straight for him, and he knew they weren't pets. Tom turned and ran as fast as he could for the wall. The wall was ten meters away when he pulled the pin on one of the smoke grenades and dropped it.

The only thing the grenade accomplished was to make finding the wall in the dark and the smoke more difficult. The dogs followed their noses and ignored the smoke. Tom reached the wall, and as he began to climb up and over it, the first dog leaped up and bit into his upper thigh. The second dog bit into his left ankle and he fell to the ground screaming.

The dogs backed off and growled a warning at him, *Don't move.*

Tom slowly assumed a squatting position with his back to the wall. Tom knew he had to get over that wall before security arrived on the scene. He tried talking to the dogs and he tried commanding them to sit. Nothing worked. Then he remembered that he had a roll of "Lifesavers" candy in his jacket pocket. He reached in his pocket and pulled the candy out and flipped a couple of pieces to the dogs. The alpha dog ignored the candy, but the beta dog picked up the candy and began chewing. The alpha dog then picked up the candy and began chewing it. While the dogs were momentarily distracted, Tom spun around and leaped for the top of the wall. Instantly both dogs were on his legs again.

At that moment, Steve reached over from the top and grabbed Tom's collar, pulling him up and over. Tom was a heavy load because both dogs were still biting and pulling his legs. Both men hobbled as fast as they could to the idling chopper. Steve pushed Tom into the open cargo area behind the pilot's seats and quickly slammed the cargo door. The dogs found a way around the wall and were barking their brains out at the chopper door, just as Steve closed the cockpit door. Steve hit the throttle, and the chopper lifted off.

Steve could see another chopper lifting off at the back of the property. He called Dave on the secure phone and said, "Mission abort! I just saw a copter lift off at the back of the property. The Fox is lost."

Dave said, "The hell it is! Get on their tail, and I'll catch up with you as soon as we clear ground zero and get our people down safe."

Steve said, "There's another complication. Tom is dog-bit pretty bad. He's moaning and groaning and bleeding on the floor."

Dave asked, "Find out if he can wait for medical attention until we figure out where the bastards are headed."

Steve looked in the back and Tom had passed out, so Steve figured Tom wouldn't have a problem. "Dave, Tom said he can hang in there, so I'm on their tail. Let me know when you're in a backup position."

"Okay, will do!"

Steve looked back at Tom and he seemed to be breathing fine. He switched on the helo's navigation radar so he could easily track the fleeing copter. He had been in pursuit for thirty minutes. When he checked the course, it was pretty clear they were headed out over water. He wondered, "Where the hell are they headed?"

Dave hailed Steve on the secure voice link and said, "Steve, I'm ten kilometers behind you, and it looks like you are about ten kilometers behind the quarry. Do you have me on your navigation radar?"

"Dave, I see you clearly on the radar display. My question for you is: 'Where the hell are they going, and do we have enough fuel to follow?'"

Dave responded, "I think they are on this course to confuse any possible tail. I expect them to change course back toward land shortly. Stay with them, and I'll stay on your tail. How's Tom doing?"

"He's sleeping quietly and he's breathing okay. I don't see a huge puddle of blood so I think he's fine for the moment. He's going to be a hurting puppy tomorrow though."

Sir Paul's navigation radar indicated that there were two contacts approaching from the rear on the same course. Sir Paul went to a secure channel, picked up the microphone, and asked, "Charlie, are you there?"

"Paulie, I'm about sixty meters directly above you. Do you see what I see on the display?"

Sir Paul said, "I see two bogies, on our course, ten clicks and twenty clicks back."

"That's exactly what I see too."

"Well maybe you'd better explain it to them."

"10-4, old buddy!"

Wing Commander Charles W. Rutherford brought the Sea Harrier AV-8V10 to a dead stop in mid air. He then turned the ship around so it was pointing toward the on-coming lead copter and he hovered in waiting. The Sea Harrier AV-8V10 was about twenty meters above the altitude of the lead bogey. The Sea Harrier was about seventy meters above the ocean, and the on-coming lead chopper was about 35 meters above the ocean. The Sea Harrier AV-8V10 was the latest edition of the venerable Vertical Take Off and Landing (VTOL), thrust-vectoring jet aircraft that had been so successful in the 20th century. The 21st century V10 was all the more potent.

Steve said, "Hey Dave, I think you're right. They're slowing down. No, wait they're moving out faster. No, they're at a dead stop. Oh, hell! There is something wrong with this stinking navigation radar."

Wng Cdr Charles W. Rutherford flipped on his fire control radar and armed a heat-seeking air-to-air missile. He knew at this range the missile's infrared seeker head wouldn't activate because it would be too close to the target, but people often get the message when an air-to-air missile goes screaming by. Wng Cdr Rutherford simultaneously flipped on his landing lights and fired the missile at a spot high and to the left. The missile would harmlessly self-destruct, but the explosion and the near miss should have the desired effect.

The lead copter, with Steve at the controls, was making 120 knots. Steve was straining his eyes to catch sight of the chopper ahead. Out of nowhere the Sea Harrier's landing lights flicked on and he was momentarily blinded. To avoid what he mistakenly thought was a head-on collision, Steve instinctively pushed the chopper's stick down hard, too far down, and held it too long. When he saw the Harrier's lights reflected in the sea, he instantly realized his error and promptly pulled the stick back. This time he over compensated in the opposite direction. He almost made it, but the tail rotor dipped into the sea and the chopper was pulled out of the night sky by the ocean's drag.

The chopper was filling up with water and sinking fast, but Steve managed to get off a distress call to Dave. He quickly put on a life jacket and struggled to get one on Tom before the sinking chopper made the point moot. Finally, the preservers snapped into place for Steve and Tom. They were both bobbing in the water, wondering what the hell happened, as the last bit of chopper slid beneath the waves.

Off in the distance Wng Cdr Rutherford had extinguished his landing lights and was watching the events unfold with the infrared night vision display.

Charlie reported, "Splash bogey one, Paulie. There are two swimmers in the water and the rescue activities should occupy bogey two. If it doesn't, I'll explain it to them too."

"Thanks a million, mate. See you at polo next weekend."

"I wouldn't miss it! This time you guys are going to be buying the ale."

"Win or lose, I'm buying!"

"I copy that!"

When Dave, in chopper two, arrived on the scene, he saw the smoke trail and the strobe lights flashing on both men's life jackets. He turned on the chopper's landing lights and brought the craft down to where the wheels and runners were just touching the sea. Shamus Green slid the cargo door open, snapped his safety belt to the door frame, and leaned out to try to pull Tom into the cabin. The two men in the water were loaded down by weapons and hardware and were at a severe disadvantage. Tom was weak as a kitten from blood loss and was virtually helpless.

Steve reached around and released Tom's weapons belt and at the same time released his own too. Shamus and Steve were struggling to get Tom into the cabin, but with each attempt it got harder, as their strength dwindled. Steve was shouting at Shamus and Shamus was shouting at Dave to get the copter closer to the water. Dave eased the chopper down to where the water was just lapping at the cabin door, with the wheels and skids submerged. Only then, were they able to pull Tom into the cabin. At that very moment the turbo intake sucked in a splash of sea water, and the chopper momentarily lost power. She immediately settled into the sea with a thump and a splash!

Wng Cdr Charles W. Rutherford called in an SOS to the RAF Air-Sea Rescue and provided the coordinates. He indicated that he had been tracking two bogies when they apparently collided and disappeared from the tracking index. He proceeded to the coordinates and when he arrived on the scene he discovered four survivors in the water. He would remain on station until the rescue team arrived.

Charlie went to the secure channel and said, "Bogey two just splashed trying to rescue the survivors. I notified S&R. I'll stay on station until the rescue team gets here. I wish you fair weather and following seas. See you on the polo field. Charlie out."

"Many thanks from all, and give my love to Sandy."

Chapter II

Europe on Six Billion Euros

Larry May sat the Gulfstream down on the tarmac at Heathrow and they taxied to the General Aviation Terminal. The last secure message Larry had from Tom was 24 hours ago and it read: "Talley Ho! The hunt begins!"

John noticed Larry checking his PDA and asked, "Still dark?"

"Yeah, all quiet on the Western Front."

John said, "Let's wait to be contacted, I don't want to take a chance that they might be in custody or under surveillance. We'll check into the London Hilton and get refreshed."

They caught the Hilton's courtesy van to the hotel and checked-in. It was 3:00 A.M. and they were beat, but John never let lack of sleep slow him down. Larry had booked a suite with adjoining rooms. John opened the refrigerator and said, "I'm having a screwdriver, how about you?"

Larry said, "Me too, only hold the vodka. If I have any alcohol now, I'll be out like light."

John poured two glasses of orange juice and handed one to Larry. He then opened a miniature bottle of Gray Goose and poured the contents into his glass.

"Cheers!"

They clinked glasses and John took a drink, while Larry drank his down in one gulp.

"Now that really hits the spot."

John said, "Have the desk give us a wake up call at six in the morning and deliver breakfast at seven."

"You've got it!

John grabbed a quick shower and hit the silks. Larry called the front desk, put in the wake-up call, and ordered breakfast. He then poured another orange juice, clicked on BBC for the news, and promptly fell asleep in the easy chair. It seemed as if he had scarcely closed his eyes when the phone rang announcing that it was six. He gave John a call and hit the shower. He walked out of the shower feeling like a new man. He dressed, opened the room door, retrieved the *London Times*, and sat down at the table to catch-up on the news. He actually preferred the hard copy paper to the PDA, but he kept that to himself.

BBC was still on the tube from the night before, and he was half listening when he looked up and noticed the scroll across the bottom, "Helicopters collide over North Sea, four men pulled from sea." Larry immediately had an eerie feeling. He opened the *Times* and started thumbing through the pages. There, at the top of page three, was the same headline. The story read, "Anonymous sources with Her Majesty's Coastguard revealed that RAF Air-Sea Rescue pulled four men from the North Sea last night after two helicopters apparently collided. Three men were treated for exposure and released. Their names have not been released. The fourth man, Thomas Preston of Lincolnshire, remains hospitalized with non-life-threatening injuries."

John entered the suite and asked, "What's news, did we miss anything?"

Larry replied, "Apparently we did! Listen to this."

Larry filled John in on the news. John asked, "Do you think it's our Tom Preston?"

"Do you really have to ask?"

John started laughing and said, "I guess not."

John returned to his bedroom to finish dressing. He continued making crude and cold comments that suggested he could care less about what happened to the men he had hired.

Larry felt entirely different about the turn of events and the apparent failure of Operation Fox Hunt. Larry felt partially responsible for the failed mission. After all, he and Tom Preston knew that with the short timeframe, the lack of planning, and their unfamiliarity with the target's modus operandi, more luck would be involved than skill. Still, he was a little shaken that things had apparently gone so wrong. Plus, he still didn't know how many operatives had been involved, or whether anyone had lost his or her life, including the target. He was anxious to get a debrief from Tom.

As he was waiting for John he couldn't help but consider how "John his friend" and "John the business tycoon" could be so different. John the billionaire genius was ruthless, tenacious, and single-minded in the pursuit of all research or business ventures.

Conversely, John the family man was kind, generous, and accommodating to all friends and family. There were aspects of John's personality and his nature that often made him seem to be more like a machine than a person.

Larry was right about John being more like a machine than a human. John was wildly successful, beyond anyone's expectation, including his own. As a child John was withdrawn and introspective to a fault. His father was career military and wasn't around much. When he was around, he tended to apply his military skills for troop management to raising his son and communicating with his family. John's mother was overly protective of John, especially when his father was around. John's father appeared cold, loveless, and indifferent to the boy. It was as if his wife and child were members of his platoon and, as Platoon Leader, he must train them to be good Marines; to show kindness would have been a showing of weakness.

Colonel Applegate set goals that the boy simply couldn't achieve. Then, he berated the lad for not being man enough to accomplish them.

John learned to handle his father's pressure by retreating to his beloved microprocessor-based games. John was one of those nerds that spent nearly every waking hour playing computer-based games. But unlike most geeks, this geek began to create, program, and sell computer-based games on his website. At first the game manufacturers sought to force John to cease and desist in improving and modifying their games. They even tried to charge him with patent infringement. That approach didn't work because John had actually created totally new games that weren't based on any of their software or algorithms.

John's initial success in computer game development led to further successes, such that, while in junior high school he was under contract and providing consulting services to several major computer-based game firms.

John was making so much money and having so much fun that he sought early emancipation from his parents, and won the right to conduct his own business affairs as a sixteen year old. John remained close to his mother, but he was never able to communicate with his father on any level.

John entered the Massachusetts Institute of Technology as a seventeen year old and by 22 he had completed all the requirements for a Doctorate in Computer Science.

John related to the world via computer and software. So it was only natural that he used his understanding of microprocessors and their associated programs as a way to relate to people. He looked at the logical functioning of his own brain as the Central Processor Unit. He considered his education as the Operating System software that facilitated the operation of his brain.

He then broke every component of his life down to discrete application programs that were applied according to circumstances. John's application programs included the "family/wife/child protocol"; the "exotic car collection protocol"; the "Americas Cup Challenge protocol"; the "dealing with employees protocol"; the "dealing with software/micro processor business competitors protocol"; the "human emotions protocol"; the "charity protocol"; the "patriotism protocol"; the "religion protocol"; and on, and on.

John developed his "religion protocol" during high school and college. John's mother had insisted on Sunday school for John. When he became an adolescent, he was familiar with the Christian experience at the Cecil B. De Mille level. Once he hit the teen years, and especially after he became emancipated, he considered the religions of the world as harmless fairy tails for children and summarily dismissed them.

When John began to date in high school and college, he realized that to declare that you are an atheist or an agnostic could be detrimental to ones dating success. So John developed his "religion protocol" and responded, when asked, that he was a Christian and that he believed in God and the Bible, but didn't belong to a church. He married Jennifer in a huge church wedding and they took their sacred vows with their hands on the Bible.

John generally avoided church, except when Jennifer insisted, and then he attended to please her and to act as a role model for the children.

Most of John's application protocols were developed the same way as the religious protocol: to accomplish an end game, one had to develop the appropriate protocol to ensure the desired outcome. Some might think of John's philosophy as "the means justifies the end," but John's philosophy was more complex than that. He considered all elements when developing a strategy to attain an objective. He always made sure that his end of the deal was squeaky clean, but he didn't mind if his partner got down and dirty while executing the plan.

Unfortunately, just like a science fiction machine-based Monster with the heart of a computer, John's humanity was often seriously absent in some applications and over done in other applications. And just like a microprocessor, John's application of logic triumphed over all and usually at the expense of people, including colleagues, best friends, or even family. His ego would never let him apologize or admit that he might be wrong.

John Applegate lacked a moral foundation for his genius. Genius without a moral foundation can be a dangerous tool in the hand of a man with unlimited power. Extreme wealth often places the possessor above the law. John clearly saw himself as above the law.

Sometimes John's Operating System applied the logic algorithm in a complementary fashion to the emotional/human application program. The result was that John seemed kind, compassionate, caring, and almost like a genuine human being when in a social or family environment. The main problem with John's Operating System software was that there was no "moral application program" concatenated to the various application programs.

In some situations, John's cold logic circuits could deliver a perfectly logical conclusion that could unnecessarily and cruelly destroy innocent people. Many times the cruelty John delivered to other people wasn't that much different from the dispassionate thrashing he received, as a child, from the Colonel. John couldn't be reasoned with because the tools he routinely applied to life and business were at the foundation of his phenomenal success. So he knew they were right and proper.

Larry wanted to contact Tom Preston and express his concerns, but he knew John would consider contact with Tom, at this point, too risky. Larry knew John's position would be to wait until Tom made contact with them, and then ensure they were dealing with a secure situation and not a set-up.

John joined Larry for breakfast and he mixed one of his high-protein powder concoctions in the fresh orange juice, then knocked it back.

Larry said, "Well, how do we get back on track with Operation Fox Hunt without getting in contact with Tom Preston?"

"Operation Fox Hunt is lost. I don't know where those guys went wrong, but they clearly went way wrong and we don't have a clue as to what happened to the Fox after they botched the mission. Operation Fox Hunt has been overtaken by events. I don't want Tom to take a loss, but there can be no bonus payout on a failed mission. Make sure he knows we appreciate the effort and we look forward to working together in the future. You can cover all this with him via secure voice when we are back in the States, but absolutely no contact while we're in Europe."

"Larry, get a hold of the concierge and book the earliest train to Southampton. Book a rental car in Southampton and reserve passage on one of the ferries to Cowes, Isle of Wight. Try to get a suite in the Fountain Hotel overlooking the River Medina. After all, if we're going to go, we might as well go first class."

"Give Jason Smith, the *Dream*'s manager, a heads-up that we should be there by two this afternoon. Remind him that all we are looking for is a status report on *Applegates's Dream* and that a dog and pony show is not required."

"Larry, I know this is your first trip to the Isle of Wight. While we could fly there, I think you'll enjoy the car trip because, first off, we're only about an hour away and, secondly, there is a lot of beautiful scenery on the way."

"While I'd like to Captain the *Dream* around the Isle, I'm not sure the weather will be conducive to sailing while we're there. There's no point in risking the ship just because it would be fun."

Larry said, "Plus, I get sea sick."

Larry picked up a brochure entitled, "What's happening in the UK" and began to read out loud. "The Isle of Wight was the scene of the original 1851 regatta when the schooner *America* won the cup that has ever since been called the Americas Cup. The race was to circumnavigate the Isle of Wight. The one American boat challenged sixteen English ships and won."

"The Royal Yacht *Squadron* of Cowes, England, was the host. The New York Yacht Club entry was the schooner *America*. The schooner's designer, W.H. Brown, was so confident of his design that he refused payment if *America* did not win. The oft-quoted remark by the Queen was..."

John interrupted, "I know, she asked, 'Who is first?" *America* has won, she was told. 'Who was second,' asked the Queen? The reply still echoes—'Your Majesty, there is no second.'"

"You see Larry, that is exactly what I mean about the immortality issue. We must solve the problem because second place is death."

While John was talking, Larry entered data into his PDA and then clicked the send button. Within ten minutes the concierge sent a response indicating that all reservations were confirmed. The two men packed their gear and headed for the lobby to catch the courtesy van to the Heathrow Train Station and connections to Southampton.

John was anxious to get the full report on the *Dream* and the applied nanotechnology project. He considered the nanotechnology project to be so secret that he wouldn't even risk discussing it over a secure link. John knew that if the concept and technology could be demonstrated in the real world aboard the *Dream*, then John Applegate's current successes would scarcely be more than a footnote to his nanotechnology program.

When they disembarked from the train in Southampton, they picked up the rental car and headed for the Red Funnel Ferry.

Larry drove the car aboard the ferry, and the two men got out of the car to enjoy the fresh sea breeze.

Larry observed, "John, you really haven't shared the dirty tricks you guys have installed aboard the *Dream*. I know you well enough to know that you plan to secure an unfair advantage in the next Americas Cup race Challenge Series."

John said, "Now, I am hurt! You wound me with your words. Unfair advantage? Dirty tricks? How can you suggest that I would break the rules? I assure you, any dirty tricks or unfair advantages will be applied within the rules."

Larry said, "Well, you have inferred that the *Dream* will be outfitted with nanotechnology, and I was just wondering how the technology can be hidden, and how the *Dream* can pass the technical inspection?"

John said, "You haven't researched the history of nanotechnology or you would have asked different questions. Okay! Here is a thumbnail sketch:"

"Control of applied science and technology is the underlying theme of my company's nano technology program. My company, or ME for short, has developed and engineered nanosystems that we believe will demonstrate the viability of mechanical functionality of engineered nanosystems operating at the molecular scale."

"Now, just what the hell does that mean?"

"The nanotechnology concept has been around for years, but the applications have been on bulk manufacturing rather than on the nano scale of engineered systems. Our concept enables programmable, positional assembly to atomic specifications."

"Okay! Now just what the hell does that mean?"

"In simple terms, it means microscopic machines and electronic systems that require microscopic amounts of energy. These tiny machines can replace large-scale machines and electronic systems. One nanometer (nm) is one billionth, or 10-9th of a meter. A nanometer is the amount a man's beard grows in the time it takes him to raise the razor to his face. We're talking really, really tiny here."

"ME's nanotechnology has been applied to the *Dream* in a liquid as paint and as a rinse. The sails, mast, and rigging use the same rinse. The hull, rudder, and flying keel use a Teflon-based paint with the nanotechnology suspended in the paint solution."

Larry asked, "Okay, I get super small but what can it do for the *Dream*?"

John replied, "Each individual nanotech component is individually programmable and we can change the function of each nanotech component to perform as an accelerometer, thermometer, stress detector, sound collector, or any other data gathering sensor that we might need."

"We can use a PDA to program the nano sensors to become whatever kind of sensor we need. For example, we have programmed the nano material to provide air speed, sail loading, mast loading, and rigging stress on the surfaces above the boat's water line. Below the water line we have programmed the nano material to measure rudder angle/stress, water temperature at the keel and the waterline, flying keel-wing position, and thousands of other bits of data. The nanotech sensors are powered by sunlight based on the photoelectric principle. The nanotechs communicate with each other and the PDA microprocessor via wire free technology."

"Incredible, but what do you do with this data?" asked Larry.

John said, "The PDA's microprocessor acts as the central processor and the individual nanotechs are part of the distributed processing system with each nanotech acting as an on-site microprocessor and sharing data with each other and the PDA's CPU. This technology allows us to change the angle of the flying keel to optimize how much sail area we have deployed, to reconcile stress data from the mast/rigging and rudder angle, and to use nanotech robotic syncho-servo technology to change the dynamics. The result is we go faster because we can dynamically change the boat to optimize the way we sail it. By applying a mechanical bias to the lines and stays we can warp the mast and we can warp the sails. We can also manage the coefficient of friction between the water and the hull by electrically changing the molecular structure of the hull paint, to take advantage of the temperature differences in different parts of the channel."

"Wow! This is way beyond me, but does this all work?"

"The technology is sound, but are we there yet with applying the technology to the real world of Americas Cup racers? I don't know yet. That's what Jason Smith is going to tell us after three months of testing and gathering data."

The ferry gave a couple of whistle blasts, signaling that docking was imminent. John and Larry got back into the car. When the ferry docked, Larry drove off while John gave him directions to the *Dream*. When they arrived at the pier, Jason Smith waved "hello." The *Dream* was at a private pier and was the only ship there. They went aboard, and Jason gave them a quick tour. The tour was quick because the *Dream* was all racing sailboat and there were no amenities of any kind. Even the interior cabin was bare except for the head and a refrigerator.

Jason said, "Well, there you have it! What do you think?

Larry said, "She certainly is a *Dream* and she is aptly named, but she sure isn't a pleasure craft."

John said, "Nope! The pleasure will be mine when Jason and I hold that Americas Cup high and give it a kiss! I can't wait to return that Cup to its rightful place on the mantle at the New York Yacht Club."

Jason said, "Let's go back to the office and I'll share the test results collected during the last three months."

They returned to the office where the three-man security team was waiting. Jason made the introductions and the security team returned to the ship. The ship was always under the watchful eye of security, 24 hours a day.

Jason said, "I won't burden you with the false leads and the dead ends we ran into. We pick-up three knots when we use the microprocessor recommended optimizations."

John said, "Excellent! What about the hull paint?"

Jason said, "The hull paint tests will be done in the next three weeks. Computer modeling predictions suggest an additional three knots in speed."

John said, "Now we're talking. If we can achieve a six-knot advantage over the leading competitor, we'll blow them away. The key will be how we actually apply the advantage during the race. I don't want to blow by them with a six-knot advantage, I want to sandbag them and just barely beat them in each race of the series. On the final leg of the race to the finish line, we'll apply all the tricks and show the world the power of ME nanotechnology in action!"

Jason said, "You are always strategizing and that's what makes you number one in the world. What are your plans for tomorrow? Bill, my brother, and I have a tea time at St. Andrews, and maybe you guys would like to complete the foursome?"

John said, "We'd love to! I haven't played Andrews in five years. How are you getting there?"

Jason said, "We'll take the company plane. It's an older Gulfstream, but it's still comfortable."

John said, "Fine. We're staying at the Fountain Hotel. What time should we be out front to meet you guys?"

Jason said, "We'll pick you up at 7:00 A.M."

John said, "Great! See you then. Tonight we're going to turn in early and get a full night's sleep for a change."

The men took their leave and headed directly to the Fountain Hotel. They checked in and the view from the room was spectacular. As they sat around the patio table on the little porch, enjoying a pint of English ale and a couple of good cigars, Larry couldn't help but think that the life of a billionaire was pretty grueling.

Larry observed, "John, I envy the way you are able to clear stuff off the table and move on."

John asked, "What do you mean, Larry?"

"Well, for example, you launched Operation Fox Hunt and you dropped everything to pursue a slim opportunity that required incredible timing to work. Then when it crashed and burned, you were able to brush it off without recriminations or second thoughts."

John said, "The opportunity was there, and the opportunity may pop up again. It's just that we aren't tracking the opportunity anymore. The chance for immortality is still the most important objective there could be, and I don't have any second thoughts about chasing it. My only regrets are that we didn't have better information or more time to qualify the opportunity. I'm not angry with our team here in England. I'm only disappointed in the outcome. I know they did the best they could, and I appreciate it. I think of Operation Fox Hunt as one bad hand in a marathon poker game. Let's see how the next hand plays out. Maybe we can double down and win twice as much during the next round."

"After all, what's the point in being wildly successful and living better than 99% of the people in the world, only to end up turning to dust just like the beggar in the street? I intend to stay on this pursuit until either we run it to a dead end or until we are successful. I assume you would also be interested in immortality? If not, I'll strike your name from the list."

Larry laughed, "Make no mistake; I want my name as high up on the list as I can get it. I'm a team player, and I too, have no regrets."

"Good! Then it seems as if we are two of a kind and in agreement on the way ahead, if we should suddenly flush the Fox from hiding."

John poured them both another round, lit up a cigar, and blew smoke rings into the night with great satisfaction.

Larry asked, "John what inspired you to develop and apply nanotechnology to the *Dream*?"

"Larry, I could give you a lot of mumbo-jumbo about technology and deep thinking, but it was really just a simple thought. I was sailing the *Dream* alone, when we got caught in a squall—a pretty bad squall. It was touch and go for a while, until I got just a little ahead of the front. I knew, if I could wring every knot of speed out of the boat, I could make a safe harbor."

"The handicap was I was alone and I needed a crew of ten to optimize all the variables. As I gained a little on the front and began to get a little comfortable, I started to think about micro sensors and servos at the critical points."

"You see? I modeled the nano servos on the *Dream*, in the same way as nerves and senses are arranged in our own bodies. Our brains are the CPU and our nerve endings are sensors. The big difference between the system on the *Dream* and the one contained in our bodies is we can't program the sensors or nerve endings in our bodies to meet the changing environment."

Larry said, "Cool! I see! So our muscles are the servos, our senses are the feedback loop, and our brains make the decisions. You know? The whole concept is kind of like Sean's idea of how DNA and molecules are connected."

"Well, I'll be damned! You were paying attention at the BBQ. I thought you were just checking out the single babes."

Larry smiled.

Chapter 12

St. Andrews and the Old Course

Jason picked them up at the hotel promptly at seven.

"Good morning, gentlemen! I trust you slept well. We're only minutes away from the airstrip, so I dropped Bill off to perform flight checks while I fetched you guys."

John replied, "Good morning to you as well, Jason."

John and Larry settled in the backseat, and they were quickly on their way.

When they arrived at the plane, Bill was in the cockpit and motioned everyone aboard. As they climbed in, Jason said, "Bill, say hello to John and Larry!"

Bill said, "Welcome aboard guys. It's great to meet you. Make yourselves comfortable, and we'll be on the course before you know it."

Larry asked, "Hey, Bill what airport are we flying into?"

"We'll be flying into the RAF base at Leuchars. Leuchars accepts commercial aviation and it's only eight miles from St. Andrews, so we can't miss."

John said, "Excellent!"

Jason turned to John and said, "I've made reservations for you and Larry at Rufflets Country House Hotel. Naturally, it's a five star resort and is just one mile west of St. Andrews. Tee-time is 10:00 A.M. on the Old Course."

The Old Course has been the home of golf for the past 600 years, and the British Open is played there every five years. It can take up to a year to get a tee-time, unless you know someone. John Applegate didn't know it, but Jason's original tee-time was on the Jubilee course. When John agreed to play, Jason contacted the reservations clerk with The Royal and Ancient Golf Club and, on the power of John Applegate's name, secured a tee-time on the Old Course. Wealth does indeed have its perks.

They were scarcely in the air before Bill was rolling to a stop at the commercial hanger at Leuchars. The waiting limo delivered the four men to the clubhouse in minutes. Jason instructed the driver to deliver John and Larry's luggage to Rufflets.

If you are a golfer, then there is nothing better than golfing at the holy grail of golf. The course was immaculate, the weather was perfect, and they just couldn't have had a better day. Each player was a near scratch golfer and well versed in course etiquette. They had a marvelous eighteen holes, with John Applegate prevailing over Larry by one stroke at the eighteenth hole, when Larry's put rimmed out.

They returned to the clubhouse for some nineteenth-hole libations and relived each stroke of the day with the "might-have-been" and "if-only-I-had" scores. John Applegate invited everyone to dinner at Rufflets, but Jason and Bill had previous plans with family in Edinburgh. The men split up at the clubhouse entrance, with John and Larry heading to Rufflets via the courtesy van, and Jason and Bill taking the limo to their family home in Edinburgh.

As John and Larry were checking in at Rufflets, they bumped into Sir Paul Gibbs and Clancy Mason. Sir Paul and John knew each other professionally and, of course, they were both members of the League of Red-Headed Men.

John said, "Paul Gibbs, you old dog, it's good to see you!" They shook hands and everyone introduced themselves. John said, "I know you own most of Scotland, but do you own St. Andrews too?"

Sir Paul said, "I don't, but I'll check with the family genealogy clerk, maybe one of my ancestors still holds title."

John smiled, looked around and asked, "Where's Lady Gibbs?"

Sir Paul replied, "Muffy plays polo, but golf bores the poor thing to death. Anyway, ladies aren't allowed on the course here at St. Andrews, so it's just as well."

John said, "Now, that is one rule I wouldn't want to change!" All four men laughed in agreement.

Sir Paul said, "Clancy and I are here for a couple of days of golf and a little rest and relaxation. St. Andrews gives us a chance to get away from the everyday chores around the farm. Are you in England on business or pleasure?"

John replied, "A little of both. We were down to Cowes checking on the *Dream* and decided we should take some time off too. Do you have dinner plans? You're welcome to join us."

Sir Paul said, "We do have dinner plans, but perhaps we could get together after dinner for a chat in the lounge, say about nine?"

John said, "Great! We'll see you then."

Sir Paul said, "I'm anxious to hear about your new technology. By the way, what do you have up your sleeve? I'm sure you think that old tub of yours can best Lord Grimthrope on the course."

John said, "I'd love to tell you my secrets, but then, I'd have to debrief you and put you in quarantine until after the race! The next time you see Grimthrope tell him the Cup is going home with me." Everyone had a good chuckle.

John Applegate was a self-made man and he would not call anyone Sir, Lord, or Her Majesty. John believed people born to wealth and privilege didn't deserve their titles or their special place in society as an accident of birth. John believed a man must do something extraordinary to merit the title. John wouldn't have any problem referring to Mr. Winston Churchill as Sir because Sir Winston earned the award.

John and Larry had a five course dinner in the Terrace Restaurant, but they didn't catch sight of Sir Paul so they surmised he had dined elsewhere.

John stood up and said, "Let's adjourn to the library and wait for the royalty."

They made their way to the lounge and sat down in the leather easy chairs arranged around the great fireplace. The waiter took their order for two glasses of The Glenlevit 18 Year single malt scotch whiskey, on ice.

Larry asked, "Aren't we committing a social faux pas by ordering whiskey on ice? I know the English consider it a sin to serve whiskey over ice"

John said, "We are indeed socially bereft by adding the ice, but probably more so by selecting commercial scotch whiskey. I'm willing to bet Paul has a family label single malt scotch that we will be drinking as soon as he arrives. Hey! Here he is now."

John and Larry stood up and shook hands with Sir Paul and Clancy, then everyone settled into comfortable chairs around the fireplace.

Sir Paul said, "I see you gentlemen are about ready for another round. I wonder if you would indulge me by allowing me to call for the family label scotch. I think you'll find it very smooth and enjoyable?"

John said, "I was just reminding Larry that the Gibbs distillery has a world renowned reputation for scotch whiskey. By all means, I'm looking forward to a taste of the finest whiskey in the British Isles."

Sir Paul called the waiter by name and requested the Gibbs blue and red label whiskey with set-ups. Sir Paul assumed that some may want to sip, some may want it over ice, and some may want a hot toddy.

John said, "We had an excellent surf and turf in the Terrace Restaurant. I hope you gentlemen fared as well."

Sir Paul said, "We did indeed. We shared dinner with my cousin, Nigel Hornbeak, and his lovely bride, Wendy. They're just back from an eighteen-month archeology dig in Peru, and they shared with us some remarkable stories about the artifacts they found in a pre-Incan dig."

John said, "I'm no archeologist, but it has always seemed to me that Egypt gets all the attention and the pre-Columbian sites in North and South America are largely ignored. Were there any breakthroughs in the dig?"

Sir Paul replied, "To Nigel and Wendy there were. I must admit I don't have enough background to really appreciate what I was being told, but I think most people's impression of the pre-Columbian cultures are based on bad movies depicting the Aztecs or Mayans as savages, rather than stressing their science, astronomy, technology, humanity, and religion."

"Nigel explained that the pre-Incan civilization was extremely advanced in society and culture, and should be ranked with the early civilizations of Egypt and Mesopotamia. Nigel and Wendy were particularly fascinated with a pre-Incan God called Viracocha. Apparently he was an enlightened God in white robes and was the source of knowledge. He was also a warrior God with weapons in his hands and a sun symbol around his head, much like Egypt's Sun God, Ra. Interestingly enough, Viracocha first appeared after a great flood had killed most of the inhabitants, except for those living high in the mountains above the flood waters."

John asked, "Speaking of Egypt, were you on-line for Professor Fitzgerald's presentation last week? There was some sort of technical snafu, and I lost the signal. What did I miss?"

Sir Paul replied, "There wasn't a technology snafu. The presentation was halted by Dr. Munkey, at the request of the Director of the Museum of Egyptian Antiquities, due to security concerns. The director was uncomfortable with the information being released in any way, but was totally against releasing information in an electronic format."

Larry May said, "The encryption is so good these days that I'm sure the director was overly concerned."

Clancy said, "I agree with Larry. If Professor Fitzgerald was using approved encryption algorithms there really was no risk."

Sir Paul said, "I agree, but we are working as guests in their country, and we have to honor their requests or we'll be asked to leave."

John asked, "Paul, aren't you the major sponsor of the Egyptian project? I'm sure you could prevail on the director. By the way, what is the nature of the find, and why all the hush, hush?"

Sir Paul said, "I am one of the sponsors, and I see no reason to restrict the information. But then, the West has a long history of plundering Egypt's artifacts in the name of science. There are still many artifacts in the British Museum that Egypt has been trying to have returned for years, so I can see why the director wishes to control access to the information."

"If you really want to know about the find I would recommend that you visit the director and offer a grant to support the dig. I wouldn't be surprised if the director offered a tour of the site, and then you could see the wonders for yourself."

John looked at Clancy and said, "There's always a catch, isn't there?"

Clancy laughed, "Money makes the world go around!"

John said, "Paul, if you would be so kind as to introduce me to the director, I would like to visit the site and make a substantial grant."

Sir Paul said, "I would be glad to. I'll contact the director tonight. When do you plan to visit?"

John said, "I plan on being in Cairo sometime in the next few days. Go ahead and send the director an introductive email, and I'll contact him when we are checked into the hotel in Cairo."

Sir Paul asked, "Should I mention an amount for the grant? The amount just might ensure that the director's schedule is open. By the way the director is a she. Her name is Fatima Boutros."

John said, "Let's start with $2 million. If I'm impressed by the tour, the grant is subject to change."

Sir Paul said, "You may as well check your resources because, believe me, you will be impressed!"

Sir Paul reached into his jacket pocket and pulled out his PDA and generated an email to Fatima on the spot. He turned to John and said, "I blind copied you on the email. When I get a response, I'll forward it to you."

John said, "Paul, thank you so much for the introduction."

The rest of the evening's discussion centered on sports, the world market, and beautiful women, but not necessarily in that order.

Sir Paul's limousine arrived at Rufflets early the following morning to carry them to the family's castle in Scotland. Nigel and Wendy's overview of the Peruvian project was intriguing, and Sir Paul was anxious to hear their detailed report. The Peruvian archeological dig was the hottest project Sir Paul had going, until the astonishing discovery in Egypt up-staged it.

Sir Paul was convinced the experts were wrong about the rise of modern man, and he was sure conventional wisdom regarding the accepted timeline was wrong too. But to prove that the timeline and the rise of technology had not begun with the retreating ice age 10,000 years ago, he needed fossil proof, archeological proof, or the discovery of an unknown ancient civilization. Sir Paul was afraid that the Mediterranean Basin had already given up its secrets and that ancient tomb robbers had destroyed the vital information.

So he hoped that the jungles of South America might yet reveal the proof that would set the archeological world on its ear. Sir Paul suspected that an ancient civilization, with perhaps an arts and science base similar to the Egyptians, may have once existed on more than one continent. He believed that some unknown calamity destroyed that civilization. He didn't know what destroyed the ancient world before, but he was sure that it wasn't an angry God. If it was a LEE, such as the one that ruined the dinosaur's day, then today's world remains vulnerable. If it was pestilence or disease, then there may be lessons from the past that could benefit today's civilization. Plus, the past may hold secrets related to people living in harmony with nature.

The Nile Valley and the Fertile Crescent had been host to the rise and fall of any number of civilizations in the last 10,000 years, some large and some small. The settlements contained in the Nile Valley ranged from fishing settlements, to villages subsisting on agriculture, to independent city-states, to connected and organized civilizations like the Egyptian dynasties.

Each civilization, as it grew, was likely to have been built atop the ruins of the previous civilization. Given the rebuilding and the activity of tomb robbers, Sir Paul had been reasonably certain Egypt was all out of startling revelations. Professor Fitzgerald's discovery only proved how wrong Sir Paul's assumptions had been.

Still, Sir Paul believed North and South America had buried secrets that virtually no one had even bothered to look for. Most archeological research in the Americas had concentrated on recovering artifacts from the Olmec, Toltec, Maya, Aztec, Inca, and other pre-Columbian civilizations. While he found the pre-Columbian civilizations interesting, Sir Paul was concentrating his research activities on the civilizations that predated the Aztecs and Inca. He hoped to discover evidence of civilizations on the scale of the classical Egyptian period nearly 5,000 years old.

Now, with the professor's discovery, he planned to encourage Nigel and Wendy to expand their search beyond 5,000 years. That meant if they found evidence supporting a civilization 5,000 years old, they would immediately assume that there must be an older one beneath it and they must dig deeper.

When the limo arrived at the castle, Sir Paul and Clancy went straight to the library to discuss the finds in South America and Egypt.

Sir Paul said, "Nigel, I think your discoveries in Peru are incredible. If it wasn't for Professor Fitzgerald's astonishing find in Egypt, your Peruvian find would be the hottest subject in the archeological world. I suggest we sit tight and hold your news close to the vest until we see how this Egyptian find pans out."

Nigel said, "I concur. The part that I alluded to last night is that we have found evidence of what appears to be 18th century glass shards in the debris of our dig. The local researchers are convinced that tomb robbers from the 20th century have contaminated the site. I don't think so because the site looks untouched to me. I didn't try to convince anyone because the rainy season was starting, and I didn't want to give anybody an incentive to dig while we were gone. We have the site guarded while we are away."

Wendy said, "The site is under an Inca temple that was built on a pre-Inca temple. We are digging beneath the pre-Incan site. There is no evidence to suggest that anyone has excavated there before. If we can find a pre-Incan temple or tomb intact, then we will have a good chance to define the timeframe."

Sir Paul said, "I want you two to enjoy your time off, and I want you to relax. I also wanted you to know that Sean Thornton and his fiancé, Corinne Cannon, have visas and identification papers that use your last name. The story is that Sean Hornbeak is your younger brother and he is an amateur archeologist. It's a long story but "Sean and Corinne Hornbeak" are currently aboard the Observation Island in route to Egypt. Nigel, their background applications document their relationship to you as a brother and sister-in-law. I can't imagine this little caper hitting the newspapers, nor can I envision a situation where you might be asked questions regarding your 'brother,' but if you are, you'll know those questions aren't out of the blue."

Nigel said, "Please let my 'brother and sister-in-law' know that we welcome them to our family. Remind them that should they find anything remarkable in the tomb, we taught them everything they know about archeology, and we will gladly share the by-line with them."

Everyone laughed and Sir Paul said, "Professor Fitzgerald's reports are available in the library. Please take the time to review the data, and see if you see any similarities with architecture or artifacts you've come across in Peru. For the next few days let's plan on meeting each day for high tea on the veranda. Now off you go!"

After Wendy and Nigel left the library for a previously scheduled appointment, Clancy poured himself and Sir Paul a spot of tea. Sir Paul noticed that Clancy seemed to have an unresolved issue.

"Okay, Clancy! You look troubled. Out with it!

"Paul, I don't know anything about anything other than security, but your response to Applegate's question last night, about the find in Egypt, is bound to send him straight there!"

Sir Paul asked, "Was I that transparent? I hope John Applegate doesn't figure it out."

Clancy said, "You don't have to worry about that. Applegate has an ego that can only be photographed from the air. Paul, if you wanted that guy to go to Egypt, then you played him like a trout. You gave him just enough information to pique his interest but not enough to reveal the essence of the find."

"Exactly, my friend!"

Clancy said, "Now that bugger is going to go straight to Egypt and insert himself right in the middle of everything. He's a known loose cannon, and you won't be able to muzzle him either."

"Clancy, I don't want him muzzled. I want complete buy-in by Mr. John Applegate. John possesses one of the most brilliant minds of the 21st century. With his Manufacturing Enterprises he is the only member of industry that has mature nanotechnology that is ready to produce products. I want Applegate to go to Egypt and think the whole idea is his. With Applegate and ME on board, the rest of industry will follow like lemmings."

Clancy said, "Why not ramp him up and only let him into the tent when you are ready for the implementation phase? He will be hard to control."

Sir Paul said, "Don't forget that old line that goes, 'It is better to have the faithful opposition in your tent peeing out, than to have them on the outside peeing in!'"

Both men chuckled.

Clancy said, "I can see the method to your madness!"

Sir Paul said, "The success of 'Operation Jupiter' depends on nanotechnology. The tiny size is an important consideration, when you are building and operating spacecraft beyond the Jovian orbit, but the most important benefit is the very tiny power consumption required to deliver enormous computing power. If John Applegate is convinced the Earth is facing a crisis, then he will be convincing when he implores others to support the goals and objectives of Operation Jupiter. The way we convince John is to make him part of the team that defines the problem and recommends the solution."

"Brilliant! Wait a minute, Operation Jupiter? What is Operation Jupiter?"

St. Andrews and the Old Course

Chapter 13
Big Oil and the Double-Helix Conspiracy

Off in the distance Corinne could see the blinking navigation lights of a mammoth North Sea offshore oil platform. As Sir Paul circled the oil rig Muffy asked, "Paul, why are we going to the oil platform at this time of night?"

"Muffy those weren't fireworks you saw. It was a firefight between our security force and whoever the uninvited guests were. Clancy made it clear that we were not available for callers, at that time of night and they withdrew. However, when our chopper lifted off I think their objective changed."

Muffy asked, "Were they looking for Sean and Corinne?"

"Probably, and that's why we're here at the company oil platform."

Paul keyed the radio and asked Art Clark, the platform manager, for landing instructions. Art provided a landing vector, and Paul began his approach.

The demise of the North Sea oil field had been predicted since the construction of the first platform, the Beryl Alpha in 1975. However, additional oil finds and an abundance of natural gas continued the North Sea operation well into the 21st century, and the fields were still pumping crude at nearly the same level produced in the 1980s. Life aboard the oil platforms was still two weeks on and two weeks off, and the living conditions were no worse than life aboard a ship. The platforms were notoriously dangerous, with instant death for the careless, but the successful riggers wouldn't trade the job for any other, anywhere.

As the chopper approached the light of the rig, Paul could see Art standing, with lighted wands, on the helo pad. Paul skillfully set the chopper down in the center of the helo pad. Art's crew secured the bird to the platform and immediately they began to refuel the chopper for its next flight. Art grabbed Sir Paul's hand in greeting and guided them to the executive suites where all the amenities were set-up and waiting. Everyone settled into chairs clustered around the large screen display.

As they watched the satellite news, they clinked glasses and Sean proposed a toast, "To oil riggers, choppers, and Red-Headed Men!"

And Corinne added "And Red-Headed Women too!"

Sir Paul said, "I'll drink to that! Okay guys, I think we have some privacy now so let's hear about Corinne's DNA field test!"

Corinne described how simple the field test was and described the minimum laboratory equipment needed. Sean explained that they would like to hook up with Professor Fitzgerald at the Great Pyramid and try the test on the DNA of the mummies in the new tomb.

Sean said, "We want to compare the 5,000 year old DNA with today's DNA to see if there is a significant difference. We can then determine if the difference represents a degraded condition. If we discover that the genetic code has degraded over time perhaps we will be able to develop a controlling gene sequence correction splice."

"If the comparison shows a significant degradation, then the stagnant genome theory may have merit. Depending on how many generations of mummies are available for sampling, this group of royalty may be just the kind of historical gene pool that will allow scientists to develop a conclusion that makes sense. If we can isolate the problem, we can develop a correction based on science rather than preconceived notions of either Dr. Death or Dr. Munkey."

Sean said, "I believe if Dr. Death is armed with scientific research, he can persuade Dr. Munkey to consider an alternate solution. With the power of the government behind them and with Dr. Munkey pushing a joint solution, science can solve the problem of any gene pool degradation without looking like the government is advocating eugenics or using the 'hand of man' to replace the Hand of God. The solution would simply be repairing a birth defect and thus the men of God shouldn't oppose the correction either."

"Paul," said Sean, "You and I have discussed parts of my theory before but lately I've expanded my theory a little. We've always been skeptical regarding a literal interpretation of the Bible and I've never been one to consider it the Word of God. But recently Dr. Death has convinced me that his DNA degradation theory has merit. But where Dr. Death thinks the degradation of the genome is a result of the stagnant gene pool, I believe that the double helix is the implementation arm of the Collective Intelligence. I believe the CI is, at some level, manipulating the human genome with the express purpose of dethroning, from the top of the food chain, mankind or at least this latest version of civilization."

"I initially thought we Homo sapiens were being dethroned because of our inability to solve the asteroid threat. More recently I've come to believe we are being dethroned because our species represents a bigger threat to life on this planet than an asteroid. I hope that continued research into the double helix will reveal the code that is apparently retracting our life span and perhaps our civilization."

Paul said, "Sean, you are suggesting that today's civilization is self-destructing because we can't get along as nations. And as industrial giants, we are destroying the environment that supports life on this planet."

Sean said, "Paul, that is exactly the point. The problem is I can't prove the Collective Intelligence exists, nor can I prove that, if it does exist, it is manipulating the double helix."

"So, degradation of the human genome is only degradation from the point of view of Homo sapiens. From the point of view of the CI it is simply erasure of a failed experiment."

Paul and Muffy laughed and Muffy said, "Sean, your proposition is the classic 'does God exist or doesn't he' argument, restated with the double helix playing the part of both a benevolent God and an avenging God."

Sean said, "It is indeed, but there is a difference. My theory doesn't have a group of demigods pretending to be in contact with the double helix and speaking for the double helix. What I'm saying is the double helix is a force of nature or a life form, if you will, that exists on this planet because the conditions are right. As the environmental conditions change, the Collective Intelligence takes action to modify the double-helix template to adapt to the changing environment."

"You see, I think Darwin's 'natural selection' of survival of the fittest is correct, but I think it needs to be applied at the double-helix level rather than at the species level."

"I believe each double-helix molecule is a discrete intelligent life form, but that all double-helix molecules together form the Collective Intelligence. I theorize that the Collective Intelligence is greater than the sum of its parts. The individual DNA life forms are like a distributed processing system that is controlled by a federated, over-arching operating system, which in this case is the CI. I suspect that the CI then manipulates individual species on this planet to respond to the environment."

"Perhaps six billion years ago the Collective Intelligence adapted to the changing environment, but by now, via Darwin's theory of evolution, the Collective Intelligence has evolved and created a species that can change, protect, or, perhaps, inadvertently destroy its own environment. I think the unintended consequence of a species that can protect the planet from a LEE asteroid is a species that can destroy the planet via uncontrolled industrialization, war, and weapons of mass destruction."

Corinne said, "The Bible says man has free will to sin or not sin. Are you suggesting the double helix and/or the Collective Intelligence have the free will to sin or not sin?

Sean replied, "I don't believe morals or sins have anything to do with the Collective Intelligence. I think survival of the Collective Intelligence and the double-helix molecule is the only imperative, and only those species that are directly contributing to that imperative are safe."

Corinne said, "Your concept is an interesting idea and could be as true as anything in the Bible, but it remains a concept without adherents besides yourself. How would you prove it?"

Sean said, "Corinne, I think if the tomb at Cairo is all Professor Fitzgerald says it is and, if your genetic test proves reliable, the data we collect will go a long way to either eliminate my theory or point to my theory as plausible."

Corinne said, "I'm looking forward to helping collect and analyze the data, but I'm not ready to believe that God or the double helix is trying to dethrone human beings. I accept your idea as viable, and if the data is there, I'll help you prove the theory."

Sean said, "Hey! Wait a minute! Why should my concept have to shoulder the burden of proof when the great religions of the world get a pass?"

Corinne said, "The burden of proof for the scientist is equal to the burden of proof for the devout. Still, you've got an easier argument. You don't have to prove a negative. All you have to do is prove a positive."

Sean replied, "Corinne, I agree and I'm anxious to collect the data. The double-helix molecule exists and it is a template for life. That has been demonstrated. I don't have to prove that the Collective Intelligence exists, nor do I have to prove that it is sending orders to the double helix. All I have to prove is that the double-helix molecules communicate with each other. Once that communication link is established, I can than deduce that the whole of DNA-based life on this planet is likely conscious. Therefore, that consciousness may very well represent a sentient being."

Corinne said, "I see what you mean. But what is the nature of the communication link and what are its characteristics?"

Sir Paul asked, "Corinne, let me propose a concept for the link. Einstein's 'general and special theories of relativity' are based on the observable world and they can be, and have been, demonstrated physically and mathematically through scientific experiments. For example: Einstein's theories defined the speed of light and the likelihood that a large object's gravitational mass would bend light in proportion to its mass. The actual experiment confirmed Einstein's theory."

"Einstein, Plank, and the other scientists that developed quantum mechanics to define the observation of subatomic particles at the atomic and subatomic level, found that particle behavior was acted upon by 'hidden variables.' In other words, matter and electrons at the atomic and subatomic level behave contrary to the general theory of relativity. They developed quantum mechanics to define the behavior of matter at the subatomic level."

"I think many of us believe that, if there is a Collective Intelligence, it would most likely communicate at the atomic or subatomic level, so we can't use conventional theories of communication to define or detect the link. This communication link may not be able to be directly established, but we may be able to infer that the communication link exists as a 'hidden variable.'

Corinne said, "Okay, guys, here is the problem. Once you demonstrate the subatomic link and we actually prove that data exchange occurs between the molecules and ...."

Sean interrupted Corinne and said, "I know! You're going say it merely proves that nature behaves according to God's plan."

Corinne said, "No! I was going to say that the communication link between the CI's initial command to the eventual implementation by the double helix may span generations and centuries. It may be your great, great grandchild that either proves or disproves your theory."

"Corinne, you make an excellent point! We have data to collect! Now, how do we get to Egypt?"

Paul said, "Well, now you've asked a question I can answer. With your permission, I propose we create alternate identities for you both."

Sean said, "That sounds okay to me. I'd be delighted to be someone else right now."

Corinne said with a laugh, "Me, too. I want to be someone that no one is looking for."

"Sean, do you remember my cousin, Nigel and his wife Wendy Hornbeak?"

Sean replied, "Oh, sure. I met them one time at Stonehenge Manor a few years back. If I remember right, they are professional archeologists. It seems as if they are almost always in the field."

Paul said, "You are exactly correct. You will be Nigel's younger brother, Sean. You and your bride, Corinne, will be on your honeymoon. Here's the cover story. Sean and Corinne Hornbeak, Sir Paul's cousins, will take the family owned oil company chopper to the company refinery in Aberdeen, Scotland. There you will trade the chopper for a Gulf Stream 10 for the trip to Rota, Spain. From Rota you will jump back on a company chopper for the flight to the Observation Island, which is underway somewhere in the Mediterranean. When you report aboard the Observation Island, you will be Sir Paul's cousin, Sean Hornbeak and Sean's wife, Corinne. The Hornbeak's are amateur archeologists and will be on their honeymoon and interested in the sights and sounds of Egypt and the Great Pyramids. You will be taking tours wherever the Observation Island might dock.

"When," Paul said, "you arrive aboard the Observation Island and Captain John Smith-Davies shows you to your cabin, you will present the Captain with your passports, visas, and identity papers. Your papers will be ready for pick up when you arrive in Rota."

"Just blend in with the crew, which you will find are a great bunch of guys, but maintain your new identities, and trust no one until you hook up with Professor Fitzgerald. Good luck, and off you go. I will take care of everything, and we will remain in contact via encrypted PDA text messages. I will let the professor know when to expect you in Cairo."

When Sean and Corinne arrived at the company refinery in Aberdeen, Scotland, they got showers and a full night's rest, for a change. The two of them, along with their luggage, climbed aboard the Gulf Stream at three the following afternoon and settled in for the trip to Rota. They used the morning to pick up all the clothes, toiletries, and other items they would need for the trip. Sean sent Sir Paul a text message list of what they still needed, so it would be waiting for them when they got to Rota.

Corinne asked, "How come we are flying to Rota, I thought the Navy Station at Rota was a joint US-Spanish military base?"

Sean said, "You are right. I forgot that your family lived in Madrid for a few years. The joint operation of the Rota Naval Station began in 1953 and is still going strong. The US Navy Supply Center at Rota supports the Navy's 6th Fleet in the Mediterranean. The station has several other resident commands, as well as a CIA office. Sir Paul's company has offices on the base and they also have hangar space. So Rota makes for a good base of operations for Sir Paul's Mid-East operations and is a natural stop-off on the way to the Observation Island."

Corinne started to say something but Sean put a finger to his lips and pointed to the PDA. They began to text message back and forth. Corinne wondered how they would manage to get off the Observation Island without sticking out like a sore thumb. Sean replied that when the Observation Island docked in the Gulf of Suez at the company oil rig, he planned to book a weekend tour of the Egyptian monuments and holy sites just like regular tourists.

Corinne and Sean collected the gear Sir Paul had stationed for them, and they boarded the chopper early in the morning for the flight to the ship. They were in the air for an hour or two when Corinne spotted a speck in the distance. The speck began to grow larger by the minute. Corinne said, "We're not going to land on the back of that moving ship, are we? It is so tiny!"

Sean said, "Oh, don't worry we're not going to land on the ship."

Corinne said, "Oh good! I was getting worried."

"The chopper is going to hover above the ship, and we'll climb down a rope ladder!"

Corinne said, "Oh, great! What a relief! I feel better now!"

Sir Paul's ship was an ex-USN and Military Sealift Command ship. In its former life it was a missile test range ship used by the Navy since the 1950s. Because it was a stable platform with anti-roll capabilities it had been perfect for converting to a research ship. While the ship looked like a speck to Corinne, it was huge—564 feet in length and a beam of 76 feet. The Observation Island was equipped with its own helo and the ship's helo deck could easily accommodate helo landings, but the ship was currently rigged for the sonar search function, and clearing the deck and moving the cargo stored on the helo deck would be too labor intensive.

As the helo matched speed with the ship, Sean lowered the rope ladder. Two seamen on the ship's deck grabbed the dangling rope ladder and pulled it tight. Sean helped a brave and fearless Corinne climb aboard the ladder and showed her how to wrap her arms around the ladder for extra security. As Corinne made her way to the deck, Sean quickly followed. The noise of the helicopter's engine was fierce, and the rotor wash was powerful enough to sweep them off the deck. The first mate, Cris Sauer, escorted them to the bridge to meet Captain John Smith-Davies. The captain welcomed them aboard. Captain John, Sean, and Corinne stood on the bridge wing watching the ship's helo detail grab the cargo and their luggage as the helo crew dropped it on to the ship's deck. Captain John said, "Follow me, I'll show you to your cabin. Then you can join me in the galley for coffee, and I'll give you a sitrep."

As Corinne and Sean were putting their stuff in the locker in their cabin, Corinne asked, "Sean, what's a sitrep?"

Sean said, "Nothing special, Corinne. A sitrep is a Navy term for situation report." Corinne laughed, "Oh, I knew that. I just forgot for a second. It's like a snafu."

"Corinne, that is exactly right!"

They joined the captain and other members of the research crew in the galley, where they learned that the ship had been running a grid pattern for weeks off the northern coast of Africa. The pattern included towing two side and bottom scanning SONAR fish to map the sea floor's topography. The captain indicated that the average depth of the Mediterranean Sea is less than 5,000 feet but that Africa's continental shelf extends out many miles from the shoreline. While they often couldn't see land, they were generally within fifty miles of land.

Corinne asked, "Captain just what are you hoping to find?"

The captain explained that they were mainly looking for signs on the sea floor of volcanic activity, earthquakes, craters, volcanic cones, or anything that looked unusual with regard to the rest of the sea floor. The Mediterranean Basin has a long history of seismic activity through the ages, from tsunamis, to volcanoes such as Vesuvius, to major earthquakes. Except for the occasional apparent shipwreck, they hadn't come across anything that would merit taking a core sample to try to determine age.

Just then the intercom blared, "Captain to the SONAR shack!"

Captain John said, "Well maybe our luck is changing. Follow me to the SONAR shack, and let's see what they've found." As they entered the SONAR room the large-screen display depicted a debris field that showed the outlines of man made buildings.

Captain John asked, "Are we seeing this live?"

Bill Evans, the SONAR operator, said, "We are indeed. We'll continue on this pattern, north and south and east and west, until we determine the boundaries of this site, but it is already at least two miles long and doesn't show any sign of tailing off."

Everyone was glued to the large-screen display as toppled buildings and columns continued to roll by. The debris field to the east began to diminish and the sonar operator asked the officer of the deck to turn the ship north to map the northern quadrant. There were excited whoops as new images appeared and faded.

As tradition holds on the Observation Island, the captain broke out congratulatory cigars for all hands and declared, "The smoking lamp is now lit!" Corinne looked at her cigar, sniffed it, and handed it to Sean.

Mike Nelson, the expedition's chief diver, was anxious to get overboard and start exploring. However, due to the nearly 400 foot depth, all exploring would be conducted very carefully with a gas and oxygen mixture. While diving in hardhats and suits was possible at a depth of 400 feet, it would not be a feature of this particular expedition.

The ship's navigator, Bill Smith, entered the SONAR shack and joined in the jubilation over the discovery. Then Bill said, "Captain, I hate to throw a wet blanket on this party, but you may have noticed the sea is getting a little rough. Global weather has issued a storm warning for the Eastern Mediterranean, and they are predicting a five day category four storm so we've got about eight hours to find safe water."

As everyone was experiencing a little disappointment Mike Nelson yelled, "Take a look at that! Is that the remains of a pyramid? It looks like the very top of the Great Pyramid only under 400 feet of water."

Just then the ship took a heavy hit from a large wave and the captain said, "We'll review all the digital images later, but for now retrieve the sonar fish, secure topside gear, rig the ship for heavy seas, and let's head for port." The crew stepped lively and began carrying out the captain's orders.

Sean asked, "Captain, how can we help?"

The Captain said, "Sean and Corinne, I would like you guys to review the digital images and flag all the important elements that you believe we should take a closer look at. Don't worry about the storm. We are hours ahead of the bad stuff, and by the time the bad stuff arrives we'll be transiting the Suez Canal and you'll never know a storm is raging out here."

The Suez Canal was opened in 1869 and is slightly more than 160 kilometers long. It connects the Mediterranean Sea with the Red Sea. The ancient maritime peoples of Egypt and the surrounding countries had been trying to build the canal for at least a thousand years. Unlike most canals there are no locks, and because the Red Sea is slightly more elevated than the Mediterranean, the Red Sea actually flows into the Mediterranean Sea. The Red Sea water is also saltier and brings along the pollutants and the flora and fauna of the Red Sea.

Corinne and Sean were on deck wearing tourist mufti shorts, hiking boots, neckerchiefs, and broad brimmed hats to protect themselves from the setting sun. The heat from the setting sun was almost as fierce as the mid-afternoon swelter. Sun protection was vital. Corinne was wondering how the Egyptians ever began wearing robes for heat avoidance.

As they stood on the fantail of the ship, watching the sun slip below the horizon, Corinne asked, "Sean, what do you make of the apparent ruins they've found on the sea floor?"

Sean said, "Well, we don't know how old the ruins are, or to which civilization they belong. This whole Mediterranean Basin is called the cradle of civilization for good reason and many civilizations have risen and fallen along the shores of the Mediterranean Sea. The true significance of the find is just too hard to call without an artifact to establish a timeframe. Regardless of how old the ruins are, the find constitutes a tremendous discovery, and certainly our history of the Mediterranean is about to change in a big way."

"Archeologists have found the remains of Roman harbors and temples along the shorelines of the Mediterranean before, and they've been able to connect the ruins to historical records and nail down the timeframe of when the land or sea shifted, burying the harbor. However, I don't know of an historical reference to any city or civilization at these coordinates. Perhaps there was an ancient isthmus that earthquake activity suddenly relegated to the sea floor."

As the sun slipped below the horizon, Sean and Corinne began to realize just how dog-tired they were. It was almost 8:00 so they decided to grab sandwiches and retire to their cabin to catch up on their sleep. They were asleep as soon as their heads hit the pillows.

At 2:30 A.M. Sean was awakened by the call of nature. He nudged Corinne and said, "I'll be right back, I'm going to take a walk on the fantail and have a cigar, so no worries."

Corinne mumbled, "Okay."

Sean pulled on his shorts, shoes, and shirt and took off for the after head on the huge ship. After completing the necessaries, Sean found the up ladder and made his way to the fantail to have that cigar. The moon was a bright light, the night was crystal clear, and the smells of the sea were intoxicating. Sean greeted the fantail watch and said, "Ahoy mate, do you have a light?"

The fantail watch is posted to make sure the bridge crew is not surprised by the approach of canal traffic from behind. The watch stander usually wears sound-powered headphones that are connected to the bridge so the watch stander can alert the officer of the deck of any ships that might be overtaking them. Because the night was so bright, the bridge crew and the fantail watch were both a little lax in their duties. The watch stander fumbled in his pocket, produced a lighter, and lit Sean's cigar.

Sean introduced himself and learned that the watch stander's name was Yusef and that he had just joined the Observation Island, as an ordinary seaman, a few days ago. The ship had put in to the Port of Alexandria to admit a crewmember to the Alexandria hospital for appendicitis symptoms. The first mate decided to add on an additional ordinary seaman for the duration of the voyage. He contacted the Alexandria Port Authority for a list of available seamen and selected Yusef.

Yusef told Sean that he was standing the midnight watch, and the only ship's lights he had seen belonged to the vessel eight kilometers behind them. He then asked Sean if everyone on the ship was English and Sean said that he hadn't met everyone and didn't know. Yusef then began to rail against the English and the Americans for being responsible for all the trouble in the Mid East.

Sean didn't like how the conversation had turned, so he wished Yusef fair weather and moved toward the port side of the fantail to enjoy the rest of his cigar, without further discussion of the Mid East. That sixth sense that sometimes works in one's favor caused Sean to turn his head to the right just slightly and his peripheral vision picked up motion at the same time his ears heard bare feet on the deck. Sean quickly spun around, pivoted to the left, and just narrowly avoided a dagger in the back.

Sean instinctively assumed a defensive crouch with his knees bent and his arms outstretched. Yusef lunged at him with the knife a few times, and Sean effectively dodged the thrusts. Neither combatant said a word to the other. There was no time for that. Sean scanned the deck looking for something he could use as a weapon and found a coil of rope with a monkey fist on the end. He picked up the rope and parried each thrust with the rope. Sean quickly separated the rope covered metallic monkey fist from the coils of rope and began to swing the weighted ball over his head like a primitive slingshot. When Yusef tried another thrust with the dagger, his reward was a hard whack in the temple with the monkey fist. Yusef went down on one knee.

Sean shouted, "Drop the knife! Drop the knife!"

Yusef stumbled like he was going to pass out, and Sean moved toward him. Yusef sprang from the couching position and lunged hard at Sean. Sean backpedaled and tripped over a cleat in the deck. Yusef was on Sean instantly with the knife raised above his heart.

Yusef growled, "Die, English, die!" At that moment Yusef suddenly collapsed on top of Sean unconscious.

Sean looked up and Corinne was standing over both of them with a steel marlinspike in her hand. She had just knocked old Yusef senseless. Sean rolled Yusef off him, and Corinne extended a hand and pulled Sean to his feet.

Sean hugged her and asked, "Did I ever tell you that you have perfect timing? I'll call the bridge and alert them to the criminal in our custody." At that moment Yusef began to revive a little, and he stood up near the ship's lifeline.

Sean said, "Stay where you are and don't move!" Yusef flipped himself over the lifeline and appeared to jump into the Red Sea but they heard a dull thump rather than a splash. Corinne and Sean rushed to the side of the ship and looked down. Yusef had landed on the heavy gauged piping that extended out from the side of the ship to protect the propeller. He was slightly dazed, with the breath knocked out of him, but he seemed to be regaining his wind.

Sean shouted, "Hold on I'll throw you a lifeline!" At that moment Yusef made another bad decision and tried to push off the screw guard into the sea. Unfortunately he didn't push off hard enough, and when he hit the water he was sucked directly into the ship's propeller. Corinne could see a red froth covering the white caps in the ship's wake.

Corinne said, "Oh my God!" and turned her head away.

Sean pulled her to him and said, "Let's go back to bed. I guess it just wasn't Yusef's day!"

Corinne asked, "Do we report this to the captain or what?"

Sean said, "Come on Tiger; the answer is or what." Sean patted her on the butt and they returned to their cabin.

As they were lying in bed, Corinne was a bundle of nerves. Sean said, "Sweetheart, that's twice your quick thinking and perfect timing has delivered us from imminent danger."

Corinne said, "Well, your quick action on the streets of Georgetown and your quick thinking in the Smithsonian has kept us free and on the run."

Corinne asked, "I thought you were going to have a cigar. How'd you manage to get into a fight with that guy?"

Sean said, "It seems that Yusef harbored a personal vendetta against the English, and I guess he felt I was close enough."

Sean said, "The part that kind of makes me mad is I'm not even English, but I couldn't even tell Yusef that without blowing my cover."

Corinne said, "Not to worry, he would have hated you just as much anyway when he found out you were American."

"I guess you're right." He pulled her to him and they fell asleep in each other's arms.

At the morning breakfast in the mess hall the conversation was abuzz about how an Egyptian crew member had apparently slipped away in the night and swam to shore.

Sean asked, "Isn't that kind of dangerous?"

The first mate said, "Well, the swim is not for me, but it was a clear night and a calm sea, and if he was any kind of swimmer, he wouldn't have had any problem making it to shore. Besides he probably had his brother meet him with a boat anyway. He volunteered for the mid watch, so he had something up his sleeve for sure."

Sean and Corinne returned to the scene of the crime on the fantail to catch the sunrise and the morning breeze. The shoreline was a bustle of activity with fishermen in papyrus boats casting nets just like their ancestors did before the time of the Great Pharaohs. The Red

Sea's shoreline is a continuous line of fishing huts and boat building facilities to keep the fishermen well supplied.

An approaching tugboat gave two blasts on its whistle as it matched speed with the Observation Island. As the two ships touched, an Egyptian pilot leaped aboard and made his way to the bridge.

Corinne asked, "Is that the customs agent?"

Sean said, "No, that's the pilot. The immigration officer will board the ship after we dock. Before anyone is allowed to leave the ship, everyone's papers will be examined and then the immigration officer will issue shore permits for the crew."

Corinne asked, "What's the name of our next port of call?"

Sean said, "I wouldn't exactly call it a port of call, but it is the Sultan of Swat oil transfer station, and we should reach it in an hour or so."

Corinne asked, "Who is the Sultan of Swat and where is Swat located?"

Sean laughed and replied, "That's just what the sailors call it; the official name is Abdul Nasser and the Prophet of Islam's Royal Oil Transfer Station.

Corinne said, "I'll go with the Sultan of Swat."

"Okay, but don't say it out loud because the Sultan of Swat was the great George Herman 'Babe' Ruth and you don't want to take a chance on offending our hosts."

The Sultan of Swat had three birthing areas where huge tankers could tie up to the oil transfer buoys. Once secure, a ship's tank system would be connected to the oil transfer pipes and the transfer of the crude oil from the storage tanks on shore begun.

The Observation Island slipped between the at-sea berthing areas for the tankers and began docking maneuvers with the Sultan of Swat's pier. Once the Observation Island's seamen doubled up the mooring lines, the immigration officer came aboard, met with the ship's executive officer and reviewed everyone's paper work, finding everything in order. The immigration officer had scarcely left the pier when the local vendors appeared in skiffs and boats offering 5,000 year old antiquities, monkey meat on a stick, cigarettes, fresh fish, and cold beer. The ship's chef made a deal for some fresh fish for the evening meal, and the crew bought switchblades and other contraband.

Waiting on the pier were the commercial vendor trucks stacked up to replenish the Observation Island for its continuing voyage. Also on the pier, was Malcolm Smith-Jones, the Sultan of Swat's manager, and he welcomed the captain and invited the research group, including the Hornbeaks, to dinner at the station. Sean asked Malcolm for a recommendation on a tourist agency, and Malcolm said that Father Reynolds, from the Monastery, would be joining them for dinner and would have the best recommendation.

After a wonderful feast on local Egyptian dishes, Sean asked the good Father for a recommendation on tourist agencies, and Father Reynolds told them that any tour should begin with St. Catherine's Monastery. He invited them to spend the weekend and said that he would introduce them to the best tour guide in Egypt. The Hornbeaks accepted the invitation and told Father Reynolds to expect them tomorrow afternoon.

Later that night Corinne and Sean were standing on the fantail of the ship watching the moonrise over the water, and Sean revealed that Father Reynolds was also a member of the League of Red-Headed Men. He pointed out that they would be safe at the Monastery, and Father Reynolds would help in any way he could to get them to the Great Pyramid.

When the taxi dropped them off at St. Catherine's Monastery, Corinne was amazed. "Sean, this is not what I pictured at all. This looks like a medieval castle, wall and all!"

Sean said, "I know! I don't know what I expected, but I didn't expect a walled city."

Corinne said, "Where is Mt. Sinai?" Sean pointed in the distance to a very unimpressive barren peak that would have looked more at home on the moon.

Corinne said, "From the Bible, I know Moses climbed Mt. Sinai and that is where God presented Moses with the Ten Commandments. Sean, do you think we can climb Mt. Sinai?"

At that moment Father Reynolds joined them and answered, "Indeed you may, my child, but before you follow in the footsteps of Moses, you must be aware that it takes about three hours to climb the 2,285 meter peak. One follows the path of Moses, a stairway of nearly 4,000 steps, and then one must retrace one's steps."

Corinne said, "Father, it is so good to see you, and I think maybe we'll enjoy the other sights of the Monastery first and save Mt. Sinai for last."

Sean agreed and said, "Father we were just discussing the Monastery and how surprised we were that it is like a city or castle including the wall." The good Father went on to provide them with a walking tour and a little history of the Monastery.

The walls are referred to as Justinian's Wall. In 527 A.D., the Byzantine Emperor Justinian ordered the construction of the walls and the basilica to protect the monks from the local Bedouin tribes. The walls are nine feet thick and sixty feet tall.

The Basilica is the heart of St. Catherine's and contains three naves with many distinctive pieces, including impressive mosaics and many antique lamps that hang from the ceiling. Lying next to the main altar is the sarcophagus that holds St. Catherine's remains. The little city also includes the Burning Bush through which God spoke to Moses. The original bush is still flourishing after all these years. The courtyard includes the fountain where Moses met his wife, Zipporah. The fountain is supplied by an underground spring that has never run dry. The charnel house contains the bones of thousands of monks that have lived and died within the walls of St. Catherine's Monastery.

Corinne and Sean were most impressed with the Monastery's Library and Gallery of Icons. The library contains the largest collection of Christian manuscripts and icons outside of the Vatican Museum.

Father Reynolds said, "We are a self-contained city. We grow our own food and tend our animals. We could hold out here for an indefinite period of time. When the occasional Bedouin tribe decided to lay siege, we had the ability to wait them out. Let me show you to your rooms. Dinner will be at six. Feel free to explore and enjoy yourselves. Tonight you will meet Jamal Mohamed, the best tour guide in Egypt."

Dinner was a delight and Jamal spoke perfect English so communication was no problem. Sean and Corinne said they wanted to start with the Museum of Egyptian Antiquities and that they would like to meet Professor Fitzgerald, the leader of the archaeology team on the new tomb. Jamal was familiar with recent research activity and assured them that he knew the professor personally. He said he would pick them up in his taxi the next morning.

Father Reynolds, Sean, and Corinne were having coffee and discussing the new find at the Great Pyramid when Father Reynolds asked, "How much do you know about the find?"

Sean said, "We only caught the first part of Professor Fitzgerald's report when it was cut short due to technical difficulties. But we are excited about the find and we would like to see it, and, where we can, help with the research."

Father Reynolds said, "Be prepared for the surprise of your life!"

Chapter 14

London to Cairo Before the Sun Sets

John Applegate was still very pleased with himself for working Sir Paul in such a clever way to obtain an email introduction to Fatima Boutros, the Director of the Museum of Egyptian Antiquities. As he and Larry were relaxing in the hotel suite, he continued to replay his witty repartee in his mind. John's ego would never allow for the possibility that he had been out maneuvered by Sir Paul.

John's PDA began to buzz and vibrate. John picked it up, read the email from Sir Paul to Fatima Boutros, and smiled.

Then John browsed the web to get an overview of the Egyptian Museum and its contents. John stood up, walked over to the light switch, and dimmed the lights in the suite. Then his PDA used the web images to create 3-D holographic image files of the Tutankhamun treasures. A 24 inch tall image of Professor Fitzgerald was hanging in mid air describing the Tutankhamun collection and the 1922 Howard Carter discovery. As he continued with his presentation, the various treasures began to appear and slowly rotate so that all sides of the objects were displayed.

Larry said, "Wow! Where's that button on my PDA?"

John laughed, "You asked about nanotechnology before, so I thought I would give you a simple demonstration of one small advantage of nanotechnology."

Larry asked, "You can do all that with a PDA? I thought holographic projections required multiple processors operating at extremely high speeds? What else can it do, iron my pants?"

John said, "Here is another little routine for email display that I've been tinkering with. John moved a finger over the PDA and the holographic image immediately changed to Paul Gibbs standing in front of the fire place at Rufflets, delivering his email message to Fatima in 3-D and orally."

Larry said, "How the hell did you do that?"

John said, "When we were having drinks with Paul earlier, my PDA scanned everyone and collected their mannerisms and their expressions of speech while we chatted. Look! Holographic Paul is wearing the attire he had on tonight. If his email had been more complex or contained more words than he used last night, my program could have accessed the dictionary to automatically assemble words and attach the appropriate inflections to his voice."

"This is a simple application program when you have virtually unlimited processing speed and unlimited storage. I think this little program has the potential to change the way everyone uses and relates to email and text messaging, not to mention on-line pornography."

Larry said, "On-line pornography! Why the potential is unlimited!'

"See! I told you not to mention on-line pornography!"

Larry asked, "Well, what if you... I mean could you....?"

John said, "Now, now...I don't want to over load you. I'll share more nanotech stuff when the time is right. Now, let's get back to the business at hand. Based on Paul's email and the director's response, we're all set for Cairo. Do you have a man on the ground in Cairo?"

Larry replied, "Absolutely! Ali Badawi is his name but everyone calls him Ali Baba. He is retired CIA, and although he is manager of the Four Seasons Hotel in Cairo, he works the floor as the concierge. As concierge he ends up knowing everyone's business without having to ask directly. Ali has his finger on the pulse of Cairo. Nothing gets by him, and, just like his nickname, he does indeed know forty thieves. I'll send him a message to book our suite for tomorrow night. If anybody knows what the director's sweet spot is, it will be Ali."

The next morning John was back on his protein and orange juice shake for breakfast and was vigorously exercising. When John was at home he preferred to swim a hundred laps in the pool each morning. While a pool was available at Rufflets, his schedule was too tight for the pool today. Larry was drinking coffee and eating a bear claw watching John exercise.

As John completed fifty push-ups, he looked up at Larry and said, "You know, you'd be better off to toss that bear claw and do fifty push-ups."

Larry replied, "John, I have a theory that when you are born you have a finite number of heart beats to use before your final exit. I'm pacing myself. I don't want to use up my heart beats too early."

John shook his head, "Well, at least you don't smoke cigarettes."

Larry asked, "Are we really going to Egypt and give those clowns two million bucks? If they had anything to hide they wouldn't encourage you to sponsor it, would they?"

John said, "It's because Paul encouraged me to sponsor the dig that I now know I definitely need to go to Egypt. So, I consider the trip a must! There is something in that pyramid that they are keeping from us. I'm not worried about the two million; you have to be able to afford the ante if you are going to stay in the game. Once we know what's in the kitty, we'll find a way to make a dollar off of it."

The best and fastest way to connect with Heathrow from Edinburgh is by air. Larry and John were up early to catch the Rufflets courtesy limo to the Edinburgh International Airport to connect with the daily shuttle to Heathrow. John wanted to be in the air and on the way to Cairo as soon as possible. John asked Larry to check with the Cairo International Airport Authority to determine if they had to jump through any special hoops to schedule a visit to Cairo.

Larry completed his on-line research and said, "European airports require no early notification and neither does Cairo International; no additional customs hassle either. Of course, there will be the usual fees. Customs processing is as simple as presenting a copy of your passport and identification papers or a certified electronic file, unless you are on their list of undesirable characters. We're not, so as soon as we submit our flight plan, we should receive almost immediate approval."

"It says here that Cairo International has just competed a billion dollar renovation and they have the latest accommodations for jet service in terms of maintenance and hanger space. So we are good to go as soon as we file the flight plan."

"File the flight plan and ask Ali Baba to confirm a dinner reservation with the museum director for tonight, if possible. Let Ali and the director pick the restaurant. Also contact Heathrow General Aviation and make sure the Gulfstream is flight ready."

Larry said, "I've already made the arrangements with Heathrow, and I'm waiting on an answer from Ali. The flight plan goes out, now!"

John said, "Excellent! Let's pack up!"

Ali Baba was looking forward to seeing is old pal, Larry May. They had worked together for years collecting intelligence for "The Company." Ali Baba and Fatima Boutros were once very close. They met on campus at Oxford University when they were both undergraduate students. Oxford had an active Arab community and nearly all the Middle Eastern students were acquainted with one another. In the past, Fatima Boutros and Ali Baba were very well acquainted; and, on occasion, they sometimes still were.

Fatima Boutros' family had arranged a marriage for Fatima when she was six years old with one of the most important families in Cairo, so the star-crossed lovers knew that whatever happened in Oxford must stay in Oxford.

Fatima Boutros often dined at the most famous restaurant in Cairo, Paris on the Nile. This restaurant was reputed to be the Prophet of Islam's favorite restaurant and many important business deals were brokered in the restaurant's secure dining rooms. The restaurant was located at the top of the Four Seasons. In fact, Ali Baba had just booked a lunch reservation for Fatima. Sir Paul had included Ali as a blind copy when he had emailed the director about John Applegate's meeting request.

Ali Baba knew Larry May worked security for John Applegate and Manufacturing Enterprises, and he wanted very much to help seal the deal between ME and Fatima. Ali Baba knew that, one way or the other, he would profit by arranging the dinner meeting.

Fatima and her daughter would be arriving within the hour for lunch. He planned to speak privately with Fatima and explain that Mr. Applegate was as rich as a member of the royal family of Saude and, like a Saudi Sheik, Mr. Applegate was anxious to share his good fortune with the people of Egypt to support the archeological discovery in the Great Pyramid.

Ali Baba glanced at his pager and saw that it was an alert that someone was entering the Four Seasons via the VIP entrance. He checked the time and guessed that it was Fatima and her daughter. Ali quickly made his way to the VIP entrance, welcomed them to the Four Seasons, and escorted them to the private VIP express elevator to the restaurant above.

Ali said, "Fatima, today your favorite table overlooking the Nile is reserved for you, if it pleases you, or you may want to enjoy a quiet lunch with your lovely daughter in the Calif's private chamber."

Fatima said, "Ali, you always take good care of us. Today, we will enjoy the sights and sounds of Cairo."

"Very well, please come with me." He led them to their table. Three waiters were pulling out the western style chairs, taking their orders, and making sure both ladies were comfortable.

As Ali was seating Sima he commented, "Sima, you are more beautiful every time I see you. The young men at Oxford will follow you from class to class."

Sima smiled and said, "Ali, while I am away, I will miss you like a father."

Ali seated Fatima and leaned close to her ear and whispered, "If I could have but a moment of the director's time for a very private matter, I would be most grateful."

Fatima looked into Ali's eyes and barely nodded. She turned to her daughter and said, "Please excuse me, Darling. I must speak to Ali; he has something to show me." Her daughter nodded to her mother, and Fatima followed Ali Baba to the private chamber.

When Ali closed the door, Fatima turned to Ali and said, "What's up?"

"Do you remember Larry May, the guy I used to work with before I retired?"

Fatima said, "Oh, yes, the crazy American."

"Exactly! Well, he works for John Applegate, the American billionaire computer mogul, and Applegate wants to meet you and tour the Great Pyramid."

Fatima said, "This, I know. I got an email from Sir Paul telling me the same thing. Sir Paul mentioned a possible grant of $2 million. I wonder if he would be good for more than $2 million."

Ali Baba replied, "Fatima, Applegate is one of the five richest men in the world. I'm sure $2 million is a mere drop in his bucket. If you charm him, you can do a lot better. I have a suite booked for him tomorrow night. Shall I reserve the Caliph's private and secure chamber for you and your guests?"

Fatima smiled, "Ali, as always, you are a treasure. Yes, please do and let your friend, Larry May, know that I will have dinner with them tomorrow night. Now, I better get back to the table before little Sima thinks I have been kidnapped."

Ali returned to his station and pulled his PDA out of his pocket and hit the send key. As he was standing at the concierge's information kiosk Ali Baba's brother, Jamal, came into the lobby, saw Ali, and waved.

Jamal said, "Today, I must drive to St. Catherine's Monastery. Father Reynolds has a tour for me. He said his very best friends are arriving tomorrow and he has invited me to dinner and to spend the night. The Father told me he has already made reservations with you for them for tomorrow."

Ali said, "Yes, Father Reynolds asked me to have you call if he wasn't able to track you down. These people are Sir Paul's relatives. Father Reynolds assures me they are very nice people. Be sure to take good care of them. When are you leaving?"

Jamal said, "I plan to leave in the next few minutes. Their ship is expected sometime today."

Ali said, "Allahu Akbar!"

Meanwhile, John and Larry caught the shuttle from Edinburgh to Heathrow and by 9:00 A.M. they were standing in front of the Gulfstream doing a pre-flight check. The Gulfstream checked out fine, and within ten minutes they were in the air on the way to Cairo. Larry clicked the autopilot on and said, "Flight time to Cairo: four hours. I checked the weather forecast, and it is clear and calm all the way."

John said, "Great! You know I still can't imagine what could be in that tomb that could be so damned important that security is a must and that it takes $2 million to get a glimpse of it."

Larry said, "If the secret is 5,000 years old, what kind of impact could it possibly have on people in the 21st century?"

John said, "Well, for one thing, it could be is proof that extra-terrestrial life forms visited the Earth 5,000 years ago."

Larry said, "Space aliens? How could it be? Who the hell believes in visitors from another planet?"

John said, "While I don't believe in the supernatural, I do know, given the vastness of the universe and the fifteen to sixteen billion years since the big bang, that we are a long way from knowing all the possibilities that are out there."

Larry said, "Good point! Let's assume that the tomb does contain hieroglyphics suggesting contact with extraterrestrials 5,000 years ago, then what? What impact could that have on Earth today? Does that mean that all the religions of the world are based on fiction, or does it mean that man was not created in God's image? What could that information mean?"

John said, "Well we don't have to go too far to consider the possibilities. For example, if we look at the science fiction literature of the last one hundred years, and if we eliminate the monster driven plots and the plots centered on the aliens desiring to eat us or steal our world, we are left with the benevolent aliens that bring advanced technology, greater understanding, and, perhaps, immortality through medical advances."

Larry said, "And there we are, full circle to immortality again!"

"Exactly! I have to follow-up on this just to satisfy my curiosity. If it costs $2 million to find out what's behind the door, then that's what I need to do."

Larry said, "I'm with you. While our assumptions may be faulty due to lack of concrete information, we might be able to confirm or eliminate some of those assumptions after we meet the director."

John and Larry continued to discuss all kinds of wild scenarios until late that afternoon when they were cleared to land at Cairo International Airport. Ali Baba had arranged to have the Four Seasons courtesy limo meet them at the general aviation terminal for transport to the hotel. When the limo pulled up under the hotel's canopy, Ali Baba was waiting to welcome the weary travelers.

Ali Baba stepped forward and opened the limo door. Larry stepped out and grabbed Ali by the hand and then they embraced and kissed each other on the cheek. Ali exclaimed, "Larry, my friend, it is good to see you!"

Larry said, "Ali it has been years! Say hello to my friend, John Applegate!"

John said, "Ali, it is good to finally meet you. If even half of those stories are true, you two had one hell of a good time working for 'The Company.'"

"Ah! We did indeed, Mr. Applegate."

"Please, no 'Misters' here, John is just fine!

"Okay! John. Gentlemen, come inside, you must be tired. Join me in the Caliph's lounge and let us have some refreshments."

John said, "That would be great. The engines are still ringing in our ears."

The Caliph's room was a private, soundproof room for VIPs. It was lavishly decorated in the style of the 18th century, with hanging fans, satin drapes, and oriental carpets. It was, of course, equipped with every amenity.

Ali asked, "Gentlemen, what's your poison?"

John said, "Make mine a screwdriver."

Larry said, "Me too!"

Ali clapped his hands. The waiter bowed and said, "As you wish!"

Larry asked, "Ali, what arrangements have you made for tonight?"

Ali replied, "I have reserved the Caliph's private and secure dinner chamber for your party tonight. I have asked the chef to prepare the director's favorite cuisine for the feast."

"The director will arrive at 8:00 P.M." Ali looked at his watch and said, "It is six now, so you have time to rest and relax before dinner. I will be waiting for you at the entrance to the Prophet's favorite restaurant to escort you to the Caliph's chamber."

John said, "Excellent! Larry assured me you would cover all the details. Ali, my Arabic is nonexistent, does the director speak English?"

Ali Baba replied, "The director is fluent in English, but she has asked me to attend the meeting as her translator, if that meets your approval."

John said, "Ali, I was just going to ask you to join us, but the director has upstaged me. We would be delighted to have you participate and resolve any translation difficulties."

Larry remarked, "Ali, the purpose of the meeting is to discuss the recent discovery in the Great Pyramid and determine if the director would be interested in having John's company, ME, sponsor the dig. ME sponsors many philanthropic causes around the world, and John has a strong interest in supporting the archeological activities in Egypt."

Ali Baba replied, "The director is familiar with ME, and she noted that many schools throughout Egypt are still struggling with inadequate and primitive computer resources. She has assured me that the poor people of Egypt would be most appreciative of updated computer laboratories."

John replied, "Ali, ME has an abundance of computer resources that we would be delighted to share with the people of Egypt. Can you tell us what you know of the find in the Great Pyramid?"

Ali Baba's eyes darted from side to side and then he replied, "I know little of the actual details because of the tight security imposed by the director herself. I know that it is of enormous size and of tremendous value for all of the people of the world. But I can say no more. The director is the only information source at this time. I'm sure she will reveal more when you and ME become partners in sponsorship."

John said, "Ali, thank you for your candor and all the arrangements you have made on my behalf. I'm looking forward to further discussions with you and the director tonight."

Larry said, "Man! I feel dirty and gritty. Ali, if you will show us to our suite, we will meet you at eight."

Ali said, "This way, gentlemen. If there is anything you need, just ring."

When John and Larry were alone in the suite, Larry started to ask a question, but John shook his head side-to-side and pointed to the PDA.

Larry nodded and began to text, "We don't know any more now than before."

John texted, "I was hoping Ali could give us some idea of what is happening at the site."

Larry texted, "I'm sure he is under a strict gag order from Madam Boutros."

"I know; I was just hoping."

At ten minutes before eight John and Larry took the elevator to the Prophet's favorite restaurant at the top of the building. When the elevator doors opened, Ali Baba greeted them and motioned them to follow.

Ali asked, "Well gentlemen, have you shaken the journey's dust from your eyes?"

John replied, "I must say the Four Season's amenities are world class. Has the director arrived yet?"

Ali said, "I just received word that the director is delayed ten minutes. Make yourselves comfortable and order a round of drinks. I will wait in the lobby for Madam Boutros."

Ten minutes had grown to half an hour and they were on their second round of drinks when, at the far end of the chamber, John saw the curtains move and Ali entered the room. He then motioned for them to stand and he said, "Gentlemen, may I present Madam Fatima Boutros, Director of the Museum of Egyptian Antiquities?"

Fatima entered from behind the curtains and she was a vision from *A Thousand and One Arabian Nights*. She was attired in the traditional 18th century silks and looked like a genie fresh from Aladdin's lamp. Her hair was piled in a coif and she wore a traditional veil.

Both men stumbled to greet her and bumped into one another as they simultaneously tried to escort Fatima to her chair.

Fatima said, "I'm afraid the people's business detained me. I just left a cultural affair that required me to dress in a traditional costume, and I didn't have time to change to my regular clothes. A thousand pardons."

John said, "Not at all, the people's business must come first. Madam Boutros, I want to thank you for finding the time in your busy schedule for me. And I find your costume most enchanting."

Fatima said, "Thank you, Mr. Applegate, for your kind words. Your professional standing in the world is well known, and the information technology provided by ME is the world's standard. When Sir Paul advised me that you wished to offer support to the archeological research in the Great Pyramid, I knew the Hand of Allah was at work."

"Madam Boutros, I have accessed the on-line information available that describes the Egyptian Museum's treasures, and I was particularly impressed with Professor Fitzgerald's description of the Tutankhamen headdress and sarcophagus. I don't know who develops your web site presentations, but I must say they do a very professional job."

Fatima Boutros said, "Mr. Applegate, I would be honored if you would address me as Fatima. We are all friends here."

"Thank you, Fatima, we are indeed all friends; and please, call me John."

"Thank you for taking the time to visit our web site. I have been too busy to access the site lately but I did approve the script, and I know Professor Fitzgerald to be an engaging speaker."

At that moment, John activated his PDA and a holographic image of Professor Fitzgerald presenting the King Tutankhamen treasures immediately began to hover over the center of the table.

Fatima gasped and said, "How wonderful! Your technology is extremely advanced. I know enough about our web site to know that you did not obtain that 3-D holographic image from our site. How did you do that?"

John replied, "When I accessed your site I simply employed my holographic image routine to synthesize Professor Fitzgerald's presentation and to create a 3-D holographic image by filling in where the actual data was lacking. It's a simple process."

Fatima replied, "If the holographic imaging technology was available to our school system, I would predict an immediate improvement in test scores across the board. Plus, this is the kind of technology that would inspire our students to seek careers in science. You and ME are an incredible resource that I would like to make available to Egypt's children.

The meeting continued with a general discussion of archeology, history, and modern technology. The attentive waiters were very busy delivering and retrieving the many courses of traditional Egyptian favorites. When the final course was cleared, the waiters brought Egyptian pastries and coffee for after dinner treats.

Ali Baba produced two cigars and asked Larry, "Do you still enjoy a fine cigar?"

Larry replied, "Ali, I have no other vices, but a good cigar can always tempt me."

Ali turned to Fatima and John and said, "Please excuse us. We will be on the balcony considering the view and the benefits of a good cigar."

Fatima replied, "Ali, thank you for your consideration. The cigar smoke is an odor I just cannot tolerate."

John was familiar with the time-honored custom of avoiding any semblance of haste in broaching business discussions. Once the two men left the room, John said, "Fatima, thank you so much for such an enjoyable evening. The traditional cuisine was amazing and your company was so refreshing. I don't want to make a social faux pas by introducing business at dinner, so can we get together tomorrow to discuss the archeological dig and the grant from ME?"

Fatima replied, "John, discussing business tonight is no social faux pas. What did you have in mind?"

John replied, "I asked Sir Paul if he could share the details of the dig with me, and he mentioned that you have a very tight security level invoked on the project, so we left the discussion there. Sir Paul mentioned in his introductive email to you that I would be willing to support your project with a $2 million grant. Before we proceed, I would like you to share the nature of the project with me."

Fatima replied, "John, the find is so significant that I would ask that you sign a non-disclosure agreement with the museum before we proceed. Plus, your generous offer of a $2 million grant will get you added to the official museum press release distribution list such that you will have all press releases 24 hours before the public."

John laughed, "A $2 million grant only gets me on the distribution list. What else comes with it?"

Fatima smiled, "I did fit you into my schedule, and I took time out to discuss your interest in our program."

Now John smiled and said, "Please tell me more. What are the thresholds to partnership that you have in mind?"

"John, this archeological site is at least the size of a football field. The contents are so incredible that the world will be astonished. If you want to be part of it, you need to make a serious commitment to the Egyptian Museum and to the people of Egypt."

John said, "I do want to be a part of it. How does a $25 million grant sound to you? I would need to gain more information and do an evaluation, but I think $25 million is do-able."

Fatima replied, "John, $2 million got you dinner with me; $25 million gets you 48 hours notice of planned press releases. If you are serious about a partnership, we will need to hold a joint press conference tomorrow morning announcing a $500 million grant to the Museum of Egyptian Antiquities, and the details must include another $250 million grant of computer technology for the Egyptian public school system."

John pursed his lips and emitted a low whistle.

"Fatima, if we proceed in this partnership, I would expect that the Egyptian people and the Museum of Egyptian Antiquities will turn to ME for all information technology and computer resources for the next 25 years. I would expect to be a voting member of the Egyptian Museum's board with regard to developing the plan of action and milestones associated with the contents within and around the Great Pyramid and to any other site connected or associated with this archeological dig, regardless of whether the contents takes us to the past or to the future."

Fatima replied, "John, I see no road blocks in your conditions."

"One more question, Fatima. Is the possibility of immortality a factor in this archeological dig?"

Fatima raised an eyebrow and said, "John, Egypt and immortality have been coupled since the beginning of time. This find underscores life's continuity and the immortality of men. Immortality has always been the focus of the Egyptian civilization. The content of this archeological site defines the key element of immortality."

John said, "Excellent! I will prepare a memorandum of understanding between ME and the Museum of Egyptian Antiquities. We can then announce the partnership and the grant at a photo opportunity at your office tomorrow morning, at ten, when we sign the documents."

"When can I tour the site?"

"Plan to meet with Professor Fitzgerald tomorrow afternoon at four for indoctrination and a tour of the site. The professor usually leaves for the Great Pyramid around dusk. Dress in warm clothes because the median temperature is 68 degrees F."

Ali Baba and Larry returned from the balcony, and John and Fatima shared the information that they had reached a partnership agreement that would be finalized tomorrow morning.

John Applegate lifted his glass and said, "To a long and prosperous relationship between the people of Egypt and ME!" They raised their glasses together and saluted the new partnership.

John said, "Fatima, thank you for including ME as a partner in this most important of all projects. Your hospitality and understanding are unparalleled and I look forward to working with you and your team. Now, I will retire to my suite, and I will have the documents ready by tomorrow morning. Shall we meet at the museum?"

Fatima replied, "Yes, I will schedule a news conference, and I will prepare a news release too. I'll do that tonight and email it to you for your concurrence."

"Great! See you in the morning!" They embraced and shook hands. Then Fatima and Ali made their way to the back of the room and the exit.

Larry said, "I see she was putty in your hands."

John gave Larry an annoyed look and said, "Get your tomb exploring clothes ready. We tour the Great Pyramid at dusk tomorrow!"

Larry asked, "I still can't believe its costing $2 million to tour some creaky old tomb."

John said, "Oh! Don't worry; $2 million is the least of the cost!"

John picked-up his PDA and accessed ME's secure corporate records file to choose a suitable template to execute the terms he and Fatima Boutros had agreed to. ME was a major sponsor of many philanthropic causes, not only because ME cared but also because it was cheap advertising, tax deductible and just plain good business. John completed the document in about thirty minutes and forwarded the draft to Fatima along with a draft of the proposed press release. ME and the Museum of Egyptian Antiquities would release simultaneous press releases once both were satisfied with the content.

Larry was reading the draft agreement and he said, "I guess Fatima spilled the secret of the Great Pyramid to you; so what is it?"

John said, "We won't know for sure until we see for ourselves during the tour of the tomb tomorrow, but she did characterize the find as larger than a football field. She also confirmed that immortality was a key component of the find."

Larry replied, "Immortality, in what way? You mean like a potion or the secret to eternal life in the book of the dead? If the Egyptians had the secret to immortality we'd be up to our asses in Egyptians right about now."

John said, "She was evasive and I was reluctant to push her. I was willing to agree to anything by the time we were on the brink of an agreement."

Larry said, "You have committed ME to nearly a billion dollar grant. How do you slip out of that agreement if the find is bogus?

John said, "Even if the find turns out to be nothing, the agreement and the grant will return a lot more than my three quarters of a billion dollar investment. If ME gets a monopoly agreement for IT resources with Egypt, the rest of the Islamic countries won't be far behind. When ME books the business from the rest of the Middle East, it will be all sole source to ME. So, I have guaranteed the future of ME in the Islamic countries by making a tax-deductible contribution. Hell! I can't lose!"

Larry said, "I'm stunned! This whole archeological dig thing is more about cornering the IT business with the Islamic countries than it is about what may or may not be in that tomb, isn't it?"

John grinned and replied, "Of course it is. Discovering the secret of immortality would be icing on the cake, but a monopoly business position will make you smile in your sleep."

Later that night John received email confirmation from Fatima that the document looked good and that she expected to see them at the Museum of Egyptian Antiquities in the morning for the ceremony.

While John, Larry, Ali Baba, and Fatima were having a five-course dinner in the Caliph's secure chamber, Sean and Corinne were having dinner on the terrace at the Prophet of Islam's favorite restaurant. Little did either group know, but their destinies would cross violently deep beneath the sands of ancient Egypt in less than 24 hours.

Chapter 15

Mad Dogs, Englishmen, and the Noon Day Sun

All travel in Egypt is conducted early or late to avoid the intense heat of the midday. Jamal was up at dawn ready and waiting for Corinne and Sean. Father Reynolds packed a bag of goodies full of fruit, light sandwiches, and, from the Fountain of Moses, bottled spring water. As they stood at the car, the good Father blessed Corinne and Sean, Jamal, and the taxi and wished them God's speed on their journey to Cairo. They piled into Jamal's taxi for the five-hour trip to Cairo and with a lurch and a jerk they were off.

As they were rumbling along, Corinne asked, "Jamal, you smiled when Father Reynolds wished us God's speed; are you Christian, too?"

Jamal replied, "No, I am Muslim, but I gladly accept the blessings and benedictions of all Holy men."

Corinne said, "Jamal, I think your policy is a good one. Sean and I feel the same way."

If Jamal's driving skills and the way he attacked the road to Cairo was any indication, then God's speed was being achieved, and Jamal was indeed blessed.

The five-hour trip was concluded in less than four hours as the taxi squealed to a stop in front of the Four Seasons Hotel–Cairo at Nile Plaza. Jamal was out of the cab in an instant, opened the taxi's door, helped Corinne out of the cab, and conducted them to the hotel's foyer.

Jamal said, "Please, wait right here and I will return with my brother." Jamal then disappeared into the interior of the Four Seasons Hotel to find Ali, the Four Seasons concierge.

While Jamal was gone, Corinne and Sean were marveling at the artifacts on display in the glass cases in the foyer. As promised, Jamal was back in a flash and said, "My brother will be with us in a minute, he is finishing up business with a very important government official. I did have a private moment with him, and I used my great influence to secure for you, the finest suite in the hotel, the Caliph's suite."

Sean said, "Jamal, you are the finest guide and taxi driver in all of Egypt! Thank you very much."

Ali appeared almost immediately. He was all smiles and with outstretched hands he welcomed them as if they were family.

Ali said, "Welcome! Welcome, to Egypt my friends! You will find that Cairo is Paris-on-the-Nile and is truly the world's eternal city! Come with me to the Four Seasons Hotel's media room, and enjoy the full-up tourist media event. All of the highlights of Cairo and the Giza Plateau are presented in an interactive media room. You must remember that Cairo was a grand city when many of the world's huge metropolises were but mere crossroads."

Ali was absolutely the very best ambassador for Cairo and was a wealth of knowledge about the city and Egypt. Ali said, "Cairo is cloaked in excitement and mystery, with many dark secrets and bright celebrations to discover for first time visitors. Cairo mixes the many cultures of the world with the many ages of the world. You can find French cuisine from the French residents, new age culture from the Germans, enterprise from the Americans, all the while embracing Egyptian heritage from the dawn of civilization. Cairo mixes modern religion with ancient traditions as easily as the streets accommodate automobiles and donkey carts. America has no claim as a melting pot in relation to Cairo, for Cairo melts both time and culture into one city that can embrace civilization as no other."

Ali noted that, "Most scholars believe that the tales from the *Thousand and One Arabian Nights* took place in Cairo during the period of the Burgi Mamluks, rather than in Baghdad. Edward Williams Lane made the original English translations and he believed that a Cairene wrote the stories in the late medieval period. For example, in *The Tale of the Jewish Physician*, there is a description of Cairo:

"He who hath not seen Cairo hath not seen the world: her soil is gold, her Nile is a marvel; her women are like the black-eyed beauties of Paradise; her houses are palaces; and her air is soft, more odorous than aloes-wood, rejoicing the heart. And how can Cairo be otherwise when she is the Mother of the World?"

Ali said, "My brother, Jamal, is at your disposal and is prepared to give you a personal tour of Cairo and the Giza plateau."

Ali finally, took a breath and, Corinne asked, "What do you recommend Ali?"

Ali was again at no loss for words, "First, we will get you settled in the Caliph's suite where you can rest and prepare for dinner. The Caliph's suite is located on the thirtieth floor and has a beautiful view of the Nile and Great Pyramids. Jamal will call for you at seven this evening and take you to the Prophet of Islam's favorite restaurant for dinner, where you will experience the finest cuisine in all of Egypt. After dinner Jamal will give you a moonlight tour of the Giza Plateau. Tonight there is a full moon, and you will discover the most beautiful sight in the entire world, shimmering in the moonlight, just five miles south of the city."

Ali said, "I have taken the liberty of making dinner reservations for you tonight at the Prophet's favorite restaurant, Paris on the Nile, which is located on the top floor of the tallest building in Cairo. The choice of dining areas includes a secluded private room, an open dining area, or al fresco dining on the terrace. I can secure a table in any area for you now, if you have a preference."

Corinne looked at Sean and said, "Ali, please make the reservation for the night air. We want to get to know Cairo."

Ali touched the screen on his PDA and said, "Excellent choice. You will not be disappointed!"

Later that night, as they sat sipping after-dinner drinks and enjoying the beauty of the Nile and the bustling city at night, Corinne asked, "Sean, when do we visit the museum and meet Professor Fitzgerald?"

Sean said, "I just checked the PDA before we left for dinner, and we're scheduled to meet with the professor and his staff late tomorrow afternoon. I think we should arrive at the museum about an hour before our meeting so we can get a tourist's eye view of the treasures and educate ourselves a little bit. That way we aren't so far behind the learning curve with regard to Egypt's antiquities. We need to know what has been found to-date and what today's archeologists are still looking for."

Corinne remarked, "I know the Egyptian Museum houses the Tutankhamen tomb treasures and many mummies. I'm anxious to see the exhibit, but can we tour Tutankhamen's tomb also? How close to the Great Pyramid is his tomb?"

Sean said, "I'm looking forward to seeing the Tutankhamen exhibit too, but remember Tutankhamen's tomb is located in the Valley of the

Kings funerary complex, and that complex is in Luxor. Luxor is located up the Nile 450 miles south of Cairo. It is easy to think of Egypt, the pyramids, and the tombs as one place, but it is actually many different sites covering thousands of years and very different time periods. The Great Pyramid and the Giza complex is the earliest complex. It predates Memphis, Luxor, Karnack, and the other famous historical sites of Egypt. We may be amateur archeologists, but we have to visit the museum first so we don't appear to be worse than amateurs."

The waiter approached their table and asked if they would like another round of drinks.

Sean said, "No, a check will be fine, and we will be going as soon as we locate our driver."

The waiter said, "Oh, you mean my brother, Jamal! I will ring for him to bring the van to the front of the restaurant. By the time you reach the street level Jamal will be waiting."

As they walked out of the hotel, Jamal waived and asked, "Did you like the Prophet's favorite restaurant?"

Corinne said, "Jamal, everything was just exquisite. We will never forget our visit to this beautiful restaurant. You and Ali are Cairo's finest ambassadors."

As Corinne and Sean climbed into the van, Sean asked, "Jamal, how long will it take to get to the Great Pyramid?"

Jamal said, "We are twelve miles from the Giza Plateau so we will be there in about 45 minutes."

As they relaxed in the van, Corinne opened the tourist brochure from the hotel center and reviewed the information as Jamal darted through the suburbs of old Cairo.

Corinne said, "Sean, here is an Arab proverb that is really cool: "Man fears time, yet time fears the pyramids!"

"That is cool! I like it! What else does the brochure say?"

Corinne read aloud, "The Giza Necropolis stands on the Giza Plateau, on the outskirts of Cairo. This complex of ancient monuments is located five miles inland into the desert from the old town of Giza on the Nile, twelve miles southwest of the Cairo city center."

"This Ancient Egyptian Necropolis consists of the Great Pyramid, the somewhat smaller Pyramid of Khafre, and the relatively modest-size Pyramid of Menkaure, along with a number of smaller satellite edifices, known as "queens" pyramids, causeways, and valley pyramids, and most noticeably the Great Sphinx. Current consensus among Egyptologists is that the head of the Great Sphinx is that of Khafre. Associated with these royal monuments are the tombs of high officials and much later burials and monuments from the New Kingdom onwards, signifying the reverence to those buried in the Necropolis."

"Of the three, only Menkaure's Pyramid is seen today without its original polished limestone casing. Khafre's Pyramid retains a prominent display of casing stones at its apex, while Khufu's Pyramid maintains a more limited collection at its base. Khafre's pyramid appears larger than the adjacent Great Pyramid by virtue of its more elevated location, and the steeper angle of inclination of its construction—it is, in fact, smaller in both height and volume. The most active construction phase on the Giza Plateau was in the 25th century BCE. The ancient remains of the Giza Necropolis have attracted visitors and tourists since classical antiquity, when these Old Kingdom monuments were already over 2,000 years old. It was popularized in Hellenistic times when Antipater of Sidon listed the Great Pyramid as one of the Seven Wonders of the World."

As the van approached the Giza site in the dusk of nightfall and they first caught sight of the pyramid in the moonlight, they were astonished. The physical size of the Great Pyramid was astonishing. Oh, they knew it was called the Great Pyramid but to see it in all its magnificence, in the brilliant moonlight, was overwhelming.

The tourist brochure presented the vital statistics: the Great Pyramid weighs 6.5 million tons; the base covers 13 acres; and it is 481 feet tall. The Great Pyramid was the tallest man-made structure in the world for 3,000 years until the Eiffel Tower was built in Paris. The blocks are 5' x 8' x 12' and weigh anywhere from thirty to sixty tons each.

Jamal said, "Most Egyptologists date the construction of the Great Pyramid to 4,600 years ago with the Sphinx slightly older. But many Egyptians believe the Great Pyramid and the Sphinx may be 10,000 years old or older still. Of course, the Western experts point out that there is no evidence for ancient peoples or civilizations with the technological know how to create a city, much less a structure, on the scale of the funerary layout at Giza. The Egyptian people shake their heads because they know that Western experts don't have all the answers. Western historians insist that modern people were at the hunter-gatherer stage 10,000 years ago and cities remained thousands of years in the future. The Egyptian people know the Western experts are foolish."

Jamal parked the van at the north side of the Great Pyramid where the security team and the official entrance are located. Corinne and Sean weren't the only tourists enjoying the night air and the spectacular sights of the Egyptian desert. The Great Pyramid's guides and security staff were very busy answering the same questions that they field every night. Jamal grabbed the senior security guard and they greeted each other with a hug and a kiss on both cheeks.

Jamal waved and said, "Corinne and Sean, I wish to introduce you to my brother Hashmet."

Hashmet bowed to Sean, hugged Corinne, kissed her on both cheeks, and said, "Welcome to the Great Pyramid complex. If you have any questions or need anything, I am at your disposal. Our security team provides 24-7 security to the complex, and if you need anything just come to any one of several large tents and trailers just outside the entrance."

They thanked Hashmet for his kindness. Jamal suggested that they take a van tour of the major sights of the complex and then return to the Great Pyramid. Corinne and Sean agreed with Jamal's plan and they climbed back into the van.

As they drove around the complex Jamal asked, "Do you know the story of how the entrance to the Great Pyramid was originally discovered?"

Corinne said, "No Jamal, we don't. Please tell us the story."

Jamal began, "In the 9th century, the Governor of Cairo, Caliph al Ma'un, had his workmen use chisels and hammers to knock a hole in the pyramid's outer limestone casing to find out if a great treasure was hiding within. By the will of Allah, the original entrance to the pyramid was located on the north side and had a hinged stone that could be swung open. Of course, no one knew of this secret entrance. The Caliph's workmen just happened to pick the north side for their assault on the pyramid, and they began their tunnel under and near the original opening. Their work dislodged a capstone in the original tunnel. When they heard the capstone fall crashing to the floor, they decided to investigate by tunneling toward the sound. Their new tunnel then intersected the original descending tunnel. That is how they discovered the original entry way and tunnel."

"The Caliph explored the interior of the pyramid and found that the King's Chamber and sarcophagus were empty and that there were no treasures, hieroglyphs, or decorations of any kind within the pyramid. Finding the interior of the Great Pyramid devoid of decorations is unlike all the rest of the structures and tombs within the Egyptian Dynastic period and remains a mystery today. One explanation is that the Great Sphinx and the Great Pyramid predate the Egyptian Dynastic period by thousands of years, and that the Egyptians appropriated the Giza plateau site and simply built their monuments on top of the existing complex."

Corinne said, "Jamal, what an amazing story! Can we tour the inside of the Great Pyramid tonight?"

Jamal said, "Corinne, night time tours were possible until a few months ago, when the new chamber was discovered, but now all tours must be coordinated and approved by the Director of the Museum of Egyptian Antiquities."

When Jamal circled back around to the entrance of the Great Pyramid, everyone got out to experience the size of the pyramid.

Corinne asked, "Is it possible to climb to the top of the Great Pyramid?"

Jamal said, "Climbing the Great Pyramid is forbidden without approval by the Director of the Museum of Egyptian Antiquities, but I will ask my brother if it will be permitted."

Jamal returned and said, "My brother said climbing the Great Pyramid at night is not permitted. Hashmet also told me that those who disregard the law often choose the southwest corner, for it is the safest way."

Corinne and Sean made their way to the southwest corner and looked up.

Corinne said, "Just look at all those steps, and they seem to be going straight up. I'm not sure this is a good idea after all."

Corinne invited Jamal to climb with them, but Jamal said he would wait at the bottom and ward off other lawbreakers, and should they slip he would catch them.

Sean said, "Corinne come on, show a little courage! Let's get going!" The climbing was straight forward because the polished limestone casing is missing. The granite blocks form a huge staircase and the stones on the southwest corner are in better shape, with less crumbling, then at any other point on the pyramid. Still, climbing the equivalent of 48 stories takes time. They stopped and rested a few times on the way up, and Sean was glad he had bottled water in his backpack. Jamal had cautioned that while climbing is prohibited, nevertheless, several bloody heaps are found at the base of the pyramid each year, and he begged them to take care.

When Corinne and Sean reached the top, they felt like they had just scaled Mount Everest. To the west was the darkness of the desert, and to the northeast they could see Cairo's lights twinkling in the distance.

A sudden gust of cool desert wind rocked them both and Corinne said, "Sean, hold me, I'm scared."

Sean pulled Corinne close and said, "Scared? There is no reason to be afraid. There is no one anywhere except for about 480 feet down."

"Let's make our trip to the top of the Great Pyramid a great experience in more ways than one!" Sean pulled a blanket from his backpack and spread it out on the flat granite and pulled Corinne down beside him. She tilted her head up and kissed him.

As Sean was luxuriating in the afterglow, he was thinking he had never in his life felt as close to a woman as he felt to Corinne. As he cradled her in his arms at the top of the Giant Pyramid, he again had a sense of déjà vu. Could the two of them possess old Ka's or souls from thousands of years ago? Is reincarnation possible? How many times had they been reincarnated, and how many times had they been lovers in past lives? As he lay quietly in semi-sleep with his arms around her, he was jolted back to the 21st century by Corinne's voice: "Hey, Sean, I think it's time to go. Can you get us back down off this heap of rocks without killing us?"

Later that night, after Jamal returned them to the Caliph's suite, Corinne and Sean were lying in bed discussing the day's events. Sean was still fascinated by the sophistication of the location, construction, and the technology that resulted in the Great Pyramid. Sean was using his PDA to research far more details than were available in the tourist brochures.

"Corinne, listen to this! I can't believe all these points related to the Great Pyramid can be mere coincidences. If a student in a physics class was given a problem to measure and examine all the continents or land masses on Earth and to come up with the exact point that would represent the exact center of all those combined land masses, then that point would just happen to be where the Great Pyramid is physically located. Forget for now that whenever the Giza complex was constructed, somewhere between 10,000 and 7,500 years ago, allegedly the people of that time did not have knowledge of the continents of North and South America, Antarctica, Australia, or Indonesia. Perhaps the same physics student would be asked to determine true north rather than magnetic north in laying out the Great Pyramid. Here again, one would have to assume that the people of that time probably wouldn't have the knowledge to know the difference between true north and magnetic north. However, the people that laid out the foundation markers for the Great Pyramid just happened to lay out the pyramid exactly on the cardinal coordinates for true north, south, east and west."

"Corinne, there's more! You know how today's bridges and buildings are constructed with joints or rollers that allow the bridges and buildings to expand or contract with extreme heat, wind, or even earthquake activity? Well, so, too, was the Great Pyramid. The limestone covering of the Great Pyramid uses a ball and socket system at all four cornerstones to allow for heat expansion and for movement of the entire limestone casing during earthquakes. Even today we don't construct our buildings with the kind of attention to detail the Ancients used with the Great Pyramid; even in an area subject to earthquake activity. The mortar used between the stones is of an unknown origin and is stronger than the stone, and it still can't be duplicated today. Here's the part that is right up my alley. As you know, when the Giza complex was first built the desert was nowhere to be found. The entire complex was lush gardens, green courtyards, and temples. The Great Pyramid itself was used as a sundial. At noon the pyramid casts no shadow. The temples, as located around the pyramid, told the time of the day based on the pyramid's shadow."

"Corinne it doesn't make sense that the pyramid builders would expend the enormous resources necessary to construct the Great Pyramid, but then leave it unfinished, undecorated, unused, and empty with no apparent purpose. The ancient Egyptians may have been the most technologically advanced of all the ancient peoples because there has been no other archaeological records discovered to indicate that they had competition, so leaving the pyramid unfinished suggests to me the builders must have perished due to disease rather than being destroyed by barbarians or a competing city-state."

"Corinne? Corinne? Don't you agree?

Corinne said, "I'm sorry I was daydreaming. I was thinking about how the ancient complex must have really looked and how beautiful it must have been. I bet ancient Egypt did seem like Eden to the people of the time. But yes, I agree, perhaps they were wiped out by a natural disaster like fire, earthquake, or flood."

Sean said, "I see what you mean, but the natural disaster left the temples, pyramids, and the Sphinx unscathed. Oh well, I think now would be a good time to consider the present rather than the past. I love you, Corinne. I know we are working and running for our lives, but I've never had a better time in my life."

Corinne said, "Wait a minute! Is that Cleopatra's needle? I thought the needle was moved to England.

Sean said, "Please don't say needle, say obelisk."

Chapter 16

The Museum of Egyptian Antiquities

The next morning Sean ordered room service. Over breakfast, he suggested, "Corinne, let's go straight to the museum. How's that sound to you?"

"Okay, let's do it! I'm anxious to see everything."

"I'll give Ali a call to see if Jamal can meet us outside."

Sean rang the concierge station and asked Ali to relay a message to Jamal.

Ali said, "My friends, when you are ready to go, Jamal will be waiting under the hotel canopy."

When Corinne and Sean reached street level, Jamal shouted and waved. He then pulled the taxi under the hotel's canopy and jumped out of the cab to assist Corinne into the back seat.

They were off in a cloud of smoke, screeching tires, and a blast of horns.

Corinne said, "Jamal, how did you ever learn to drive an automobile in Cairo?"

Jamal said, "Learning to drive an automobile was very easy. Learning to drive my father's donkey cart was very hard. The donkey was very stubborn and refused to respect me."

They were in front of the Egyptian Museum in fifteen minutes. Jamal said, "I can wait for you or you can call Ali at the Four Seasons when you need me.

Sean said, "Thank you, Jamal. There is no need to wait. We will skip lunch today, and we'll be in touch after our meeting with Professor Fitzgerald."

Corinne and Sean entered the Egyptian Museum's main entrance and began viewing the interactive displays to get an overview of the history of the museum and an idea of where they wanted to start. The first display provided the following information: The Egyptian Museum was built in Boulak, in 1891. It was then moved to the Giza Palace of "Ismail Pasha" and was later moved to the present building. The current building was constructed during the reign of Khedive Abbass Helmi II in 1897. It has 107 halls. The huge statues are located on the ground floor. The upper floor houses small statues, jewels, Tutankhamen treasures, and the mummies.

"Sean, listen! This is interesting about the scarabs: During and following the New Kingdom, scarab amulets were placed over the heart of the mummified deceased. During final judgment the heart scarabs are weighed against the feather of truth. The amulets are inscribed with a spell from the *Book of the Dead*, which entreats the heart to 'Not stand as a witness against me.' Sean, I wonder if my scarab once covered the heart of a mummy?"

Sean said, "We have no way of knowing, but it could have." Corinne touched her amulet and looked lost in thought. Sean said, "Corinne, it may have once covered the heart of Nefertiti or Cleopatra, but the heart it covers now is beyond compare."

"Oh Sean, you say the sweetest things. I love you, too."

Corinne began to carefully read the section on the mummification process. She said, "Sean, this is fascinating. First the embalmers wash the body with wine and Nile water. Then they remove all of the internal organs, except for the heart. They place the organs in canopic jars. I knew they removed the internal organs, but I didn't know they left the heart in the body. I was planning on taking the DNA samples from the hearts. I guess that is out. The four canopic jars are as follows: the falcon-headed jar protects the intestines; the jackal-headed jar protects the stomach; the baboon-headed jar protects the lungs; and the human-headed jar protects the liver. I think I'm in the mood for liver. If the site is undisturbed, the jars should all be intact so finding the human-headed jars should be a snap."

Sean said, "Well let's tour the museum by the numbers and start with Tutankhamen's treasure."

They were strolling among King Tut's treasures, marveling at the display, when a panel in the wall opened and out stepped Professor Fitzgerald.

Sean immediately grasped his hand and said, "Professor Fitzgerald, I presume!"

The professor laughed and said, "Corinne and Sean, so good to see you, too. You should have let me know that you were arriving early."

Corinne said, "Professor, I am very pleased to meet you. We were simply enjoying the wonderful treasures of the museum before our meeting. We know that you have a very busy schedule."

The professor said, "It is indeed busy, but with you two on hand, I'm looking forward to sharing some of the work load. Sir Paul sent me an encrypted message to expect you today, and I'm glad to see you have arrived safely."

Corinne said, "We've spent a night with Father Reynolds at St. Catherine's Monastery, and last night at the Four Seasons–Cairo. We had a marvelous visit with Father Reynolds. The monastery is incredibly beautiful."

The professor said, "I think you will find the above-ground accommodations here on par with the monastery but off the mark where the Hilton is concerned. You will also be pleased with the underground accommodations."

Corinne said, "Underground? Oh, that's right, deep underground. What about the ventilation?"

As the professor led them towards the conference room he continued talking, "Come and join me and the staff in the secure conference room. I will share with you what we have learned so far and answer all your questions in turn. I also want you to meet Mr. John Applegate, the newest addition to the team. Mr. Applegate, and Manufacturing Enterprises have agreed to become a sponsoring partner with the Museum of Egyptian Antiquities. It was announced just this morning that Manufacturing Enterprises and John Applegate made a $750 million grant to the Egyptian Museum. John will be touring the dig for the first time today, so we have arranged a joint presentation for the three of you."

As Corinne and Sean were following the professor they exchanged concerned looks and Sean said, "Terrific! We're looking forward to meeting everyone."

Corinne, Sean, and the professor entered the conference room and the professor said, "Everyone! Please welcome Corinne and Sean Hornbeak. Sean's brother, Nigel and his wife, Wendy, have been leading Sir Paul's Peruvian archeological dig. Sean and Corinne are anchoring the London-based analysis of the Peruvian material, and they wish me to express to you that they are amateur archeologists. And, more importantly, they are on their honeymoon."

There was a loud round of applause and many happy wishes from the members in the group.

Professor Fitzgerald remarked, "Sean tells me Nigel and Wendy just left Peru for England and are on their way home. It is now the rainy season in Peru, so they are on hiatus for the next three months."

"Sean and Corinne are anxious to learn about our little dig here, so that when they return to England they can share stories with Nigel and Wendy. Plus, Sir Paul has asked Corinne to conduct a special research project for him."

Corinne and Sean went around the room shaking hands with everyone. When they got to John Applegate, John said, "Corinne and Sean, it is such a pleasure to meet you. Sir Paul and I ran into each other just last week on the golf course. Sir Paul shared some of the remarkable progress your cousins have made in Peru. I am delighted to meet you both."

Corinne and Sean both took a silent breath of relief as everyone took seats around the conference room table. They were hoping John wouldn't inadvertently divulge their true identities.

The professor explained, "As you know by now, the Egyptian government has put a gag order on all information regarding the find, other than what the government has officially released regarding the new chamber in the Great Pyramid. The information concerning the most remarkable part of the find has not been released by the government, and probably won't be for years to come. It is still hard to believe that we found this Necropolis in a virtually unmolested and pristine condition. The surprising aspect of the new chamber is the accidental discovery of a hidden door, inside the chamber, that opened to a descending staircase. The staircase led to another chamber located well below the base of the pyramid, within the actual bedrock foundation of the Great Pyramid. That chamber has a connecting corridor that leads to an enormous Necropolis that is physically located under and around the Sphinx."

Corinne, Sean, and John all had looks of stunned disbelief on their faces. After a few seconds of contemplating what they had just been told, all three leaped to their feet and applauded the team.

As Sean began to grasp the enormity of the discovery he said, "Professor, I don't know what question to ask next."

The research team chuckled in unison. The professor said, "Don't worry, the whole team has been just as overwhelmed as you are. In our mutual excitement we have been working virtually around the clock."

Corinne asked, "How do you light the way and provide ventilation for the research team?"

The professor said, "That is very easy because the lighting and ventilation exists from the time the Necropolis was built!"

The look of wonder showed on their faces, again, and it was the same look that everyone displayed when they heard that news.

Corinne asked, "What kind of lighting technology lasts 5,000 years?"

The professor said, "The kind that is 10,000 years old! We were stunned when we entered the Necropolis and realized we didn't need torches or battery-powered lights. The Ancients developed a radium powered lighting system that is perpetual, at least, so far. We passed a Geiger counter around the globes to determine if the lights presented a personnel radiation hazard, and the radiation level is safe. We also discovered that an underground branch of the Nile, or a tributary to the Nile, powers the bathhouses and restrooms and provides drinking water, too. The river's underground cavern and channel is also the source of the fresh air."

As Sean got his scientific feet under him he asked, "How large is the Necropolis, and how many mummies are contained in it?"

The professor replied, "The Necropolis contains three large chambers, with each being the size of a football field. The Necropolis was designed as a destination and a memorial park where the dead could be prepared for their journey, honored prior to entombment, and visited and revered after entombment. Much like some of Europe's catacombs but on a much grander scale. Body preparation and the mummification process took place in the temples above ground. Each chamber of the Necropolis is distinct. The first one is for the pharaohs; the second one is for the royal family and the third one is for the important noblemen. The sarcophagi range in age from 10,000 years BCE to about 5,000 years BCE. Our initial research and documentation has only scratched the surface. All of what I've told you remains to be verified through on-going research."

Corinne asked, "Professor Fitzgerald, you said 10,000 year old mummies; how can the mummies be that old? I thought modern humans were lucky to be in the hunter-gatherer phase 10,000 years ago? Ten thousand years ago would mean a highly sophisticated civilization more advanced than the three Egyptian Dynasties and on the brink of the ice age, too. Wasn't most of Europe covered with ice during that time period?"

The professor explained, "Many scientists and historians will now have to reevaluate the evidence for early man and the generally accepted timeline that currently exists. Not only were the Ancients advanced from a technology standpoint, they were also deeply religious. They believed in reincarnation of the soul. The Necropolis is covered with the ancient civilization's history, up to the point where a cataclysmic event occurred that apparently resulted in multi-generational destruction. At this point, with the limited research we've done so far, it appears that the Dynastic Egyptian civilization was founded on the remains of the ancient civilization, rather than being a direct evolution of the earlier civilization."

"Based on a review of the hieroglyphics in the Necropolis, the Egyptians may have borrowed the hieroglyphic writing system and much of their original knowledge, if not their practical technology."

"The Necropolis contains the civilization's history in picture art and hieroglyphics so the immortal soul, the Ka, can stay centered or connected to the mortal life until the soul is reincarnated in a living body."

"The history of the civilization and what we can learn from it is far more important than the golden statues and artifacts that tomb raiders desire. The most amazing thing about this Necropolis is that it has not been looted or robbed by the ancient tomb robbers like most of the Egyptian era tombs have been. Contemporary tomb robbers robbed most, if not all, of the Egyptian Dynastic tombs. The gravediggers and the embalmers themselves robbed many of the tombs. The Museum of Egyptian Antiquities is fearful that the richness of the new find will be leaked to the criminal element and the site will be looted or vandalized. I will now introduce Dr. William O'Neil, our resident hieroglyphics expert. Dr. O'Neil?"

Dr. William O' Neil said "Thank you, Professor. The hieroglyphs refer to the City in the Lake as just that, but the research team has taken to calling the City in the Lake, Atlantis. While Atlantis may or may not be historically correct, it is metaphorically correct. This Atlantis was the first city-state in the Mediterranean and perhaps in the world. The Mediterranean's water acted as a natural moat to isolate and protect the city from the barbarians and other competing fledgling city-states.

The Atlanteans developed a maritime trade with the region's people and, through maritime trade, created other satellite city-states along the Nile. Possibly, what later came to be called Alexandria was Atlantis' first trading post on the continent."

"We believe the Atlanteans constructed the Sphinx and the Necropolis under the Sphinx, during their civilization's high point. The best guess at a timeline for Atlantis is that they achieved critical mass sometime earlier than 10,000 years ago. How much earlier is unknown at this time. We do know that they were excellent astronomers, and they laid out the Sphinx and the Great Pyramid to greet the morning sun. The Sphinx points to true north rather than magnetic north, so their original measurements are extremely precise. The glyphs show a fireball from the sky sent by Ra to create Atlantis. The glyphs predict that the fireball will return and destroy Atlantis, if the people do not live by the Sun God Ra's commandments."

Professor Fitzgerald said, "We don't know if Atlantis was wiped out by the predicted fireball, but it could have been."

Corinne said, "An asteroid strike in the Mediterranean could have been the source of the Biblical flood as well."

The professor said, "Corinne, that is a good point and many of us believe in that possibility, including Sir Paul. Sir Paul's Observation Island is doing the research on the coordinates we consider to be the most likely location of Atlantis."

"Our research team is woefully understaffed due to the director's insistence on tight security and limited dig publicity. Director Boutros is the only one aware of the magnitude of the find or that the true find is located outside the Great Pyramid. She is concerned that treasure hunters, masquerading as scientists, would swarm in and blast holes all over the Giza Plateau. The director has imposed a gag order on all news and has not allowed a significant increase in activity at the site, lest the curiosity of the tomb robbers be piqued. Because the Necropolis is such an important find and would create great international interest, she is concerned that she would lose control of the dig."

John Applegate remarked, "Surely the tomb robbers aren't sophisticated enough to threaten Egyptian governmental authority?"

The professor said, "The director doesn't fear local thieves, she fears the richest men in the world, who finance high technology tomb robbers, and also have connections at the highest levels of the government. The unbounded enthusiasm of the world's scientists to assess the find might jeopardize the scientific aspects, and the historical aspects are, of course, far more important than the gold artifacts."

Professor Fitzgerald continued, "The director reluctantly acquiesced to Sir Paul's request to allow Corinne and Sean access to the site because, one, she knows we desperately need the help; two, because you are blood relatives of Sir Paul's; and, three, Sir Paul was the primary resource sponsor of the dig until John Applegate became a partner earlier today. We know you are on a special assignment for Sir Paul, but we don't know the nature of your mission. How can we assist the two of you in your data gathering?"

Corinne said, "I need access, in the tomb, to the canopic jars containing the pharaohs livers from the earliest pharaoh to the latest. I only need enough material from each liver to create a slide for microscopic analysis."

The professor said, "We have concentrated on the pharaohs and we have documented all of them from the beginning of the Neolithic period, from 10,000 BCE to 5,000 BCE."

"There is either another Necropolis yet to be found, or perhaps Atlantis was conquered or destroyed when this Necropolis was nearly completed. Either way, the Necropolis has enough capacity to accommodate an additional thousand-year reign of pharaohs; so there is probably not another Necropolis yet to be discovered. The period between 5,000 BCE and 2,500 BCE is largely unknown, just as Atlantis was unknown until this discovery."

Corinne said, "I don't need to sample every mummy, just one each at 500 year intervals."

The professor said, "The pharaohs are easily mapped because they are laid out in chronological order. We can direct you to the numerical sequence you need. Also, we have a lab set-up with enough slides and microscopes for your project. While the entire tomb has 10,000 years of dust and debris, we have left things virtually untouched except in the areas where we work and live. We are in the process of creating a detailed digital scan of the entire complex. We won't actually remove anything from the tomb, beyond dust, dirt, and debris, for many years to come."

"John, Director Boutros indicated that she wanted you to have an overall understanding of the site, but she did not expect you to work the site. Is that your understanding as well?"

John replied, "Exactly so, Professor. I have no archeological skills, and I'm sure I would be more in the way than help. I am willing to pitch in wherever you might need some labor. If I can lend muscle, please don't hesitate to bring it to my attention. I doubt that I can offer any intelligent observations that would enlighten anyone in this room."

The professor said, "Excellent! We do need muscle power to help carry in the supplies tonight."

"We will enter the site after sundown, so please utilize the museum's facilities to get ready for the journey to the Necropolis and to get a bite to eat before the trip to the Great Pyramid."

When Corinne and Sean were behind closed doors, Corinne started to ask Sean a question and he put his finger to his lips to suggest that security might be at risk. She picked up her PDA and they began secure text messaging. Corinne wondered how much the professor knew about their identities. Sean said not to worry, the professor is fully aware and knows what they know, but Sean believed that the room may be bugged by the criminal element that the professor had alluded to, so they couldn't take a chance on talking freely unless they were in the professor's secure conference room.

Corinne texted, "You could have knocked me over with a feather when Professor Fitzgerald told us John Applegate was in the conference room and was a patron of the dig!"

Sean texted, "Me too! I was further surprised when John didn't blow our cover."

Corinne texted, "What do you make of his presence here, and do you think it has anything to do with Dr. Munkey?"

Sean texted, "If he is here, there is an angle to this whole find that has a dollar sign attached to it because that is John's biggest motivator."

At sundown the professor knocked on the door, and they all climbed aboard the project van for the five mile trip to the Great Pyramid. When they arrived at the Great Pyramid, Corinne was once again stunned by its shear size.

The three men sitting in the fifteen-year-old utility van parked two blocks away from the museum, nodded to each other, and took off their headphones. The leader pointed to the driver and said, "Jamal, drive the van to the pyramid."

The Museum of Egyptian Antiquities

Chapter 17
Sphinx for the Memories

As the Great Pyramid came into view, Corinne and Sean were amazed at the magnificence of the entire complex. They couldn't help but imagine how stunning the three pyramids must have been thousands of years ago. The white limestone casings and the full moon would have turned the Giza complex into daylight at midnight.

During the 17th century, the Caliph of Cairo used the Giza complex as his personal quarry to construct the modern buildings in Cairo. As a result, the pyramid's brilliance, in the natural moonlight, was somewhat toned down due to the missing limestone casings, but the grandeur still endured.

Jamal's brother and the security team met the group, and the bearers began carrying supplies from the professor's cargo van down the four foot square shaft to the entrance of the passageway to the Queen's Chamber. The only access to the interior of the Great Pyramid is via the entrance on the north face. The Queen's Chamber was built beneath the King's Chamber and is somewhat smaller. The name Queen's Chamber is actually a misnomer, because the chamber was never intended for the Queen, and its true use is unknown. The other mystery chamber is the so-called Subterranean Chamber, which is located below ground level and cut out of the bedrock that forms the foundation for the Great Pyramid.

In the King's Chamber, the large rectangular box carved out of stone is referred to as the King's sarcophagus, but all of the terms are casual guesses of what the original constructors might have had in mind for the various chambers. The contents and interior of the Great Pyramid remained a mystery for thousands of years until 820 CE when Caliph al-Ma'mun's workmen blasted a hole into the side of the north face. When the Caliph's workmen entered the pyramid for the first time, they were stunned to discover that none of the chambers were finished and that there was not one hieroglyph, or any writing of any kind, to be found. The Great Pyramid was abandoned before it was completed!

The senior site leader briefed the professor on the day's work, and the guests were briefed on the "do's and don't's" inside the Great Pyramid. Just inside the pyramid entrance was a descending passageway leading down into the interior. The original access to the pyramid was a twenty-ton stone on the north face that fit so perfectly that it was undetectable for thousands of years. The twenty-ton portal was so carefully counter balanced that, from the inside, it could be opened with a simple push. But the portal was never intended as a day-to-day access port. The descending corridor was lit with a series of incandescent bulbs, rigged with extension cords. The professor had reminded Corinne and Sean to dress comfortable because the average temperature inside the Great Pyramid was 68 degrees Fahrenheit. As they began the descent they proceeded in single file and carefully placed each foot one after the other.

The corridor was 345 feet in length and sloped downward at 36 degrees. At 36 feet the corridor splits into two corridors, with the ascending corridor providing access to the upper chambers. The ascending corridor was accessed through the ceiling of the descending corridor and led to the Queen's Chamber, the Grand Gallery, and the King's Chamber. Today, the research group ignored the ascending passageway and continued down the descending corridor to the Subterranean Chamber and a dead end.

When the group arrived at the Subterranean Chamber, they found the supplies stacked up, but the bearers were nowhere to be found. Corinne exclaimed, "Hey, where did everybody go? This can't be the Queen's Chamber. I thought we were going to the Queen's Chamber?"

The professor laughed, "Dear Corinne, I'm afraid you have been a victim of our little misinformation game. Our security program is based on limiting information to only those individuals that need it to do their jobs. The Subterranean Chamber also has an airshaft that connects to the ascending passageway via the ceiling. Look above you! The bearers were instructed to stack the supplies and to exit via the air shaft in order to return to the pyramid's entrance. Using this technique allows us to avoid traffic in these close confines."

"Now, the magic will be shared with the three of you, but the cost of this knowledge is that you, Sean, and John must pitch-in and assume the duty of the bearers to help cart the supplies to the Central Necropolis."

Corinne looked at Sean and John and said, "Okay, Professor, no problem."

The professor extracted a coat hanger from his pack and inserted it into a tiny hole near the ceiling of the chamber saying, "Corinne dear, would you be so kind to keep pressure on this rod?" Corinne reached up and pushed on the coat hanger. The professor then pushed on the largest visible stone, and it easily swung open to reveal a chamber on the other side of the Subterranean Chamber.

Corinne and Sean both gasped in amazement, and Corinne said, "Wow! This is just like a Hollywood mummy movie."

The professor said, "Indeed! But this plot was staged 10,000 years ago." The professor removed the rod, and the stone door remained open while the team transferred the supplies to the other side. Then everyone slipped through the opening, and the professor closed the door from the Necropolis side.

Corinne, Sean, and John each picked-up a box of supplies. John said, "We'll come back for the rest later."

The professor replied, "No need to return, I'll have the chef send his two kitchen helpers back for the supplies. Actually, you don't have to carry anything; the kitchen help can get it all. I was just teasing before, when I said manual labor was the price of learning the magic."

John said, "No problem, Professor, we're all here to work."

The corridor was lit with the soft glow of the ancient radium lights. Each lamp was the size of a beach ball. The orbs were located every few feet to maintain the light. After 300 yards the team came to another dead end. They stacked the supplies and the professor reached for the magic coat hanger again. Corinne assumed the position to put pressure on it. As the professor leaned on the huge stone, it swung open to take them deeper into the solid rock.

As they walked down the corridor, the soft glow of the corridor lighting gave way to a fully lit mausoleum. John Applegate said, "This ancient radium lighting system rivals modern florescent lighting but without the harsh glare."

John reached for his PDA and made a note that ME, in accordance with the agreement signed this morning, owned the production rights to the lighting system.

The Pharaoh's Chamber of the Necropolis was the size of a football field. The supporting posts were carved out of the living rock. The entire chamber had been cut out of the solid granite with the same precision evident in construction of the Great Pyramid. The surrounding walls were covered with beautiful hieroglyphs and the colors were still vibrant after centuries of being hidden. The hieroglyphs looked like Egyptian hieroglyphs but were much more detailed and obviously contained more information per square foot than the Egyptian glyphs.

Each pharaoh's sarcophagus was located in a granite enclosure. The walls of each cubical were decorated with hieroglyphics celebrating the pharaoh's accomplishments.

The professor said, "The basic complex has numerous administrative offices and laboratories, as well as dormitories for visiting mourners. We have appropriated several ancillary rooms for use as laboratories and office space. There are ten people on site right now that are continuing to document the site, and I will introduce you to the team as they come to the main office to report their progress."

"The Necropolis has a map room that has a three-dimensional model of the site, and we have been using this 3-D model to acquaint ourselves with the mysteries of the site. I'll give you a tour of the map room and you can begin to lay out your approach to data collection. There are numerous marble tables and benches that we have been using to spread out our laboratory equipment. I'm glad the Ancients chose marble for the basic furniture, because if the furniture had been made of wood, it would be dust by now. Here are two tables for you to do your work from. Place all your things here on the floor. Well, tell me now what do you think of our little discovery?"

Sean said, "This discovery defies description. Howard Carter and Lord Karnack must be smiling down with satisfaction. This find means we still have a lot to learn about the past. No wonder Director Boutros, Dr. Death, and Dr. Munkey are at odds on what to reveal, when to reveal it, or whether they should reveal it at all. I guess I'm still in a state of shock from trying to assimilate all this information in such a short time. I have so many questions, but I don't know what to ask first. I just want to ask them all at once, but then I wouldn't be able to absorb the answers."

The professor said, "If you want to be stunned again, take a look at the 3-D site map depicting the surface layout. It shows the three pyramids, the Sphinx, and numerous buildings and temples. Those above ground buildings and temples are long gone."

"According to the model, the Nile ran much closer to the Giza Plateau 10,000 years ago than it does now. Delivering the quarry stones, to construct the three pyramids, would have been an easier task than today's topology would suggest, because the stones could be delivered to the construction site via a water channel from the Nile to the Necropolis."

As Corinne, Sean, and John were discovering the secrets of the 3-D model, various members of the research team began to trickle into the main work area. The professor stepped over to the kitchen and asked the chef to send the kitchen helpers to collect the remaining supplies from the entry chamber. He also asked when dinner would be served. He then turned back to the group and said, "Everyone! I want to introduce Corinne and Sean Hornbeak. They are here on a special assignment for Sir Paul and may need our help to collect data. Please also welcome John Applegate of Manufacturing Enterprises, Egyptian Museum's newest sponsor. This announcement resulted in a spontaneous round of applause.

The professor looked at his wrist watch and said, "It's just about time for lunch, dinner, or breakfast, depending on whatever time schedule you might be on. The chef tells me dinner will be ready in about thirty minutes, so everyone has time to relax and get acquainted."

The new arrivals were immediately besieged with a thousand questions all at once. Professor Fitzgerald said, "Whoa! Whoa! Please hold up the questions for now. There will be plenty of time to get everyone's questions answered. Let's be good hosts by answering John, Corinne, and Sean's questions first."

The personal introductions began, and John, Sean, and Corinne became the questioning inquisitors. The site team workers were delighted to see fresh faces from the world above and they were just as fascinated with the dig as the new visitors were.

Sean turned to the professor and asked, "Have you developed a timeline to place the Necropolis in its proper place in time?"

The professor replied, "We have not yet directly correlated the modern calendar to the ancient calendar in any detail. My guess, at this point, is that the Necropolis, the three pyramids, and the Sphinx date to approximately 5,500 years ago; plus or minus a thousand years. The Egyptian Old Kingdom Dynasty picks up about 5,000 years ago. The Old Kingdom Egyptians were not aware of the Necropolis located under the Sphinx, so the Necropolis construction must have begun much earlier."

Corinne asked, "If the Egyptians are the descendents of the Atlantean people, how was the connection with the Necropolis lost?"

The professor said, "My guess is that the catastrophe that befell the Atlanteans, probably befell everyone in the Nile Valley. We know that there have been terrible floods and earthquakes over the last 10,000 years. So, if two generations were killed by the flood, then the civilization's infrastructure would have been destroyed, too. That destruction would be enough to set the culture back a thousand years or more. The Nile Valley would have experienced a multi-generational break in human occupation. If you then assume chaos and the barbarians held sway for a thousand years, then the rise of the Old Kingdom would be on target. Don't forget what we are looking at here is the Necropolis of a great civilization, not its library, civic center, engineering center, or seat of government. The Atlantean Hall of Records or the library may still be out there waiting to be found, but the 3-D site map doesn't show a library here."

"Anthropologists generally key on the human being's ability to use tools, the possession of opposable thumbs and a large brain, and the ability to communicate orally as the most important discriminators in the rise of Homo sapiens over his cavemen contemporaries. I think the most important discriminator is language, and not just verbal skills, but the written language."

"When a civilization must rely on oral skills to pass the tribe's history, technology, and lessons-learned from one generation to the next, then they are vulnerable to any natural disaster that wipes out the knowledgeable leaders of the current generation. When a civilization can create a written repository, that is independent of the humans in charge, then their progeny can capitalize on that repository of knowledge should a natural disaster occur."

Sean asked, "Who is the team's anthropologist?"

The professor replied, "Sean, meet Dr. Mick Heffernan."

They shook hands and Sean asked, "Dr. Heffernan, how does the Necropolis fit into the Atlantean's culture? It would seem that the Atlanteans committed an enormous amount of resources to recognize, preserve, and praise their dead. Are we looking at culture based on ancestor worship?"

Dr. Heffernan replied, "We are, of course, in the most preliminary stages of the find, but these Atlanteans believed whole-heartedly in reincarnation of the soul or Ka but, unlike the Egyptians, they didn't have a complicated explanation of what the Ka did when not incarnate. They believed the Ka's long-term memory was lost at the death of the body. They also believed the Ka lingered with the body for up to seventy days. The celebration of life lasted seventy days. During that period, the Ka could seek a suitable family infant to complete his/her reincarnation. The purpose of the detailed hieroglyphics, and the family's life celebration, was to complement the Ka's short-term memory by providing a pictorial representation of the deceased's accomplishments, so the Ka could remain cognizant of his position in the past life. This allowed the deceased's Ka to be able to tune-in to his family's unborn infants, so as to not miss the opportunity for a timely reincarnation. This belief is one of the important reasons each male member of royalty kept a harem of pregnant wives."

Corinne said, "If I understand you correctly, then the Atlantean people believed the Ka was eternal but without the ability to retain the memory of mistakes and triumphs. The Ka, even if reincarnated, may be destined to repeat the same mistakes again and again."

Dr. Heffernan said, "Corinne, I'm just guessing at this point. I'm relying on my knowledge of Egyptian religion, and I am liberally extrapolating. I only have superficial knowledge of the Atlantean's religion based on a quick scan of the hieroglyphs and incomplete translations."

Corinne turned to Sean and said, "Sounds a little like your Collective Intelligence concept but limited to human beings rather than all life."

Sean said, "It does, and you must know by now that great minds think alike."

John asked, "Dr. Heffernan, are you saying the ancient's idea of immortality is based on reincarnation and not on extending the life span of the people?"

Dr. Heffernan said, "That is exactly the case. They believed in immortality of the Ka or soul but not of the physical body."

John said, "It sounds like their religion is closer to Judeo-Christian ideas than pagan ideas."

There was a sudden rumble and a shake like a minor earthquake or tremor. Everyone looked at each other and simultaneously looked up.

Corinne asked the obvious, "Was that an earthquake?"

The professor said, "Perhaps, but I hope not. Earthquakes are rare in Egypt these days and earthquakes usually begin with tremors followed by a sudden spike."

Sean said, "That sounded like an explosion followed by rubble falling."

John said, "I agree with Sean, definitely an explosion."

Dr. Heffernan said, "Come on team we need to do some exploring."

The professor said, "Hold on, everyone! Sean, Corinne, Dr. Heffernan, Tom, and John stay here and hold down the fort. I need two volunteers!" The professor turned to two kitchen workers and asked, "Charlie, Frank are you game?'

They both answered, "Sure! Let's go!"

The professor turned back to the group and said, "If you haven't heard from us in a hour, come and find out why."

The three men headed down the corridor toward the Subterranean Chamber.

Corinne asked, "How could there have been an explosion? I thought explosives were prohibited from the antiquities."

Dr. Heffernan said, "They are, Corinne. If it was an actual explosion, it could only be sabotage."

John asked, "Who would sabotage the site? Doesn't everyone in Egypt benefit from exciting new finds?"

Dr Heffernan said, "There is a fundamentalist group that believes that exploration of the antiquities is grave robbing, and grave robbing is sacrilegious."

Corinne asked, "Sean, could our friends, like Dr. Munkey, be behind this?"

Sean said, "Corinne, Dr. Munkey, and Dr. Death may want to know what you know, but they certainly don't want us entombed in Egypt. Plus, they wouldn't do anything to jeopardize this amazing find. Let's see what the professor and his team find out. We may be jumping to unnecessary conclusions at this point."

Sean asked, "Dr. Heffernan, please continue your observations on the Atlantean's religion and how the Necropolis was most likely utilized. I find it extremely interesting."

Dr. Heffernan said, "If you look at the 3-dimensional model, you can see that each chamber has a grand staircase to facilitate access from the temples above to the Necropolis below. You see, the Necropolis was about mourning, but more importantly, it was about the celebration of life and it was more focused on the future. The Necropolis was a transfer portal for the family to time the reincarnation of the Ka to the family's anticipated newborns. The tents above ground were where the embalmers worked to prepare the body for mummification. The embalmed bodies were then moved to the temples for the interment ceremonies."

"Remember, this was a Royal complex so no shortcuts were taken. If a pharaoh was to be reincarnated here, then there was no reason to spare the expense. After all, what if the new pharaoh remembered any slights or disrespectful behavior and exacted revenge, when he returned to the throne? So the Necropolis was built on a grand scale to accommodate the bereaved family for up to seventy days and to cover sleeping arrangements, bathing, and dining functions."

"Pharaoh's baths are the one's we have been using while we have been on site, and they are quite remarkable by any standard. As a matter of fact, the whole team has been working, eating, bathing, and sleeping on site here, without a break, for the last two weeks."

John asked, "You mean you haven't been out of the pyramid for fourteen days?"

Dr. Heffernan laughed and said, "That's right, John. But remember we aren't in the pyramid. We are under the bedrock near the Sphinx. And don't act so horrified, we have hardly been deprived. Come and see pharaoh's bathing facility."

They walked down the corridor, made a left, went down a staircase, and entered the pharaoh's bathhouse. Corinne, Sean, and John were stunned. The room was extremely large and contained three large pools. There were alcoves with golden statues all around the pools.

Each wall was decorated with beautiful frescoes and mosaics depicting slaves bathing the pharaoh and the royal family, as well as other scenes from everyday life. The first pool had steps leading into the water and submerged marble benches were arranged in a semi circle where people could sit and bathe. The second pool was like the first except steam was rising off the water.

Dr. Heffernan said, "Before you ask, yes, that is a heated pool. It is apparently still fed by a water tank buried somewhere near the surface of the desert, where it captures the heat from the sand."

"But where is the water supply?" asked Corinne.

"The water is supplied from either an underground branch of the Nile or from a natural spring aquifer."

Dr. Heffernan asked, "Are you thirsty? Watch this!" Dr. Heffernan stepped up to a pedestal and when he placed a finger over a hole on the edge of the pedestal, a stream of water sprang from the rim and fell perfectly in the center of the fountain and he took a sip. "This is clean, potable water and is completely safe. Here have some."

Sean, Corinne, and John tried the fountain and they all looked at each other and smiled.

Sean said, "Well, I hate to be too nosey, but where is the little pharaoh's room?"

Dr. Heffernan said, "I'm glad you asked, step this way."

This room was like the baths in that it was unisex. There was a row of marble seats along opposite ends of the room, and each seat had a hole in the center of it. One could clearly hear water running.

Corinne asked, "You mean they have flush toilets too?"

Dr. Heffernan laughed and said, "Well, they were certainly advanced but no, no flush toilets. However, they had the next best thing because the soil was carried away by the moving stream of water under the seats."

The water in pharaoh's pool began to ripple and flow from side to side, almost imperceptibly. Then there was another jolt or tremor from the direction of the previous explosion.

Corinne looked at Sean and asked, "Did you feel that? Was it another explosion?"

Sean replied, "No! I don't think it was an explosion."

Dr. Heffernan remarked, "It didn't have the intensity of the first blast either. Maybe it was a cave in."

Corinne asked, "How long have they been gone?"

John looked at his wrist watch and replied, "It hasn't been an hour yet."

Corinne said, "I don't care, I have a bad feeling! I think we'd better go check on them, now."

Someone coughed. Then another person coughed. Then everyone began coughing, as a plume of dust and smoke rolled into the pharaoh's bath chamber.

Someone in the corridor cried out, "Oh, God! We're buried alive!"

Chapter 18

Up the Ruin Without a Paddle

Sean said, "John, Mick, let's go find the professor and his team."

They headed back down the corridor, only now it was slow going because of the thick dust hanging in the air. The soft light from the radium orbs did little to penetrate the heavy dust.

Mick said, "This lighting just isn't doing the job. I'll go back and get a couple of the battery powered spotlights. Wait here, and I'll be back in five minutes."

Sean said, "Okay, but hurry!"

Mick had been gone maybe five minutes and John said, "Listen! Did you hear that?"

Sean replied, "It sounds like someone moaning."

As their eyes adjusted to the dim lighting and the dust settled a little, they became a little more confident. John said, "Come on, let's follow the sound."

The men inched carefully toward the moaning sound and the radium lighting seemed to become a little more effective. Sean could see lights coming from main center and he shouted, "Hurry up, we found someone."

When Mick caught back up with them, John grabbed the spotlight and cast the light toward the sound. There in a heap on the floor, half way in the corridor and half way in the chamber, lay Professor Fitzgerald. His legs were pinched by the stone block that served as the secret door. John pushed on the hinged door while Sean and Mick pulled the professor free.

Mick said, "John, shine the light over here!"

John released the door and held the light above their heads so they could check the professor for injuries. The professor was bleeding from a wound on the forehead. Sean held a compression bandage to the professor's head, while Mick examined his legs.

Mick said, "I'm not an MD, but I didn't feel any broken bones. How's his head?"

Sean lifted the bandage and said, "The bleeding has stopped and his pulse and respiration seem normal. John, look in the first aid kit and hand me the smelling salts."

John set the spotlight down and handed the salts to Sean. Sean broke the capsule and held it under the professor's nose.

Mick said, "John, shine the light into the chamber. Can you see anyone else?"

John turned the spotlight toward the chamber but found that the stone door had closed on its own. He pushed on the stone, but it wouldn't budge. He asked, "Mick, how does this thing open?"

The professor coughed a couple of times and was beginning to regain consciousness. Mick tucked the first aid bag under the professor's head. Then he took the spotlight from John and looked around for the coat hanger key, but found nothing.

The professor roused up on one elbow and said, "You'll have to go get another coat hanger, but I've got a bad feeling about Frank and Charlie. They were in the first chamber when the second cave-in hit. They may be buried under ten tons of rock."

"Just before the second cave-in, Charlie called out that they found Juan and Pablo in the rubble in the second chamber. So they are likely lost too."

Mick said, "Professor, can you stand?"

The professor said, "I think so."

"Good! We need to get you back to main center. Then we'll return here with the key and see if we can rescue anyone."

Once the men were back at the center, the professor felt well enough to sit up and drink a cup of coffee.

Dr. Heffernan asked, "Professor, can you tell us what happened? What did you find?"

"When we got to the first chamber, we had no problem getting into it. But when we tried to enter the second chamber, we had to force the door open because it was obstructed by debris. Once we got into the second chamber, we could see that the chamber's exit was completely blocked. Juan and Pablo were lying among the fallen stone, and they weren't moving. Apparently, they were in the process of moving the supplies through, when the explosion went off. They didn't have a chance, poor devils."

"Everything appeared stable and safe, so after we checked for life signs we started moving the supplies into the corridor. Then, the second cave-in hit. The reinforced doorway protected me from the main cave-in, but when my legs were caught, I thought I was finished. I threw up my arms to protect my head, and that's the last thing I remember."

Mick said, "Thank God you were spared, Professor." Mick picked up a coat hanger and said, "Come on, guys. Let's go back and see if we can help anyone."

"Okay Mick, let's go!"

The men were gone for about 45 minutes. When they returned, their faces told the story even before they spoke.

The professor asked, "What did you find?"

Mick reported, "We couldn't get into the first chamber. The magic key worked okay because we could hear the release mechanism click, but there was no moving the stone door, no matter what we did."

Sean added, "The cave-in rubble must be blocking the door."

Professor Fitzgerald said, "Those poor men, they didn't deserve this. In all my years in the field, I've never lost a man until now."

Mick said, "Professor, don't blame yourself, it is either an act of providence or an act of saboteurs."

The professor said, "You're right, of course, but still I'm heart broken. We have a lot of work to do to make sure everyone gets out alive. Let's continue this discussion, in private, at the pharaoh's bath. My muscles and bones are aching. If one of you will help me to the bath, I think I'll be able to contribute more to the discussion, after I soak in those hot waters."

Once the four of them were neck deep in the soothing waters, Professor Fitzgerald, Mick, Sean, and John began to assess their plight and to discuss options and the way ahead. Professor Fitzgerald said, "The last thing I want to do is spread panic and despair. We need to stay up-beat and exude confidence. I believe we will be rescued, in time, but it may take a while. Remember, only the director and Sir Paul know our true location. Everyone else thinks we are in the Great Pyramid. In the meantime, we need to keep folks here occupied and focused on their work. The rest of us need to look for escape routes and do what we can to come up with a plan to keep everyone involved. Does that sound reasonable to you guys?"

Sean, John, and Mick nodded their heads in agreement.

"Now, let's get everyone together and put our plan in action! I need you to follow my lead and ask positive and leading questions, okay?"

Once again, everyone was in agreement.

Professor Fitzgerald gathered the team together at the command center and said, "Friends, here's what we know. The corridor that connects to the Subterranean Chamber is clear and we can access that chamber, but the exit door is blocked by rubble on the other side of the door. Charlie, Frank, Juan, and Pablo were lost in the two cave-ins."

A shocked hush fell over the group. Dr. Melissa Prickett asked, "Can we take a moment to say a prayer?"

Professor Fitzgerald replied, "Melissa, will you lead us in the Lord's prayer?"

Melissa led the prayer and many people mumbled along with her, but everyone said, "Amen."

Professor Fitzgerald continued, "Folks, we don't know how much rubble is there, how much of the corridor collapsed, or even if the corridor still exists."

John Applegate, on cue, asked, "How long do you think it will take for the rescue crew to dig us out?"

The professor said, "Hopefully, we'll be freed soon, but the down side of our security program is that no one knows where we really are, except Sir Paul Gibbs and Director Boutros. All topside workers believe we are trapped inside the Great Pyramid. If they begin to excavate and shore-up the passageway, rescue may take a while considering that the rescue team will be taking the long way around to reach us. The shortest route to us would be to drill a shaft straight down right here. Still, we don't know exactly how much sand and bedrock is above our heads."

Melissa said, "Ye Gads! We're trapped like rats in a tomb!"

Professor Fitzgerald said, "It's true, we are trapped for the time being, but not like rats. We have provisions to last six weeks, even if we don't ration, we have plenty of water and air, and we are comfortable. Plus, there are also things we can do to find our way out. We need to look for alternate ways out of the Necropolis based on the original entrance ways from above."

Sean said, "If there is a branch of the Nile that runs under the complex, then we might be able to find a hole to fish through so we can catch Nile perch and tilapia. Also, we may be able to trace the water source to the surface."

Dr. Grant Jones said, "Sean, we don't need to look for a hole. Take a look at the 3-D site model. See the descending staircase here? That staircase leads to an ancient dock that must have, at one time in the past, been a canal that connected the Necropolis to the Nile. I'm a pretty good fisherman; I'll make a fishing pole and try my luck."

Dr. Carol Stewart said, "I'll conduct a supply inventory and develop a plan for stretching the supplies for as long as possible, with and without Grant's additional fish."

Dr. Cindy Kessler said, "I'll study the 3-D site model and look for prospective escape avenues that might show promise. I'll take Dr. Mick with me and we'll conduct preliminary exploratory visits to each candidate site to investigate viability."

Corinne asked, "How can I help?"

Professor Fitzgerald replied, "Corinne, first I would like for you and Sean to concentrate on your mission for Sir Paul. We have a database of scanned and translated hieroglyphics from each pharaoh's granite cubicle. We have them in chronological order and we know how long they reigned and who they are related to. The database also has a locator for each pharaoh. I recommend that you start with a review of the pharaoh database to plan your data collection efforts. Armed with the information from the database, you can easily accomplish your task in an efficient manner."

John Applegate asked, "How can I help?"

The professor said, "I would like you and Sean to support Melissa and Corinne's data collection project by scanning the hieroglyphic panels that line the outside walls of the Pharaoh's Chamber. These panels tell the story of Atlantis from the beginning until the Necropolis was abandoned, and they haven't been scanned yet."

Sean asked, "What do you think the panels will reveal, professor?"

"I hope the panels contain a clue to an escape route that the 3-D site model doesn't show. Once the panels are scanned, we'll need to translate the hieroglyphs to English. When you have completed your scanning effort, we can up-link your scans to our computer for translation to English. Hopefully, there will be some reference to other ways in or out of the Necropolis. Yes, I know it is a long shot, but at least it will answer some questions."

John Applegate said, "Come on Sean, let's not waste any time. If there is a way out of here, I want to find it."

Sean said, "I'm with you."

Professor Fitzgerald said, "Okay Corinne, now back to you and your project. Melissa can help you lay out your data collection plan. The DNA material you need will be found in the pharaoh's canopic jars. Once you have the specimens you need, there are slides and microscopes in the laboratory for your analysis. Our microscopes are extremely high tech, and all the images can be imported to your PDA or to our on-site processor, for post-scan analysis. Our processor is capable of DNA sequencing and mass spectrometry analysis, too."

Corinne noted, "Dr. Fitzgerald, you are so calm. Aren't you worried?"

"Corinne, I am concerned, but we have some of the best minds in the world, here in the Necropolis and on the outside, determined to help us. I don't believe we are in immediate danger, but I don't think we should sit on our hands either."

Corinne laughed and said, "Come on Melissa, we have work to do!"

Melissa said, "The pharaoh's database is located on this computer. Sit down and browse the data."

Corinne said, "Okay, that sounds like a good approach."

Corinne took a seat and began browsing through the files. She was surprised to note that each pharaoh's reign on the throne averaged sixty years for the first thousand years. Then, as the empire's time wore on, the reign duration of each pharaoh began to decline.

During the second thousand years, the average reign began to drop from fifty years to forty years to thirty years, and was down to twenty by the time the record ended.

Corinne finished her review and selected ten pharaohs for DNA analysis. She and Melissa then used the 3-D site model to map the prospective pharaohs for data collection. They wanted to use the organic material from sealed canopic jars containing the pharaoh's livers. So, they would be looking for the jars with a human head on top. Corinne was certain that, if the seals on the jars were compromised, the chance of collecting viable DNA material would be slight. Corinne was sure that any organic material exposed to the air for 5,000 years would be harder to process.

Corinne picked the earliest and latest pharaohs and then spread the other eight out equally along the total timeline. She and Melissa began their mission. The first three canopic jars were intact and once the samples were collected they resealed each jar. After cleaning the surfaces of each jar, they simply used a candle to heat the wax to effectively re-seal each jar. One of the storerooms contained a supply of sealing wax, so they didn't have to rely on the original wax seal.

Melissa said, "Corinne, modern Egyptian embalmers still use the same wax today. And the burial ritual has changed little. Many Egyptians insist on being buried using the ancient burial techniques."

Corinne replied, "Melissa, I didn't know that, but I'm not surprised. I don't think I'm ready to choose my burial preferences right now; how about you?"

They both laughed and Melissa said, "Me neither! I just hope we aren't already buried and entombed."

When they got to the fourth pharaoh, the canopic jar was broken and laying on its side. Corinne rejected that pharaoh and chose the canopic jar of the prince regent. The rest of the data collection went smoothly until they got to the last pharaoh. The last pharaoh's sarcophagus was empty. Corinne said, "I must have missed something in the database when I selected this one."

Melissa said, "Let's look at the database to see what we missed."

Corinne said, "Okay, but first let's make the slides, while the samples are fresh. Then we'll recheck the database."

Corinne and Melissa returned to the lab and prepared a tiny portion of each specimen for mounting on a slide. Melissa carefully labeled everything and Corinne checked each slide and entered the finding into her PDA's main memory.

As they worked, Melissa said, "I assume you are concerned with the Atlantean's genetic DNA string and you intend to determine what people might carry that same gene marker today. I know that the female genetic history indicates that all modern humans are descended from a single area or tribe on the African continent. I'm wondering if you think that tribe might be the Atlanteans contained in this Necropolis."

Corinne replied, "Melissa, I'm more concerned with the development of civilization and modern man since the last ice age, than I am about the beginning of civilization and/or prehistoric villages or settlements. I'm not concerned with the genetic beginning of Homo sapiens and the subsequent migration of Homo sapiens from the African continent to the other continents. So, while the African continent may be the original cradle for Homo sapiens, I'm more concerned about the cradle of civilization here in the Middle East and how the individual genes and gene strands may have mutated over the last 10,000 years."

"I would be very interested in the Babylonian civilization or any of the earlier civilizations that thrived between the Tigress and the Euphrates, but those civilizations are without the Necropolis and the preserved mummies."

Corinne continued, "Melissa, of course, we assume there is a 99.9999% genetic connection between the Atlanteans in this Necropolis and modern people, but it is the subtle differences at the individual DNA strand that is of interest to me. Even that information won't help me in my analysis until I can access my database and conduct some studies. Therefore, we're really just collecting data for future analysis at this point. The unique aspect of the Necropolis is that 5,000 years worth of intact DNA specimens doesn't exist anywhere else—at least as far as we know."

Melissa said, "Okay, I think I understand."

Melissa completed the slides for the pharaohs and said, "Now let's check the data bank for the missing pharaoh, with the empty sarcophagus."

Melissa sat down at the computer and began the data check again.

Corinne said, "It's puzzling why the last one was empty. Apparently, the hieroglyphs recorded the beginning, but then, there are no follow-on glyphs."

Melissa read from the database, "Okay, here it is. Listen to this. The pharaoh was a child when the sarcophagus was begun. Apparently he didn't live long enough to accomplish a lot, or perhaps he is buried elsewhere."

Corinne said, "Well, that explains it. I guess we'll never know what happened to him. Let's collect the DNA specimen from the pharaoh just before him, probably his father or uncle anyway."

Melissa said, "You're right. Both pharaohs' names were Zahra. Of course, that's not their royal names, just their birth names."

A cold chill swept over Corinne and she grabbed the scarab amulet around her neck and began to weep.

Melissa asked, "Corinne, is something wrong?"

Corinne said, "No, nothing's wrong. I guess I just felt a little too much compassion for all the people that are so long dead. I know it doesn't make any sense. Don't mind me," and then she laughed.

Later, Melissa and Corinne returned to the Pharaoh's Chamber to collect the remaining specimen from the next to last pharaoh. While Melissa was resealing the canopic jar, Corinne began to closely examine the hieroglyphs and she paid particular attention to the pharaoh's seal. Either this was one heck of a coincidence or her scarab must have once been connected to this long dead pharaoh. She thought to herself, *Just wait till Sean hears about this.*

Corinne and Melissa finished up and returned to the laboratory to make the final slide. Once all the slides were complete, Corinne captured the digital images of each and began a side-by-side comparison. At first, she couldn't believe her eyes. She stopped what she was doing and she revisited the 3-D map. Then she went into the Pharaoh's Chamber and retraced their progress of the morning's data gathering. Then she went back to the microscope and viewed each slide again. There was no denying it. All the Atlantean pharaohs, at least the ones they collected DNA on, had been women.

Corinne was thinking about the cover story she had told Melissa and she felt a little guilty. But, she told herself, she just didn't know with whom she should share her information. After all, Sir Paul had told them to maintain their story with everyone, unless Professor Fitzgerald told them otherwise.

Corinne was reluctant to share with anyone the real reason why she was collecting the pharaoh's DNA. She didn't need a mass spectrometer analyzer or a high-speed processor to analyze and sequence the discreet strands of DNA that were critical to her analysis. All she needed was the ability to dye or stain the genes in question, and to compare the pharaoh's gene sequence with her baseline gene sequence. It's not as if she was attempting to sequence the pharaoh's double-helix molecule all by herself and in the field, too.

Corinne's preliminary review of the DNA specimens already collected indicated that the aggressive gene sequence, that was tailing off in the modern genome, was very much intact in the pharaohs. Also the gene sequence that she suspected as the controlling string, that turned the aggressive gene string on and off, had two segments that were reversed when the pharaohs' data string was compared to today's A-type personalities.

This controlling gene sequence transposition might be the difference between controlled aggression and "out of control" serial killer aggression. The test now would be to gain access to the human genome database and compare this gene sequence to selected serial killer files. She was anxious to share her findings with Sean.

Atlantis had not been wiped out by a lack of "will to power" or by change or degradation in the human genome brought about by Sean's Collective Intelligence; they must have been wiped out by some natural disaster. Still, if they had not been wiped out by being in the wrong place at the wrong time, would the gene sequence reversal in the controlling gene have led to their eventual failure as a civilization? Sean's theory was neither proved nor disproved.

Corinne believed the decline of the pharaoh's reign was evidence that the Atlantean civilization was trending to failure. She knew that later Egyptian royal families routinely married brothers, sisters and other close family members. Most likely the Atlantean royal families interbred too. Was incest and gene failure responsible for the decline of the Atlantean civilization? Or was the decline evidence of Sean's Collective Intelligence at work? Or was the decline, as promised by their priests, the vengeance of Ra?

Corinne's mind was spinning, considering the multiple possibilities. Naturally, she rejected the Sun God Ra as being a false God and thus not a factor. Then, she thought, the Atlantean's God was as real to them as her God to her and might even be the same God. Wasn't it St. Paul that said there are many paths to the one truth?

When Melissa suggested that Corinne must have been tracking the female mitochondria of the mummies for the purpose of establishing the original African tribe from which all modern humans are descended, Corinne let Melissa believe that was the link she was trying to establish. Corinne realized that she was so focused on the aggressive serial killer gene sequence that she was missing the obvious.

The Atlanteans could be the single African ancestor tribe after all. There could very well be two genetic strains that have been passed down through the millennia. One with the correct controlling gene sequence, and one with the gene reversal sequence that has resulted in individual serial killers and national mass murder on a global scale and subsequent civilization destruction. All the descendents of this tribe could be carrying the serial killer gene sequence in the dominant, subdominant sequence.

Depending on a range of conditions from both parents having the dominant sequence to the standard genetic crap shoot of hit or miss, four offspring from a given family could produce two males with the problem or two males without the problem or any other combination. Yet, there must still be something that triggers the sociopath beyond the gene sequence. Corinne believed that with the DNA samples from the Necropolis and the NIH gene data bank, she could eventually solve the problem. Corinne considered the solution might be as simple as swapping the controlling gene sequence between the type-A DNA strands, based on whether the parents were either dominant or subdominant in the controlling sequence.

The clanging sound of a spoon on a pot broke Corinne's concentration and jolted her back to the present. She thought to herself that, while she didn't know the time, she certainly knew she was starving.

Corinne turned to Melissa and said, "Melissa, I'm starving. Let's find out what's for dinner."

Melissa said, "Me, too. Smells like beef stew."

After dinner the professor gave a quick status report on escape and rescue efforts.

"Okay, everyone, nothing has changed. We need to redouble our efforts and continue to look for escape routes. Does anyone have any thoughts?"

Everyone began to talk at once. The professor said, "Hold on, you all have your assignments. Please go back to work and let's see if we can come up with a plan. Be back here in four hours with your report."

It turned out that Grant was either a great fishermen, or the fish in the Nile branch under the Necropolis were very hungry. The cook took the catch and began to prepare a feast for the next meal. Sean asked, "Will we be dining on sushi or does the kitchen have charcoal?"

The cook replied, "We do indeed have charcoal and the stove is vented, God knows to where, but there is a draw in the flu so smoke is not a problem."

Sean asked, "Is that 10,000 year old charcoal based on camel dung?"

The cook shook his head and said, "It is fresh charcoal that you helped carry in last night."

Sean said, "Go easy on it; we don't know when the next batch will be coming through."

After dinner, Corinne and Sean decided to take some time to do a little exploring in the Pharaoh's Chamber, and Corinne shared some of the information she found in the pharaoh's database, particularly the fact that all the early pharaohs were women—male pharaohs were the exception.

Sean said, "I guess I'm beyond being surprised or astonished at this point, Corinne."

Corinne said, "Maybe you just think you are. One of the pharaoh's cubicles was empty. The database shows that she apparently died young and wasn't entombed here in the Necropolis. Her name was Zahra and her royal seal is exactly the same as the name and seal on my scarab amulet."

Sean said, "Wow! I guess I'm not beyond being astonished just yet. That is an amazing coincidence."

Corinne said, "I thought you didn't believe in coincidences?"

Sean said, "Technically, I don't. If we want to be scientific, your scarab could have belonged to the missing pharaoh of Atlantis. But again, if every trinket and shard of pottery with Nefertiti or Cleopatra's name on it belonged to them, then they would have owned a hell of lot stuff."

"I'm not trying to be negative. I think it's really fun to think your scarab did, at one time, actually belong to Pharaoh Zahra. I'm just trying to be objective."

Corinne said, "I think my scarab did belong to Zahra, and until someone proves otherwise, that's my story."

Sean laughed and said, "Hey, it works for me."

"I'm not shocked that the pharaohs of Atlantis were women. I'm familiar with the theory that the original pagan Gods are thought to be Goddesses and that somehow, war-like males began to dominate the individual tribes at some point. So your discovery supports that theory. Also, the ascension of the male pharaohs to the throne is consistent with aggressive, war-like behavior too, and perhaps, is responsible for the aggressive gene sequence. It is well documented in Egyptian history that pharaohs often produced large numbers of progeny. Rameses the Great is reported to have fathered at least sixty offspring."

Corinne said, "I know that theory too, and I've always considered it just a myth, but the data contained in this Necropolis might change the myth to reality overnight. Also, your point about male pharaohs fathering numerous offspring fits right into the gene sequence reversal problem, with all the in-breeding running rampant in royal families."

Sean said, "If I remember the theory correctly, the premise is that, in a land of plenty, like the ancient Nile Valley with its abundant water, fish, and crops from the lush green fields, there was little to fight over and all the people had a high standard of living, as though they were living in the Garden of Eden."

Corinne asked, "What do you think upset the Atlantean's life in Eden?"

Sean said, "Perhaps the have-not nomadic tribes of the desert lived a fight-to-eat life style, and rather than putting their wealth into art or beauty they instead invested in weapons and tactics that facilitated their take over and eventual conquest of Atlantis."

John Applegate was doing a little exploring, too, when he noticed Sean and Corinne, and shouted out, "hello," as he caught up with them.

Sean asked, "Do you come here often? I don't think I've seen you here before."

John said, "I'm beginning to think I come here way too often because I always run into you."

Sean said, "Now is that anyway to talk to Sir Paul's cousin?"

John asked, "Well, that is an interesting observation. Just when did you become Paul's cousin anyway?"

Sean said, "It's a long story, we'll fill you in later. I'll tell you this, I don't know if you were surprised to see us, but we were certainly surprised to see you!"

John replied, "Oh, I was surprised to see you all right, especially when I found out you had new names."

Corinne and Sean laughed and Sean said, "Thanks for not blowing our cover."

John said, "After all, what are friends for?"

Corinne said, "My main concern is finding a way out of here."

John said, "Me, too. Anyone have any ideas?"

Sean said, "Well, like the professor said, sooner or later we'll be rescued, so there is no reason to panic."

John said, "Me and my goofy business deals. Something like this was bound to happen. Next time I'm going to send Larry May to explore the tomb, while I tend to the fender-bender at the Cairo airport."

Corinne asked, "What happened?

John said, "We had just completed the grant announcement and the photo opportunity with Director Boutros, when Larry got an email alert that someone had bumped into the Gulfstream. Larry thought it was prudent to check it out in person, to make sure the damages were evaluated and repairs made. So he blew-off the tour of the pyramid. Larry doesn't like to admit it, but he's just a little claustrophobic. I told him, 'Okay, you can dodge this bullet.'"

Corinne said, "I wish we had gone with Larry. By the way, have you guys completed the scan of the hieroglyphs? I think it's important to translate them as soon as possible. I know it is a long shot, but at the moment, it's the best lead we have at finding a possible exit."

John clicked on his PDA, and the professor appeared again hovering in the air as he began his presentation.

Corinne exclaimed, "Wow! Now that's a PDA!"

Sean said, "Corinne, the short answer to your question is, yes. John's PDA made the whole project a snap."

John chuckled, "This is a preview of ME's newest product line. Corinne, this PDA is faster, larger, and has more memory capacity than any university mainframe computer."

Corinne asked, "Can you upload the scans to the professor's data bank for translation to English?"

John said, "Oh, I can do better than that. On the way to Cairo, I had my lab people update the standard Egyptian hieroglyph translation program. So, the absolutely latest language translation software program responds to any scanned hieroglyph by comparing the new image to well documented and decoded hieroglyphs and their accepted English translations. The program notes any concerns with the interpretation and, if necessary, provides alternate translations when the program encounters new symbols or the syntax suggests ambiguity. I have no idea how accurate the translation will be on these unknown, undocumented, and non-Egyptian hieroglyphs; but it's definitely worth a try."

John's language translation software translated the first panel to English with an 80% accuracy confidence level and presented the original hieroglyph and the translation side by side in the holographic format.

Corinne said, "An 80% translation accuracy is pretty good."

John said, "The 80% confidence factor is not a reliable factor for this translation because the factor is based on the known Egyptian translation. I think we should not rely on these translations as anything other than guides at this point. I assume the hieroglyphic experts will have the final word on translation, probably years from now."

"However, this is the best we have to go on, right now, so let's see what it tells us."

The three of them began to review the story, panel by panel. The hieroglyphs told the story of the people's creation by the Sun God Ra, when Ra sent a huge fireball into the lake and created Atlantis. The Atlantean's worshiped Ra and they prospered and their empire grew. Because Atlantis was located in the lake, they became a maritime power connected to other people via the sea. The glyphs identified a specific pharaoh as a direct incarnation of Ra. This pharaoh brought the greatest achievement to Atlantis in terms of wealth, technology, and growth of the Atlantean empire. As Atlantis prospered and matured, they eventually began work on the Necropolis at Giza. The glyphs depicted the regular pilgrimages from Atlantis to the Necropolis, by royal yacht, for entombment, celebration of life and celebration of rebirth. The glyphs were clear that Ra's original incarnation had been reincarnated many times, so the prosperity of Atlantis was unbroken for the 2,500 year reign of Ra.

The glyphs also showed a point where Ra was not reincarnated, because the last reincarnation of Ra was murdered and a rival family-line produced a male pharaoh. The priests pronounced that Ra was angry with the people of Atlantis. The priests predicted that, as foretold in the beginning, Ra would destroy Atlantis with fire and brimstone. It was at this point that the story was interrupted, although there were, at least, another thousand years of additional unfinished panels with sparse or incomplete glyphs.

Sean said, "The Great Pyramid was unfinished, the Necropolis was unfinished, and the people and the civilization were suddenly finished. I wonder if the researchers will find the missing pieces to complete the picture."

John said, "As soon as the hieroglyphic experts translate the missing 20% of symbols, I'll have the application program updated and maybe we can fill in the details. I didn't see anything to make me think the missing stuff might address a way out of here. Did you?"

Corinne and Sean looked at each other and shook their heads no. The three headed back to the group for an assessment of where the various groups stood with their activities of the day and to share the evening meal.

After dinner, while people chatted about the day's work, the work planned for tomorrow, and the prospects of rescue and escape, Sean spent the time reviewing the glyphs he and John had collected. He found that, with the PDAs digital enhancement and restoration, he could retrieve and add some of the missing detail and symbols to the glyph panels that were partially damaged. It became obvious that the glyphs were once complete and, at some point in time, someone had been in the process of revising history when they were apparently rudely interrupted.

As Sean scrolled through the hieroglyphic history of the 5,000 year span, from the beginning to the last entry, he began to see a pattern. When Ra cast the creation fireball, there were also a dozen additional fireballs ranging in size from the largest that hit the lake, to various smaller fireballs. Three appeared to strike simultaneously with the large creation fireball. The remainder of the fireballs passed through the heavens but didn't strike the Earth. Scrolling forward 2,500 years, a collection of fireballs appeared in the sky above Atlantis again, but none struck Atlantis. The Priests of Ra described these fireballs as "warnings from Ra." Scrolling into the future, the Priests of Ra again predicted the destruction of Atlantis by fireballs from angry Ra, should the people fail to honor Ra. The people of Atlantis rededicated themselves to the worship of Ra. To confirm their covenant with Ra, they began construction of the Pyramids and the Great Sphinx as a tribute.

The three pyramids and the Great Sphinx were lined up with the cardinal coordinates to greet Ra each morning. Ra is symbolized by the sun and the sun rises in the east. The head of the Sphinx was meant to depict the face of Ra. There were rays shooting either from the sun to the Great Pyramid or from the Great Pyramid to the sun.

The fireballs always appeared in the east, so that is why people attributed the fireballs to Ra. Sean was thinking, when Corinne and I get some down time, I'll have Corinne review the images and get her take on what she thinks the hieroglyphs are trying to say.

Corinne gave a low whistle and Sean looked up. Corinne crooked her finger and motioned "come here" and they left the dinner gathering for a little walk that ended up at the pharaoh's bathhouse. In the blink of an eye they had disrobed and were submerged to their chins in the hot pool.

Corinne said, "I'm still stunned that all this exists in such pristine condition, just a few hundred feet under the desert sands. I know it is a Necropolis and a place of mourning, but it seems like a place of happiness and promise for the future, too."

Sean said, "Corinne, any religion worth its salt has a payoff for believers. Each major religion has some form of rebirth, resurrection, and/or reincarnation tied to living your life according to the golden rule. The payoff for some may be meeting their maker, seeing the face of God or experiencing the love of God, cheating death, or just participating in the miracle of life. Then again, for other people a love of life and a desire to share that joy with like-minded people is enough. The people with faith are the lucky ones because their questions are fully answered by their faith."

Corinne asked "Where do you fit in Sean? Do you have the faith?"

Sean said, "I'm a simple guy and I don't need much, but I do have questions that I'm sure I can never answer to my own satisfaction. To me, the greatest appeal of an afterlife would be realizing you get another chance to do things right. I don't know whether that means in heaven or back on Earth through reincarnation. Realistically, if you look at the other species of life here on Earth, whether it is the seventeen-year cicada or the summer butterfly, I find it very hard to believe that the cicada that died seventeen years ago is reincarnated in the cicada that crawled out of the ground today. When I see these guys mating, laying eggs, dying, and being born, I take comfort in the continuing cycle of life. I know I'm a product of a similar life cycle. The miracle is the continuing cycle of life. There were people here before me, and I know there will be people here after me. I think that is a good thing. Those of us that are here now must do our best to secure a safe future for the people that come after our time. After all, the Earth and life belongs to the living—not to the past. That is our reincarnation life cycle—reincarnation of the species not reincarnation of individuals. I find that attributing a value above and beyond the summer butterfly, to the human being, might take the arrogance of man to make it believable."

"However, I'm afraid that the only chance a human gets, is a chance to perpetuate love of life by making babies with the love of his or her life. If the Atlantean's concept of reincarnation in the offspring of your family holds up, then I would be delighted. If the fairy tales of the major religions hold water, then I would be delighted, too. The only problem for me is, I won't have a sarcophagus or the hieroglyphics to keep my Ka centered until I can wedge myself into some unsuspecting newborn, so my Ka will be destined to haunt some pyramid for eternity."

Sean said, "Unfortunately, I keep waking up from a daydream and finding myself in the middle of a nightmare about being buried alive in an Egyptian tomb. I hope I haven't already begun to haunt the Necropolis all over again."

"Oh! You're impossible!

Chapter 19
Holmes: The Game is Afoot

As Sean mused on his predicament, he thought about how the 21st century anthropologist can only guess at how ancient societies must have operated the same by analogy with today's societies. There is the official position on everything for the masses, and then there are the special circumstances for the privileged. Maybe the best approach to thinking about the glyphs on the walls of the Necropolis was not to place a literal interpretation on the glyphs but rather to look at the glyphs as metaphors and conveyers of ideas.

Sean decided to apply the "Holmesian deduction," or the "argument to the best explanation" methodology, to deduce what all the data from the glyphs in the Necropolis really meant for the people of the present and for the generations to come. The venerable Sherlock Holmes quotation came to mind: "When you have eliminated the impossible, whatever remains, however improbable, must be the truth."

Sean began a mental exercise to think about what he knew, and what he didn't know. Then he tried to apply a little deductive and inductive reasoning using the Holmesian deduction methodology.

He thought, *Okay, here is what we know:* The Earth is six billion years old. To create the Necropolis and the pyramids of the Giza Plateau complex would require a civilization with a technology beyond any historical civilization known to exist as contemporaries of the Atlanteans. The existence of the Atlantean Necropolis proves that at least one civilization with advanced technological know-how existed at the conclusion of the last ice age, 10,000 years ago. The men of Atlantis constructed the Giza Plateau complex, not supernatural forces, God, or an advanced race of space aliens. One can't help but wonder if the Atlanteans had outposts beyond the Mediterranean, or perhaps, there were competing contemporaries in other parts of the world. Sean immediately thought about Nigel Hornbeak's South American archeological dig.

The Necropolis was complete, with room for at least a thousand years of future pharaohs. The Great Pyramid was still under construction when abruptly stopped. The Atlanteans knew and feared the fireballs from the sky and recognized the fireballs as potentially

Life Extinguishing Events. The recognition of the asteroid threat and the fear of the fireballs hitting Earth are depicted in the glyphs in the Necropolis. Did the Atlanteans simply run out of time, or did they realize they lacked the technology to deflect the asteroids, or both?

What we don't know: The Atlantean civilization must have been wiped out by a significant event of nature and probably not by warfare, pestilence, or civil war, because there is no evidence of a comparable competing civilization and no record of pestilence in the hieroglyphic record. They had weathered the murder of the pharaoh's incarnation, and they had tolerated an out-of-bloodline interloper assuming the throne. Most likely the predicted fireball from the sky either directly or indirectly destroyed Atlantis.

The Great Pyramid and the Necropolis may have had multiple functions, such as: safety bunker for the royalty; time capsule and scientific repository for disaster recovery; monument to honor Ra; mount for the crystal laser to harness the sun's energy to deflect or destroy the fireball; or any other need we haven't thought of yet.

Analysis: The hieroglyphs indicate that Ra created the civilization with fireballs and the priests promised that Ra's fireballs would destroy the civilization, if the people broke their covenant with Ra.

The glyphs depict the priests as angry when the covenant with Ra was broken by the murder of the unborn reincarnation of Ra. The chosen people breaking their covenant with God is consistent with many religions, including Judeo-Christian beliefs, which explain creation of the world via a supernatural power from outside the solar system. In this case, God. Even 21st century scientists suggest life on Earth is likely a result of asteroids impacting the Earth. So, as metaphor, the Atlantean explanation is as good as any other religion's explanation and, as the dinosaur's fossil record suggest, so is the Atlantean religion's prediction of world destruction via fire and brimstone from above.

The Old Testament describes a flood that destroyed the sinful Earth and a God that promised fire and brimstone from the sky for the next world's destruction, if the people broke their covenant with God.

Corinne's supposition that the Biblical flood may have been the result of an asteroid impact has strong merit. Maybe the New Testament's Star of Bethlehem was part of that group of asteroids or a precursor to that destructive group. Is today's civilization any better prepared to live through an asteroid LEE than the Atlanteans were?

What we need to know: Is there a group of asteroids, on an elliptical orbit, that lines up with the Earth on some kind of a predictable timetable?

Is there a group of Halley-like asteroids already on a 2,500-year trajectory to return to Earth and do damage again?

How much time do we have before the next asteroid LEE? Are Argus and mini-Argus looking in the right part of the night sky?

Are the ruins discovered on the sea floor of the Mediterranean Atlantis?

If those ruins are Atlantis, do they contain the library of Atlantis?

Do we have the technology that could place an asteroid deflector beyond the orbit of Jupiter?

Is there enough time left to deploy an asteroid deflector?

Sean decided to try the results of his Holmesian deduction on Corinne. Sean and Corinne sat down, and Sean presented the methodology of his analysis and his conclusions on a point-by-point basis.

Corinne said, "Sean your theory is as good as any other at this point. What we still need are a plan of action and milestones to pursue the next leg of your analysis."

Sean asked. "What do you mean?"

Corinne said, "Well, I said your theory is as good as any other. What I mean is, if we assume your theory is worth further investigation, what do we do next? For example, let's assume your theory is 100 percent correct. Let's say you and I believe the theory you have stumbled onto is way more than theory. Let's say we believe you have uncovered the truth. The question then becomes one of what steps do we take, as a group, to prove your theory is more than hypothetical? How do we first verify your theory and, second, change the theory to a proof that the scientists and theologians of the 21st century can accept? Let's say the world buys into your theory, then what? What do we recommend as the next step to save our civilization from the asteroids? How does our civilization avoid the same fate suffered by Atlantis? These questions are more than rhetorical and the answers have to be the plan for the way ahead."

"Why don't you present your methodology, analysis, and conclusions to the group and solicit their input for alternatives or refinements? We have an educated group of people that are, excuse the pun, a captive audience. If we can't get by them, we won't be able to get by the world's scientists either. These experts can shoot down your analysis as flawed, recommend that you modify your methodology, or they may have questions that send you back to the drawing board. We should take advantage of their knowledge while we can. You and I may be too close to the forest here, so we may be missing a tree or two."

Sean said, "Corinne, that is an excellent idea. We'll drag them into the whole thing, right after dinner, when they least expect it."

Sean waited for everyone to finish the evening meal before presenting his findings. The group listened intently and many people nodded their heads in agreement.

Professor Fitzgerald said, "I believe you are right that all civilizations have reached for the stars in one way or another. For example, some have tried seeking heaven via the construction of the Tower of Babel, others by seeking an afterlife, and still others by climbing Mount Everest or through space exploration.

"Our civilization is the only one to achieve space flight, including construction of a moon base, but at what cost? We have the technology for space flight, space exploration, and the ability to colonize other worlds, but we still don't have a vision."

"There is evidence that our civilization's technology may be destroying or degrading the Earth's environment, and the degradation of the environment may be directly responsible for extinguishing a large number of species. Is the alarming rate at which we are losing species the direct result of reckless industrialization? Even our space program is focused on industrialization goals and capitalization of space. Are we simply carrying our greed and environmentally destructive ways to new worlds? Isn't there a difference between greed and need?"

"When I look at the crater evidence around the world, then I know that the asteroids will be back. Perhaps, in the near term, the short term, or the long term, but I know they will return. The destruction may be small, large, or a LEE event."

"We're in the same position the Atlanteans were in. We know the asteroids are coming, and we think we have asteroid countering technology, but will time run out before we can put the technology in place? We have one advantage over the Atlanteans—we don't blame God for our predicament. But, as a people, we remain extremely superstitious. If we take no action to mitigate the asteroid threat, then we must blame ourselves. We must present the challenge to the people of the world in such a way that governmental inaction will require the consensus of civilization as a whole."

Sean said, "When we are rescued, we can present our findings and the compelling evidence we have collected to the scientific councils of the world. The evidence makes a case for our predictions, so we should be able to forge an international agreement to commit resources to asteroid deflection technology."

Corinne said, "If we can pinpoint the night sky coordinates where we should be concentrating our telescopes, then Sir Paul can redirect mini-Argus to scan the sky to identify asteroid activity beyond the orbit of Pluto. If we catch the threat beyond the orbit of Pluto, we'll have time to deploy the asteroid deflection technology in Jupiter's orbit."

Sean said, "Exactly! Jupiter, with its massive gravity, will act as a natural asteroid sponge. Asteroid deflection technology will only need to nudge the asteroid into a trajectory that will lead it to Jupiter's gravity and nature will do the rest."

Professor Fitzgerald asked, "Sean, if we coordinate and overlay the timelines of the various world histories, one on top of the other, and focus on 'like events' rather than 'chronological timelines,' we may get a clear picture. For example, let your base timeline be the 'Earth's scientific timeline' created by the fossil record and the crater impact record."

"Then, overlay similar events recorded in the Old and New Testament without regard to the Bible's timeline. Then add your best guess estimate for the timeline from the glyphs in the Necropolis and also add the similar events from Asian histories without regard to their timelines. Once you have all the relevant events and timelines loaded, then you should create three models based on events rather than historical timelines."

"For example: let model one represent similar events beginning 10,000 years ago until the flood event that wiped out Atlantis; let model two represent the timeline of similar events from the Egyptian Old Kingdom until the fall of Egypt, when it was conquered by the Romans; let model three represent the Bible's timeline from Genesis to the Current Era with the birth of Christ."

"Then, coordinate the 'like events,' within each of the three models, with the baseline of the 'Earth's scientific timeline.' Finally, expand and contract your master 'Earth's scientific timeline' to see the three most likely scenarios without regard to each historian's particular chronological order of events."

Sean asked, "Professor Fitzgerald, do you have a theory you hope one of these models will substantiate?"

"No, I don't. I just hope the whole modeling exercise will help correlate data. All three models may be a bust or one of them may reveal something that we have overlooked so far."

"What you are trying to do here is to use similar global catastrophes to synchronize diverse catastrophes that were independently observed, perhaps simultaneously, around the world, while disregarding ancient calendars that may be open to error."

Sean said, "John, can you work with me to sort this stuff and to create the three models? If only we were above ground so we could access the world's libraries, we would have better access to information to populate the models."

John said, "Sure! Let's see what the PDA can do! Don't worry about access to the world's libraries. Before I left, I downloaded, onto my PDA, every technical library that was available on-line or that ME has a contractual or grant relationship with. Still, the PDA's memory banks are not even remotely challenged. I suspect that any resource you could possible want to access is located right here under the sands of Egypt. My PDA, for all practical purposes, contains the world's database."

Sean said, "I keep forgetting that we have the 'King of Nanotechnology' right here within our midst."

Sean and John went to the room that the group had been using as a media room, and, with John operating the PDA, he began projecting the data in holographic format. The PDA also had nanotech fingertip "stick-ons" capability for the user's nails.

John said, "Sean, stick the buttons on each nail of both hands and you'll be able to manipulate the holographic images in real-time."

Sean was familiar with digital gloves, and he recognized the "stick-ons" as the next generation of digital glove. Sean began shuffling the holographic timelines and the data in midair. He stretched and pushed the timeline to the right and to the left to accommodate new data. Sean was rapidly coordinating events and manipulating the timelines of the various civilizations, in order to create a master timeline that started 10,500 years BCE and came forward to the present date. Corinne was amazed at the speed with which Sean was working.

Corinne asked, "Sean, can I help by researching anything with my PDA?"

"The only thing I don't have is the timeline from the Necropolis. Would you please return to the Pharaoh's Chamber and scan the timeline around the perimeter of the chamber."

Sean said, "Give John and me a couple of hours, and we'll see if we have any models to evaluate."

After two hours of work, Sean and John had assembled three models. They began to review and refine each model. Corinne returned with the scanned timeline from the Necropolis and handed her PDA to Sean. Sean immediately transferred the data and began integrating the new timeline data into the three models.

Sean completed updating model one and two. So far, nothing was standing out as significant. Sean added the final bits of information to model three and hit the update key. There it was! The results were hanging in mid-air. John and Sean looked at each other and they both nodded in recognition.

At that moment Corinne walked back into the room and Sean looked up and said, "Corinne! We've got something. Take a look at this!"

Holmes: The Game is Afoot

Chapter 20

Me Nami, Tsunami

Sean presented the assumptions and the methodology that he and John employed to develop the three models that Professor Fitzgerald had suggested. They also provided Corinne the background analysis to support their conclusions.

Sean said, "Ok, Corinne, here goes. The fossil record is solid back to at least 250 million years. A major asteroid life extinguishing event occurred during the Permian-Triassic period off the East Antarctic ice sheet crater. This event, or LEE, is called "The Great Dying" because 95% of all life on Earth was wiped out. This was during the formation of the super continent Pangaea and, of course, long before dinosaurs. If an asteroid triggered the P-Tr event, then the size of the asteroid would have been the size of Mount Everest. This strike is way too early, but a catastrophic LEE is there, in plain sight, in the fossil record."

"Now, we ratchet forward in time to the dinosaur LEE of 65 million years ago. The asteroid that struck and ruined the dinosaurs' Garden of Eden is connected to the Chicxulub crater, near the Yucatan peninsula. The Chicxulub crater is underwater in the Caribbean Sea and is 110 miles in diameter. That impact would have been like 100 million hydrogen bombs going off at once. This strike is way too early for our analysis, but it also includes additional simultaneous asteroid strikes. For example, the Silverpit crater is twelve miles in diameter and is located in the North Sea off the coast of the United Kingdom, and the Boltysh crater is fifteen miles in diameter and is located in the Ukraine. They are all part of the dinosaur event

"So, multiple asteroid strike evidence is documented in the fossil record, too. No one alive today witnessed the events in real time, but our scientists and astronomers have witnessed similar events in real time on the planet Jupiter."

"For example, Comet Shoemaker-Levy 9 collided with Jupiter in July of 1994 and provided the first direct observation of the collision of two solar system objects. Astronomers Carolyn and Eugene M. Shoemaker and David Levy discovered the comet on the night of March 24, 1993. Comet SL9 was orbiting Jupiter and was the first comet ever observed to be orbiting a planet rather than the Sun. SL9 was in pieces ranging in size up to two kilometers in diameter. Scientists speculated that the comet had been pulled apart by Jupiter's tidal forces during a close encounter in July 1992. These fragments collided with Jupiter's southern hemisphere in 1994. The prominent scars from the impacts could be seen on Jupiter for many months after the collision. Observers described them as more easily visible than the Great Red Spot."

"Considering the direct observation, by Earth astronomers in real time, of the SL9 impact on Jupiter and the documented multiple hits, the SL9 event is likely proof that the people of Earth can expect a high probability of future asteroid encounters similar in nature to SL9."

"When you connect SL9 with the evidence of multiple impacts when the dinosaurs left this world, I wouldn't be surprised to find evidence supporting multiple impacts with every past asteroid event on Earth."

John said, "A key point of the SL9 event is that it was discovered in March of 1993, and it impacted Jupiter in July of 1994. From the moment of discovery to the point of impact was scarcely a year. Suppose we had a settlement or a base on Jupiter that would have been in jeopardy due to the approach of SL9? A year is not enough time to mount a rescue effort, let alone a mission to deflect SL9."

"To protect the Jupiter base, we would have to have astronauts on-station, beyond the orbit of Pluto, ready to go with a means to deliver massive explosives or laser deflection technology to affect the SL9 comet's trajectories. Without the manpower and technology in place, we would have been as helpless as the people in the Nile Valley."

"Of course, there is no base on Jupiter, so impacting Jupiter is a good thing. But if Argus or mini-Argus should discover a heavenly body on course for Earth, and if we are presented with a similar timeline between discovery and impact, we're going to have everyone running around here like Chicken Little with no ability to do anything about it. So, early warning would be mandatory."

Sean said, "Excellent point, John!"

Sean continued, "Corinne, the impact crater that is most relevant to our timeline is the one that occurred in the middle of the Indian Ocean and left an impact crater eighteen miles in diameter. This impact event occurred 4.5 to 5 thousand years ago. The crater is located 12,500 feet below the surface and the impact would have created a mega-tsunami. Mega-tsunamis can include a solar eclipse, torrential downpours, and hurricane-force winds for weeks, as well as, long periods of total darkness. A solar eclipse, created by the debris ejected into the atmosphere, can last from months to years and leave the Earth in total darkness. The crater size suggests an event that would have produced a mega-tsunami of at least a 600 foot high wave. This tsunami would have been about thirteen times as big as the Indonesian tsunami of the early 21st century."

Corinne said, "Oh my God! It must have been a horrifying experience for the poor people of the Nile Valley. The tsunami would have impacted the entire east coast of Africa. Its effects would have been felt in Lake Victoria and the Nile Valley would have been flooded. God only knows how high the flood waters would have risen or how long the flood would have lasted."

John said, "Corinne, in the database there are reports of a waterline on the Great Pyramid as high as 240 feet."

Sean said, "John's library data search, on his amazing PDA, identified research conducted by a doctoral candidate. The student attempted to do a similar correlation of the world's literature related to flood myths. He identified fourteen flood myths in various cultures around the world. Of the fourteen floods all described hurricane-force winds and darkness. Seven of the accounts described a full solar eclipse. Seven of the accounts describe torrential downpours. One third of the accounts described tsunamis. All of the flood myths could be part of the same asteroid impact event, depending on that particular culture's distance from ground zero."

"Based on the world's history of asteroid impacts, we must assume that there are other minor, or perhaps major, impact craters connected to the Indian Ocean impact event, that remain to be discovered. The impacts could have occurred anywhere, including the Mediterranean Basin. This revelation certainly opens the possibility that Atlantis may have been destroyed by the Indian Ocean event, either by a direct asteroid hit on Atlantis itself, or indirectly due to massive flooding or earthquakes. I'm anxious to hear the results of Sir Paul's Observation Island research probe."

"It is likely that the people had no warning whatsoever of the Indian Ocean impact. They got out of bed that morning and proceeded to conduct their business, just like any other day, when their lives and their world changed instantly forever, and in a bad way."

Corinne said, "This is fantastic information. You guys have more than enough data, so let's brief the team on your findings!"

That night after dinner, Professor Fitzgerald asked everyone to gather in the media room to discuss the three models that Sean and

John had developed. The men took turns presenting the methodology, the analyses, and the pros and cons for each of the three models.

The group agreed that model-3 presented startling information. There was universal agreement that the Indian Ocean impact site had to play a significant role in the untimely demise of Atlantis and the Nile Valley civilization. Everyone agreed that more data collection and analysis were required, and that documenting additional Mediterranean and/or Mid East impact craters needed to be of the highest priority.

Dr. Carol Stewart noted, "NASA has recently deployed a series of satellites with the capability of mapping the geological terrain down to 25 feet below the surface. Perhaps we can ask NASA to concentrate their initial efforts in the Mediterranean area. Additional craters might be found quickly."

Escape or rescue remained on everyone's mind. All three of the teams reported no progress had been made yet. The escape route team reported significant rubble and blockage at each staircase identified on the 3-D model. The team leader suggested that the original above ground temples were probably destroyed and rebuilt numerous times in the last 5,000 years and that each site may be under multiple foundations and tons of sand.

Sean said, "John and I plan to test the depth of the river and to explore the channel as for as we can in each direction."

Professor Fitzgerald noted, "I am not aware of any surface branches of the Nile near the Giza Plateau or of any tributaries to the Nile in the vicinity of the plateau. If the tributary does connect directly to the Nile, then it is likely to be an underground channel, and you'll find no light at the end of that tunnel."

The professor then turned his attention to the group and said, "Attention please, everyone! I want to thank Sean and John for their extremely interesting research. We have a lot to think about. I'm exhausted and I know all you must be worn out, too. I want to bid everyone a good night and I recommended that everyone get the much-needed rest we all deserve. There is no need for worry. We will redouble our efforts tomorrow to find a way out of here."

Sean, Corinne, and John found themselves immersed up to their chins in the pharaoh's hot pool. John turned to Corinne and asked, "Corinne, dear, have you completed the collection of DNA material from the pharaohs?"

Corinne replied, "I have completed the data collection. I'd still have another two days of work, if Dr. Prickett hadn't helped."

"Do you think your analyses will identify the gene sequence that is the key to immortality?"

Corinne laughed and said, "Oh sure! I think while I am at it I will develop the formula for turning base metal into gold, too!"

John replied, "I don't know where I got the idea, but I thought you were working on the NIH immortality project."

Corinne said, "Not me, but I am seriously interested in the formula."

Sean said, "Me too! John, what status do you have?"

John laughed and said, "Well, if I don't even know who is leading the project at NIH, or working on it, I would think any info I have would be seriously suspect. I don't want to breach any security codes at NIH, but what are you working on, Corinne?"

"Oh, no security problem here! I am working on a project to trace modern man's DNA back to the original tribe in Africa that gave rise to us. Because of this archeological find, and the age of the mummies, we are hoping to determine if we, modern man that is, are direct descendants of the residents of Atlantis."

John asked, "Well, are we?"

Corinne said, "I won't know until I get back to my office and complete the analysis."

John turned to Sean and said, "I think we need to return to the underground river and get serious about looking for a way out of this place. I don't want the pharaoh's tomb to become my tomb. I think we should get into the channel, follow it toward the Nile, and just see how far we can go. Professor Fitzgerald said we are about five miles from the Nile. Maybe we can get closer. If the tunnel or channel, or whatever the water runs through, is 100 percent water, then we might be able to float along on the surface to where the underground channel dips down to dump the water into the Nile."

Sean replied, "I'm with you, but we should probably check in both directions. The tributary comes from somewhere. Maybe there is a cave, oasis, or tunnel that leads to the surface before the main channel runs through the Necropolis. I don't have a high degree of confidence that we will find an exit in the five miles between here and the Nile. Professor Fitzgerald says there are no known surface or subsurface

Nile tributaries in the vicinity of the Giza Plateau. My concern is that we'll get close to the Nile, but then the final mile or more of the channel may dip way down and enter the Nile in a submerged part of the river's center. That would leave us lost and no better off than we are now."

John said, "All your points are well taken, but we can't know until we do the exploring."

Corinne cautioned, "Remember, Professor Fitzgerald said there is no reason to panic. Some of the best minds in the world, inside and outside, are working to get us out. Don't take any unnecessary chances."

Sean said, "Oh, don't worry about that. We know what we're doing."

"Hey John, when do you want to get started?"

John said, "I'm ready now, if you are."

Sean replied, "I need to get a few hours of sleep."

Sean looked at his PDA and said, "Let's begin six hours from now."

John looked at his PDA and said, "You've got it!"

John climbed out of the pool and said; "I'll see you then."

Sean and Corinne looked at each other and moved closer together in the pool. They kissed and then they embraced.

Corinne asked, "Immortality? What do you think that question was about?'

Sean replied, "Nothing new there, he's obsessed with that issue."

"Yeah, I guess you're right. I really don't know the status on the immortality project at NIH."

Sean said, "I know. Plus, based on the actuarial tables, whoever is working it apparently isn't making much progress."

They both laughed.

Sean and Corinne returned to their sleeping quarters and Sean set the alarm on his PDA to give him time to get cleaned-up, get breakfast and get some gear together for the anticipated Huck Finn adventure. Sean wasn't sure if John was Huck Finn but he sure felt like Tom Sawyer to Corinne's Becky Thatcher and they were all lost in McDougal's cave. He just hoped like hell that Injun Joe wasn't lurking within the tunnels somewhere.

John and Sean met at the wharf at the agreed upon time. Corinne was in tow to make sure they were both using caution. John had two flashlights and some twine. Sean was wearing shoes, shorts, and no shirt. John was dressed the same. The dock was a granite wharf where royal barges tied up to deliver the pharaoh and his entourage to the Necropolis. The 3-D model only covered the dock or wharf, and it wasn't clear how either side of the wharf might have looked 10,000 years ago. Sean guessed that part of the channel was probably underground. However, some of the channel may have also been on the surface. The 3-D funeral complex model showed that the original landscaping was more of a Garden of Eden than a desert oasis. But then a lot of terrain had changed in the last 10,000 years.

The dock area resembled an underground station on a subway more than anything else. The wide part of the station allowed access to the barges. The barges then, like a subway car, entered or exited the station in one direction or the other. Presumably, the tunnel to the left originally led to the Nile. The tunnel to the right was probably utilized to tie-up and park visitor's barges or to avoid traffic jams.

In each direction, the light from the station's radium orbs only lit the way a short distance. John said, "Let's start exploring to the right first. Maybe we can find the water's source or maybe a maintenance or air shaft that we could use to contact the world above."

Sean said, "Okay, let's go."

Sean walked down the steps and began feeling around for the bottom of the channel. He stepped off and found himself in water up to the middle of his chest. He was holding the flashlight above his head as he began moving toward the tunnel entrance. He stopped and asked, "Hey! You don't think there are any crocodiles in this water do you?"

John replied, "Let's hope there are because that means there is a definite connection to the Nile."

Sean said, "If there are, I hope they're all sunning themselves on the bank of the Nile right now!"

John stepped into the water and followed three feet behind Sean. As the light from the station faded, Sean turned on his flashlight and they proceeded at a steady pace into the dark of the tunnel. They had gone about a tenth of a mile, when the tunnel opened into an underground cavern with a large pool that was the source of the water flowing through the channel. Sean thought, "This lake would accommodate at least fifteen moderate sized barges." Sean shined the light around the walls. He saw no indication of a man-made object, any writing or hieroglyphics, or any sign that men had ever occupied the chamber.

John said, "Look at the center of the lake. It looks like the lake is fed by an underground spring." The water was bubbling up like a large-diameter fire hose was submerged under the surface.

Sean said, "That explains why this water is so cold. I don't see any help here. Let's head on back."

They returned to the dock, climbed out, and they both were shivering. John said, "I've got an idea. Let's go climb into the pharaoh's hot pool for a few minutes and warm up before we try the other tunnel."

"Now that's a great idea! Let's go!"

As they were warming in the pool, John said, "I don't know how much of this whole complex was engineered or whether the Ancients were just smart enough to take advantage of the natural resources, but someone knew a little bit about hydrology to make this whole place work."

Sean said, "I once caught a video on the construction of the Panama Canal and, while brute force was involved, the key to making the entire project work was based on utilizing the terrain to best advantage and capitalizing on the natural resources at hand. I think the Atlantean's leveraged the natural resources here, too."

John observed, "Based on what I've seen so far, the engineers of Atlantis were as good as anybody in the history of the human race. How about it, are you ready to give the other direction a try?"

"Let's do it!"

Sean and John entered the wharf, stepped into the cold water, and headed toward the Nile. The water remained chest high and, even after they had gone about two miles, the water was still cold.

John said, "You know, it would have been helpful if those guys had put those radium orbs all the way through these tunnels."

Sean said, "I agree, this flashlight is beginning to dim. Listen! Do you hear water running?"

"Yeah, I do, but it's a funny sound. Not quite the sound of a waterfall, but it does have a weird water sound. Let's keep going. Even if the batteries go dead all we have to do is follow the channel to get back."

Sean said, "Okay!

They kept going for another mile, and the noise became louder the further they walked. As they continued down the channel, the water began to change. The current picked up speed and had a strong pull, much like a wave at the beach, returning to the ocean. The water also became shallow, and now they were only walking in knee-deep water.

Sean slowed down and began to take one step at a time, and he used his foot to feel the way ahead. The channel made a gentle turn to the left and then abruptly ended. The water was flowing over a two-foot fall into a pool that was about 300 feet in diameter. Sean shined the light around the cavern. It looked as if the original channel had collapsed into a sinkhole and part of the ceiling had fallen in on top of that.

At the far side of the pool they could see the remains of the channel, continuing on. It looked like the ceiling of the channel had also collapsed. The pool water was exiting the cavern under the floor of what remained of the old tunnel. John wanted to investigate where the water was running, but the batteries in the flashlight were about to give out.

In the center of the pool was a small whirlpool where the water was draining at the bottom. Obviously trying to exit the pool underwater by the whirlpool was not an option.

Sean said, "Okay! Just like we thought; looks like another dead end. We might as well head back before the batteries are completely dead."

Just as the flashlight's batteries were expiring, they entered the wharf area and climbed up the stairs to the dock.

Sean said, "Hurry! Last one in the pool is a mummy's uncle! Come on hot pool."

In minutes they were up to their chins in the warm water.

Sean said, "Well, we'll have plenty of status to report now. I don't see wasting anymore time in the channel, do you?"

John said, "There may be a way out under the remains of the old tunnel, where the water is running. You would have to treat it like a cave and crawl on your hands and knees, but there may be something there."

Sean replied, "True! There may be more we can do there, but I recommend we leave it alone unless we get desperate."

John said, "Who says we're not desperate now?"

Sean said, "We still have plenty of potable water, all the fish we can eat and good company. Plus, I've got to believe the rescue efforts on the surface must be making some progress. Let's head back to the operation center and see if Professor Fitzgerald has any updates."

"That sounds good! I'll catch up with you at the operation center a little later. I'm not ready to get out of the pharaoh's hot pool just yet."

Sean climbed out and looked over his shoulder and said, "Don't be too long. I'll hold up on our report until you get there."

"Okay! See you shortly!"

Chapter 21

The Crystal Clear Persuasion

As John was soaking, he couldn't help but think that, given the distance they traveled, the sinkhole had to be near the Nile. If he had a good flashlight, and an hour and a half to himself, he believed he could make some serious progress toward freedom. At least he could put to rest the idea that was sticking in his head that they were just a few feet from daylight.

Then, just like that night he spent in the Smithsonian Museum, wild ideas began to dance through his mind. He saw himself using his incredible physique to swim to freedom. Then he, John Applegate, would lead the rescue team that saved the entire team without a single loss of life. The press would spend endless hours interviewing him and asking for a step-by-step description of how he, and he alone, had the vision and the determination to save everyone. The rescue would come while all the drones were standing around paralyzed with inaction. He could see all of their up-turned faces watching for the rescue team from above. He could see himself leading the rescue team from the Nile. He could see each member of the team walking out into the daylight and falling to their knees in the sand, thanking God for their deliverance. But he would know, and so would the public, that he was their savior.

Not only would the world declare John Applegate the savior of the Egyptian dig, but also his nano-based technology would be recognized as the key to unraveling the mysteries of the civilization of Atlantis. ME and nanotechnology would also be the key to saving the entire planet. As these visions danced through his head, the smiling face of his father began appearing with a look of approval for little Johnny Applegate. Finally, little Johnny Applegate would be a man. His father would have to show him respect.

Just then he was startled from his daydreams by Sean. "Hey John, come on! They're waiting for our report."

"I'm on my way!"

John and Sean finished their report to the group and they got a round of applause for what everyone considered to be effort above and beyond the call of duty, in those dark channels.

Professor Fitzgerald said, "I want to thank everyone for their hard work. The next eight hours will be a holiday. Please, try to relax, catch-up on sleep, and use the downtime to regenerate your mental well being. I assure you, things are better than they seem. I anticipate rescue within the next 48 hours."

Everyone wanted to take the professor at his word and most of the team used the time to sleep. Some people continued the research work that originally brought them to the interior of the Necropolis, because the work was so exciting to them and to accomplish it was enormously satisfying.

John Applegate decided to use the time to catch-up on his exercise program, so he began to workout. As he was vigorously working-out, the endorphins that were always generated during his intense exercise program began to sweep across his brain. He suddenly felt compelled to find a flashlight, return to the channel, and determine if escape was possible via the cave under the floor of the old channel.

John found a flashlight, checked the batteries, and made his way to the wharf. As he headed toward the sinkhole, the water was colder than he remembered. When he came to the edge of the sinkhole, he shined the light to the other side and verified that the water was running into a cave under the channel. As he attempted to cross to the other side he lost his footing and was instantly in water over his head. He sputtered to the surface and struck out with powerful strokes toward the far side of the pool. He kept an eye on the whirlpool in the middle and skirted the current that tried to drag him toward the center and, ultimately, down to the bottom of the pool.

John pulled himself out of the water and began shivering. He splayed the flashlight beam around the remains of the old channel as he walked a few feet into the interior, to satisfy his curiosity. It was, just as he thought, hopelessly collapsed and blocked. No one could guess the channel's original destination other than the surface of the Nile.

He got down on his knees and shined the light into the cave where the water was running. It appeared to be a natural crack in the rock that 10,000 years of water had enlarged. He thought the tunnel collapse had probably hastened the carving. John was sure the cave must lead to the Nile and daylight. He checked his flashlight and the batteries were holding up pretty well, so he thought he would crawl a little way into the cave just to see what he could see. The going was easy and he was making good progress when the cave began to shrink in size from top to bottom. He was now crawling on his belly like an infantryman, but it was still easy going because the water was supporting part of his weight. The water didn't seem as cold now.

The easy going part came to an abrupt end. The water was still flowing well and there was still about 24 inches of clearance between the cave roof and the cave floor, when suddenly, the cave filled up with water. The current was strong at this point and it was trying to carry him along with the flowing water. He braced himself against the wall and stopped so that he could still breathe.

He listened and he believed he could hear a low rumble or vibration coming from the water. He turned off the flashlight, and he was certain the water straight ahead was slightly lighter than the darkness behind him. He began to think that freedom was just on the other side. He thought that if he were to hold his breath, stick his head into the hole, and use his feet to anchor himself on this side, then maybe he could see if the water entered a chamber where there would be plenty of air. He ducked his head into the water and opened his eyes. He was sure, as his eyes grew accustomed to the light, that the darkness was a little brighter inside that hole. Feeling about with his hands, he believed this hole was just a short stricture that opened up after a few feet on the other side. He pulled himself back through and caught his breath. He was breathing heavily.

Then he thought, if I leave the flashlight on and wedged here, on the bottom of the cave floor, I could swim through to the other side, check things out, and then return. If it looks like the cave necks down to nothing, I can simply swim back through the hole using the flashlight as a beacon. If the cave opens-up then I can retrieve the flashlight and continue my escape.

John secured the flashlight to the floor, with a loose rock, and he began to take deep breaths to accumulate as much oxygen in his blood stream as possible. Then he ducked under the water and swam through the hole. Instead of opening up a few feet on the other side of the stricture like he thought, the cave continued at the same size for about fifteen feet and then suddenly it became larger. It also picked up a few other tributaries, of fast moving water, heading in the same direction. John became like a human bullet in a long rifle tube, and the force of the water was propelling him forward at a rapidly increasing pace. He struggled to stop his forward progress by grabbing the sides of the cave, but all that did was break his fingers and scrape the skin off his hands, arms, and knees. He was running out of oxygen, but he was too stubborn to panic. He extended his hands out in front to protect his head, but it was a little too late.

His head struck a low hanging rock, knocking him unconscious. His body continued to be propelled forward at an incredible rate. If he was conscious, he would have panicked when his body was expelled out of the cave opening on the side of an underground cliff. The force of the exit sent his body far enough away from the face of the cliff that, when he came crashing down into the pool below, he miraculously missed the rocks that had accumulated at the bottom of the waterfall.

The human body is an amazing machine. The instinct for survival is so pervasive that he wound up on the side of the pool with his head above water and his body partially submerged. The cavern he was in was above the water level of the Nile by about fifteen feet. During most of the year the cavern's entrance is submerged, but for a few weeks out of the year the entrance and the pool are exposed to the light of day. His body had found the freedom he sought but at what price? Was he alive, dead, or maimed?

When the holiday period concluded, Professor Fitzgerald announced breakfast for the crew. Everyone assembled in the cafeteria area, and the cook began serving the meal. Professor Fitzgerald asked, "Sean, have you seen John this morning? I want to see if we can tighten up the timeline on model three."

Sean looked around, "As a matter of fact, I haven't. Maybe he's still in the pharaoh's hot pool. We were really cold after spending all that time in the channel. I'll go check."

Sean grabbed Corinne's hand and said, "Let's go find him."

They gave the entire Necropolis a once over, but he was nowhere to be found. They even questioned everyone to find out when he was last seen. It turns out that it had been about six hours earlier.

Sean reported back to the professor, "Professor, we can't find John anywhere."

The professor asked, "Where could he be? You two didn't find a way out that you've been keeping from us, did you?"

Sean said, "The channel is the only place I didn't look. I'll go check the tunnels and give a call out for him."

Corinne tagged along with Sean and said, "Don't go into those tunnels again. Yell for him, but stay out of the water."

Sean said, "Pipe down. If you're worried, why don't you come along with me?"

Corinne said, "I'll be right here if you need me. Just call out and I'll go get help."

Sean said, "That's what I thought! I'll be right back."

Sean climbed back into the numbing cold water and started down the channel toward the Nile. When he reached the sinkhole, he called out John's name. He shined the light along the sides of the pool but saw nothing. Then he thought about the cave leading down under the old channel. Then he thought: *That guy must be lost in that damn cave.* He looked around and decided he could climb around the perimeter and get to the channel on the opposite side. When he got there, he climbed into the channel and looked around just like John had done and, of course, found it hopelessly blocked. He then got down on his knees and looked into the cave. It looked like easy going so he went in and called John's name a few more times. As the cave began to neck down, Sean stopped. He checked his flashlight and when he did, he turned it off. With his flashlight off, he swore he saw a light and began to move toward it. There in the water, and glowing dimly still, was a very weak flashlight. He picked it up, turned it off, and headed back toward the wharf. Sean now knew that John was dead. Dead! Just like those poor men killed in the cave-in. He wondered how many more of them would die before rescue, or even if rescue was possible. He took some comfort in the knowledge that John had perished trying to help them all. He had a sad feeling, but at least he knew John had perished trying to help them all.

Sean returned to the main work area and shared, with the team, the evidence he had collected. Everyone was devastated. Professor Fitzgerald asked for a moment of silence and said, "Please, bow your heads." He then recited the Lord's Prayer and asked for God to have mercy on John Applegate's soul.

Dr. Munkey and Dr. Death were together at the Smithsonian Museum of Natural History and they were discussing the Egyptian mission. Dr. Munkey asked, "Any word of progress yet on the rescue efforts?"

Dr. Death said, "Well, as you know it is slow going in the narrow confines of the descending passageway. Each bucket full of rubble and debris has to be sent out hand-over-hand by the workmen. It is hard work and the men are working in shifts. Plus, every inch gained requires extensive shoring. It will be a long slow process that may take another ten days or even two weeks, depending on how much damage to the tunnel there really is."

Dr. Munkey asked, "Does Fatima have any idea what group is behind the bombing?"

Dr. Death replied, "No one has claimed responsibility for the bombing and there have been no demands for money or other compensation. The Egyptian police are at a loss, at this point. Dr. Boutros personally believes a fundamentalist organization is behind it."

Dr. Munkey asked, "What are the websites and the wire services reporting? Does the story have legs, and is it being carried worldwide?"

Dr. Death said, "The world's five leading news services have crews on site at the Great Pyramid. The daily progress of the rescue effort is being reported and updated at dusk and dawn. Each network has various experts estimating how much oxygen the trapped research team might have left. They are basing the amount of oxygen on the size of the Queen's Chamber. The Nielson ratings place this news event as the most watched in history. So far, "The Pyramid Caper," as they are calling it, has collected twenty million more daily viewers than the last world soccer championship. A thirty second advertising spot is selling at an all time high."

Dr. Munkey nodded his head vigorously and said, "Excellent! Well done! This is better than we had hoped for! I would have preferred to stay on our schedule, but the fundamentalists may have inadvertently enhanced our position."

Dr. Death's PDA signaled that a text message had arrived. He read it aloud to Dr. Munkey: "We have discovery, we have content, we have a correlation of facts, and a recommendation for the way forward. Recommend rescue teams start work via the Temple of Life above the main staircase. See you soon, Fitz."

Dr. Death responded to Professor Fitzgerald with, "Well done!" Dr. Death immediately contacted Fatima Boutros, Director of the Museum of Egyptian Antiquities, and asked her to step-up the rescue efforts and to alert the media to a possible breakthrough. Breaking news bulletins began appearing on all media outlets. Around the world people were glued to their large screens. The Egyptian Air Force began airlifting bulldozers, via helicopter, to the Giza Plateau and a massive effort was begun to move tons of sand from a specific site between the Great Sphinx and the Great Pyramid.

The news services and reporters were desperately trying to come up with something new and they began interviewing people on the street. One BBC correspondent interviewed an Egyptian cleric to try to get an understanding of why the site between the Great Sphinx and the Great Pyramid was selected for sand removal.

The reporter asked, "Sir, can you explain how this latest site relates to the people trapped in the Great Pyramid? Why would the rescue effort be focused in the desert rather than within the Great Pyramid?"

The Egyptian cleric, known as Jamal, said, "I know nothing of the rescue efforts associated with the Great Pyramid. For years during prayer meditation I often slip into a deep trance. While deep in the trance, the Ka of the Great Ramses often visits me. It is as if the Great Ramses and I are sitting together on a stone bench near the Great Pyramid. Just yesterday morning as I was praying, I again fell into a trance. When I awoke, I remembered that the Great Ramses and I were again sitting in the shadow of the Great Pyramid. During this visit the Ka of Ramses the Great told me that the trapped people are alive and well and that they are not in the Great Pyramid. Ramses told me that they are below the sands where the bulldozers are now working."

The BBC reporter asked, "Did you tell the people here, conducting the rescue efforts, that they were digging in the wrong place and that the people are beneath the sands?"

Jamal replied, "Oh, no! You are the only person to ask me questions. I am a holy man; they don't care what I think or what the Great Ramses has to say. The people of Egypt have abandoned their ancestors and now they desecrate their graves. It is no time to…"

The BBC commentator abruptly interrupted the cleric, thanked him for being with them, then turned to the camera and said, "Well folks, there you have it straight from the Ka of the Great Ramses! According to Ramses the Great, the archeological team is safe and rescue will be forthcoming shortly. It is a time to rejoice!"

The activity in the desert looked like a small city was being erected. There were bulldozers, cranes, steam shovels, temporary buildings, tents, port-a-potties, kitchens, medical facilities, and communication centers filled with archeological experts, Egyptologists, news anchors, and reporters. The Egyptian Air Force had set up an airfield to accommodate the ever-present helicopters. There was so much activity at the airfield it was hard to tell how fast this new city was growing.

One particular square mile area was roped off in quadrants, and surveyors were further subdividing the quadrants. They were using tape measures and transits to mark off and establish boundaries.

Tables and drawings were set up in each area, and local laborers were busy moving sand out of the various quadrants. The entire activity was far from random and was progressing toward a specific site in the desert some distance from the Great Pyramid and the Great Sphinx. The site formed a triangle with the Sphinx and the Great Pyramid.

Three crawler cranes were positioned around an area the size of a city block. The construction engineers used bog mats with steel plates to distribute the weight of the out-riggers for each crane. The Army constructed temporary roads using the sand-grid plastic honeycomb material that allowed heavy machinery, such as large trucks, to be filled so they could carry away the sand, debris, and large stones that the cranes and workers were beginning to remove from the site.

The site leader, dressed in Arabic robes and turban, was directing all activities. With map and charts in hand, he directed the removal of each stone personally. Suddenly, he halted all crane activity and waved off the heavy equipment operators except for one crane operator. He then called in the labor force with buckets, shovels, and wheelbarrows.

As the sand was removed bucket-by-bucket, an outline of a foundation began to emerge. The site leader jumped down into the hole and directed the crane operator to lower the hook. Two of the laborers, using shovels, dug out a hole on each side of a massive stone. They then fished a cable under and around the stone. The site leader attached the crane's hook to the cable and gave a signal to the crane operator to lift the stone. The cable bisected the stone such that when the stone was lifted, it was balanced perfectly. The stone pulled free from the debris and sand began to fall into the hole. The leader motioned for the crane to swing the stone over to a waiting flatbed truck. The laborers then poured into the open foundation and began hauling up buckets of sand. It wasn't long before a staircase and a landing became visible.

Once the sand above the temple ruin had been cleared and there was now space to work, the rubble on the staircase was removed rather quickly. The rescue team broke through to the Necropolis just before dawn.

Jamal was watching the rescue effort on the big screen at the telecommunications tent. He had just completed another interview with another news agency, when the breakthrough occurred. As soon as the staircase was opened, a news anchor on site tried to get an interview with the site leader. Jamal saw the site leader shaking his head and then heading to the airfield. As the leader approached the chopper, the turbine began to spool up and the blades began to turn. The reporter trailed the site leader right up to the door of the chopper and it immediately lifted off.

Every news agency had images of the research team survivors, as they were led from the hole in the ground. An outcry of relief was heard around the world. The research team was loaded into the waiting ambulances and taken to the Cairo Hospital, as a precautionary measure. Professor Fitzgerald; Fatima Boutros; and Dr. Heffernan scheduled a news conference at the museum, for the following afternoon.

At the news conference, Professor Fitzgerald was in his element. The professor presented, as fact, that the archeological find was connected to the lost civilization of Atlantis and that the Necropolis contained the mummified pharaohs of Atlantis. The historical revelations in the hieroglyphs recorded the creation of Atlantis and the subsequent destruction of Atlantis. According to the hieroglyphs, the fireballs of the Sun God Ra had created Atlantis in the years before 10,000 BCE. The fireballs of Ra visited Atlantis again in 7,500 BCE as a warning from Ra.

These asteroids were visible in the night sky for three weeks, and the people of Atlantis were terrified. The priests predicted that, unless the people maintained their covenant with Ra, he would destroy the world. The professor, with a wry smile on his face, said, "Apparently, the people of Atlantis broke the covenant with Ra because their civilization was destroyed in the year 4815 BCE due to asteroid impacts."

Dr. Heffernan added, "We believe the great flood described in the Old Testament may have been triggered by the 4815 BCE asteroid strike. There is evidence that the great flood was a direct result of a massive asteroid strike in the Indian Ocean. That crater is located in the bottom of the Indian Ocean and is eighteen miles in diameter."

"Further, we believe that the asteroids that struck the Earth on 4815 BCE can be traced backward in time to a strike in 7315 BCE, and forward to a strike in 2315 BCE, and again asteroids were sighted in 185 CE."

"All of these historical asteroids can be tracked backward to the Ra debris field. The debris field is in a long duration elliptical orbit around our sun. The Earth is, unfortunately, subject to the asteroids generated by gravitational action on the debris as it orbits the sun. Depending on unknown variables, we may only see lights in the night sky or we may be in line for a potentially deadly asteroid impact."

"We believe an asteroid, from the Ra debris field, was observed in the night sky, as the Star of Bethlehem, near the beginning of the Current Era."

"Was the Star of Bethlehem actually connected with the return of the asteroids of Ra? No one can answer that question. However, we do believe the asteroids of Ra are due to return to Earth within the next 25 to 150 years. We can't predict any tighter timeline on their return because we have no knowledge of what gravitational fields the asteroid debris field may have been exposed to over the last 2,500 years, and to what extent their orbits may have been affected."

Professor Fitzgerald cautioned, "The margin of error of our predictions may be as high as 20%."

One of the pundits in the news conference audience noted that, with a 20% margin of error, it would behoove all mankind to start looking towards the heavens tonight. Corinne and Sean watched the news conference aboard the Observation Island, on the vessel's large media screen.

Corinne asked, "Sean, when will we see Sean Thornton and Corinne Cannon again?

Sean said, "Just as soon as we return to Sir Paul's Stonehenge Manor. Sean and Corinne Hornbeak will be debriefed, put in boxes, and slid under the bed. Sean Thornton and Corinne Cannon will complete their vacation and return to Washington on the bomber's next trip to Andrews Air Force Base."

The world's pundits were calling for an immediate reexamination of the goals of the international space programs, and the finger pointing had begun. The President of the United States held a special news conference at the National Scientific Research Foundation's project site. In attendance, and endorsing Dr. Fitzgerald's recommendations, were Dr. Munkey and Dr. Death. The President assured the international community of the full backing and cooperation of the USA in support of Dr. Fitzgerald's recommendations. The Hornbeak's spokesman read a prepared statement that concurred with the professor's recommendations and urged the backing of the European-Asian Space Consortium.

Corinne said, "My Gosh! We couldn't have said it better ourselves! Do you suppose we still have jobs?

Sean said, "Of course we do, and, more importantly, we are needed now more than ever before. We have a lot of work ahead of us. You need to continue your gene research, expand your analysis, develop conclusions, and make recommendations."

The Observation Island was back on station in the Mediterranean Sea with her side scanning SONAR fish deployed. The crew were conducting the final acoustic runs to complete the boundary definition of the underwater ruins near Alexandria.

The captain entered the media room and asked, "Are you guys all packed and ready to go? The helo will pick you up in about an hour. Sir Paul's Gulfstream will be waiting for you on the ground in Cairo."

The loud speaker crackled and everyone looked up at the speaker on the bulkhead, "Now set the helo detail! Now set the helo detail."

Corinne and Sean said their good-byes and headed onto deck to climb aboard the helo. They were thirty minutes from Cairo, and within an hour the Gulfstream was passing over the Observation Island.

Corinne said, "Sean, look! It's the Observation Island. Funny, it looks tiny from here, but I know better."

Sean said, "If I wasn't ready to be home again, I wouldn't mind being part of the exploration of that underwater city. Just think. What if that is Atlantis? The hall of records may still be intact. Wow! What a treat that would be! An entire civilization's hall of knowledge concentrated in one place. I wouldn't be able to keep my hands off the books, or should I say scrolls?"

Corinne said, "That would be fantastic. To have a civilization's complete book of knowledge at your fingertips would be daunting. I wonder how many times Homo sapiens has had to start over and reinvent fire, the wheel, the printing press, and everything else from scratch? If each generation and each civilization could begin by standing on the shoulders of the last, just think how far advanced we might be, as people, now."

Sean replied, "You are so right. If civilizations and empires had not risen and fallen over the millennia, then Homo sapiens would already be stationed beyond the orbit of Jupiter. We would already have asteroid deflection technology in place and we wouldn't be worrying about a life extinguishing event hovering over us, our children, and our children's children."

"However, Corinne, the question remains: Is life on this planet, and the rise and fall of the mighty empires of the past, a result of providence, or is the Collective Intelligence behind it? Is our discovery of the Necropolis, and the history contained therein, simply a happy coincidence? Or were we led there by the Collective Intelligence?"

"Will the revelations from the Necropolis catalyze the nations of the world to solve the threat of the asteroids and life extinguishing events? Will the Collective Intelligence recognize that this version of Homo sapiens is reaching to the heavens for the right reason and let up on attempting to reload this version of civilization?"

Corinne said, "Hold on, Sean. I'm still not convinced the Collective Intelligence, and my own DNA, is out to get me. So let's set those questions aside for the moment. Let's save the universe tomorrow!"

Sean said, "Of course you're not convinced! What chance do I have to convince you, now? Especially, since we're following the Collective Intelligence's imperative to save the double helix? The Collective Intelligence will now let up on reducing the life span of the A-type personalities because we need the A types to develop and deploy the asteroid deflection technology!"

Corinne said, "You know what? I'm ready for a little down time, at least, for a weekend, anyway."

Sean said, "Corinne, you're right! Why don't you get some rest. We'll be landing at Heathrow in about four hours. I still have John Applegate's amazing PDA here, and I'm going to send Sir Paul an email. He'll think Applegate is back from the dead!"

Corinne said, "Oh Sean! How could you? Now, that's just not funny!"

Sean said, "Well, Sean Hornbeak couldn't send that email, but Sean Thornton can. But you're wrong; it is funny!"

Corinne replied, "Okay! But I'm still sad about poor John. I guess we'll never know what happened to him."

Chapter 22

Pluto, the Scarab, and Me

Hasani, a young fisherman, and his dog, Nailah, were scavenging the riverbank near their home looking for things of value that would please his father. Nailah began barking and ran into a cavern in the side of the cliff. Hasani called Nailah again and again, but still the dog didn't come. Finally, the boy went up to the cavern mouth, and he could hear Nailah barking furiously.

Hasani said, "Nailah, you are crazy. Come right now!"

The dog continued to bark. Hasani looked around for things to make a torch out of. He found a piece of driftwood and then bundled together some dried grasses and an old rag he found on the beach. He then pulled out his Bic lighter and lit the torch and followed Nailah inside. As his eyes became adjusted to the semi-darkness, he could see the outline of a man lying in the sand, near a pool of water. He saw the man move, and he heard him mumble something unintelligible. Hasani crept closer and he could see the man was hurt and that he had been bleeding. The man reached out and grabbed Hasani by the ankle. Hasani let out a yelp, and twisted away. He threw down the torch, grabbed the dog by the collar, and ran out of the cave.

Then, dragging the dog by the neck, he ran home as fast as he could. His father was mending a net while sitting on an over-turned boat. He looked up when he heard Hasani shouting.

"Father! Father! A man! A hurt man that needs help! Help him father!"

Hasani's father, Imhotep, listened to his son and then he called his wife to hear the story also. Imhotep asked, "Hasani, where is this man and what is wrong with him?"

Hasani said, "Father, Nailah and I were following the river looking for driftwood. Nailah ran into a cave and I couldn't find him. I called and called and then I heard him barking. He was in a cavern in the side of the cliff."

Imhotep said, "Hasani, you are not making sense. There is no cavern near here."

Hasani said, "But father, the river is low now, and the cavern's entrance was just revealed today."

Imhotep said, "How bad is he hurt? Did you see blood and open wounds?"

"He looks to be almost dead, and he is bleeding from head to foot. He has a broken arm and maybe a broken leg too."

Imhotep asked, "Is he from the village?"

Hasani said, "No! I think he is English."

Imhotep's wife, Shani, said, "He is not our business. Leave him be."

Hasani said, "Mother he will die. We must help."

Imhotep said, "Wife, he is a human being and it is our duty to help him, if we can."

Shani said, "He is English! No good can come of this."

"If he is English, there may be a reward." Imhotep turned to his wife and said, "Bring the wagon and some cloth for bandages."

The little Egyptian rescue group pulled John Applegate from the cavern, loaded him on the wagon, and carried him home. Shani washed his wounds and applied honey. Honey has been used successfully for thousands of years as an antibacterial balm for burns and infections. After shooting through the granite tube, John looked like a motorcycle accident victim with a bad case of road rash. Imhotep sent for the village doctor to set John's broken leg and arm. The doctor gave him a sedative and he was sleeping quietly in Imhotep's hut.

Shani could see her husband coming from the river with a string of fish over his shoulder. Imhotep greeted his wife, handed her the days catch, and asked, "How long has he been unconscious?"

Shani said, "It is three days now. The doctor came by today and said that he should be waking up in the next day or so, if he is going to wake up at all."

At that moment, perhaps disturbed by the voices, the patient moved and groaned.

Imhotep knelt down beside the man and brought a cup of water to his lips. He began to sputter and cough, sat up on one elbow, and opened his eyes. He looked around the hut and looked at them and asked, "Where am I?"

They looked at each other with puzzled looks on their faces and Imhotep said, "Hasani, go to the village and get the doctor. He speaks English."

Sean and Corinne finally met Nigel and Wendy Hornbeak. They all spent the week together at Stonehenge Manor, with Sir Paul and Lady Gibbs, telling story after story. A week was hardly enough for all the Peruvian tales and the Egyptian tales. Sir Paul and Muffy enjoyed the stories more than anyone.

After a week of downtime, Corinne and Sean caught a space-available RAF transport plane back to Andrews Air Force Base, where the "Egyptian Caper" had actually begun just a few short weeks ago. It seemed funny that only members of the League of Red-Headed Men had a clue about Sean and Corinne's part in the whole story.

Sean and Corinne were on the Metro headed for Georgetown and Corinne's brownstone. Corinne said, "I sent Cathy an email so she knows to expect us home today."

Sean said, "We'll stop by the Smithsonian, get my car, and head to your house."

Corinne asked, "You don't really think the car is still there, do you?"

Sean replied, "Absolutely! It's legally parked and the registration is up to date. Plus, the director and I play racket ball together, so he knows my car."

The Metro pulled into the Smithsonian Station and Corinne looked up and said, "Sean, look! This is where it all began."

Sean stood up, grabbed Corinne's hand and pulled her off the Metro car just before the doors closed. Corinne asked, "What are you doing? Now we have to catch another car and drag our luggage around, too!"

Sean said, "Corinne, you forgot; this is where we left the Corvette. We'll go up a level and get the car. Come on, let's go!"

Corinne said, "Sean, get real! The Corvette is in some impound lot by now."

They took the escalator to the ground level and they headed to the parking lot. As they turned the corner, Sean said, "Oh, ye of such little faith!"

Sean pushed the button on his key chain and the Corvette answered with a beep. He opened the door, tossed their luggage in back, and then he opened the door for Corinne. Corinne just stood there in a daze. Sean asked, "Come on! What are you waiting for?"

Corinne replied, "The battery must be dead."

Sean jumped in, turned the key and the Corvette roared to life. Sean asked, "Oh, Corinne? Are you coming too?"

Corinne laughed, jumped in the car, and Sean squealed the tires as he pulled out into traffic. Corinne said, "Careful, you'll get in trouble!"

Sean laughed, "After what we've been through, I ain't scared of nothin'!"

Corinne and Sean remained incognito, as far as the press was concerned, and they were delighted. The Hornbeaks were dogged by the paparazzi wherever they went, and they couldn't get a minute of privacy anywhere but at home.

It had been nine months since Sean and Corinne Hornbeak had climbed out of the Necropolis. The world did not know that Sean Thornton and Corinne Cannon were ever in Egypt. Sean and Corinne were both back at work, and they had been married for two weeks, but they hadn't taken their honeymoon yet. Corinne had confirmed her initial DNA conclusions in the Necropolis and while there were, and always will be, exceptions to all rules, all the serial killer DNA and mass murderer DNA to date had shown the reversed sequence in the controlling DNA string for the A-type personality aggressive marker. Corinne still didn't have a clue as to what was reducing the life expectancy of the A-type personality types or, even if the life expectancy was being reduced. She really needed ten years of data to establish any real trend.

Sean was still insisting that the Collective Intelligence had a hand in the early terminations, but Corinne would need at least three years of data to say whether there was a downward trend or whether the trend was real, stabilized, or turned around. Corinne and Sean remained members of the League of Red-Headed Men and attended the quarterly meetings at the Smithsonian.

The United Nations had arrived at a unanimous decision to pursue asteroid deflection technology and subsequent deployment of it in an orbit beyond Jupiter. The big push now was to select the director of the program and his staff on Earth and on the moon base. The moon base is where the technology would be developed. The starship to deliver the technology on station at Jupiter would be built in orbit above the moon. It was critical that the team be dedicated, single minded, and goal oriented. A slate of candidates for each site was in Dr. Munkey's hand. Dr. Munkey asked Corinne to quietly run the gene sequence test on each set of candidates, to ensure there were no serial killer types applying for the jobs.

Corinne was apprehensive and told Sean of her misgivings. She said, "I feel like I'm playing God, and I wish Dr. Munkey hadn't asked me to run the test."

Sean said, "How would you feel if you didn't run the test, and we found out later that the crew to deploy the vehicle in orbit near Jupiter was full of serial killers who had knocked one another off on the way there?"

"I guess you're right."

When the appointments were announced, Corinne was stunned to note that each candidate for the director's position, at each site, was the candidate with the questionable DNA. The astronaut crew for the mission to Jupiter consisted of all the candidates without the questionable DNA, except for the commander.

Corinne asked, "Sean, Do you think Dr. Munkey misunderstood my findings?"

Sean said, "Corinne, I believe Dr. Munkey made the selections based on your findings. He cannot take a chance on selecting directors that aren't single minded and brutal in the execution of their duties. Nothing can come between fulfilling their obligations to the species by implementing the asteroid deflection technology in the most expeditious manner. Notice that Dr. Munkey took no chance that the three-year voyage to Jupiter might be jeopardized by competition of on-board serial killers."

"Corinne, you know what? I bet if you ran the DNA test on Dr. Munkey you'd find that..."

Corinne interrupted and said, "What I'd find is that Munkey isn't human."

Sean laughed and said, "I've got a theory on what makes a human being a human being, too, and it isn't based solely on DNA."

Corinne said, "I'm sure you do, but let's save that conversation for the next time we're buried alive in some 10,000 year old tomb!"

Sean said, "You know, Corinne, when we started our Egyptian adventure, in the basement of the Smithsonian Museum, I believed you and I were blazing a trail. After the whole thing wrapped-up, I began to have doubts. As I look back on it now, it almost seems like we were following a beaten path."

Corinne said, "You mean we were like two mice in a maze and no matter which way we turned, while there might be delays, we were still going to arrive at the center and discover the cheese."

"Exactly!"

Corinne asked, "Tell me, Sean, was the maze and the path constructed for us by Dr. Munkey, Dr. Death, God, or the Collective Intelligence? Or was the whole thing contained within our own preprogrammed double-helix molecule?"

Sean said, "Corinne, your analysis of the mummies' DNA proves that all of our ancestors are descended from the people of Atlantis; so anything is possible."

Corinne replied, "Sean, there is no doubt that, given, the size of the human genome, messages from the past could very well be embedded in our DNA."

Sean said, "True! But remember it was still our choice to chase the clues to a 10,000 year old tomb in Egypt."

Corinne said, "I know it sounds a little creepy, but that day in the tomb, when I realized my scarab necklace had Zahra's name on it and her sarcophagus was empty, I had cold chills running up and down my spine. I feel as if Zahra somehow reached out from the grave and touched me that day. I didn't feel afraid and I wasn't scared; I felt only a connection and a deep feeling of love swept over me."

"Sometimes reality is a combination of things including free will."

Sir Paul had been Sean's best man, and he offered Sean the use of the family castle in Scotland for their honeymoon. Sean and Corinne's schedule had finally calmed down enough to for them to schedule their honeymoon. The castle had been in Sir Paul's family for 450 years. It was fully staffed and completely modernized. Corinne and Sean had been enjoying the country-life like only Americans in Scotland can.

The housekeeper knocked, entered the suite, and began the daily housekeeping chores. Corinne stirred from the noise in the living room and nudged Sean awake.

Pluto, the Scarab, and Me

Sean asked, "Is it morning already? Are we still in the Great Pyramid?"

Corinne said, "Yes! And no!"

Sean asked, "Do you know how lucky you are to have me?"

Corinne replied, "Someone once told me that they didn't believe in luck; now I know why."

"Come here, wench, the squire of the castle will thrash you within an inch of your life."

"The squire had best get in the shower or we'll miss our tour today."

Sean said, "Let's blow off the tour and take a bicycle tour of the local towns around here."

Corinne said, "Okay! Sounds good, but where do we go and where do we get the bicycles?"

From the other room the maid chimed in, "Excuse me Madam, but I couldn't help but over hear you, and I can recommend just the tour for you two love birds. Me husband and me took our honeymoon tour thirty years ago and the romantic old fool just surprised me by returning to our honeymoon suite this past year. Trust me. You'll have a good time."

Sean and Corinne opened the door to the living room and joined the maid. She was wearing the traditional outfit and was a dead ringer for Mary Poppins, except much older. Corinne and Sean introduced themselves and said, "Mary, congratulations on your anniversary, and we would love to hear your recommendation."

The maid said, "Well, the best thing is to use the castle's bicycles and then have the gardener drop you and the bicycles off in Peebles. Peebles will be a comfortable ride back to the castle here. The bicycle trail starts in the Glentress Forest and winds its way through farmland on old drove roads and leads to the beautiful town of West Linton. Before the railroads, the drove roads were how the cattle were driven to market. Now the old droves make wonderful hiking and biking trails. There are many places in West Linton for shopping and for lunch, too. There is a little bit of a hill leaving West Linton but don't worry about it. Once you're at the top of the hill there's a gorgeous descent down the Pentland Hills and home to Edinburgh."

"There are lots of things to see and you can stop at any of the numerous pubs to refresh yourselves on the way."

"If this sounds like something you would like to do, I'll have the chef pack you a picnic lunch, with some wine, and I'll get the gardener to load the bicycles. Oh, don't mind me. I'm an old fuddy-duddy. You kids probably have more exciting things on your mind."

Sean and Corinne looked at each other and Corinne said, "Mary, it sounds wonderful. If you don't mind, we'd love to have you set things in motion. Give us and hour and we'll meet the gardener out back."

"Very well, Madam, you'll not be sorry."

They said thanks and good-bye to the gardener and Corinne looked at the hill and said, "A little hill, don't worry about it? Mary and her husband may have spent their honeymoon biking, but looking at this hill, I'll bet there was no biking this time around!"

They started off on the bikes, and the hill wasn't too bad as long as they stayed in high gear. When they got to the top of the hill, the view was a bucolic masterpiece. The herds of sheep and cows dotted the countryside on both sides of the drove. Off in the distance the village church bell was ringing the members to mass.

Sean said, "Mary was right about the downhill glide. I think all we have to do sit back and enjoy the view."

The land leveled out and they came to a clump of trees and a crossroads. On the right, the ruins of an old castle loomed. They decided to take a break to explore the castle ruins.

Sean asked, "Did you ever wonder why all the little towns have names that end in burg? I was reading a brochure last night and burg is an old word that means castle. So everywhere that there was a little bit of civilization, from farming or cattle and sheep breeding, there was a need for a castle to protect the people and their budding enterprises."

Corinne replied, "I saw the same brochure. I was amazed at how big a presence the Romans had here. I didn't realize that all the main roads and railways are constructed on or near the ancient Roman roads."

Sean said, "It's really the whole genealogy thing again. Your family and my family have roots in the British Isles, and the ancient gene pool reflects the Huns, the Tartars, and the Romans, too. It's funny how the Nile Valley civilization became mother to the modern world."

Corinne was walking around the castle ruins and she said, "You can almost feel the lost history here. I know there were lives and civilizations that were won and lost right here on these grounds. When I think back on what we found in the Necropolis, under the sands of

Egypt, I can't help but wonder about the stories that must be lost with these ruins, too."

Sean asked, "Are you ready to find a shovel and start digging?"

Corinne said, "Probably, but just not now. I would like to investigate the pagans, their world, their religion, and just how Stonehenge, and all those rocks, figured into their lives. When you think about Ra, the Son of Ra, the fireballs, and how their civilization was lost to space rocks, you can't help but wonder what happened to the pagans. I wonder how close the pagan view of the world and religion is to the priests of Atlantis."

Sean said, "Quick, get back on your bike! You are beginning to sound like Professor Fitzgerald."

They stopped about half way through their trip, when they had to give way for a shepherd and his flock of sheep. They got off the main drove and found a stunningly green meadow to enjoy some refreshments.

Sean said, "Let's stop at the pub in the next town and see if the local atmosphere is as wonderful inside as it is outside."

Corinne said, "Great, but don't they drink their ale warm? I never understood that tradition."

Sean said, "I guess you've never owned a British sports car or motorcycle then."

Corinne said, "What does that have to do with drinking warm ale?"

Sean said, "The British cars and bikes are notorious for their unreliable electrics by Lucas. The joke was Lucas Electrics produced all their refrigerators too."

Corinne said, "That's not funny!

"See! Now I know you've never owned a British sport car! Their motto was: 'Get home before dark.'"

They continued to the next town and found a pub that looked like it was off any tourist path. They parked the bikes and entered the massive front door. Inside was dark oak paneling from top to bottom. There were many tables, and the bar with brass rails ran from one end of the pub to the other. The seating or standing room at the bar appeared to be assigned, so they chose a table and sat down. The bar tender came over and asked, "What'll it be?"

They chose ale and Corinne reached for the bar nuts. Sean put his hand over the nuts and said, "Never eat anything in a bar that is not individually wrapped."

Corinne said, "You're right and I know better. I was lulled into a false sense of security."

The bartender returned with the drinks. There were no napkins for the mugs. The tables looked like they had been there since Roman times. The bartender inquired, "Tourists?"

Sean said, "We're on our honeymoon."

The barkeep said, "Americans, too. I can tell by your accent. Where are you staying?"

Sean said, "We're on a bike ride from Peebles to near Edinburgh. We're staying at Castle Gibbs."

"Blimey! Friends of Sir Paul are you? Well tell the old bloke that Johnny said 'Cheerio.' By the way, the drinks are on me and anything else you need. Would you like a plate of fish and chips? They're fresh in the kitchen. Mighty good eating!"

Sean replied, "Johnny, thank you for your hospitality, but we have a big dinner planned for tonight. I'll remember you to Sir Paul."

Sean and Corinne arrived at Castle Gibbs totally exhausted. They returned to their suite to shower and dress for dinner.

Corinne said, "Sean, I know we are in Scotland, and not Ireland, but after the bicycle trip, the picnic in the glen, and that little pub, I felt like we were extras on the set of the John Ford classic film, "The Quiet Man."

Sean said, "Corinne, I'm glad you like that movie as much as I do. While we may not look like John Wayne and Maureen O'Hara, when I'm with you, I feel like the Duke." She gave him a hug and a kiss.

Sean said, "I've got an idea! Let's skip dinner tonight and have our Merlot under the stars in the hot tub overlooking the forest."

"That's a great idea!"

They were on their second bottle of wine and in the middle of God knows how many toasts, when Sean asked, "Corinne, do you think we will ever solve the question of the environment, God, and the double helix?"

Corinne said, "I do think we can iron out the details, if we don't run out of time. And, the only way to buy time is to get the asteroid deflection technology deployed."

Sean asked, "Well then, who or what is in charge? Is it: God and God's master plan for the universe, the Collective Intelligence as a derivative of the natural laws of the universe and the double helix, nature/nurture of the species, or the self determination of humans?"

Corinne said, "I prefer to define nature as your Collective Intelligence concept and nurture as the 'Hand of God.' I believe God is love, and his nurturing of life on this planet through the human emotion of love, is the proof."

Sean said, "So! A partnership! I'll drink to that!" They touched glasses, and the golden amulet between Corinne's breasts was reflecting the flames from the candles making the scarab look like it was on fire. Sean could see the stars twinkling in Corinne's beautiful eyes, and he smiled.

As Sean was embracing Corinne he could see, over her shoulder, a red light flashing silently on his PDA. Even from across the room, Sean recognized John Applegate's avatar rotating slowly in 3-D above the PDA. Then, the avatar began to change shape as it resolved into an image of John standing on the Observation Island. He was smiling and waiving.

As Pluto completed the final leg of its apogee at the far point of its orbit, the gravity of the tiny planet created a slight nudge on a field of rubble passing near by in the Kieper asteroid belt.

Pluto, the Scarab, and Me

Acknowledgments

First I want to thank my wife, Carol, and all the other girls in my family for being the inspiration for Corinne. There is a piece of each of you in Corinne's character: strong, smart, beautiful and confident. Special thanks to Mick and Linda Heffernan for all the warmth and encouragement that made me want to finish the project when I could have easily hit the delete key or just shoved a CD into a desk drawer. Your comments and suggestions were invaluable.

A special thanks to Larry May for reading the first cut of TPOA, your favorable comments inspired me to write the Prologue.

About the Author

Larry N. Stewart, is a practicing electronics engineer and a former US Navy Cold War Warrior. He has been an electronics technology buff for decades and has written many technology related articles in the course of his day job. He lives in Silver Spring, Maryland, with his wife, and two Scottish terriers. This is his first novel.

www.ingramcontent.com/pod-product-compliance
Lightning Source LLC
Chambersburg PA
CBHW070553130626
46556CB00001B/137